The Master

The

SOUL CAGE II

David Booker

ISBN-10: 1481105728
EAN-13: 9781481105729

CONTENTS

I

A CALL FROM
AN OLD FRIEND

ONE

They sat across from each other at the scratched and battered kitchen table in the ancient astrological station they had made their home. Each picked at their breakfast of fresh pineapple and leftover mahi-mahi in the bright morning sunlight. The four mutating dogs were silently gnawing on the meaty bones of a wild boar they'd killed the previous night.

"What're your plans for the day, big boy?" asked Penelope.

Campbell glanced up from his breakfast at the striking blond woman and her blue-gray eyes. "Who're you talking to, me or Sergeant?"

"I see you're still the master sleuth," Penelope said, laughing with her beautiful smile. "I mean you, of course. I already know what Sergeant has planned—eat, sleep, poop, and pee."

"Watch it, Sargy. I think you're getting predictable," Campbell said to the huge red-and-white Malamute male at his feet.

Damn, Sergeant, you're getting so big, Campbell thought. *You and the three girls have changed so much since Penelope healed you. Hell, all of us have changed since Penelope came into our lives.*

Sergeant glanced up at Campbell with his wolfish face and golden eyes before woofing softly as if to apologize for his lame predictability.

"Well, anyway," Campbell said, "I need to work on the thermal generator in the north fissure. After that small quake we had last week, sensors show there's a slight power loss."

"Be careful. I don't like it when you work around the fissures. One false step and it's a long fall to the magma below."

Campbell opened his mouth to respond when the twerp of his recorder-communicator sounded in his office in the next room.

Damn! No one has tried to reach me on that thing since we escaped. He stared at Penelope, mirroring her expression of deep foreboding and fear.

"Who could that be?" Penelope asked anxiously.

"I have no idea, but stay here and keep out of sight of the communications monitor. I'm still hoping the military thinks you're dead."

Campbell got up and strode into his sparse office. The communicator continued its obnoxious twerp, unnerving him. He glared down at it on his desk. It appeared so innocent, this device that had once been such an essential part of his previous life as a Global Investigator. *Maybe they'll just go away if I don't answer,* he thought. *Whatever I do, it's going to spell disaster.*

Campbell gazed out his window with his black eye implants. His beautiful vision from atop the Mauna Kea volcano on the Island of Hawaii was one of serenity and tranquility. Above, the crisp blue skies were streaked with thin white clouds being blown about by southeastern trade winds. Below, the flowing black lava-rock landscape extended down to the tree line of a vast forest of pine, spruce, and ironwood. Beyond the forest and beach-lined coast, the deep blue waters of the Pacific Ocean filled the horizon. Far to the west, he spotted the cloud-covered Island of Maui.

We've had this island nearly to ourselves for so long, he mused. *I had hoped civilization had forgotten us. How could I have been so naïve?*

He decided the caller wasn't going to give up. He grasped the handheld communicator and opened its viewing screen. He was shocked to see the Japanese features of Captain Goro Sen, his old boss from the Global Police.

Campbell's past came rushing back. His mind went back to the fateful night two years ago that had changed his life forever. It was the night he'd met Penelope Preston while investigating the vicious murder of Dr. Jiro Yamamoto in New Detroit, Michigan. Penelope had introduced herself as Jiro's lab assistant. The fact that she freely admitted to being the old man's lover didn't stop Campbell from immediately falling in love with Penelope's beauty and intelligence.

He had quickly discovered that Jiro was perfecting the world's first organic teleportation device. It was funded by the military, and they were providing Jiro with death-row inmates to conduct his experiments. But Jiro wasn't working toward the military's goals. His real intent for creating the teleporter was to save his dying wife, Monica. Using the teleporter and an illegal computer with artificial intelligence, Jiro had transformed Monica into the youthful imposter, Penelope Preston.

"Burt? Burt, are you there?" Sen was asking.

"Goro," Campbell said, returning from the past. "Lord in Hades, I had hoped I'd never hear from you again."

"I'm glad to see you as well," Sen said with a weak smile.

Campbell thought his longtime friend's face appeared far older than the last time he'd seen him. His oriental features were pinched as if he were in pain.

Something is very wrong, Campbell thought. *Sen would never jeopardize our lives by trying to contact us unless it's of tremendous importance.*

"Burt, some things have come up," Goro said. He glanced at something, or someone, out of Campbell's sight.

Goro isn't alone. If he's calling when someone else is listening, that means he's been compromised. Damn, this call is traceable. I need to end this now.

"Burt, they've kidnapped me, Oki and Akio. They claim they'll kill us if you don't come back to Global Police Headquarters in Denver immediately," Goro said, and terminated the connection.

TWO

Campbell stared at the blank monitor. Oki was Goro's wife, Akio his teenage son. Campbell knew immediately who "they" were—the military.

Campbell's mind returned to the past. On the night of Jiro's murder, Jiro had teleported two inmates, Hedon Bohdan and Yo Tojo, to the moon-base teleporter. The experiment had gone terribly wrong. The artificial intelligence in Jiro's computer had become a psychotic killer. When Bohdan and Tojo were teleported back to Earth, the computer used them to murder Jiro before attempting to kill the rest of the experiment team—including Penelope Preston.

While trying to capture the murderers, Campbell and Penelope had been attacked by the inmates. Campbell thought he saw Penelope take a directed energy beam shot in the head. Miraculously, she showed no ill effects after the attack. Campbell was just learning that Penelope had remarkable recuperative abilities. He'd later learn she was virtually immortal.

Campbell had taken Penelope back to his home in Denver for her protection. While there, she fell in love with his four aging Malamutes. That's when Campbell witnessed the most incredible miracle of all. With a glowing touch of her hand, Penelope healed the dogs of their ailments. She had the ability to pass along the bioengineering in her blood to others.

Campbell smiled at the memory. He touched his neck where Penelope had healed his wounds after Bohdan had shot him with a directed energy beam. He should be dead. It was one of the blessings of meeting Penelope. She had healed him, and now he possessed her abilities as well.

He also recalled all the dangers of being involved with Penelope's remarkable life. After realizing that the corrupt military could create an army of immortal soldiers using Jiro's teleporter,

Campbell had destroyed the teleportation devices and the computer. Fearing the military could reverse engineer their super army by experimenting on Penelope, they had faked Penelope's death and escaped into hiding. They had feared the military's pursuit ever since.

The military obviously intends to draw me back to Denver by threatening my friends, Campbell thought. *At least it doesn't sound like they know Penelope is alive. There's no way they know I possess her abilities.*

Campbell walked slowly back to the kitchen table, where Penelope sat with her head down, lost in despair. The dogs glanced up from their bones with worried eyes, as if sensing Campbell's anxiety.

"Who was it?" Penelope asked.

"Goro Sen. The military has kidnapped him and his family. They're demanding that I return or they'll kill the Sens."

Penelope gazed up at Campbell. Her beautiful features were creased with pain.

"Look at the bright side," he said with a thin smile. "They're only asking for me. If Bohdan had really told the military you were alive, they would have demanded that you return as well."

Penelope frowned, obviously missing the silver lining of this black cloud.

"I'll have to go, of course," Campbell muttered.

Penelope rose to her slender two-meter height. She crossed around the table, stepping over the lounging dog hurdles.

"Burt, if you go, you know they'll either kill or experiment on you. Just by looking at you they'll know you've changed physically. It won't take them long to realize it has something to do with Jiro's experiments.

"You must not allow them to get their hands on you. That'll destroy everything for which we've fought so hard. The technology of my blood now flows through your veins."

THE SOUL CAGE II

"Penelope, you of all people know I have to go. You're a pacifist. For Jonah's sake, after all Bohdan did to us, you still tried to stop me from killing him. Surely, you can see that I have to try to save the lives of the Sens."

"Yes, I understand," Penelope persisted, "but that was different. If they capture you now, you'll provide them with the technology to create a super army. Such an army would dominate the world's population, and possibly kill millions in an all-out war. Are three lives worth risking the lives of millions?"

Penelope grasped Campbell's huge shoulders and stared up into his black orbs with pleading urgency. He turned away and started to pace. Deciding the yammering of humans didn't interest them, the Malamutes went back to chewing on their bones.

"Penelope, the military might already have the technology to create that super army. They did capture Bohdan before he tried to kill us, and they have, or had, Yo Tojo. Both Bohdan and Tojo went through that teleporter. They'd been altered much the way you've been."

"Oh, we both know the experiments on Bohdan and Tojo weren't successful. Those two came away raving homicidal lunatics with multiple personalities they couldn't control. Those experiments destroyed those men physically and mentally. You said yourself that Bohdan appeared very ill and weak the day he died. Tojo committed suicide, he was so insane.

"No matter how much information the military extracted from Bohdan and Tojo, they can't possibly recreate what Jiro created in me. They don't have all the information they need to create their army yet. Much of that biogenetic information was in Jiro's brain when he was murdered. He didn't even make any notes. The only way the military will discover that information is to capture one of us. I assume they still believe I'm dead, unless Sen told them otherwise."

6

Campbell felt hurt by the accusation of Sen.

"Goro will go to his grave protecting your secret," he grumbled. "He understood the implications of you being caught and examined."

"But would he see his own family die over my secret, Burt? Think of how much Jiro risked and sacrificed to save me, because I was all the family he had. Think of all you have sacrificed to save me, because you love me. Don't you think Goro would give anything to save his family? He's not going to care if the world is destroyed after his family is dead. The fact that he made the call today proves that much."

Campbell gazed down into Penelope's pleading blue eyes. His heart was torn over his love for Penelope and his duty to save his longtime friend.

"What would you have me do, ignore Goro's pleas? Penelope, how could I live with that?"

"How could you live with the death of millions?"

"We don't know it would come to that."

I know she's right, damn it, he thought. *But the Sens have always been like a family to me. Who's going to save them if I don't?*

"I have to go," he whispered. He hugged Penelope tight. "I have to at least try to do something."

"And what about us?" Penelope cried in his ear. "What about your family—our family?"

As if on cue, Sergeant got up and barked loudly. Cala and Amber whined and woo-wooed mournfully. They rubbed their huge furry bodies against Penelope's and Campbell's thighs. Giant Hana squeezed in. She nudged Campbell with her wet nose. Campbell dropped his hand to her brown-and-white head. She licked and slobbered all over it to show her usual affection.

"You know," Campbell said. "I think all you dogs are getting too smart for your own good."

He bent over and hugged each of their immense, furry bodies in turn. They returned his affection by curling into his embraces and lifting their heads to sniff his dark-skinned features and long black hair. Hana snuck in a huge lick across his face.

"Yuck!" he yelled as he leaped back, wiping away Hana's slobber.

"See, Burt, even they think you shouldn't go," Penelope cried.

Campbell stared at Penelope with torn anguish.

"I'm sorry, I have to go." He turned swiftly and strode into his office with Penelope close on his heels.

THREE

Campbell reached into his office closet and got out a military duffle bag. He loaded the bag with a 150-kilowatt directed energy beam pistol (DEP) and a bulky sonic blaster. After a moment, he put in an ancient Glock 20 10mm handgun and ammunition to go with it.

Penelope stood by, watching with great sadness in her pained eyes. The dogs had crowded the office doorway, where they watched with anxious concern. They knew from experience the duffle bag meant Campbell was leaving.

"Excuse me," Campbell grumbled. He pushed by Penelope with his duffle. He headed down the decaying, narrow hallway toward their master bedroom in the astrological observation dome to pack his clothes and get his body armor. He heard Penelope following close behind until he reached the kitchen, where she stopped. The dogs scrambled out of his way, but stayed behind with Penelope.

Campbell packed a minimum of clothes. *Hell. I won't need them anyway. Either I'll be right back or not at all.*

He pulled and stretched into his black cloth-like body armor. It had fit him perfectly two years ago. Now it was far too small. Its elastic qualities still allowed him freedom of movement, but the short sleeves were stretched out and barely rounded his muscular shoulders. The pant legs no longer fell to his heels. He was forced to stuff them into the tops of this calf-high assault boots.

Damn, Penelope's right. Anyone who knows me will instantly see that I've grown much taller, something that's impossible for someone my age. They're gonna know something is up.

Campbell finished dressing. He peered around the bedroom he'd shared with Penelope. He sighed as he thought of their long talks into the night while they stared at the billions of stars through the open dome. He thought of the deep friendship and love that had formed between them—of the happiness they'd shared. *Will I ever know such peacefulness again?* he wondered.

He quickly left the ancient dome and headed back into the kitchen. Penelope stopped him.

"Burt, at least take me and the dogs with you. We're your family. We're a team. We've faced all our fights together."

"This isn't your fight, Penelope. Besides, we can't risk exposing you. Obviously they think you're dead. No one even knows about the dogs."

"You can't just go in there alone. Who's going to help you if you get into trouble?"

Campbell could see she was on the verge of tears. For all her beauty and strength, he thought she appeared so incredibly vulnerable and alone. He almost dropped his bag and rushed over to hug her. He wanted to tell her he would never leave her.

"Penelope, it isn't like I'm not going to come back, and I didn't plan on going alone. I'm going to call Koko to cover my back. If anyone can get me out of this jam, it's him."

"Koko has been retired for almost two years now. You gave him your house, your land, and a vast amount of money to keep our secret. What makes you think he'll risk his luxurious retirement to save you?"

"Well, other than owing me his life several times over, I have the same ability to take away that wealth as I had to give it. I can still access the military computers and destroy his accounts as easily as I created them. So, one way or another, Koko's retirement is over as of today."

Penelope smiled weakly. It made Campbell feel better to see her face lose some of its pain. He crossed the kitchen before he bent over and kissed her deeply. He released her, and went back to his office.

FOUR

Campbell picked up his communicator off the desk. He punched in retired Global Police Security Captain Koko Sinopa's ID number. The call was answered almost immediately.

Campbell and Koko stared at each other for a long moment through cyberspace. Campbell thought Koko's handsome pale features were a little heavier. His long blond hair was a mess, as if he'd just woken up. Still, he thought Koko's brown eyes had the same intelligent intensity they'd shown since they'd fought together in the Yarv War.

"Who is it?" asked a female voice in the background of Koko's monitor.

Campbell realized Koko wasn't alone. *He better not be having sex in my old bedroom . . . in my old bed!*

Koko turned away from Campbell while speaking to someone in the background. "Oh, it's only Carlo from building maintenance, honey," he said. "Why don't you go and fix us some dinner?"

"But Koko, we weren't finished. Can't it wait?" whined the female voice.

"Go on!" Koko said sharply. "You know how hard it is to get maintenance up here. We can finish later."

Who the hell is Carlo, and why does Koko need building maintenance? Campbell wondered. *It doesn't sound like Koko's in my old Denver home anymore.*

Koko turned back to the monitor and winked at Campbell. Koko sighed in relief after a door slammed in the background.

"Burt Campbell! You're still alive!" Koko said with excitement. His expression quickly changed to one of suspicion. "Why are you calling me? There's a problem, isn't there? A big problem."

Oh, there's a big problem all right, Campbell thought. *Your retirement is over, and if I find out you've been having sex with sleazy women in my old bed, there's going to be hell to pay.*

"Hi'ya, Koko." Campbell put on his best smile.

"Stuff it, Burt. What's happened?"

Campbell skipped the pleasantries, and filled Koko in on Goro's kidnapping.

"And I suppose that you're going to return to Denver to save Sen, huh?" Koko asked with dread on his face. Campbell merely nodded. "I suppose you want me to come with you."

"You know I could never fool you, Koko. Will you help?"

Koko laughed warmly "Need you ever ask? Even if I didn't realize what all was at stake, I'd do whatever you ask of me. To tell you the truth, things have been kind of boring since you disappeared. I can't tell you how many nights I've laid awake wondering about you, Penelope, and those four mutts of yours."

"Penelope and I thank you from the bottom of our hearts," Campbell said with relief. "I'm going to come directly to my old house in Denver."

"Ah, Burt, I live in São Paulo now. You're going to have to come here if we're going to enter Denver together. It'll be safer if we go in my clipper. That way the authorities won't know you've returned."

"São Paulo? What in Hades are you doing there?"

"Oh, just enjoying my retirement. At least I was, but now it appears that's over. If I'm not mistaken, the world is about to be changed forever."

You couldn't have spoken truer words.

After getting Koko's address in São Paulo, Campbell told Koko he'd see him in an hour or two before signing off.

FIVE

Campbell reentered the kitchen, where Penelope sat at the table staring blankly at her unfinished breakfast. The dogs were nowhere to be seen. *Huh? They must have gone out on their morning hunt. Always thinking with their stomachs.*

"Koko is in São Paulo, Brazil. He's going to return to Denver with me," Campbell announced with a smile.

Penelope glanced up, but she didn't say anything.

Now comes the hardest part of all. "It's all right. I don't have any intention of getting killed or revealing our secret to the military. Koko and I will figure something out," he said, with all the honesty he could muster.

"I know I can't change your mind," Penelope said, sighing with defeat. "Won't you at least consider taking me and the dogs along? Burt, we can't survive without you. You're all we have left in this world."

Campbell couldn't bring himself to answer verbally. He shook his head with a heavy heart and went to get his duffle. When he returned, Penelope was still there with her head laid upon her crossed arms on the table.

"Penelope," he whispered. He came over and placed his warm hand on her slumped shoulder. "You knew this day would come. We couldn't have stayed here forever. Sooner or later they were going to find us again. In fact, I'm surprised we've been left alone for this long."

Still, Penelope remained a slumped figure of defeat and despair. She didn't respond.

"I want you to stay here for another three days. If I haven't either returned or contacted you after three days, I want you to take the dogs and the other clipper. Seek a new haven. I'll find you somehow when I can. I'm not deserting you and the dogs, Penelope. You are my life."

Penelope sat up with a start. Her blue-gray eyes were burning with intense emotionalism.

"If we were really your life, you wouldn't be leaving us like this," she sobbed, "running off to your death." She got up and raced off to their bedroom.

Campbell started after her, but then stopped.

Grabbing his duffle, he marched out into the morning heat without looking back. It was another beautiful day on their deserted island. The warm breeze carried the sweet smell of tropical flowers from Penelope's struggling garden. He stopped to gaze about for the Malamutes, but didn't see them. He felt deeply saddened. He made for the second of two military clippers they had hidden on the island across the rough lava rock.

While Campbell walked the kilometer to the second clipper, he peered in all directions expecting to see the dogs charging him with their usual enthusiasm. They were nowhere in sight.

Seems like everyone's against me on this one, he thought.

He found the black disk-shaped clipper sitting on the ledge above a volcanic fissure just as he'd left it. He scrambled down the rocky cliff leading to the ledge, and opened the entrance ramp beneath the starboard side of the huge disk. He stopped and studied the desolate black landscape one more time.

"Damn, I wonder what happened to those mutts. They're probably busy stuffing their furry faces as usual," he muttered, and entered the clipper.

After strapping himself into the cockpit, Campbell went through a flight checklist. He powered up the two ion engines, and gave Koko's São Paulo address to the computer.

As he took off, he gave the island one more glance. *Will I ever see this peaceful place again? Will I see Penelope and the Malamutes again?*

"Well, there's no turning back now," he grumbled. The clipper entered lower orbit for the hour-long trip from Hawaii to Brazil.

II

REUNION

ONE

Campbell felt deeply anxious about his and Penelope's future as he sat in the instrument-crammed cockpit of the clipper on his way to São Paulo. He was also confused as to who had kidnapped the Sens as he stared absently at the star-filled horizon.

Why has the military resorted to the illegal act of kidnapping a prominent police captain and his family? he wondered. *It's not like the act will go unnoticed. Has another corrupt general gone rogue?*

He knew he didn't have enough facts, and he mentally kicked himself for falling out of touch over the last two years. The clipper began its descent out of lower orbit without him reaching any conclusions.

Campbell gave São Paulo Air Space Control Koko's ID number to remain anonymous as he entered the 600-year-old city. He landed his huge clipper in a hangar atop the 280-floor building located on the outskirts of the international city where Koko owned one of the penthouse suites.

As Campbell took the glass elevator on the exterior of the building down to Koko's suite, he was in awe of the sheer size of the structure. It was over a thousand meters tall and stretched into the thin air of the clouds. He marveled at the technology used to create this self-sustaining city within a single building. He figured it contained the residences of over 200,000 people.

It would be obvious to any ambitious tax auditor that Koko didn't buy a penthouse suite in this building on a retired policeman's pension,

Campbell thought. *Maybe I should talk to Koko about his lavish spending before he gets us all caught. What am I thinking? We've already been caught!*

"My old friend." Koko greeted Campbell as the door to Koko's personal elevator opened into the penthouse. He shook Campbell's hand, and then gave him a warm hug of friendship.

Campbell stood back and stared at Koko with curiosity and a touch of apprehension about his old friend's reaction to his arrival. He noted Koko had put on a few kilos, but his wiry body still appeared muscular and ready to pull the ears off an aggravated bull. Koko's brown eyes peered at Campbell with their usual intensity. His pale face was piqued with intelligent curiosity. Finally, Koko's sharp features broke into a smile.

"Burt! What's happened to you? You must have grown ten centimeters and gained twenty kilos of muscle since I last saw you. What's more, you look fifty years younger."

"It's that noticeable, huh?" Campbell asked. "Well, let's just say life in hiding has been good to me." Campbell smiled. Koko was shaking his head in disbelief.

Campbell just waved off Koko's incredulous look. He entered the lavishly furnished living room that was complete with Abruzzi crystal chandeliers hanging from vaulted ceilings and a huge marble fireplace. He dropped his duffle, and gazed about for the woman he'd heard on the monitor. She was nowhere in sight.

Koko must have gotten rid of his playmate, Campbell thought. *Damn, I hope I didn't spoil something special.*

"Life might have been good to you, but not that good, Burt. This has something to do with Yamamoto's experiments, doesn't it? I know it does. So many strange things surrounded that teleporter. It must have done something to you."

More than I hope you ever know, Campbell thought.

He walked around the massive living room. The cream-colored walls were covered with original oil painting by Bykowski, Caldera, Gilchrist and other modern impressionists. The huge eastern windows overlooked the expansive city of São Paulo—the largest metropolis in the Southern Hemisphere, containing over twenty-five million people. In the distance, he spied the southeastern coast of the Brazilian Commonwealth and the Atlantic Ocean.

The furnishings in the room were those of the fabulously rich, made of the finest fabrics, leathers, and real wood. The woodwork was so exquisite in some of the tables and chairs they could only be antiques. It contained all the latest technology in computer and entertainment equipment. Campbell knew Koko as a fierce warrior, an excellent captain of men, and one of the best in security, but he was surprised by Koko's fine taste. He finally turned to find Koko watching him closely.

"Like I said, I could never fool you, Koko, but it's better that you don't know how or why I've been changed. Remember, you said yourself the less you know about the experiments, the less you can reveal if you are ever questioned by the military."

Koko slowly nodded in understanding. "Well, can I get you anything while we plan this rescue, or do you want to go straight to Denver?"

Campbell didn't answer.

"I made a few calls to some friends after you called, but this one's very quiet," Koko said. "It sounds like the kidnapping just took place within the last few hours at Denver Global Police Headquarters, but no one knows what's going on. Goro isn't receiving calls, and I couldn't even get through to his office. So whatever we do, we're going in blind."

Campbell nodded. *I figured as much.*

Koko peered toward the plushy carpeted floor with guilt.

"Burt, I have a confession to make. To tell you the truth, it's what I thought you were calling about earlier." He glanced up with embarrassment.

"What?" Campbell asked with suspicion.

"Well, remember that last day we were together and you gave me a few things to do?" Koko looked down again.

"Sure, I remember. I told you it could be imperative to Penelope's and my health that you caught Bohdan and Tojo before they killed again or were caught by the military. I know you failed to catch either killer."

Koko's normally pale face darkened in shame. He offered no excuse.

Campbell laughed. Koko glanced up with surprise.

"Don't worry about it, Koko. Both Bohdan and Tojo were captured by the military before you had a chance to hunt them down. Bohdan was caught by the military police trying to escape my . . . your . . . neighborhood. He was probably already gone while your agents were hunting my woods. Tojo turned himself in, more or less."

"What happened to Bohdan?" Koko asked anxiously.

"He came within a hair of killing me about a year ago. The military had tortured him and done their experiments. He told them about coming back to life after I killed him in Denver. Apparently, he also told them about going through Yamamoto's experiment and being changed by the teleporter. He made a deal with the military to lead an assault force to find me and bring me back alive. When he did find me, he killed his assault team and tried to kill me. In the end he died for good."

Koko smiled grimly over the death of the traitor. "What about Tojo?"

"I'm not too sure. We think he committed suicide. Bohdan seemed severely affected by the teleporter experiments. He was very ill by the time he came to kill me. I don't think the military learned what they wanted about the experiments from either Bohdan or Tojo. That's why they sent Bohdan after me to see if I was still alive. It's a good thing we destroyed the teleporters and computers in New Detroit and Moon Base Alfa-Tango. Now the military can never learn all the secrets of the experiments."

Koko dropped his head again. His long blond hair hid his anguished face.

Oh, no, Campbell thought.

"Well, that's part of my confession, Burt. I know you ordered me to destroy both teleporters, and I *did* destroy the one in New Detroit just like you suggested. We hauled it off-site and blew it up.

"Then, since we feared Bohdan would escape if we didn't pursue him immediately, I ordered one of my men to destroy the teleporter and computer on the moon. I didn't go there personally, and that was my mistake. The military had possession of the experiment area. There was no way we could destroy it."

"Lord in Hades! You're saying the military has had possession of a working teleporter?" Campbell asked. "Do you realize what this means?"

"I have failed you, but it isn't as bad as it seems. The computer on Alfa-Tango was a military computer. It wasn't something they didn't already have. I've learned since that it wasn't programmed with artificial intelligence like the one in New Detroit that we destroyed. I don't think they were able to reconstruct the experiments with the equipment on the moon base."

Thank the gods for that! There's still some hope.

"Are you sure?" Campbell asked, staring Koko in the eyes. Koko nodded. "Well, they're further along than I'd hoped. Still, Penelope told me Yamamoto kept the secrets of her recreation to himself and never gave all the information to anyone—including the computers. The military still doesn't know all the secrets, so maybe we're still okay. That must be why they kidnapped Sen's family to get at me."

Koko remained silent about his failure of Campbell's trust. Campbell felt sorry for his old friend.

"Let's go to my old house first," Campbell said to change the subject. "We can make any plans along the way. I think I'm just going to have to walk into Goro's office and turn myself in. This is going to require seat-of-the-pants planning, since we don't know anything. Koko, you used to be the best at this sort of thing. I just hope you haven't lost your touch."

Koko smiled at the compliment. "I think you have too much confidence in my abilities. But if there's anything I can do to help you and Penelope, I'll give my life to save you both. Lord, it's good to see you, Burt. I've been waiting for bad news about you two or that teleporter ever since you disappeared. I just want to redeem myself for my past mistakes."

TWO

Not knowing what to expect, Koko and Campbell quickly loaded Koko's personal clipper with enough weapons and equipment to take on an army.

I'm surprised how well prepared Koko has remained during his retirement, Campbell thought. *But then, he said he's been waiting and planning for this moment since our disappearance. It was a fool's hope to consider this matter over and finished just because Bohdan was greedy and took the location of our hiding place to the grave with him.*

Koko flew to Denver, never revealing to any of the authorities that Campbell was onboard. They entered Denver airspace with no problems, but they still hadn't come up with a plan of action.

"At least let me come with you to Sen's office," Koko said. "We have no idea who or how many are involved. You're going to need my help."

"No," Campbell replied immediately. "Having you along would reveal your continued relationship with me, and you could be captured. I want you to stay at the house and see what happens. If I don't return, I need you to take care of Penelope."

"Oh, no," Koko said, as he prepared to land at Campbell's old home in a secluded area at the outskirts of Denver.

"What's the problem?" Campbell asked anxiously. He came forward into the cockpit to gaze out the window.

"There's a military clipper in the backyard of the house. They must be guarding against your return."

Campbell sighed while he gazed down at the densely wooded five-acre area surrounding his old home. There was a huge disk-like clipper parked in the backyard between the house and the woods.

"Well, we're too close now," Campbell said. He knew they couldn't fight a military clipper and its personnel escort. "They'll have spotted us by now. You might as well land. I'll just have to turn myself in here."

Koko didn't argue, and did as he was told. As they got closer, and started to land on the clipper pad off to the left of the house, Campbell gazed intently at the military clipper.

"Koko, do you recognize that clipper?" Campbell asked with a scowl on his face.

"No, should I?"

"Just land," Campbell said with anger.

Koko landed his clipper with a look of apprehension as if he thought he was missing something. Campbell leaped out the clipper exit as soon as it had settled. He carried no weapons.

"Burt, wait for me!" Koko yelled, but Campbell was already at the clipper-pad gate.

Campbell marched into his old backyard with Koko running up on his heels. Suddenly a blood-curdling howl of some fierce beast pierced the quiet afternoon from the darkness of the deeply wooded forest to their right. It was answered by other eerie howls nearby. A tense moment followed when even the birds fell silent. Then came the sound of snapping branches and ruffled foliage, as if a horde of wild animals were rampaging toward them through the woods. Koko stood tensely at Campbell's side, wearing a fearful expression.

The sounds of yelping, growling, and throaty panting grew near. Abruptly the underbrush exploded as a pack of vicious wolves erupted from the forest. They charged Campbell and Koko as if driven by their instinctive need to kill their helpless victims. Their bodies were huge, immensely powerful. Their lips were curled in fierce snarls, showing off their huge white fangs. Bloody drool flew from their red tongues. Their furry faces were caked with the dried gore of a recent victim. Death twinkled in their eyes.

Koko let out a small scream and made a desperate dash for the protection of the clipper. Campbell stood his ground, wearing a wide grin.

"Hey, you guys!" Campbell managed to laugh before he was plowed over by Sergeant, Cala, Hana, and Amber.

Sergeant was barking madly. Cala and Amber woo-wooed with elation. Hana grrr'd. Burt lay on the ground laughing. He was smothered in a dog pile of fur, licking tongues, and wagging tails. Occasionally, he managed to get an arm or a leg loose as he struggled to free himself. He was no match for the dogs' love. They pummeled him into submission.

Here I was worried that I'd never see them again, Campbell mused.

Suddenly, the dogs leaped off Campbell to charge a new opponent. Campbell sat up wiping the slobber from his face. The massive dogs had surrounded Koko in a circle of terror. Koko had drawn a directed energy beam pistol. He was frantically trying to point the weapon at all the dogs at once.

"Burt! Burt! What are these things?" Koko yelled, frantic with fear.

"Don't shoot! Just put away your pistol and stand still."

Campbell saw what tremendous courage it took Koko to lower his weapon. The dogs were snarling. Growls rumbled deep in their chests. They were showing Koko fangs the length of a grown man's little finger.

Damn! Campbell thought. *They're going to rip him to shreds!*

Just as suddenly as they'd charged Koko, all four dogs stopped their attack in unison. They turned their heads toward something behind Campbell. He followed their gaze. Another wide smile broke over his face.

"Penelope, what're you guys doing here?" As Campbell asked this, the Malamutes stampeded by him and obediently sat in front of Penelope, peering expectantly up at her beautiful face as if waiting for new orders. "I wish I could get my own dogs to obey me the way they obey you," Campbell muttered.

"Hello to you, Burt," Penelope grinned. "It's that telepathic link we share, I tell ya."

"Yeah, yeah," Campbell muttered sarcastically as he approached Penelope. "All I did was give them my heart and take care of them for twenty-some years. What do I get in return? Disobedience and a slobbery beating every time I come home. But you show up, and in just one day they give you all the special treatment. Ungrateful mutts."

He smiled broadly as he parted his way through the blockade of patiently waiting dogs. "Lord, am I glad to see you." He hugged her tight. "I was sort of hoping you'd show up, but then I was hoping you didn't."

She hugged him warmly in return. "I told you, Burt, we're family now. Wherever you go, we go. Whomever you fight, we fight, and that includes the dogs."

Campbell released Penelope and stood back. "I guess I was wrong to try and keep you all out of this. You're as much a part of this as I am, if not more." He grinned again and gazed happily around at his family.

Abruptly, the four dogs whirled toward the clipper with deep threatening growls in their throats. Koko had been approaching, but now he leaped back with his hands up as if surrendering. "Burt, what're those monstrous things?"

"Easy guys, it's just Koko." Campbell said. "Don't you remember, Koko?"

The dogs stopped growling, but they crouched as if ready to pounce as they slowly approached Koko with their heads lowered, ears back, and their fur up. Koko stared at Campbell with wide, pleading eyes. The fearsome dogs fanned out and surrounded him as if awaiting the order to attack.

Well, it has been a long time since they've seen another human besides me and Penelope, Campbell thought. "Relax, Koko. Just stay calm, and they won't hurt you—I don't think. Don't you remember my dogs?"

"These are those Malamutes you took away two years ago?" Koko uttered in a terrified whisper. He looked like he was about to pee his pants. "What the hell happened to them?"

"It's okay, guys. It's just Koko," Campbell repeated, and avoided the question. The dogs relaxed and lowered themselves to the ground, but they still appeared ready to pounce at the slightest provocative move from Koko.

Koko tore his wide eyes away from his surrounding assailants long enough to look at Penelope. "Penelope, either my memory is really off, or I'd say you've changed as much as Burt and the dogs." Koko glanced around at the six of them for a moment. "This has something to do with Yamamoto's experiments, and those things you told me before you escaped, doesn't it? Yamamoto really could have created a race of superhumans."

"I think you're finally starting to realize our worst fears could happen," Campbell said, smiling grimly.

Koko gazed down at the dogs that continued to eye him suspiciously.

"But I still don't understand what happened to your beautiful dogs. They must be twice the size as they were. My God, that male must weight over a hundred kilos, and look at the muscle on them. To tell you the truth, when they charged out of the woods, I thought we were being attacked by grizzly bears or something."

The dogs apparently got tired of Koko's speech and decided he was okay. They got up and casually wondered back to Penelope and Campbell. Hana went over to wash Campbell's hand with slobbery affection.

Penelope looked at Koko. "Captain Sinopa, it's better that you know as little as possible about those experiments. If you require an explanation about us, just think of it as the next step in our evolution. You're correct. The changes in our physical and mental beings occurred because of Yamamoto's experiment. That's why we must either talk Burt out of turning himself in, or make sure he isn't captured. The information in his bloodstream will give the military all they need to create that army of superhumans."

Koko slowly nodded his head in understanding.

Campbell turned and gave Penelope a nasty glance for giving Koko too much information and suggesting he not try to save Goro and his family.

"Come in the house and let's eat," Penelope said, and turned to the dogs. "You guys can go back to the woods and hunt your own dinner."

Finally released from their protective duties, the eager dogs charged off. They disappeared into the woods with the silence of ghosts. Koko watched them disperse with an expression of anxious curiosity. He was still shaking his head in confusion as he followed Burt and Penelope into the house.

BENJAMIN "BENEDICT" ARNOLD

ONE

I hope Akio and Oki are here as well, Campbell thought, as he landed Koko's clipper in the garage next to the Global Police Headquarters in Denver. *As long as the whole family is being held in a group inside Goro's office, it'll be possible to rescue all of them at once.*

He exited the clipper and made his way toward the headquarters building, still thinking about the heated discussion he'd had with Penelope and Koko about him going in alone. He saw no reason for having Koko on site, since he doubted one more man could stop the military if they decided to take him by force. He'd won this argument. They'd finally decided that it was Koko's job to protect Penelope and organize a team to rescue Campbell if he was taken.

Neither had he been ready to allow it to be known that Penelope Preston was alive. They still didn't know who was involved in the kidnapping, or what they wanted from him. He knew if things went as poorly as he feared, Penelope would have plenty of chances to fight for their lives. Her high intelligence and physical capabilities would be invaluable to Koko if Campbell needed to be rescued.

Still, their parting at the house was one of great sorrow and dread. The dogs had been too busy with their hunt to see him off.

"Damn, my life has a lower priority rating than their stomachs," Campbell grumbled.

He approached the headquarters building as the sun was waning in the west. A cool breeze blew across the manicured lawns on the early fall evening. In the background of the five-story concrete building towered the Rocky Mountains with stunning beauty. The dying sun glistened off their snowy peaks. Although the building was constructed like a circle surrounded by a five-point star, it reminded Campbell of a bunker. The five stories above ground contained the administration offices. The other twenty floors beneath the surface housed the jails, labs, and armory.

At the moment, the building was deep in the mountain shadows. Its tinted windows peered back at him like malevolent black eyes awaiting his arrival. He hoped that most of the office personnel would be gone for the day. He expected trouble the moment he entered the building.

Campbell didn't have clearance to enter the building anymore, and was forced to go to the front entrance. He stopped and shoved his index finger up his right nostril like a child searching for a choice booger as he ensured everything was secure.

He stepped up to the entrance, and opened one of the tinted doors to allow two women in business attire to exit. The women gazed up at him in wonder and possibly fear. He realized his immense size, dark face, shoulder-length black hair, and black-marble eye implants scared the women. He quickly entered the building.

Upon entering the modern marble-floored lobby, Campbell was happy to see that it was nearly empty of personnel. He immediately noticed things had changed. There were four armored guards standing next to the chrome-plated reception desk. They were scanning the wide, brightly lit area where everyone entering was checked for weapons by a security bot standing next to a scanning device.

Two of the guards were dressed in light-gray Global Police Security Force uniforms—Koko's old unit.

Those other two goons are dressed in black army uniforms from the military base at Moon Base Alfa-Tango, Campbell thought. *What the hell are they doing here?*

He noted all the guards wore body armor, and were armed to the teeth. Although the security agents were standing apart from the two military guards, all of them came to attention and drew their weapons when he came into view. The security agents only drew directed energy beam pistols. Campbell knew his armor could handle the DEPs without a problem. It was the moon base guards that worried him. They both carried sonic blasters that would blow apart his body no matter how it was armored.

Campbell strolled up to the security bot by the shiny reception desk without missing a step. He passed his ID through the scanner.

"Oh boy, here we go," he muttered. He felt his heart rate quicken, and his palms perspiring.

The bot showed the typical lack of personality and didn't respond. Campbell handed his DEP to the bot so he could pass through the weapons scanner. It was the only weapon he carried. He figured he would never be allowed into the building with a weapon anyway.

He cleared the scanners with no problems. The bot didn't return his weapon. Campbell gazed down the wide window-lit hall past the four guards. The left wall was made up of windows peering into the vast garden-relaxation area in the center of the building. The garden was already in the shadows, but Campbell saw that the tree leaves were just starting to change, and the summer flowers were gone. He also noted there was no one else in sight down the hallway.

What in Hades is going on here? Does the military control the whole building? That's illegal!

TWO

"Burt Campbell?" a lieutenant in a security force uniform asked as he approached.

Campbell glared down at the tall, muscularly built lieutenant with a round jovial face and crew-cut brown hair.

"That's me. Am I under arrest?" Campbell asked in a neutral tone.

The man appeared uncomfortable and young to Campbell. The lieutenant glanced at his partner before he summoned his courage and threw out his chest.

"Ah, no, sir, I'm Lieutenant Baxter. I've been asked to escort you to Captain Sen's office as soon as you arrived."

"Kind of young for the rank, aren't you, sonny?" Campbell said threateningly.

Baxter's face paled before it reddened. He glanced at the floor. His lighter, smaller, partner grinned. The two military guards barked with laughter.

Campbell glared menacingly at the military guards. They went tightlipped.

Those military guards appear more like hardened veterans. They could present problems, Campbell thought. *Well, I'm not here by my own choice, and I have no intention of being cooperative. Military guards don't belong on these premises. Their presence only confirms my suspicions that it's the military behind the kidnappings. I just wonder what the garrison from the moon base has to do with this situation.*

Campbell turned back to Baxter. "Well, Lieutenant, I'm on my way to see Captain Sen right now. It's still a free world. You can accompany me if you wish, but I won't go like some prisoner."

Having dismissed them, Campbell strolled by the lieutenant as if it were just another day at the office. The two military guards weren't so easily put off. They jumped out to block Campbell's path with their bulky sonic blasters pointed at his torso. Campbell walked up until the barrels of the two weapons were squarely on his huge chest.

"You either get out of my way, little boys," Campbell said softly, "or you're going to get hurt—bad."

The hideously ugly guard on his left sneered. He had sharp pointy teeth, and his dark face with almond-shaped black eyes reminded Campbell of a goblin's. *Something's wrong with this man's face. It isn't natural.*

"Little tikes, is it, mate?" the guard said with a menacing grin. "We'll see how many little pieces you make after I pull the trig . . ."

The guard never finished the sentence. Campbell attacked with lightning speed. He swiftly swatted both guards' weapons out of their hands with one powerful swing of his right hand. Before the blasters even hit the ground, he had his left palm tightly wrapped around the uppity guard's throat in a death grip. He heaved him off the ground as his heart soared with the exhilaration of his incredible strength.

The guard's feet kicked violently in the air. His face turned purple as blood began to seep through his gaping mouth. His black goblin-like eyes bulged as he struggled for breath. Campbell held him aloft as if he were a child's toy.

"I am not your mate," Campbell said with a wincing smile.

He crushed the guard's windpipe in his giant hand before he slammed the man's limp body to the marble floor. The second military guard stared at his partner's demise with stunned silence. He seemed rooted in place by his amazement before he collected his wits. He bent for his blaster.

"That would be an incredibly stupid mistake," Campbell said calmly.

The stooping guard didn't heed the warning. After a brief hesitation, he kept going for his blaster.

Campbell swiftly stepped forward. He brought his right fist down with a powerful blow on the base of the man's neck. The guard collapsed to the floor as if he were a limp sack of garbage. He was either unconscious or dead.

If he isn't dead, he'll be in intensive care for a month, Campbell mused.

Campbell whirled around on the two security agents. Both of them were standing just where he'd left them. They stared back at him with wide-eyed shock. Neither had dared to draw their weapons.

Good, Campbell thought. *They don't appear to be as stupid as these other two.*

"Okay, you two," Campbell said pleasantly. "If you plan to accompany me to Captain Sen's office, I want you out in front of me where I can see you. I hope you have more brains than these two." He pointed to the two limp and bleeding bodies on the floor.

Both the agents scampered to get ahead of him.

"Oh, and Lieutenant, I'll take those pistols," Campbell said with a wave of his hand. "You know, just so you don't get any ideas."

"But, but . . .," the lieutenant started to protest.

The other agent didn't say a word. He quickly handed Campbell his DEP. The lieutenant shrugged in defeat and handed over his pistol as well.

"Good boys." Campbell blessed them with an evil smile. "Lead the way, please."

As the agents started down the hall, Campbell scooped up the two military guards' blasters. He tossed the bulky rifles over his shoulder, still grinning with evil pleasure. *Damn, that felt good.*

He followed the guards down to the elevators, but was surprised by the echoing rings of their footsteps. The hallway remained completely devoid of people. He'd never seen it like this before.

"Lieutenant Baxter?" Campbell asked. "Where is everyone?"

The young lieutenant pushed the up-button to the elevator and turned timidly toward Campbell.

"Captain Sen ordered everyone out of the building. I think those two secretaries you passed were the last to leave, but there should be others about."

Campbell grunted as the elevator door opened. He followed the agents into the lift.

"Captain Sen's office," Campbell said to the elevator. "What about other security agents?" he asked the lieutenant.

"Oh, all the security guards are still here, but they were ordered to stay out of sight and not interfere," said Baxter. His expression reminded Campbell of a terrified child's. His partner was peering at the elevator floor like a guilty teenager awaiting his parents' return.

The elevator shot upward and dropped Campbell's stomach to the floor. It came to a rapid halt when it reached the fifth floor before shooting sideways to go around the building to Sen's office. Campbell wanted to ask about the moon base guards, but didn't have time. The elevator came to another abrupt halt.

"Zooids, I'd forgotten how much I hate these elevators," he muttered.

The door opened into another wide and well-lit hallway. Across from the elevator was a large picture window already shadowed in darkness. Outside the window, Campbell could still make out the tops of pines and leafy oak trees that were part of the garden in the center of the building. Campbell halted the nervous agents before they made their exit.

"Hold it. How many of these military guards are in Sen's office?"

"I don't know, Inspector," Baxter said, as if expecting a beating for his lack of knowledge. "We weren't told anything. We received a call from Sen's office to wait at the entrance for you, and then to bring you directly to his office. We weren't expecting any trouble until the military guards showed up just before you arrived. They warned us that you had turned traitor and were very dangerous."

The young man had an honest face with a scared expression. Campbell believed him.

"Well, I'm hardly a traitor, and even you could be considered dangerous under the right circumstances. Obviously, those guards didn't heed their own warnings. I'm only here to see that Captain Sen and his family are freed and safe." Campbell tried to smile to show the agents he wasn't a threat, but then gave it up as hopeless when they retreated from his toothy grin.

I'm sure these agents have nothing to do with the kidnapping, he thought. *This smells too much like the treachery of a military operation. These agents are under Sen's control. I doubt an entire group of Global Police Security Agents would rebel against Sen to commit this kidnapping.* Still, he didn't return their weapons.

"Baxter, Captain Sen has been kidnapped by the military. I'm going to free him somehow, since I think it's me the kidnappers want. I want you to find Sen after he's released. If I'm not with him, I want you to tell Sen to seek Sergeant Preston at his usual spot. He's to tell the sergeant what has happened. You got that?" Campbell's black eyes burned into Baxter's.

The lieutenant appeared nervous as if he were considering collaborating with a possible traitor, but then slowly nodded.

"I'll tell Captain Sen to seek out a Sergeant Preston at his usual spot," Baxter repeated.

"Good man," Campbell said. "Now you two get lost down the hall, and wait for Sen to come out of his office. Stay out of the way. This could get nasty."

THREE

Campbell didn't wait for the agents' response. He exited the elevator, and turned right to head down the hall. When he came to an intersecting hallway, he stopped and peeked cautiously around the corner. He wasn't surprised by the reception committee awaiting him outside Sen's office doors. Sen's old Irish secretary, Galinda, wasn't at her desk, but a much bigger problem was—two problems. Two huge armored guard bots stood in their human forms, blocking the entrance. Their black heads swiveled on armor-plated shoulders as their optics searched the hallway.

"Damn," Campbell muttered. He retreated behind the corner and considered his options.

My DEPs are practically useless against that bot armor, Campbell thought. *I could try and lure them away from the entrance, but they're carrying sonic blasters that'll blow me to pieces.*

Thinking of his own sonic blasters, he determined a plan of action.

The bots were stationed only about a meter apart. This worked to his advantage. He would have to hit the bots dead on. If he missed, the sonic blast could go through the office wall and kill those inside. He didn't want to hurt Sen and his family.

"You're stalling, Burt, Just do it," he grumbled to himself.

He took the blasters off his shoulder, and put one on the floor. After ensuring the remaining blaster was fully charged, he peeked behind him to be sure the coast was clear. Without further thought, he charged around the corner with the blaster leveled.

He targeted the hulking bot to his left. He fired just as the bots spotted him and lowered their weapons to return fire. His sonic blast slammed into the chest plate of his target. The bot disintegrated into pieces with such force they exploded through the office wall. Campbell knew he was already too late. He threw himself to the floor just as the second bot fired and blew apart the wall to his left.

Campbell sat up uninjured and amazed when no shots followed the first. He glanced through the dust and rubble toward the office. The remaining bot was slowly struggling to drag its bulk off the floor. Campbell realized it had been thrown aside by his shot at the first bot. It had fired as it lost balance, saving his life.

He leaped to his feet. He quickly aimed and blasted the remaining bot before it got another chance to kill him. As the bot was disintegrated by the sonic destruction, the rest of Sen's office wall was blown apart.

Campbell waited anxiously for the rubble to settle and the obscuring cloud of dust to clear so he could see any remaining opposition. Sudden directed energy beams flashed like brilliant lights through the dust cloud in Campbell's direction. Before he could react, one of the blind shots slammed into his armored shoulder and threw him off his feet in surprised agony.

Campbell was on his back for only an instant before he was leaping to his feet. He saw he was already too late. Three raging men in black uniforms were charging down the hall firing their DEPs. He quickly fired his blaster, knowing his aim only had to come close. He was rewarded as two of the men disappeared in a mess of splattered gore.

Campbell didn't have time to rejoice as he was slammed to the floor again by a DEP shot reflecting off his chest armor. He lay momentarily winded and dazed. Before he could recover, the third guard was upon him, drilling his weapon barrel into Campbell's temple.

"Don't move, Campbell, or you're a dead man," growled the guard.

Campbell gazed up at the dark-faced guard with a burning hatred. For an instant, he was stunned by the man's resemblance to the goblin-faced guard in the lobby.

"You first!" Campbell snarled.

Campbell moved faster than the guard could react. Jerking his head away from the pistol barrel, Campbell threw up his wrecking ball fist into the guard's surprised features. The DEP blasted harmlessly into the floor as Campbell felt his knuckles shatter his assailant's face. The guard was hurled backward with his nose driven into his brain. He was dead before he hit the floor.

FOUR

"Enough, Campbell!" yelled a voice from the front of Sen's office. The man's voice sounded sickeningly familiar to Campbell.

He whirled around and cautiously got to his feet. He gazed down the bloody and ruined hallway. It appeared like a fierce battleground of shattered rubble, dusty smoke, and torn bodies.

A smallish man in a black military uniform with a general's stripes stepped through the rubble that had been the front of Sen's office.

Oh, no, Campbell thought.

Directly in front of the general was a small teenage boy of Japanese descent. The boy was Goro Sen's son, Akio. The general had his skinny left arm wrapped tightly around Akio's neck with his right hand fisting a DEP to Akio's ear. Campbell immediately recognized the weasel-faced general with dark greased-back hair and rodent black eyes.

"Been a long time since the Yarv War, Arnold," Campbell said with a nasty smile. "How far did you have to stick your big nose up someone's ass to make a general's stripes?"

Flush anger flared in Benjamin Arnold's face. Campbell knew he'd hit a sore spot.

"You were always the smooth one, Campbell. Now put your weapons down, and step into the office." Arnold glanced around at the rubble. "What's left of it at least."

"Still hiding behind other people, Benedict? You're still a traitor." Campbell pushed his luck. Again the anger flashed across Arnold's pinched, rodent features.

"You're not in a position to be making insults, Campbell. Now put down your weapons, or I'll kill this sniveling brat!"

Arnold pushed the barrel into Akio's ear to emphasize his point. Akio winced in pain.

"Burt, please do as he says!" Campbell heard Oki Sen scream from the office.

Campbell saw the terror in the boy's eyes. Rage filled his heart to see the boy's fear, but he also realized he had to do as Arnold wished or he *would* kill Akio. Arnold was a treacherous murderer—possibly worse than his greatest nemesis, Hedon Bohdan.

"I never saw you after I had you arrested for treason and collaborating with Bohdan," Campbell said, with malice dripping from his voice. "I know you led many of my troops into Yarv ambushes. A lot of good men died there—good friends. You should have gotten the death sentence like Bohdan. You must have had some pretty powerful connections to have gotten off."

"I'm getting impatient, Campbell," Arnold said calmly. "Drop your weapons or I'll kill the boy and start on Sen and his wife."

Looks like this is what this is all about, but I wonder what Arnold really wants. Campbell slowly bent over and placed his blaster on the floor. He stood up and glared at Arnold with intense hatred before he slowly walked forward.

"Put down the DEPs as well!" Arnold snapped.

Campbell stopped. He pulled the two pistols from his belt before he laid them on the floor as well. Now he was defenseless, with only his wits to save himself and the Sens.

"You'll never survive this one, Arnold. Now everyone will know what a traitor you really are." To his surprise, Arnold laughed.

"As usual, you have no idea. Now come on."

Campbell walked forward. He glared down at Arnold through his cold black eyes before he turned and smiled warmly at Akio.

"You've grown, Akio. It's great to see you, young man."

Akio's Adam's apple bobbled up and down in his skinny neck. His dark, tear-rimmed eyes peered bravely at Campbell.

"Thank you for coming, Inspector Campbell," Akio whispered. "I knew you would save us from the monster."

Arnold swiftly unwound his arm from around Akio's neck before he wickedly slapped the boy on the back of his black-haired head with his left palm. Akio's head was thrown forward, away from the pistol barrel. Campbell roared and grabbed Arnold's scrawny neck in his powerful hand. He heaved Arnold's thin body toward the ceiling with death in his eyes.

"Stop, Burt! It'll kill us all!" Goro screamed from the office.

Campbell whipped his head toward Goro's plea. The office was dark and obscured by dust particles. He could still clearly make out Sen's outline along with several other dark-clad guards. Yet what arrested his gaze was a monstrous figure that towered over Goro like some devil from Hell.

"What in Hades?" Campbell muttered. He felt the point of Arnold's DEP jab into his head.

Arnold was gasping something that Campbell figured was an order to either release him or lose his head. His anger was spent in his curiosity and fear of the thing behind Goro. He relaxed his grip on Arnold's neck. Arnold fell to the floor with a thud. Campbell ignored him.

"Goro, what's going on here?" Campbell asked. He cautiously entered the office through the ruined walls while stepping over the rubble on the floor.

Akio sprinted around him and ran into his father's arms. Campbell saw Goro's wife, Oki, was being held at gunpoint by a black-uniformed guard off to the left side of the large, dimly lit room. Goro was standing in front of his expansive desk. The office had been ransacked. Behind the desk was a window-wall looking out onto darkening Rockies.

The desk had been swept clear of Goro's monitors and communications devices. Files were scattered all over the floor. Hover chairs had been thrown aside. Goro's conference table had been tossed against the bookcase-lined wall to the right. Campbell ignored the disarray while transfixed with wonder and growing fear at the huge shadow lurking between Goro and his desk.

Damn thing looks like a huge gargoyle, Campbell thought.

Despite his terror, Campbell marveled at the gargoyle. It was immense in its structure and musculature. It was at least a head taller than him, and its body half again as wide. Its shoulders and arms bulged with strength. Its legs were bowed and thick with muscles. The thing was naked, and had dark scaly skin that appeared to be armor. It had no sex, and was standing on talon-like feet. Its powerful hands had long fingers that were tipped with dagger-like nails.

The thing had no weapons, but Campbell figured it didn't need any. The gargoyle's head and face was strangely bat-like with an upturned nose and wide nostrils. Above a mouth filled with long knife-like teeth were two eyes that burned with flickering flames from Hades itself.

The thing growled something at Campbell. It sounded like grunted words in some uncouth language that he didn't understand. As it spoke, a long, forked tongue slithered from its mouth. When Campbell only stared at it with horror and didn't respond, the gargoyle stepped forward, knocking Goro and Akio out of its way as if they were made of paper.

That was when Campbell became aware the thing had huge bat wings folded behind its massive back. Campbell stood rooted to the floor as the gargoyle came toward him with a purposeful slowness. As it stepped forward, the gargoyle spread its immense black wings. It shrouded itself in such darkness that Campbell could only see the flames of its red eyes. It folded its wings again and continued forward. To Campbell, it seemed as if the creature had the density of stone. The floor trembled beneath the thing's weighty steps.

"For Jonah's sake, what are you?" Campbell whispered.

Could this be some off-world creature I've never seen before? Campbell thought. *I doubt it. The thing's structure is too familiar to human history. It's like something out of a horrible human fairy tale. Like something created out of a human's mind to instill fear in the human soul. But who would have been insane enough to have made this monstrosity? And why?*

As if to confirm Campbell's suspicions, he felt the incredible black aura of the beast coming before its physical presence. Deciding this thing was the creation of man gave him the resolve to stand his ground.

The gargoyle stopped in front of Campbell and glared down him. For a moment, he was hypnotized by its flickering red eyes. He shook off the feeling.

"Lord, you stink! I'll bet you don't get too many dates," Campbell said.

The thing opened it hinged jaw before Campbell's face and roared with a stenchy breath that made Campbell retreat a step. Then it moved with a terrifying swiftness that nearly caught Campbell off guard.

The gargoyle reached out to grasp Campbell by the throat, but he caught its thick scaly forearm in between both his hands. He felt the creature's terrible strength like nothing he'd encountered before. Not even a guard bot could rival this power. Campbell thought he was holding his own for a moment before the gargoyle's expression changed into what he thought might be a demon smile. Suddenly, a thick snake-like thing whipped out from behind the creature and roped around Campbell's legs.

Damn! This thing has a tail!

"You're just full of un-pleasantries," Campbell managed before the gargoyle tossed him back and off balance as if it were child's play. As Campbell crashed to the floor, the gargoyle gurgled with a new noise that he decided was laughter.

FIVE

"That's enough, George!" Arnold yelled. The creature stopped and glanced up at where Arnold stood in the ruined entrance to the office.

Campbell was already kneeling and preparing for a nasty death as he turned his head toward Arnold. "George? You called this, this thing, George?"

Arnold appeared surprised by the question. "Well, yes, that's his, its name."

"George?" Campbell turned and gaped at the most sinister, fearful creature he'd ever seen. Suddenly, he felt wild laughter building in his sore chest before he squelched it.

"George, your job here is done for now," Arnold said. "Go back to the roof and wait for our arrival. Oh, and don't let anyone near the clipper."

To Campbell's disbelief, George grunted once and then turned back to the huge window behind Sen's desk. For the first time, Campbell noticed that the window was gone, smashed inward as if something immense had crashed through it. He considered the possibility of this, since the window was on the fifth floor. Then he recalled the gargoyle had wings.

Everyone scampered out of George's path as it slowly made its way forward. Once George arrived at the window, Campbell was again surprised when it didn't take flight. It reached out with its talon-like fingers and grasped the concrete wall outside. Then the thing crawled out and up the outside wall with effortless strength before it was gone. The entire room seemed to lighten with the passing of the thing's evil presence.

Campbell slowly got to his feet again. Arnold strolled by him with his DEP pointing at the Sens huddled near the right side of the desk. Campbell feared he would kill the Sens, having captured his prize.

There were three stern-faced guards left in the office. One was standing behind the Sens. The other two were pointing sonic blasters at him from a safe distance. Campbell knew he wouldn't surprise them again. He was at Arnold's mercy.

"Let the Sens go, Arnold," Campbell said. "You have me now. That's what you wanted, isn't it?"

Arnold turned his beady black eyes on Campbell. "You must care about this family a great deal, Campbell. Why else would you have turned yourself in and risked certain death?"

"It's called love and loyalty for one's fellow humans, Arnold. Feelings you obviously wouldn't understand," Campbell sneered.

Rage surged in Arnold's face.

Uh-oh, Campbell thought. *I may have pushed too many of Arnold's buttons with that one.*

Arnold's body shook with anger as he whipped his DEP around to point at Campbell's head. Campbell squinched his face waiting for the intense heat of the energy beam that would kill him.

It never came. Instead, Arnold sighed and lowered the weapon.

"Come over here and sit down in this chair, Campbell." Arnold pointed at a high-backed steel chair with metal cuff bands welded to the arms and legs.

That's obviously not some new furniture Goro brought in to persecute the poor performance of his employees. Arnold brought it with him for the sole purpose of restraining me. He obviously wants me alive for some reason.

"There?" Campbell pointed at the chair, but didn't move toward it.

"Right now, Campbell!" Arnold yelled. He turned his weapon on Akio again.

Campbell slowly moved to the chair and planted his rear. Arnold put away his DEP before he stepped forward and backhanded Campbell across the face. Campbell barely flinched. It was Arnold who was wincing with pain.

"That was stupid," Campbell said with a smile. "You must be used to picking on women and children—or shooting men in the back."

Arnold whipped back his hand with snarling rage to strike Campbell again before thinking better of it.

Campbell calmly brought his hand up to wipe his face as if he were checking for blood. With little show of manners, he snuck his index finger up his right nostril.

"I see you haven't lost your social graces," Arnold commented dryly.

Campbell pulled his finger out of his nose and examined his fingertip. Arnold turned away as if afraid Campbell might pop the finger into his mouth. Campbell wiped his finger off on his armor before he pinched his nose and wiggled it around a bit.

"Put your wrists and ankles into the manacles," Arnold ordered.

"Turn the Sens loose, and I'll do whatever you say."

"Not until I'm sure you're secure and helpless to escape."

Campbell glared at Arnold with malice. His face softened as he turned to look at the Sens. He saw the pleading in Oki's eyes, but there was defiance in the faces of Goro and Akio. He knew such defiance was useless at this point. He placed his wrists and ankles into the restraints.

"Secure him, Sergeant," Arnold ordered one of the guards pointing a blaster at Campbell.

The sergeant approached Campbell with caution.

"Boo!" Campbell yelled. The sergeant jumped about a meter into the air.

Arnold huffed while Campbell laughed.

The sergeant appeared embarrassed as he stepped forward and slapped Campbell's restraints closed before retreating. He picked up his blaster again, and pointed it at Campbell's head as if he feared Campbell was capable of freeing himself. To test the theory, Campbell yanked and struggled in his chair to see if he could free his arms. It was useless.

"Sergeant, check the Inspector for transmitters," Arnold ordered.

The sergeant approached Campbell cautiously while pulling a small black box off his belt. Starting at his feet, the sergeant began to search Campbell's person. When he got to Campbell's chest, the black box beeped loudly. The sergeant glanced over at Arnold for instructions.

Campbell wore a disgusted expression as Arnold stepped forward and unzipped his armored shirt. He reached inside Campbell's shirt and felt around. Arnold's face turned triumphant as he pulled out his hand and held up a device the size of a sewing needle.

"A transmitter!" Arnold shouted. "Who were you transmitting to, Campbell?"

"No one. My recorder is in my clipper. I was hoping to gather evidence against the kidnappers," Campbell said with disgust at being caught.

"Ha!" Arnold said. He snapped the transmitter in two in front of Campbell's nose. "Even if you were able to record this conversation, no one would believe you," Arnold said, laughing obnoxiously. "Search the rest of his body, Sergeant. I want to make sure this transmitter wasn't a decoy."

"I thought you weren't worried about being recorded, Arnold."

"It never hurts to be safe," Arnold grinned.

Campbell began to seriously worry about the Sen's safety. *What's stopping Arnold from killing the Sens to ensure their silence?*

In the meantime, the sergeant was waving his box around the rest of Campbell's body. The box beeped again when it got to Campbell's head. The sergeant glanced up again at Arnold, who was shaking his head.

"Don't worry about it," Arnold said. "It's just his implanted eyes that were linked to the Central Police Computer through his personal recorder. His eyes have a limited transmission range, and since his recorder isn't on him, it can't pick up the video transmission. Check his ears and mouth just to be sure."

The sergeant gave the general a nasty look before taking a small flashlight off his duty belt and peering into both of Campbell's ears. When he was satisfied that Campbell's ears were clean, at least of transmitters, the sergeant stood before Campbell impatiently waiting for him to open his mouth. Campbell childishly glared back at him with his lips sealed shut.

"Don't make me injure one of the Sens, Campbell," Arnold threatened. "If you have nothing to hide, open your mouth."

Campbell glared at Arnold before saying, "Ahhh," and opening his mouth wide while sticking out his tongue.

The sergeant squinched up his face and peered into Campbell's mouth with his flashlight. Satisfied by what he saw, the sergeant backed away.

"Check his teeth and make sure none of them are false," Arnold ordered.

The sergeant gave Arnold another disgusted look before turning back to Campbell who had clammed up again.

"Campbell!" Arnold shouted.

"I don't have any false teeth," Campbell said, but opened his mouth anyway.

The sergeant sighed and leaned forward. Using his index finger and thumb, the sergeant wiggled each of Campbell's teeth with what he thought was a bit too much vigor and roughness.

Finally, the sergeant stepped back while shaking his head and wiping his hand on this tunic. Campbell made a disgusted expression and spat out the sergeant's foulness on the floor before him.

"He's clean, General," said the sergeant.

SIX

Arnold finally seemed satisfied and nodded.

"Well, you have me where you want me, Arnold. Set the Sens free," Campbell said. He wanted the Sens gone before the conversation turned to something incriminating against Arnold, and Arnold decided to have them killed.

"You're in no position to make commands, Campbell. I'll let the Sens go, but only after they hear the charges against you. The young man here seems to admire you a great deal. I want to enjoy his expression when he hears what you've done and what kind of a criminal his father has been protecting." Arnold smiled as he said this.

"What charges? You've got nothing on me." Campbell was outraged that this criminal had the gall to point a finger at him.

Arnold's smile grew into outright laughter. "Burt Campbell, how can you be so naïve? Just walking in here you killed five military personnel. We have witnesses to those murders. That alone would be enough to sentence you to death."

"I only killed three of your men, and they fired on me first. The two guards at the front lobby were only seriously injured, but they'll live. I have witnesses that these attacks were provoked as well. Your charges will never stand up in court."

Again Arnold laughed.

Boy, that laughter is really starting to get on my nerves.

"Still, those charges alone would be enough to put you under arrest, and I don't think you want to be arrested by military personnel, do you?"

Campbell didn't answer, so Arnold continued. "Perhaps you don't realize it, but you've been one of the most sought men by the military police for the past two years. First, there's the destruction of a top military project. You destroyed Dr. Jiro Yamamoto's teleportation experiment, and killed General Stenwood. Furthermore, you abused the authority Stenwood gave you and misappropriated huge amounts of military funds. The government wants their money back, and the military wants to see you executed for multiple murders. Do I need to continue?"

"You can't prove any of that," Campbell said, shocked by the lying accusations. "Stenwood was killed by the security around Yamamoto's experiment. And it was Stenwood that embezzled those funds."

"Do you deny the rest of it?" Arnold asked, apparently not concerned whether Campbell denied anything.

Campbell didn't respond.

"Well, I'll continue anyway," Arnold said. "I want you to realize just what a hopeless position you're in right now, and how much power I hold over your future.

"Then there is the stealing of a government military clipper from Captain Koko Sinopa. That in itself is very suspect, and Sinopa is under suspicion. The only reason they haven't picked up Sinopa yet is because the military is waiting to capture you first to find out what really happened. But don't worry, he's being watched. He'll be arrested if the need arises. That'll be the end of an excellent career for Sinopa. No telling what'll happen when he's put in prison along with all those criminals he helped put away."

Campbell frowned, but he remained silent.

"I see some of this is starting to sink in, Campbell. Besides the destruction of Yamamoto's experiment, the largest charge hanging over your head is the destruction of the *USS Smith* and the killing of twenty-three sailors including its captain—a Captain Grant."

"I did no such thing!" Campbell was outraged. He wiggled desperately in his confinement.

"Oh, but you did, Campbell," Arnold smiled again. "You see, there's visual evidence that you were aboard the military clipper that attacked the *Smith*. Your communications with the *Smith* just before your attack were recorded. It clearly shows an image of you along with an unidentified woman.

"The survivors of the *Smith* swear you fired multiple missiles into their ship hull. Then, to cut off all communications the ship might have sent out to report you, or beg for assistance, you shot away their communications tower and killed the captain. That makes you a traitor, Campbell. A traitor and a murderer! You catching all this, boy?" Arnold glared at Akio with an expression of glee.

Akio remained silent behind Campbell. Campbell couldn't bring himself to look at the Sens. He didn't know if Goro knew all this, but he was sure Goro would have never told Akio about his and Penelope's fight to escape.

Campbell knew he could defend most of these charges. It was missiles fired from the *Smith* that had destroyed their own ship. His clipper didn't even carry missiles. However, he *had* provoked the attack and been acting illegally while trying to escape with Penelope and the dogs. Neither could he defend the fact that he'd fired at the ship's communication tower to keep the ship from firing more guided missiles at them.

This was the first news he'd heard that so many men aboard the *Smith* had died. He was devastated that he'd been the cause of it all. He could only justify the action by thinking of the alternative. He couldn't allow Penelope to be captured by the military, and he was defending their lives.

Arnold gloated over at Campbell's dismal expression.

"Next," Arnold persisted, "there's the murder of Hedon Bohdan and the security detail that were sent out to capture you about a year ago. While there's no proof they didn't meet up with some sort of foul play, things point to the fact that they were probably able to locate you and you killed them."

Oh, you're really searching on that one, Arnold, Campbell thought.

He kept his mouth shut. If they really were watching Koko, they'd find the clipper Bohdan and the security team had used sitting on top of Koko's building in São Paulo. Things were appearing worse and worse for Koko, and Campbell had been the one who'd dragged Koko into this mess.

"Your silence only proves your guilt, Campbell . . ."

"What's your point, Arnold?" Campbell interrupted. "Did you bring me here to listen to a bunch of fabrications of your wild imagination? Do you still feel guilty about your treachery during the Yarv War, and this is some sort of payback? I know what you did!"

Campbell's outburst seemed to annoy Arnold, but he quickly had himself under control.

"You still don't get it. I own you now." Arnold smiled. "With everything I have on you, you'll do whatever I want. That's why I brought you here."

Campbell laughed. "I wouldn't work for you, even if you could prove all your allegations. You'd have to kill me first."

"That can be arranged!" Arnold bent in front of Campbell and shouted before he settled down and added, "But that won't be necessary. See, I know you've always been willing to risk your life, but are you willing to risk the life of the woman you love?"

SEVEN

"What're you talking about?" Campbell whispered with dread.

"I think you know," Arnold said, as if he were enjoying Campbell's discomfort a great deal. "It all goes back to Stenwood and Yamamoto's experiment. Stenwood never told you I was his assistant during the Yamamoto experiment, did he?" Arnold smiled broadly at Campbell's silent shake of his head.

"I was privy to all the knowledge Stenwood had about the experiment, including what he guessed was Yamamoto's real purpose behind the teleportation device. Yes, Campbell, I know all about Monica Yamamoto. I even met her once after her life was saved by Yamamoto and his teleporter. I met her after she became the beautiful Penelope Preston. You have to admit, Campbell, hers isn't a face one forgets."

"Again, what's your point?" Campbell asked lamely. "She was killed by Bohdan and Tojo."

"Ah, but you, Sen, and possibly Sinopa would know best. I read Sinopa's report that she was one of the murder victims at the Yamamoto Teletech Building. At first I believed it. Then I was amazed when I saw her during the communication recordings from the *USS Smith*. I realized she was alive. She was alive, and you were risking everything to escape and save her. You gave up your life, your home, and were willing to waste your life's work to save one woman. I think you'll risk even more to keep her safe."

Although Arnold doesn't appear to realize the reason why I'm willing to risk it all for Penelope, Campbell thought, *the reasoning is pointless. It all comes down to the same thing. Arnold knows Penelope is still alive, and I'm caught.*

But I don't understand what Arnold wants from me. He obviously doesn't intend to turn me in or kill me. Arnold has some use, some special purpose for me.

He sagged in resignation.

Arnold saw Campbell's defeat and strode about the office beaming in his glory. Campbell lowered his head and closed his eyes, unable to watch. His mind was whirling for Arnold's purpose and how he was going to get the Sens out of danger.

Arnold laughed in near hysteria before shouting, "Yeah!"

"Let the Sens go, Arnold," Campbell whispered.

"What's that, Campbell?" Arnold asked with exuberance. "Is that how you address your superior officer?"

Damn! This ass isn't going to be satisfied with anything less than a total victory.

"General Arnold, sir, please allow the Sens their freedom," Campbell said, glaring at Arnold with rage and defiance burning in his eyes. "They have suffered enough, and are no threat to you now, sir. I promise I will do as you wish with no hesitation, sire."

"That's better, but I still hear the fight in your voice. I guess that's to be expected, since I doubt a man of your great military record could be broken, yet. Still, have it your way. I don't want Goro around to hear what I have to say next. Sergeant, come here."

Arnold pulled the sergeant over to the far side of the room out of everyone's earshot. They had a short conversation before they both returned. The sergeant strolled toward the Sens, who were still huddled together against the wall behind Campbell. The guard motioned the Sens toward the exit with his blaster.

Campbell twisted around to look at the Sens and exchanged glances with Goro. "I can't say how sorry I am to have brought you all into this. Watch your back, Goro."

Akio stared at Campbell with something akin to horror. Oki looked at him with a mixture of fear and pity. Goro wore an expression of great sorrow.

"No, Burt, old friend," Goro said. "Someday, if I can, I'll explain to Akio how all that you have done was for the good of the many. You've only done what I wish I had the courage to do. It is I who am sorry for betraying you." Goro appeared as if he was going to say more, but the sergeant prodded him with his blaster to get them moving.

Campbell watched the Sens leave with great fear in his heart for what Arnold had planned for them. He feared it was the last time he would see his second family alive. He felt totally helpless to do anything about it.

"Oh, Sergeant," Arnold said. "Find Inspector Campbell's clipper and his recorder. Destroy the recorder, and then follow us in his clipper. I want to leave as little evidence as possible."

"Yes, sir," answered the sergeant before he followed after the Sens.

"Arnold, if something happens to them, I guarantee I'll find some way to kill you," Campbell warned.

Arnold smiled. "Oh, this is wonderful, Campbell. You have all the bite of a toothless old dog."

I wish Sergeant could get his huge fangs around your neck. Still, Campbell thought Arnold's smile was false this time and there was a flash of fright in Arnold's appearance.

Campbell turned to watch the Sens walk slowly down the hall with the sergeant following behind them with the blaster in their backs. They took a right turn toward the elevator and disappeared from his view.

Arnold reached into his pocket and pulled out a small communicator. "George, I still don't trust Campbell. I need you back down in Sen's office."

Campbell listened to this ominous request with growing terror. *What does Arnold mean to do with that monster?*

A huge shadow appeared at the broken window before the gargoyle flew into the office. The evilness of the black demon was palpable in the air. Even Arnold backed away.

"George, please incapacitate Inspector Campbell so we can transport him to the clipper without any mishaps," Arnold ordered with a calmness that terrified Campbell.

Campbell's heart leaped into his throat. "Incapacitate! What in Hades does *that* mean?" he yelled, and cringed away from the approaching creature.

The gargoyle towered over Campbell. It shrouded him in total darkness before it reared back its mighty claw, ready to hammer Campbell's skull.

Suddenly, a single sonic blast shook the walls from down by the elevator. Just before the gargoyle pummeled the side of his head and he lost consciousness, Campbell realized what had happened.

IV

PLANS REVEALED

ONE

Campbell slowly began to regain consciousness, and cracked open a puffy eye. He was on his back. There was a dark ceiling and confining walls all around him. He felt groggy and bruised all over. He didn't understand where he was.

Oh, damn, I feel like crap, he thought.

A sledgehammer was rhythmically pounding an anvil inside his skull, threatening to explode it like a rotten melon. The right side of his head felt as if he'd been swatted aside by a rusty wrecking ball. But his intense pain inspired his memories of what had happened.

"The Sens are dead!" he yelled, and struggled to get up.

Campbell quickly discovered he was restrained. His wrists and ankles were locked to a metal bed and he could barely move. Glancing around, he found himself in a tiny jail cell in the rear of a military clipper. He heard the whine and felt the vibrations of the engines. They were traveling somewhere. Before him, the nearly transparent pulsating door of the cell was activated. He knew from experience that there could be no escape even if he was able to break out of his restraints.

"Arnold, I'll kill you!" he screamed.

Before the echoes of his scream subsided, Arnold strolled through the door of the jail compartment.

"I thought I heard you bellowing, Campbell. How's your head?"

His head felt twice its normal size and his jaw hurt to talk. As he struggled, he felt the soreness of bruises in his shoulder and chest where he'd been struck by the DEP blasts that had reflected off his armor.

"I'll see you pay for the death of the Sens," Campbell growled.

"Oh, you'll see things my way soon enough." Arnold waved off the threat as meaningless.

Arnold started pacing before the cell as if considering what to say. Campbell watched him with hateful and hooded eyes. He began to work his wrists in the restraints to see if he could get free. It was hopeless.

"Where are we going?" Campbell asked.

"To your new home."

"The moon base?" Campbell asked. Arnold nodded as he paced.

"How much do you know about Moon Base Alfa-Tango?"

"Just that it's a military base and a mining colony," Campbell recalled. "I've been there a few times to change ships to other planets. It's not a very hospitable place, and requires a full security force just to control the miners. It's also where they send the worst military personnel. You're proof of that."

"Not exactly your Hawaiian sanctuary," Arnold commented.

Campbell didn't fall for the trick to confirm his hiding place. *Not that it matters anymore.*

"Things have changed a great deal on the moon base since you disappeared," Arnold continued. "You know I was made the commander of the base about the same time Yamamoto's experiments began. That's why Stenwood decided to set up the second teleporter at Alfa-Tango. It was the best place to keep the experiment secret and under military control.

"Since you disappeared, I've also taken command of a new penal colony on the moon base. The maximum security prison was moved there to keep the world safe. I did a great deal of lobbying to get it there."

"So you would have an unlimited source of experiment victims for the teleporter, right?" Campbell asked.

Arnold glanced up.

"You're very shrewd, Inspector," Arnold smiled. "You're much smarter than the politicians who saw it as a means of public safety and a way to get more votes. Of course, no one had any way of knowing we were experimenting on death-row inmates—inmates who are no longer given a choice on whether they wish to take part in the experiments."

Campbell was starting to forget his pains due to his interest in the conversation. *This is our worst fear. They've figured out the teleporter without Yamamoto.* "So the teleporter is still working?" he asked.

"Teleporters, Campbell. There're three of them now." Arnold smiled at seeing Campbell's dismay. "Oh, yes, I bought some of the top scientists that weren't too ethical about how they gained their fame in research. They analyzed the experiment and created two more teleporters."

"But they don't understand everything Yamamoto was doing, do they?" Campbell asked.

It was Campbell's turn to smile at the flicker of dismay that crossed Arnold's face. Arnold didn't respond, but he didn't need to. Campbell knew Arnold hadn't been able to recreate the experiment that had saved Monica Yamamoto and given her immortality as long as her body wasn't completely destroyed.

"Do you understand the potential of those teleporters, Campbell?"

"Better than most." He smiled, thinking Arnold didn't realize the half of it.

"Maybe you do, Burt," Arnold said, nearing the cell and examining Campbell closer. Campbell didn't care for the niceness in

Arnold's tone. "When I first saw you, I thought either my eyes or my memory were deceiving me. Then I saw the same disbelief in the Sen's eyes.

"Burt, you've physically changed in drastic ways since the last time I saw you. You've grown dramatically in size and muscle mass. When I thought about your relationship to Yamamoto's experiment, it occurred to me that somehow you were altered by that experiment. I don't understand how, but maybe I should find out."

Campbell didn't answer.

"I guess it's not too important now," Arnold continued. "I have other things planned for you, but maybe you'll tell me in the future as we become better acquainted."

"What makes you think we'll get to know each other better, Arnold? You're dead as soon as I get my hands around your skinny neck."

"Oh, you'll come around to my way eventually," Arnold said, smiling evilly. "If not for your precious Penelope, then we have other ways."

"What're you using the teleporters for?" Campbell asked to change the subject.

Arnold started pacing again. "It's all part on our master plan, Campbell."

"You haven't been able to create an artificial intelligence, have you?"

"No." Arnold shook his head with a frown. "But then that isn't part of our design. I don't plan on using the teleporters to teleport organic material or make any grand discoveries. That would require teleporters in remote areas, and I already have all I need."

"Teleporters in remote areas would be discovered."

"Exactly," Arnold nodded. "No, we have other plans."

"The creation of alternate life forms—super soldiers like George."

Arnold stopped and gazed at Campbell before nodding slowly. "Excellent, Burt, I always knew you were smart. That's why I selected you. Yes, George is one of my creations, a super soldier, if you will."

"How'd you do it? Did your scientist create a program that used the teleporter to alter human physiology into these monsters?"

Arnold nodded again. "That's one way, but we perfected a program that creates these beings out of the particle reservoir without the use of human subjects. George is one of those creations. He's much more specific to our needs than what we can create out of humans and their limited resources alone."

As Campbell understood it, a high-powered computer could use the teleporter to molecularize together a living being from a reservoir of particles using a detailed description of the being's intended structure. That was the way Monica Yamamoto's body had been recreated into Penelope Preston.

Arnold had his scientists create a molecular-level description of the most frightful being he could imagine. Then the teleporter created the being from a particle reservoir. As long as he has the necessary particles available, there's no need for the restructuring of a human's body. But what about this new creation's intelligence and controllability to form the army that I assume Arnold is attempting to create?

"And what's the specific need you have for such an evil creation?" Campbell asked. "Certainly not the betterment of mankind."

"Use your head, Burt, you're an intelligent man. Isn't it obvious?" Arnold huffed.

Campbell thought it was, but he decided to play stupid and let Arnold spell it out. He shook his head.

"Our goal is to create an army powerful enough to take over the planet Earth," Arnold said with exuberance. "We want to rule the world, and then maybe the Universe."

Campbell laughed nervously at the outrageousness of Arnold's statement. He got serious when he saw the craziness in Arnold's expression combined with the knowledge that Arnold's plan was quite feasible.

If Arnold isn't stopped, Campbell thought, *I could be looking at the next ruler of Earth. Millions, if not billions, of lives could be lost if this madman is able to complete his plan.*

"I see you're impressed, Inspector," Arnold smiled, misreading Campbell's expression.

"You're a lunatic!" Campbell shouted.

"Isn't that what they say about all men who aspire to greatness that none before have achieved?"

Campbell went silent and thoughtful for a moment.

"You've gone to a great deal of trouble and inconvenience to bring me here and tell me all this," Campbell said. "What's your point?"

"Haven't you figured it out yet?"

Campbell shook his head. He really had no idea why Arnold wanted him if it wasn't to do tests on him. But Arnold didn't appear to want him for a test subject, or even to care that he might possess powers beyond his abnormal physical dimensions. Arnold had shrugged off the notion that he'd been altered somehow by the teleporter.

"Campbell, you came back from the Yarv War as the most highly decorated commander alive today. Your heroism is the stuff of legends. Your battle tactics are required teachings at the military academies, and you did all this while fighting incompetent military leadership and traitors among your own ranks. It was your leadership that brought the Yarvs to their knees—if they had knees." Arnold laughed before he continued. "If not for your retirement from the military, you would be sitting at the President's side as one of her top advisors," Arnold said with too much enthusiasm.

Damn, I wonder how long he practiced that speech. "You haven't answered my question," Campbell pointed out.

"I want you to command my forces to conquer Earth!" Arnold shouted while flapping his arms up and down like the chicken he was.

"Ha! That proves it! You really are insane!" Campbell hooted with laughter.

Arnold glared at him from across the cell door. His weasel-like face was flush and creased with frustration.

He looks like a child holding his breath in a temper tantrum. This impression only made him laugh harder.

Arnold went back to pacing. Campbell settled down. It hurt too much to laugh.

"Look, Arnold—and I really should be calling you Benedict now—once a traitor, always a traitor. No matter how much I loved Penelope when she was alive, no single person is worth the lives of billions. I would never lead your army."

Arnold's rodent features grew more scarlet at the mention of him being a traitor, but he appeared to calm down at Campbell's confidence about not leading his army. This worried Campbell.

"Oh, but you will—you will." Again Arnold showed his evil smile of small teeth. "Have you considered what makes brutes like George obey me with their very lives? If I ordered George to kill itself, it'd do so without hesitation.

"Campbell, you haven't realized the full potential of my scientists and the power of the teleporters. We have developed many new ways to condition the human mind over the last two years. If we can't convince you one way, there're other ways. Remember, the teleporter can re-molecularize human organs, including brains. You will lead my army in the end. Now rest up. It'll be a couple more hours before we land on the moon. Consider your options carefully." Arnold did an about face and left.

Campbell watched him go, thinking he only had one option—suicide. Even that seemed impossible. Plus, he doubted he would ever get the chance.

TWO

While traveling to the moon base, Campbell spent his time lost in thought. Giving up on his thoughts of suicide, he thought about his only other alternative—escape. He considered what he knew about Moon Base Alfa-Tango. He swore at himself for not keeping up with current events since escaping to Hawaii.

He knew the original moon base had been built at the Sea of Tranquility, the site of the first Apollo lunar landing. It'd been heralded as being Earth's savior due to its tremendous mining potential for ores, hydrogen, and nitrogen. The mining colony had been built using hydrogen fusion plants and solar power. With the perfection of compressing moon dust into water and oxygen, the colony had become self-sufficient by growing plants and producing its own oxygen with the help of multiple atmosphere-forming facilities.

He also knew that the mining colony had become the collection point of all the Earth's undesirables seeking wealth and adventure. This had created an explosive drug and crime problem. It required a large security agent force to keep the miners under control.

I wonder if Koko could use the security force on the moon to assist in my escape from the military, he thought.

Campbell turned his attention to the moon's military presence. Originally the force had been minimal, but it had grown quickly as the moon had become a universal spaceport. If he could believe Arnold, a prison was also now a part of the military facility. That meant an even larger military presence. He realized he had no idea what was on the moon base now, nor what to expect.

Damn, what have I gotten myself into?

It looks like my only hope is for Koko and Penelope to find and rescue me before Arnold succeeds in doing whatever he has planned.

Campbell felt the clipper engines slowing down. After the door zipped open, George hulked into the cramped jail area like a black nightmare from hell. Campbell's pulse quickened beneath the monster's fiery gaze. Arnold popped out from behind George and approached the cell.

"I see I wasn't dreaming," Campbell said. "Dr. Frankenstein and Igor have returned."

"Who?" Arnold asked. His face was pinched with confusion as if he were trying to decide if he'd been insulted again.

"Forget it, Arnold. You obviously don't read much. Are we about to land at the moon base?"

"Yes, and I need your cooperation. Either you come along peacefully, or I'll have George sedate you again."

Campbell peeked around Arnold to peer at George's evil face. Its red eyes seemed to be on fire. Its black lips were curled in a snarl showing off rows of dagger-like teeth. Campbell could have sworn the monster was grinning.

"That's a tough one, Arnold. I think I'll cooperate—for now."

"I knew you would see reason," Arnold said. "We'll be entering the hangar in a moment. Out you go."

Arnold turned off the door, and George squished its bulk into the cell. Its evil aura and rotting stench preceded it.

"Remember, no trouble, Campbell. George wasn't programmed for compassion. It *will* hurt you if you try to escape." Arnold removed a remote key from his pocket and pushed a button to release Campbell's restraints.

Campbell groaned with soreness as he stood up. He tried to stretch out some of his stiffness, but George grabbed his arm with crushing force and hurled him from the cell. Campbell wheeled on George with lightning speed. George was ready for him. It cuffed Campbell on the side of the head hard enough to make him wobbly with dizziness.

"I warned you," Arnold said.

Campbell gazed up with smoldering hatred. Arnold had his DEP pointed at his head. Campbell sighed and reluctantly raised his hands in the air. Arnold waved his pistol to motion him through the door.

Campbell moved forward through the long and narrow fuselage with George and Arnold on his heels. Since no one stopped him, Campbell continued toward the cockpit so he could see where they were going. He gazed over the heads of the two pilots in wonder at the desolate lunar landscape. He was amazed at what he saw.

The military had indeed been busy the last couple of years. The clipper streaked over the huge pyramid shape of a hydrogen fusion reactor alongside a sea of solar panels reflecting brightly beneath the sun. Campbell knew this immense power plant was new. They quickly flew over a high wall and into the central military complex. It was packed with dusty low-level buildings set beneath a black sky twinkling with millions of stars. Campbell estimated the area to be about twenty-square kilometers in size.

What in Hades is going on here? he wondered with awe.

Off away from the central complex, surrounded by a large open area of small craters and gray moon dust, he saw what appeared to be a group of modern buildings similar to any small city on Earth. The city was complete with skyscrapers, a monorail system, and even had outside gardens, walkways and streets. Obviously the gardens weren't real. The whole urban setting appeared totally out of place in the surrounding barrenness. He wondered with deep anxiety what the purpose of the Earth-like city might be. He saw no signs of life and doubted it was even habitable by humans.

"What's the fake city for?" Campbell asked.

"That's all part of our grand scheme," Arnold answered from behind him.

They were quickly over the city and approaching the main military complex. The buildings were obviously the low-level prefabricated type that'd been brought from Earth and constructed here. They were bunched together to form a massive single lunar complex that spread out in seemingly uncoordinated directions. The once light-colored structures were dulled by moon dust. Their bright windows twinkled like stars in a night sky. The rooftops bristled with communication and detection antennas. Only the occasional rotating scanning disks broke up this overstuffed pincushion illusion. Campbell noted that the buildings increased with size and height until they reached an apex surrounding a huge dome in the center of the complex. He was stunned with amazement. The military base and prison were now at least triple the size of the old complex he remembered.

"I'm impressed," Campbell said as they approached the clipper hangars.

"Oh, this is but a small portion of the moon base," Arnold said. "The real treats will come later after I'm sure I can trust you."

THREE

Campbell watched anxiously while they entered the green plasma door of the hangar. The pilot gently set them down on the hangar pad before Campbell turned toward the starboard clipper door. Arnold lowered the clipper ramp, and motioned him forward with his DEP.

"Time to begin your indoctrination into our little society," Arnold said, as they moved down the ramp into the large shadow-filled hangar. It stank of filth and mustiness.

Campbell didn't respond. He was too surprised by his welcoming committee. Six huge soldiers dressed in black military uniforms stood at attention while bearing their sonic blasters before them. They were divided into two lines along each side of the ramp. At first Campbell mistook them for an honor guard. Then he realized they weren't there to honor him and they weren't human.

Now there're some faces no mother could love, he thought.

Campbell examined the muscularly built brutes more closely while he walked through their formation. Although they had human forms with thick bowed legs and powerful torsos, they had pitch-black, scaly skin similar to George's. He found their demon-like features repulsive. Their heads were nearly bald with lanky dark hair and small pointy ears. They had misshapen noses, unaligned eyes, and huge fangs that were barely contained in their crudely shaped mouths. Yet each face was as different and individual as one human being's from another's. The only similarity he noted in all their faces was the pale redness of their eyes, which shown like candles behind red-stained glass. He thought their evil eyes blazed with a barely contained hatred of anything human. Their gazes struck fear in Campbell's heart.

But how does Arnold control these monsters, and what keeps them from tearing us apart? he wondered.

Campbell came to the end of his honor guard, and noticed two people dressed in white medical uniforms. The person to his left was a tall Asian woman who appeared to be hiding behind the last guard. Next to her stood a short, overweight Caucasian male with thinning blond hair and a jowly face. His lab coat was rumpled and food stained. He smelled of a rancid old fart.

Campbell stopped at the end of the line, not sure where to proceed. He gazed down upon the Asian woman, but he had trouble seeing her face. She continued to peer at the dirty floor as if searching for the universal mysteries, but he did notice her beautiful long black hair and her willow-like body.

Damn, Campbell thought, *this woman is on some powerful stimulants. She's wasting away.*

"I'd like you to meet two of my top scientists," Arnold announced. "You'll be working closely with them for a short time. This is Dr. Kevin Blake. Blake is a biochemist who specializes in human physiology."

Campbell turned to Blake. He found Blake staring at him intently with pale-blue eyes as if he were an interesting specimen. Campbell stuck out his hand to shake Blake's. To his horror, Blake grabbed his hand between sweaty palms before bringing it up to his eager features to examine it closer. His grasp was soft and weak like a rotting piece of fruit. Campbell quickly retracted his hand with disgust. He made a show of wiping it off on his pants. Blake's eager expression collapsed into one of a rebuffed child.

"Now, Blake," Arnold broke in, "you'll have plenty of time for your examinations after we get Campbell to his, ah, quarters."

Arnold turned to the female. "This is Dr. Ai Eto. She is a biologist who specializes in human brain physiology. Eto and Blake assisted Jiro Yamamoto with his original teleporter experiments. They came here after he discharged them."

Campbell considered the doctors' backgrounds. He wondered how much they knew about Monica Yamamoto's recreation into Penelope Preston with her new genetic makeup.

They must have been discharged from Yamamoto's experiment before Penelope's transformation, Campbell thought. *They obviously haven't been able to recreate Yamamoto's superhumans here on the moon.*

"Dr. Eto performs the mentally programing our new creations," Arnold said, stopping to wave toward the soldiers, "and is an important key to the success of our entire operation."

"Obviously she hasn't studied *your* brain recently," Campbell said. He was taken back when Dr. Eto raised her face from her floor examination.

Eto had recently been severely beaten about her face. Her full lips were split, her high cheekbones were swollen, and her dark eyes were bruised. She quickly glanced down again as if embarrassed by her appearance.

"Dr. Eto had an unfortunate incident with one of our newly created soldiers," Arnold said with a small laugh.

Eto whipped up her head to glare at Arnold with intense hatred.

Eto didn't have an unfortunate accident, Campbell thought. *Arnold beat her.*

Arnold ignored Eto's evil glare as he grabbed Campbell's arm to lead him forward. "Time to take you to your new home where we'll teach you the meaning of the words submission and subordination."

Campbell ripped his arm out of Arnold's grasp. He immediately received another knock in the back of the head from George, along with a shove that almost knocked him off his feet. He regained his balance and whirled around. The six horrid guards had moved forward and were pointing their sonic blasters at his chest. Campbell stopped, glanced evilly at George, and turned around to face Arnold.

"I'd be glad to see my accommodations now, Arnold. I believe I reserved the luxury suite."

Arnold ignored him, and showed the way toward the hangar exit. George gave Campbell another shove to get him going. He followed Arnold, and glanced behind him to see that the entire party was following.

FOUR

Campbell decided escape was impossible at the moment and walked forward, concentrating on his surroundings. The dark-walled hangar appeared like any military hangar he'd seen. It was filthy and ill kempt. Here and there were multiple craft under repair surrounded by bright lights. These brightly lit areas left much of the hangar in dark shadows, obscuring his observations. He did spot shadowy storage bins of smaller spare parts and maintenance areas full of discarded tools. There were mobile repair computers, unused bots, and diagnostic equipment. The stained and battered walls were lined with spare engines, landing struts, and armor plating. But what captivated his attention were the various types of creatures at work. None of them appeared human or like anything he'd ever seen before. They all appeared like some nightmare created by Arnold's experiments.

Nearby, creatures were working on overhauling a large disk-shaped clipper. Campbell was fascinated and horrified by huge green-skinned beasts with bushy mops of dark hair, wearing shabby, ill-fitting overalls. They appeared twice the size, weight, and musculature of George. One was lugging an ion propulsion unit that should have required a crane to lift. Their appearance reminded Campbell of trolls from children's fairytales.

He tore his eyes away from the trolls at the heightened sound of grunted yelling from the top of the clipper wing. A being similar to one of the honor guards was standing rigidly on the wing. It was cursing down at a small yet hairy spider-like creature that had a tiny bald human head. The spider was desperately tangled in some loose wiring from the partially dismantled wing. As Campbell peered closer, he spied spider creatures crawling all over the craft. It made his skin crawl when he noticed they had little human hands on the tips of their eight hairy legs.

Suddenly, something swooped down from the hangar ceiling at the yelling guard, making it duck for cover. Campbell gazed upward with horror. He spotted a variety of black bat-like creatures of various sizes. Some were flying around carrying parts onto the clipper. Others were sitting on perches awaiting orders, or just flying around for no apparent reason. They had huge muscular legs with talon claws for feet. A few of the bats appeared large enough to carry a man on their backs.

Damn, these creatures are more suited for battle than clipper maintenance, Campbell thought.

As Campbell thought about this, he noticed the great number of armed soldiers that appeared to be guarding the hangar. He didn't get the impression they were there on his account. They appeared more like guards of a prison detail, as if they were guarding all the creatures in the hangar to keep them in line.

His suspicions were confirmed when they neared a large double door that apparently led to the interior of the complex. He saw the soldier that had been yelling at the spider go irate with rage before pulling out a DEP and vaporizing the spider.

Immediately, total mayhem broke loose. The spider creatures erupted in a frenzied riot while screaming in tiny high-pitched human voices. One of the larger bats flying over the clipper dropped a heavy armor plate, killing some of the rioting spiders. It screeched with angry hatred as it swooped down and grasped the offending soldier's head with one of its talon claws.

Campbell stood there gazing in horror as the gigantic bat lifted the struggling soldier off the clipper wing. While madly flapping its huge leathery wings and screeching earsplitting cries, the bat violently shook the soldier's body back and forth until the body was torn from the head. The beheaded body flipped through the air before landing on the hangar floor with a bloody splat.

The air became filled with screams, yells, and angry oaths. All the bats took to the air like a flock of birds from hell. They started swooping at everything that moved. The huge trolls carrying engine parts threw aside their burdens. They became entangled in bloody hand-to-hand combat with each other while bellowing with unintelligible rage.

Arnold screeched like a frightened girl before he made a panicked dash for the exit. The surrounding guards began screaming orders and opening fire with their sonic blasters. George pushed Campbell forward, but Campbell didn't need any prodding. He outran Arnold and was through the door as it opened. He dove for cover on the other side as directed energy beams shot by his head.

Arnold whisked breathlessly around the door and closed it as Eto, Blake, George, and two of the guards ran through. Campbell saw that Arnold's face was ashen and his eyes were huge with fear.

"I always knew you were a coward, Arnold," Campbell said with a sneer. He heard a laugh escape Dr. Eto.

Arnold whipped toward Campbell. His rodent features were consumed by shaking rage. He was pointing his DEP at Campbell with a trembling hand. Campbell was sure he'd gone too far this time.

"You can hurt him now, George," Arnold said in a shaky voice.

Campbell started to scramble to his feet to protect himself, but George pounced on him. With one mighty swing, George pummeled his head. Campbell fell unconscious to the floor.

FIVE

Campbell woke up with a jolt as if from a terrible nightmare. He couldn't move. He was terrified to discover he was confined by restraints in a standing position. He appeared to be strapped into in an upright coffin-shaped contraption like nothing he'd ever seen.

Damn, I'm naked! he thought with terror.

To compound his embarrassment and fear, he couldn't move his aching head. His peripheral vision was partially blocked by some sort of a helmet he was wearing, but he was able to peer down. The bottom of the coffin was hinged to a lid that could be moved up to seal him into the contraption. This hinged lid was covered with needles, cutters, probes, and a few other nasty-looking items he didn't recognize. He didn't hazard to guess their gruesome purpose. He felt exposed and terrified by his restrained helplessness.

Campbell tried to scan the brightly lit room. Dr. Eto suddenly moved into his vision from his right. She began to examine his face closely through her dark, bruised eyes. Dr. Blake approached from his left, holding an intravenous injector at his side. There was a faint smile on Blake's jowly features. Even from this distance and in his current state of mind, Campbell was revolted by Blake's body odor.

My whole body feels strange, jumpy, like there's a low voltage current running through my veins, Campbell thought. *My skin feels so sensitive, my mind so alert. My god! I'm getting an erection!*

To his relief, Eto showed the good grace to appear not to notice his aroused state. To his horror, Blake did. Blake nodded with an appreciative grin on his stubble-covered face.

"What did you inject me with?" Campbell asked. His voice seemed to boom, hurting his oversensitive ears.

Blake's smile widened to the point of showing off a green scrap of food wedged between his filthy front teeth.

"This is the first stage of your mental conditioning, Inspector," Blake said.

Although Campbell could tell by Blake's expression that he was speaking in normal tones, his entire body flinched at the sound of Blake's voice as if zapped by an electrical current.

Campbell's terror increased. He gazed around the room with wide eyes. He was in a lab containing small computers, monitors, and biotables that appeared to be made for human torture. This stirred his heightened senses and imagination to a point of pure panic. He imagined what kind of terrible pain these torture devices could inflict on his electrified nerves.

Calm down, Burt, calm down. Lord, this erection is so embarrassing.

"What, what're you going to do to me?" Campbell asked. He fought his confinement with all his brutal strength. The tight restraints around his wrists, chest, and ankles seemed to burn his skin with searing pain.

"Please, Inspector, do not fight your restraints. You will only injure yourself," Eto said. "They were designed to confine the most powerful beings."

Campbell stopped struggling. Dr. Eto was correct. There was no way he was going to free himself through brute force and it was causing him more pain.

What are Eto's motivations for being in this torture room? Campbell wondered. *She doesn't sound or act insane like Blake and Arnold.*

"The first stage of your conditioning will teach you submission, that disobeying commands will cause you severe pain," Blake said.

As if to prove his point, Blake reached over and pushed something on the side of Campbell's coffin.

Immediately, Campbell's entire body was jolted as if a bolt of lightning had been shot through his brain. Every muscle tightened in full-strength contractions before his body burned with lactic acid build-up. His chest muscles drew so tight that he couldn't draw a breath. His heart was about to explode. Campbell wanted to scream with the mind-crippling pain of his every nerve ending being lit on fire, but his jaw muscles were clamped shut like vises.

After an eternity of agony, Campbell's muscles suddenly relaxed. He was able to take in huge breaths of air. With his entire body covered in sweat, Campbell could hear Dr. Eto pleading with Dr. Blake.

"Kevin, it doesn't have to be this way," Eto was saying.

Campbell could see the pain of his suffering reflected in Dr. Eto's face. Again he wondered about her motivation for being here.

"Ai," Blake whispered, "be quiet. You know everything you say is being watched and recorded. Look in the mirror, Ai. How many times does Arnold have to beat you before he kills you?"

Blake turned back to Campbell. "So, Inspector, how did you like your first sample of Arnold's conditioning methods?"

Campbell glared at him with intense hatred.

"Didn't care for it, huh?" Blake asked. "Well, the fun's only beginning. That was the minimal setting you just experienced, but I must say that you're more resistant than most of our subjects. Many of them pass out on even the lowest setting. Many of them eventually go completely mad and have to be destroyed. This system is far from perfect, but I think your resistance to pain confirms my first impression of you. You were altered somehow by your involvement with Yamamoto, weren't you?"

Campbell thought, *I wonder if the microprocessors and nanotechnology in my blood from Penelope's healing will be destroyed by this conditioning? If they aren't, they may keep healing me enough for me to escape from this alive. My eye implants don't appear to be damaged. Maybe the technology in my veins will remain unaffected.*

He didn't answer Blake, but continued to glare at him with a stare that meant Blake's death if he ever got loose of his restraints.

"Answer me, Campbell!" Blake yelled. His loud voice seemed to tear at Campbell's every brain cell. "Fine, but you will learn obedience." He pushed the control on Campbell's coffin again.

Campbell couldn't ready himself. His body was electrified with even greater pain than the first time, and for a longer period. He was sure he would smother from his own constricted chest. Darkness consumed his agony. Suddenly, his body relaxed again. As he heaved in deep breaths, his entire body went lax in his restraints.

"I'm impressed, Inspector," Blake said. "You're going to be a tough subject to condition. I'm sorry Arnold has forbidden experimentation on your body so I can discover what has altered your physique. Unfortunately, he seems to think there isn't time to see what makes you such a tremendous physical specimen."

"He isn't a specimen, Blake!" Eto screamed, jolting Campbell's head with sound waves. "He's a human being."

Campbell was able to open his eyes. He saw Blake eying Dr. Eto with a look of caution before Blake glanced at the ceiling as if someone were looking down at him.

Blake turned his attention back to Eto. "Oh, come off it, Ai. This process is your creation."

"That might be, but it isn't meant for human beings. I created it for mindless, hateful beings that couldn't be controlled otherwise," Eto said, peering at the floor.

"It's a little late to eradicate yourself now, Ai," Blake said with what Campbell thought might have been pity in his voice. "Okay, Campbell, we don't have much time. Ready yourself for the worst experience in your life. It's an experience that will alter your very way of thinking, and the rest of your existence."

"It looks like you should try a little of this experience yourself, Blake," Campbell grumbled.

His heart leaped when Blake pushed another control on the side of the torture device. The instrument-laden bottom of the coffin began to rise to seal Campbell in his tomb of pain and terror.

Campbell began to scream when he saw bright-blue electrical currents shooting between electrodes in the closing lid. They were directed at his groin area. He felt his testicles trying to crawl up into his abdomen. Campbell began to struggle with inhuman effort, but he quickly realized there was no escape.

Suddenly his body relaxed. He knew Arnold wanted him alive. He believed the technology in his blood would heal his body. If he could endure the agony of his torture, and control his fear, he would survive. He began to feel at peace over the inevitability of his suffering and the impossibility of his escape. He stared at Blake with intensity.

"I will escape, Blake. You are a dead man."

Campbell had a chance to see the expression of terror that crossed Blake's face before the lid closed and he began his real conditioning. To his surprise, he discovered he could control his fear. He could survive the agony. Yet he knew that change was inevitable. It was this change and the fear of what lay ahead that terrified him.

V

AN UNEXPECTED MEETING

ONE

Penelope sat anxiously next to Koko in the darkening cockpit of the military clipper in the backyard of Campbell's old Denver home. They'd been listening to the transmitter Koko had inserted in Campbell's right nostril before he'd left for Global Police Headquarters. Penelope and Koko had heard everything that had happened to Campbell up until Blake had started the conditioning program. Then, the transmissions had suddenly terminated. Penelope was near panic.

"You don't think they killed him, do you?" she asked.

"No. I think he's undergone some severe trauma that has disabled the transmitter," Koko said after a moment. "I don't think Arnold's intentions involve killing Burt. He went through too much trouble to get him."

"We have to go save him, Koko. We have to do something to stop Arnold. He obviously intends to attack Earth."

"*We*? What's this *we* stuff?" Koko asked, peering at Penelope. "You're not even supposed to be here, and I can't afford to get you involved in a deadly rescue operation. *I* have to do something, not you."

Oh, men can be so demeaning! Penelope thought. *Why do they always have to treat me like a helpless woman?*

"I have to go, Koko. Whatever they're doing to Burt may make him very vulnerable. I'm the only one who has the ability to save him."

Koko seemed confused by this remark.

"Look, Penelope, we might not even be able to get close to Burt. I've been hearing all sorts of rumors about the military portion of the moon base for years now. The military doesn't even let security agents near their complex anymore. I think it all started when Jiro installed that second teleporter there. Since then, it's been locked up tight to everyone except a few select military personnel. I couldn't even sneak someone in to destroy Jiro's second teleporter, and believe me, I tried."

"Well, you're just going to have to try harder, Koko," Penelope said stubbornly. "If you refuse to help me, I'll go by myself." Penelope reached over. She placed her hand beneath Koko's chin and lifted his eyes to hers. "Koko, I have to go. Burt's my life. He's the only person who has cared about me for who I am now that Jiro is dead. We both owe him our lives."

Koko smiled at Penelope. He got out of his seat without saying anything. He began to pace the clipper while deep in thought.

Penelope watched him closely. *What sort of man even has to think about going to save a longtime friend who has saved his life so many times?*

Finally, Koko turned toward her. "It's not a matter of me going, Penelope. It's a matter of how we're going to do it. I don't know what we're facing. It's obvious that Arnold has created an army of beings using that teleporter. These creatures sound rugged enough to conquer Earth. We're not going to just march into one of the most heavily guarded bases in the solar system and demand Burt's return."

At least he said, "We," Penelope thought.

Koko continued to pace in thought.

"Can't you organize a security force and attack the base?"

"Penelope, how in Hades am I supposed to do that? I've been out of the service for two years and haven't really kept any ties. I've been hiding out since I retired, because I wanted everyone to forget me. I can't organize a force large enough to attack the moon base, and even if I could, it would be impossible to do in the short time we have to save Burt."

"Can't we go to the authorities of some kind? We have the recording of the transmission. It's obvious that Arnold is planning something treacherous."

"That's an excellent idea, but I wouldn't know who to tell about this. The obvious choice would be the military. But who do we trust, and how do we keep the rest of the world from discovering about you?

"Burt risked his life and ruined his career to save you and keep you a secret. I think it was with good reason. By letting the military discover your existence so we can destroy Arnold, we might just be exchanging one rogue general for another. Someone else would take up the teleporter experiment, except then they would know how to create more humans like you. We'd be in a worse situation."

"I wish Captain Sen were still alive," Penelope said. "He could organize a global police force."

"Goro couldn't even save himself when the time came," Koko said with a sad shake of his head. "Still, he was a great friend, and we could use his help right now."

Koko went back to pacing.

Pacing and talking doesn't seem to be getting us anywhere. I thought Koko was a man of action.

"We have to do something very soon," she said. "It won't be long before they discover Burt's amazing recuperative powers and strength, if they haven't already. If they discover Jiro's secret, there'll be no saving the world."

TWO

Penelope left the clipper with a deep feeling of foreboding. She gazed longingly into the peaceful dark woods. *I wish I could just walk into the woods and escape all these troubles. Why couldn't everyone just have left us alone? Why does the whole world have to depend on what we do?*

She thought of how she'd lived her whole life first under Jiro's direction, and then under Burt's. There'd always been someone there to help her. Now there was no one. She was at a loss. Most of all, she ached to feel Burt's powerful arms around her, and hear his comforting voice saying everything was going to be all right. He'd always seemed to have had a plan that would keep them alive no matter how terrible the danger. He'd never failed her, until now.

Penelope walked toward the woods. The young evening was cold compared to Hawaii. There was a faint smell of pine in the air. She gazed up at the full moon rising above the changing fall trees. It showed with a silvery light, and seemed so close that she could reach up and touch it. She thought of how Burt was on that moon—how Burt was suffering. She felt a shiver rise along her spine. The hairs rose on the back of her neck when an eerie howl arose from nearby in the forest.

"Yes, Sergeant, your friend's in danger on that moon," she whispered. "I promise we'll go to save him, but I don't know how."

As she gazed back up at the moon, it was suddenly overshadowed by a huge black disk.

"Oh, no!" Penelope yelled. A military clipper was approaching. *Arnold told Burt that Koko was being watched. Someone has followed Koko.*

As Penelope began to race back toward their clipper, she realized she was too late. She'd never make it without being seen. Elated howls erupted from the woods.

The dogs! If they come running out thinking it's Burt returning home, whoever is in the clipper will try to kill them.

She did an about face. Penelope plunged into the dense and dark woods racing toward the sounds of the dogs. It wasn't hard to find them. All four of the dogs came crashing through the underbrush with Sergeant leading the way. The gleam of his golden eyes and huge fangs were shining in the moonlight.

"Shhhhhh!" Penelope hissed, when the three girls started to woo-woo impatiently at the sight of her.

The girls sensed her apprehension and fell silent. She wondered if the mental link she'd formed with the dogs would allow her to control them in silence. The huge dogs instinctively sensed danger and sat obediently before her as if awaiting instructions. Their wolf-like faces bristled with intelligent alertness.

Penelope anxiously considered whether to run into the woods and hide, or go back to the house. Again she was too late. The clipper landed a few hundred meters away on the house clipper pad. The dogs stood up and started to whine with apprehension, but they stayed at her side.

Oh, I have to see who this is, Penelope thought nervously.

"Come on. Let's go see who's here."

Penelope started to move cautiously forward when Sergeant and Amber stealthily snuck ahead of her as if they were acting as her guardians. She turned to see Cala and Hana moving silently behind her as if to protect her rear. Their dark eyes twinkled with intensity in the darkness. Their furry ears were perked forward with alertness.

They reached the edge of the woods before the manicured lawn. She wasn't surprised to see Sergeant's and Amber's fur rise along their rigid backs. Both dogs lowered their bodies into the underbrush as if they were stalking some prey. They stopped at the tree line with a perfect view of a military clipper sitting on the clipper pad off to their left.

Penelope hid behind a tree trunk. The immense long-legged dogs stayed out of sight camouflaged by the darkness and the underbrush. They were perfectly silent, but Penelope could sense their tension.

They must know that it's not going to be Burt stepping out of that clipper this time, she thought.

Penelope glanced at Koko's huge, disk-shaped clipper to her right, about twenty meters away in the backyard. The cockpit was now dark. Both the house and the clipper appeared deserted.

Where'd Koko go? At least he had the good sense to hide.

THREE

The whine of the ramp being lowered on the side of the military clipper caught Penelope's attention. Dark figures started to scramble down the ramp beneath the clipper shadow. Initially, Penelope couldn't make them out. She could see that they carried heavy weapons, but she thought their shadows were all wrong. They didn't appear like men.

Penelope drew a sharp intake of breath when the leader of the assailants stepped into the moonlight. He appeared like a demon from Hell dressed in a black military uniform. She heard a deep growl rise from Sergeant's chest. She leaned down to calm him. Every muscle in his body was trembling with emotion.

Four more demon-shaped beings walked out behind their huge leader. Even from her hiding place, Penelope could see the demons' flaming red eyes glowing in the darkness while they searched the grounds. They had broad muscular bodies with bat-like heads and black scaly skin. Penelope knew she and the dogs were in terrible danger.

This must be the horrible type of creature Burt faced at Global Police Headquarters, she thought. *No wonder he didn't return.*

"What in Hades has this Arnold done?" Penelope whispered.

As if hearing Penelope's murmur, the giant leader held up a talon claw. The whole group came to a halt. Penelope held her breath. The creature turned its bat-like face this way and then that way as if it were waiting for the sound to be repeated. To Penelope's horror, the leader lifted its repulsive face and appeared to be sniffing the air to sense its prey. It motioned the group toward the forest. They headed directly toward Penelope and the dogs.

Penelope was terrified, and began to slowly retreat into the forest. *These things don't appear too intelligent or fleet of foot. Maybe we can outrun them.*

Sergeant's growling deepened. Penelope stopped in her tracks. She knew the dogs would want to protect her. She couldn't leave them behind to fight these terrible creatures alone. They carried sonic blasters that would blow apart the dogs before they even had a chance to attack.

The leader must have picked up Sergeant's growl. Once again it held up its claw for the group to stop. The group was close enough for Penelope to make out their frightening faces more clearly in the moonlight. There were lumpy black growths on their horrid features. Their open mouths bristled with terrifying fangs. And Lord, did they stink!

They're like something out of a nightmare! Penelope thought.

"Please come forward. We mean you no harm," said the demon leader. As it said this, it lowered a sonic blaster in Penelope's direction. She was sure the demon's glowing eyes could spy her even in the dark, but she had to choke back an insane desire to giggle. The demon's voice had sounded like that of a dapper Englishman. It sounded totally out of character spewing from that foul mouth.

"Penelope Preston, Inspector Campbell sent us to take you to him. We mean you no harm."

The demon smiled, showing his fangs in the moonlight. Even if Penelope hadn't known the demon was lying before, the chill sent through her heart by that evil smile convinced her it was time to flee or die.

Not getting a response, the assailants slowly began to advance on Penelope and the dogs.

"Run!" Penelope yelled at the dogs, and turned to flee.

She heard the dogs charging after her as the leader crashed through the trees.

Suddenly, the side of Penelope's face was illuminated by a brilliant light. She heard a terrible scream that sounded inhuman.

That was a directed energy beam cannon from our clipper! Penelope thought. *Koko must have gotten one of them.*

Suddenly, a sonic blast off to her left blew her off her feet. She painfully rolled on her back, winded and dazed. Another sonic blast exploded in the woods beyond where she'd been standing.

Penelope rolled over and peered toward the edge of the woods. The blazing eyes of the leader were searching for her from only meters away. The remaining three creatures had whirled back toward Koko's clipper in defensive positions. The two directed energy beam cannons on the clipper bow blazed again and two of the creatures exploded. The third creature clumsily trotted toward the cover of the woods. Koko fired the cannons again. The creature was vaporized in mid-step.

Penelope was terrified to see that the leader ignored the demise of its assault force. It was bounding through the woods directly toward her. She was paralyzed with fear for a moment. She knew she was defenseless against such a powerful monster. The dogs were nowhere in sight. The sonic blasts must have scared them away. Realizing she must fight or die, her paralysis broke. She got up to run.

The creature was upon her with an angry roar. It had dropped its blaster as it grabbed her torso with powerful arms that crushed her like steel vises. It lifted her from the ground as if she were a child. Penelope screamed in agony and terror. The demon's horrid laugh hissed in her ear. Its odor was staggering. It threw her against a tree trunk, knocking her senseless.

She became aware of being lifted in the air by her throat. Her legs kicked uselessly in the air. She gagged and choked while staring into the flaming eyes of the demon, which was now nose to bat-nose with her. She could smell its awful breath. Desperately, she kicked out at the demon's body and punched at its terrifying features. She might as well have been beating an unfeeling rock.

For all her strength, her savage attempt to escape was in vain. Her chest burned for breath. Her eyesight began to darken as consciousness slipped away. The creature continued to hiss with laughter, its cold, forked tongue licking her cheeks. It increased the tremendous crushing force around her windpipe.

Suddenly, Penelope was thrown to the leafy ground. In her daze, she heard the roaring barks and vicious growling of a ferocious dog attack. The dogs had come to her rescue.

Gagging for breath, and holding her bruised throat, Penelope rolled over. The demon leader was on its back, fighting for its life. The four huge dogs covered it in a squirming-struggling pile of fur, muscle, and teeth. The noise was terrifying. The demon couldn't defend itself against such a fearless, mindless assault. The dogs were wild in their fury at her attacker. But for as much damage as the dogs were inflicting upon their victim, the demon continued to fight with a ferocity that was causing them great injury.

Cala began yelping in fear and pain. The creature had her pinned to its chest in a mighty double-arm squeeze that was crushing the life from her. Sergeant had buried his fangs into the demon's neck and was thrashing his massive head back and forth. Black blood poured out from around Sergeant's growling mouth. The creature howled in pain. Hana and Amber were darting in and out attacking the demon's legs that were kicking in the air trying to fend them off.

The demon threw Cala aside to try and rip Sergeant off its neck. Cala landed with a lifeless thud and didn't move. The demon landed an iron fist on the side of Sergeant's head with a sickening crack. Sergeant's body went limp and fell aside. The demon kicked out its legs to drive Hana and Amber away while they tried to avoid the sharp claws of the creature's feet. The demon was up and roaring in defiance before any of them could move.

Penelope took in the horrible sight of the mangled, bleeding creature in all its ferocious rage. Its fierce cry echoed through the forest like some primeval beast. She knew they were dead.

Suddenly the beast exploded. Penelope was flattened by the blast. Pieces of gore pelted her as if she'd been hit by hail in hurricane force winds.

The next thing Penelope knew she was staring into Hana's chocolate eyes while the huge Malamute licked her face.

"Yuck, Hana!" Penelope said. She fought off the mutated dog and sat up.

"I thought you and Burt were lovers, Penelope, but now the truth is out," Koko said with a smile. He was standing behind Hana with a sonic blaster resting over his shoulder.

"It's about time you showed up, Koko. Do the dogs and I have to fight all the battles?"

Koko smiled again and leaned over to help Penelope to her feet. "Are you all right?"

"I think so. I'm just a little bruised," she grumbled.

Penelope saw a mound of black fur with a white underbelly and legs laying silently a few meters away. It was Cala. Penelope rushed to Cala's side. The huge brown-and-white Hana was already there licking Cala as if attempting to wake her. Penelope looked up and saw that Hana's smaller sister, Amber, was pawing at Sergeant's body off to their right. Amber was whining at Sergeant, but he wasn't responding, either.

"Quick, Koko, we have to carry these two back to the house," Penelope cried. She lifted Cala in her arms.

Koko stood there shocked at Penelope's ability to lift a dog that obviously outweighed her.

"Move it, Koko!"

"But, but, aren't they dead?" he asked. He dropped his blaster and moved quickly toward Sergeant. Amber growled at Koko as he neared. Koko backed off.

"Amber, it's all right. He's here to help," Penelope said. Amber moved back while giving Koko a wary eye.

Koko cautiously kneeled at Sergeant's side and touched his chest. "I'm sorry, Penelope, but I think this dog is dead."

"Move it, Koko!" Penelope yelled with such authority that Koko jumped.

Without another word, Koko slipped his arms beneath Sergeant's body. With tremendous effort, he lifted the still dog into his arms and struggled to his feet.

"Lord in Hades!" Koko said, grunting beneath Sergeant's weight. He staggered toward the house with Amber and Hana on his heels watching his every unsteady step.

As Koko wobbled and weaved toward the house beneath his tremendous burden, Penelope zipped by him with a smooth confident walk that belied Cala's weight in her arms. Koko staggered forward through the door of the house, which Penelope had left open.

"Bring him in here," Penelope yelled from the living room.

Koko carried Sergeant through the kitchen and into the living room, where Penelope had returned to kneeling over Cala after turning on the overhead lights.

"Set him down within my reach," Penelope said without turning around.

Koko sagged to his knees and unceremoniously dumped Sergeant's limp body next to Cala's. He dropped onto his back, heaving from exertion. Amber was behind Koko with Hana at her side. Amber woo-wooed at Koko's mishandling of Sergeant.

"Koko! You're an uncaring oaf!" Penelope said.

"What! They're dead, Penelope."

Hana grrr'd at this statement. Koko gave her a nasty side glance. Penelope sat back on her heels and glared at Koko for a moment. In a voice so quiet that Koko had to lean forward to pick it up, Penelope said, "You still don't understand, do you, Koko?"

Koko gazed at her with bewilderment.

"Never mind," Penelope said, "we have a bigger problem. Obviously, those were Arnold's creatures that just attacked. I don't know if they were here for you or for me, but Arnold must know we're here. Others will come. We have to leave as soon as possible."

Koko got to his feet. "I agree with that. A plan occurred to me as to how we can approach the moon base if I can find some sort of ID on those creatures. That clipper must have come from the moon base. We can use it to get there, but I need an ID to start it."

"What are we going to do once we get there? The six of us can't attack an entire army of those things. We were lucky we got away from a few of them."

"Six of us?" Koko asked with another confused look.

Penelope sighed. *Is he really that dumb or does he just like frustrating me?* "Just go find some ID to start the clipper. I'll be out shortly."

"You're one of the most perplexing women I've ever met," Koko said, shaking his head and leaving the house.

VI

THE DEMON'S CODE

ONE

Penelope found Koko an hour later hurriedly transferring their mass of weapons and scant belongings from their clipper into the one from the moon base. "What did you find on those, ah, creatures?" she asked.

"Not much. The four I shot from the clipper were mostly vaporized, but I found a few pieces of their leader. They were wearing black moon-base uniforms, but I'm not even sure what they were made out of. They seem to have been silicon based, but I don't understand how something like that can be made to live."

"It's obvious that Arnold's people have found a way. Did you find an ID to start the clipper?"

Koko sighed. "I found the leader's ID card, but it was partially destroyed. That's going to be a problem."

"Then why are you transferring our things to their clipper if we can't get it started?"

Koko grinned bashfully, as if he knew she wasn't going to like his answer.

Oh, no, Penelope thought. *That's the same stupid grin Burt used to get just before hatching some plan that would almost get us killed.*

"I thought I'd let you work out the ID number while I finished packing," Koko said.

He pulled out an ID card that was shredded along the right side and smeared with some black substance. Penelope took the card gingerly as if it might infect her with some deadly disease.

89

"A military ID can be any number of digits in any sequence," Koko said. "They're supposed to be random and have no mathematical solution, so no one can figure them out by knowing some of the digits."

"You sound like you don't believe that in this case."

"Well, military personnel are supposed to memorize their ID in case they're lost or stolen. This creature was still carrying its ID, which leads me to believe that it wasn't that intelligent, that it couldn't remember its ID number.

"Look at the digits on that card: 1524336 . . . and the next partial digit looks like a six. It looks like there's supposed to be at least one more digit after that, but I can't make it out."

"Well, there can only be ten possible answers for that last number. Why don't we try using zero through nine for the last number and see which one works," Penelope pointed out.

Koko shook his head. "The clipper will only accept three miscues. That means we only get three tries at the last number. If we're wrong a third time, the clipper shuts down. Then it sends out a warning signal that it's being tampered with and they'll know we're here. Besides, there may be more than one number that's missing."

Penelope changed the subject. "Do you think it's safe to stay here overnight and leave in the morning?"

Koko was shaking his head, but asked, "Why?"

"Sergeant and Cala could use the rest."

"What?" Koko asked, with a startled expression and disbelief in his voice.

"Koko, they aren't dead. They need time to heal themselves. They should be able to move around by themselves in the morning. I'd feel much better if we gave them a little time before we take them on another dangerous clipper ride like the one Burt took us on when we tried to escape."

"They're not dead?" Koko asked. Penelope shook her head.

Koko stared at Penelope to see if she was trying to joke with him, and apparently decided she wasn't. After a moment his face illuminated with understanding.

"This has something to do with what happened to Hedon Bohdan after Burt killed him the first time and he came back to life, doesn't it?"

Good God, Koko. It took you long enough to figure that out. She nodded her head with a look of disgust at the mention of Bohdan.

"It's not the same process, but the results are the same, yes," she said.

"I don't like the idea of waiting here all night, but we might not have a choice if we're going to leave in that clipper and my plan for getting to the moon base unnoticed is going to work. We need that clipper, and we don't know the ID yet."

"So we're not going anywhere until I figure out this number, huh?"

"I think I have a pretty good idea of what it is, but I'd like you to come to the same conclusion on your own so we don't screw this up," Koko said. He picked up some cargo boxes before heading to their new clipper.

I wonder if he really knows what it is, or if he just wants me to figure it out for him?

"Can't you give me a hint?" she called after him.

"Think simple. These creatures weren't too smart."

"Huh," Penelope muttered. She stomped back into the house.

TWO

She went back into the spacious, well-lit living room, filled with comfortable furniture. Sergeant and Cala still lay on the tan-carpeted floor close to the unlit fireplace. They appeared just as she'd left them.

Amber and Hana were both perched on the brown fluffy couch watching over the other two. Penelope sat on the couch between them and stroked the two furry sisters, both for her comfort and theirs. Hana reached her huge head over and licked Penelope's hand until it was washed. Penelope absently removed her hand to wipe it off on her pants.

She gazed long and hard at the semi-destroyed ID card. Nothing occurred to her, but then she remembered that Koko had said to keep it simple. Suddenly, a possible answer occurred to her, yet she thought it didn't make sense.

"I'll watch over Sergeant and Cala for a while," she said to Hana and Amber. "Why don't you two go out and find some dinner?"

Amber turned to gaze at Penelope with her light brown eyes. Hana jumped off the couch at the mention of food and grrr'd at Amber. Amber peeked mischievously at Hana and then back at Penelope.

"Go on. I promise they'll be all right until you get back."

Amber hopped off the couch and followed Hana to the kitchen door. Penelope went with them and let them out. Koko was on his way back in as the dogs disappeared into the darkened woods.

"Stay close," Penelope yelled after the dogs.

"Where are they going?" Koko asked.

"Dinner."

Koko nodded. "What about our dinner?"

They were in the middle of eating their own meal before Koko said, "All our things are loaded into the new clipper. We can go as soon as the dogs are loaded and we have the ID number. Did you figure it out?"

"I think so, but it doesn't make that much sense to me," she said, as she finished her warmed rehydrated beef and broccoli.

"Tell me what you've got. If you came up with the same thing, I think I can explain the rest."

"Well, if you take the numbers in twos, the first six numbers add up to six. One and five equals six. Two and four equals six, and three and three equals six. The next number is six, and the partially destroyed number is six. So I think the last number is six. Am I right?"

Koko smiled, and nodded. "That's what I figured out as well."

"But why are the last three numbers six, six, and six? That doesn't make sense to me," Penelope asked.

Koko smiled again. "Well, what gave it away for me was the creatures' appearance. I saw immediately that the coupled numbers added up to six, and how easy it would be to remember the number as long as you remembered the first number was one."

"So you end up with three sixes at the end," Penelope said. "Three pairs of numbers add up to three sixes, right? What does that have to do with the creatures' appearance?"

"That's one way of doing it, but I also thought of Arnold's vanity of creating beasts that appear like demons. What's the biblical sign of the beast?"

"Six, six, six," said Penelope, nodding at Koko's logic. "That sounds too simple."

They cleaned up their dinner in silence. Penelope peeked in on Sergeant and Cala. Koko followed her into the living room.

"Those two look the same to me. Are you sure they're going to be all right?"

"Yes, Koko." Penelope sighed.

"If we're going to be here the rest of the night, why don't we test our theory and see if we can get the clipper working? We might have to get out of here in a hurry."

Just then, Hana came marching in with Amber close on her heels. Each dog carried the bloody, mangled body of a dead rabbit in their drooling mouths. Hana gently laid her rabbit in front of Sergeant with what Penelope thought was reluctance over losing a dinner. Amber hesitantly left her treat in front of the recovering Cala.

"You opened the backdoor by yourself again, didn't you, Hana?" Penelope accused. Hana gave Penelope a guilty glance before she crawled back up on the couch to resume her vigil. Amber licked her rabbit, and eyed it closely before returning to her perch on the couch.

Koko shook his head at the scene before leaving for the clipper with Penelope close behind.

THREE

"Do you want to do the honors?" Koko asked once they were seated in the cockpit seats.

"What happens if we're wrong?" Penelope asked with concern.

"If the first code is wrong, then we have ten seconds to try again. If we're wrong a second time, we have another ten seconds. If we're wrong a third time, an alarm will go out to all the security organizations and the military with the universal coordinates of the clipper that it's being stolen."

"Will someone respond immediately?" Penelope asked.

"Probably not right away, but the computer will shut down the ship. I might be able to override the computer, and I might not. Either way, it would take hours for me to override it, and it might not work. I think we better get the code right the first time."

Penelope shook her head. *This sounds too risky. Burt's life, all our lives, may be resting on a simple guess.*

"Don't worry, Penelope. Have some confidence in me," Koko assured her.

Again, Penelope shook her head. *How many times did Burt say that exact same thing only to end up nearly killing us?*

Koko leaned forward and punched the code into a numerical security pad on the front console of the cockpit. Immediately an alarm went off and the numbers on the pad started blinking.

"You have ten seconds to enter the correct security code," an animated voice said over a loudspeaker.

"Koko! I thought you said this would work?" Penelope screamed.

"It didn't," Koko muttered while staring at the flashing key pad in anxious thought.

"I can see that! Punch in another code!"

Koko hesitantly typed in a second code. The pad continued to blink as the obnoxious alarm went off again.

"You have ten seconds to enter the correct security code," the loudspeaker repeated.

"Uh-oh," Koko muttered, and sat back to think.

Penelope peered furiously at Koko. She reached forward and quickly entered another code. Suddenly, the alarm went silent.

"We did it!" Penelope said with triumph.

The entire cockpit console went blank.

"Oh boy, we're in trouble now," Koko said. He buried his face in his hands.

"What happened?" Penelope asked anxiously.

"It was the wrong code. The computer has sent the alarm and shut us out of the system."

"What do we do now?"

Koko didn't answer right away. Finally, he said, "I think it would be a waste of time for me to try to hotwire this thing. If I mess with the computer, all sorts of things could go wrong on the way to the moon. That means we lose our way to enter the military moon base undetected on one of their clippers. We'll have to find another way."

"We still have our other military clipper. Can we use that?"

"Well, it won't get us into the military section of the moon base, but it will get us into the mining colony at least. Come on, I think we still have time to load everything back onto that clipper and get out of here."

Penelope and Koko scrambled to reload their clipper as quickly as possible. Penelope made a brief visit to the living room to see how the dogs were doing. She wasn't surprised to see Hana and Amber curled up on the couch sound asleep. Sergeant and Cala were still on the floor, but she was encouraged that they'd both moved to other locations, and the rabbits were gone.

"I just wonder who ate the rabbits," she muttered.

She went back outside, and left the backdoor open so the dogs could get out to take care of their business when they woke.

"There are a few more loads. Let's hurry up," Koko said. "This has taken too long, and I'm getting worried."

Penelope and Koko rushed inside the moon-base clipper, and started to remove the last of the weapons. As they started to exit, Koko dropped his load and held up his hand. "Listen."

FOUR

Penelope heard the engines of a small craft approaching. "What is it?" she asked with desperate fear, feeling like a cornered animal.

Koko rushed to the cockpit windows and peered out into the night.

"Damn, we've been caught! It's a local police shuttle."

"What do we do?" Penelope asked, feeling the instinctive need to flee.

"It's too late now. These will be either security agents or the local police. Hopefully, I'll know them and we can bluff our way out of this. Just follow along with whatever I say."

"Now I know we're in trouble," Penelope groaned.

Koko gave her a nasty look, and left the clipper with Penelope behind him.

Koko and Penelope rushed out onto the lawn. They peered up in the early morning sky as a small, boxy craft painted silver with the Denver police insignia on its sides passed over and landed in between the two clippers. Penelope watched anxiously as two large men in dark blue police uniforms exited the tiny shuttle. They were lightly armed with DEPs, yet neither one wore a suspicious expression. They even smiled when they recognized Koko.

"Captain Sinopa, good to see you," said the dark haired, middle-aged officer on Penelope's right. He confidently stepped forward and warmly shook Koko's hand.

"Officer Piper, I haven't seen you in what . . . about a year?" Koko said, while smiling so broadly Penelope feared his face would crack. "How's that woman of yours and your kids?"

"Old news, I'm afraid, Captain," Piper replied, with his flush trim features pointing to the ground.

"I'm sorry to hear that," Koko said mournfully. "Officer Valentine, isn't it?" He reached over to shake the hand of the smaller officer, who sported a trimmed blond moustache and boyishly curly hair. Valentine appeared to be the much younger and less experienced of the two by far.

"Yes, sir, it's an honor to see you again, Captain," Valentine said with a huge smile of horse teeth.

"I'm Monica Rose, officers," Penelope said quickly before Koko could screw it up.

"Ma'am," the officers said politely. Piper returned his attention to Koko, but Valentine gave her a curious look with dark eyes.

"Is something wrong, Officer Valentine?" Penelope asked.

"Ah, no, ma'am. Your name seems familiar to me for some reason."

Koko and Piper turned to examine Penelope. It was her turn to gaze at the lawn as if embarrassed.

"What brings you officers out here this late at night?" Koko quickly asked to change the subject away from Penelope.

"Oh, ah, we received an alarm that a military clipper was being tampered with at this location," Piper said, pulling out his communicator recorder. He checked the data on his recorder, and turned around to look at the moon-base clipper. "That's the clipper there."

Koko laughed, and shook his head. "Is that what this is all about? I'm sorry. I just got back home, and that thing was parked on my pad with no one around. I waited all day for someone to come pick it up, but no one returned for it. Finally, I tried to break into the computer to find out what it's doing here. I must have set off the alarm."

Penelope saw both the officers were nodding at Koko's story. She glanced away when she noticed that Valentine was still staring at her.

"Why didn't you call it in?" asked Piper. "We would have taken care of it for you, Captain. Someone is obviously trespassing."

"Well, I guess that's what I should have done, but I honestly thought someone would be here to pick it up. When they didn't show, I thought I wouldn't have any problems figuring out who it belonged to by looking at their computer, and well, now here you are."

"Lord in Hades, what's that!" Valentine cried with high-pitched fear. He started to reach for his DEP.

FIVE

Penelope glanced up to see Valentine's huge eyes staring over her shoulder toward the rear door of the house. She realized what had terrified the officer. She saw that Valentine already had his weapon drawn. He was about to shoot one of the dogs.

"No!" she yelled. She kicked out at Valentine's hand as he aimed his weapon.

The DEP sailed out of Valentine's grasp. Valentine turned on Penelope, his eyes filled with rage. Koko lunged toward Valentine to stop him from attacking Penelope, but he was violently knocked aside as Hana raced by him to attack Piper.

Penelope stepped back into a defensive stance when she saw Valentine's expression of rage. Amber flashed between them and leaped at Valentine. Penelope watched in horror as Amber hammered Valentine to the ground and went straight for his groin with her huge fangs. Valentine screamed like a woman giving birth. He viciously rained blows about Amber's massive head and shoulders, trying to save his manhood.

"Hana, no!" Koko yelled.

Penelope turned to see that Hana had Piper pinned on the ground. He had his arms and legs wrapped around Hana, wrestling with her bear-like body. He was screaming in terror. Hana had her mouth securely around his neck. A simple squeeze of her huge fangs would rip out Piper's throat. He desperately tried to reach for his DEP, but Koko stomped on his hand. Hana closed her teeth more tightly around Piper's throat. Piper went limp with fear.

"Hana! Amber! Come!" Penelope yelled.

Amber remained latched to Valentine's injured crotch for a moment, and then gave it one last headshake before she released him. She trotted back to sit obediently at Penelope's side while wagging her bushy tail as if to say: That was fun.

Hana held onto Piper's neck as if considering the consequences of disobeying Penelope's command, but finally released it. Piper didn't dare move; his eyes were still wide with terror. Hana leaped back and grrr'd playfully at him. Piper slowly turned his head to stare fearfully at his exuberant attacker. Hana leaned forward and licked his face.

"Oh, ick," Piper muttered. He swiped his hand across his offended features.

Koko reached down and scooped up Piper's weapon while Penelope picked up Valentine's. She aimed it at him before he got any more stupid ideas. Valentine was in no condition or mood to make any further advances toward Penelope. He grabbed his wounded groin and moaned in pain.

"That was a stupid move, Officer Valentine," Koko said breathlessly. "You should know better than to raise your weapon in a non-threatening situation. You brought this on yourself. These dogs meant you no harm."

"Dogs?" Piper said incredulously. He carefully got to his feet, eyeing Hana.

"They're my bodyguards," Penelope said. "You threatened them."

"You should feel lucky, officers," Koko said. "They would have killed you both."

Piper continued to watch Hana closely while she strolled out into the yard and peed. Valentine moaned and rolled around on the ground holding his crotch.

"We have to get out of here now, Monica," Koko said. Penelope nodded. "We'll have to get back to Brazil." Koko turned to Piper. "I'm going to have to tie you both up. I can't have you reporting in until we're long gone."

Piper only nodded before he turned toward movement at the rear door of the house with a renewed expression of terror.

Penelope peered behind her. Sergeant and Cala were ambling sleepily out of the house, like bears after a long winter hibernation. She rushed toward them wearing a joyous smile of relief. Sergeant woofed as if to say hello. Penelope knelt before them and gave them each a loving hug.

Sergeant and Cala suddenly perked up and struggled out of Penelope's tight embrace when they noticed Valentine and Piper.

Sergeant growled half-heartedly at the defenseless and wounded attackers. Piper threw up his hands in terrified capitulation. Valentine only groaned louder with rolling agony. Apparently deciding everything was in order, the two dogs left to take care of their personal business.

"Monica, please finish loading the clipper while I take care of these two," Koko said.

"What about Valentine?" Piper asked.

Koko gazed down at Valentine, and smiled. "Oh, I think he'll live as long as he behaves himself while I'm tying you up. Help him to his feet and let's move it. Oh, and give me your communicators."

Penelope quickly finished loading the military clipper, while Koko securely tied up the officers in their shuttle.

SIX

"They aren't going anywhere fast," Koko told Penelope after they were finished.

"I made a mistake," said Penelope. "I told them my name was Monica Rose. I didn't realize until after I said it that it was the same name I used when we were attacked by the *USS Smith*. No doubt the authorities will realize who I am after these officers are rescued."

Koko shook his head with a weary smile. "Don't worry about it. They were going to be pursuing us anyway. You don't get away with assaulting police officers, and I doubt their story will be anywhere close to the truth that they provoked the assault.

"Come on. Collect the dogs and get them aboard while I lock up the house and get the clipper ready to go."

Once they were ready in the clipper, Koko filed a flight plan for Brazil with the Denver Spaceport. They left Denver heading southeast. Once they were a safe distance, Koko took command of the clipper and changed course.

"We're not going to Brazil, are we?" Penelope asked from the copilot's seat.

"No, that was just to throw off anyone chasing us. We're going to Hawaii. You're going to have to show me where you and Burt have been hiding out."

"Hawaii? Why are we going back there? I thought we were going to the moon base to save Burt," Penelope said.

"We are, but my plan has been changed, since we don't have a way into the military base on one of their clippers. I'm going to have to find out what's going on with the security agents who work the moon mines. Hopefully, I still have some loyal friends there who can help us. I don't want to just show up in what might be a hostile situation that gets us all killed or captured."

"But all that will take time, Koko. They're torturing Burt now. There's no telling what they're doing to him or how long he'll survive."

Koko turned to Penelope with a frown. "I'm just as aware and anxious about the situation as you are. I still think Arnold wants Burt alive rather than dead. We won't do him any good if we're both dead or captured. We have to go into this with some strong support and a plan."

"I only hope we're not too late," Penelope muttered.

VII

DEFEAT

ONE

Campbell awoke in a cell that was so dark even his black implants couldn't pick up any light. He slowly moved his head and instantly regretted it. His neck muscles clenched in soreness. Terrible pressure increased behind his eyes as the nauseating headache that had been hammering away at his brain since the onset of his conditioning returned with a vengeance. Through his private nightmare, he heard the tormenting recording of Arnold's droning voice spewing out submissive messages over the loudspeakers. He'd been subjected to this continual verbal barrage the entire time he was locked in his cell. He was going insane.

Damn, he thought, *are those messages really playing over the loudspeaker or are they part of my every thought now? I'm losing the battle to control my own mind.*

He felt mentally and physically drained to the point of breaking and pleading for them to stop. His entire body was like a massive bruise. He was surprised that, even with his body's amazing recuperative powers, he was still alive. But it was the mental anguish of his continual conditioning more than his physical pain that was defeating him.

Campbell lay there and concentrated on one of the mental escapes he used to relieve his eternal suffering. He thought of his peaceful existence on Hawaii. He tried to envision Penelope's beautiful face— her long blond hair and lively blue-gray eyes. He despaired when at first it didn't appear. It was taking more and more concentration to see anything in the consuming blackness of his mind. He desperately tried to see the beloved dogs, but failed miserably. He sought to imagine the brilliant and beautiful Hawaiian sunsets that had brought him so much peace from high atop the Mauna Kea volcano. He saw only darkness.

"Damn! What's happening to me?" he raged. He slammed his fists into his aching forehead. For a brief moment he saw bright lights behind his eyes. His intense pain cleared his confusion.

"Arnold! I'll kill you!"

Immediately his body erupted in a convulsion of severe agony that was nauseating and debilitating. He knew the pain stemmed from his conditioning. To revolt against Arnold crippled him mentally and physically.

The door to his cell suddenly opened. He was blinded by the bright light from the hallway.

"Inspector, it's only me," said a soothing voice.

Campbell recognized Dr. Eto at his side. He felt her touch him briefly on the arm in a gentle manner.

His pain eased when he thought about the strange relationship he'd developed with Eto in their long sessions during his conditioning. He'd felt that she was different than the others from the first time he'd seen her battered and frightened face. Her expression had always shown compassion and caring for his plight. It was something he'd never seen on any of the other faces around him. He felt comfort around her, and pity for her, since he didn't get the feeling that she was there of her own free will.

"I have to give you your injection," Eto said. "We'll continue your conditioning in a few minutes."

At first Campbell tensed when Eto injected him, but then he began to relax. This wasn't the first time that he felt the easing of his pain after one of Eto's injections.

What's in those injections? he wondered suspiciously. *They seem to help with the pain of my conditioning, but they could be something that reduces my resistance and makes my mind more susceptive.*

Four guards appeared at Campbell's cell door.

"Dr. Eto, we are here to escort the prisoner to the lab," one evil-eyed guard announced.

Eto quickly backed away as the four goblin-like guards entered the cramped cell. Two of the scaly-skinned guards roughly hauled Campbell to his feet while the other two stood safely aside, aiming sonic blasters at him. Campbell had always seen his transfer as an opportunity for escape, but the guards had been extremely careful.

The guards pushed Campbell to the lab next door before they restrained him in his coffin-like torture chamber. Eto had quietly followed them in. Blake was already there preparing his usual injection for Campbell after he was securely restrained and helpless. Campbell had noticed that Blake never approached him unless he was incapacitated and unable to retaliate.

"Blake, happy to see you this morning, or is it night now?" he asked with mock cheerfulness.

Blake laughed nervously. "One loses their sense of time here, Campbell. Now be a good boy while I give you your injection."

Campbell thought of a worthy retort, but suddenly he was struck by a bolt of pain.

"I see your conditioning is working," Blake said, showing a smile of filthy teeth. "You mustn't think nasty thoughts about your superiors."

"You'll never be my superior, you spineless worm!" Campbell hissed through clenched teeth. Another bolt of pain shot through his already tormented body.

Blake laughed. "Oh, I'm not only your superior, but I'm your better." he said. "You'll do whatever we ask. After a couple more sessions the guards won't even be needed to escort you from your cell."

Campbell struggled against his restraints before his mind and body were set ablaze with agony. He nearly passed out, but not before he saw the doubt and fear in Blake's face.

Ha! I haven't lost yet, Campbell thought.

As Campbell sagged, Blake snuck up and injected his arm. Immediately, Campbell felt his body tense and his senses heighten. Blake pushed the control that closed his coffin to begin his torture. His muscles clenched in readiness as his breath became short in anticipation of the agony to come. After a moment the conditioning resumed.

TWO

Campbell was vaguely conscious of the light in the lab when the coffin was opened again. He didn't know how long he'd been in there, but it seemed like his entire life. He had no memory of how he'd even gotten there.

His body was drenched with sweat. He hung limply in his restraints. The helmet had been removed, and he saw Eto standing off to his right. Blake was lost in thought while surveying results on a computer monitor. Campbell peered up to see the weasel-faced Arnold standing directly in front of him. Arnold was staring intently at him with his black beady eyes.

"How are you feeling, Campbell?" Arnold asked.

Another blot of pain shot through Campbell's body as he attempted to respond. Nothing came out of his mouth but a hate-filled hiss.

Arnold smiled. "Dr. Blake tells me you're an excellent subject, and that your conditioning is nearly complete. That's good. Time is of the essence. We have so much to do and plan for our future together."

Campbell tried to clear his mind of possible responses. He knew the results would be painful.

"No answer, Campbell?" Arnold sneered. "Excellent, really excellent. You're learning."

Arnold started to pace the room as if in thought. Campbell watched him with hooded eyes. He wondered if it was really possible for Arnold to make him do as he wished. One part of his mind still revolted at the horrid thought, but his body didn't seem to respond to his true desires. At the same time, another part of him wanted to do whatever Arnold wanted, anything so that Arnold would stop the pain.

"I think it's time to test your resolve, Campbell," Arnold said. "Blake, remove the inspector's restraints."

Campbell saw fear spread across Blake's pale, fat face. He turned to Eto and saw she was smiling. Glancing around the room, he didn't see any guards present. It was just the four of them.

"But, General, what if . . .?" Blake left the rest unsaid.

"Come now, Dr. Blake. You just assured me he was about ready."

Blake slowly came forward. Campbell noticed that Arnold retreated to the door, and was fingering a DEP in his holster. He took a deep breath and prepared himself.

As Blake undid the restraints, Campbell tried to tense his muscles for the attack. They remained as loose as boiled noodles. He was horrified to find that his body wouldn't respond to his mind. Blake undid the belt around Campbell's waist. He fell limply forward.

"Oh!" Eto yelled.

Blake quickly got underneath Campbell and caught him before he fell forward enough to impale himself on the instruments of the coffin lid at his feet. Arnold laughed with an evil harshness that pained Campbell down to his soul.

"See, Dr. Blake? The man has no ability to resist, much less the desire. Help him down to his cell."

Blake got his arm around Campbell and struggled to get him into the next room. Even when Campbell thought about escape, he could only make one foot step in front of the other. The wave of pain that followed his thoughts seemed dimmed by his anger at his inability to respond.

Blake let go of Campbell. He collapsed onto his cell bed. Dr. Eto was instantly at his side and tried to arrange his limbs in a comfortable position.

"That's enough, Eto," Arnold snapped. "Sometimes I wonder about your loyalties. Even the Master is concerned about you and your vocal criticism about Its methods."

Eto backed away from Campbell with an expression of pinched fear before she held her head down in submission. Her long, black hair fell over her bruised face. Campbell watched her with pity and concern as she scurried out of his cell.

Arnold stepped into the cell, rubbing his small, thin hands together.

"Campbell, you see now that escape is impossible. You are completely under my control. I believe this calls for a celebration.

"In three days' time, after you have completed some more sessions with Dr. Blake, we'll allow you to participate in a little training session with George. That'll give you a chance to work out the rest of your hostilities and convince you once and for all that you have no will left to oppose us."

Campbell had just enough strength to wonder what Arnold meant by a training session with George and a chance to vent his hostility. He didn't respond to Arnold, and Arnold left the cell followed by Blake. They closed Campbell in the blissful darkness of his cell.

As Campbell felt his body recovering and sleep coming on, he reviewed Arnold's statements in his head. *What did Arnold mean by what he said to Dr. Eto? Who is the Master, if not Arnold? Does Arnold have a superior that I don't know about?*

THREE

Campbell again awoke in the lonely blackness of his cell. He wasn't sure how long he'd been asleep, and decided Blake had been correct. One lost all sense of time on the moon, but maybe it was just his mental state after all his anguish. Maybe he desired to escape time completely. He could only tell that his horrible experience since arriving had been the worst nightmare of his life. Oddly, he now felt strangely refreshed, as if some major conflict in his mind had been resolved in his sleep.

He stared into the cold darkness and again tried to remember his wonderful life on Hawaii with Penelope and the dogs. He was angered and frustrated that he couldn't remember a single vision from that life. He knew it had happened. He knew he'd been happy and at peace with himself, with the decisions and actions of his life, but he couldn't generate the images of his past in his mind.

I have lost my battle against Arnold. My entire existence before arriving on the moon has been obliterated from my mind. I can only hope that my memories and happiness will return with time.

VIII

A FINAL TEST

ONE

Campbell realized he'd fallen asleep again when he was awakened by a gentle shake on his shoulder. He opened his eyes only to screw them shut again as the light from the open door burned his eyes.

"It's okay, Burt. It's only me," Dr. Eto said softly in his ear.

Campbell kept his eyes closed, and whispered, "Is it time for another session? I don't know how many more I can take."

I wish there was some way I could kill myself and be rid of this agony, he thought. *With my image of Penelope and my peace gone, this pain has become unbearable. I don't want to live.*

"Have hope, Inspector," said Eto. She gently rubbed up and down on his arm with her warm hand to comfort him. "Your last session was two days ago. The time has come for your final test."

"Two days ago?" he asked with surprise. To him it seemed like he'd just left the torture lab hours before. He didn't even remember the session or being brought back to his cell.

"That's right, Campbell," Arnold said.

Campbell opened his eyes a crack. He could make out Arnold standing in the cell doorway. He groaned with pain at the sight of his tormentor.

"Today's the day, Campbell," Arnold said gleefully. "I let you rest yesterday so your body will be ready for the grand competition and your test against George."

"I beg you to reconsider, General Arnold," Eto pleaded. "The inspector isn't physically ready for the competition. You'll be wasting all our work if he's killed."

"That may be true, Doctor," Arnold said, "but time has run out. He's either ready or he isn't. If he isn't ready, he'll be killed in one manner or another. Guards, come prepare the inspector for the arena."

The same four goblin-faced guards came in and hauled Campbell to his feet. Lost in his terror and confusion about what was happening, he didn't even offer resistance when they cuffed his hands behind his back and placed a hood over his head so he couldn't see.

As the foul-smelling guards pushed Campbell out of his cell, Arnold said, "You know, Eto, I still wonder if you're behind us with all your heart. Remember what the cost will be if we fail. You're part of this team, and there's no denying your participation."

Again Campbell feared for Eto's life as he was led down the hallways in the total darkness beneath his hood. He quickly lost count of the twists and turns along his way. It was obvious to him that Arnold still didn't trust him. He was deeply anxious about his final test against George.

Abruptly, the guards brought Campbell to a halt. He could distinctly hear the muffled roar of a crowd close at hand. He'd never heard so many voices clamoring and yelling with mad excitement all at once. It reminded Campbell of screaming fans at a ballgame. His nervousness deepened.

"Guards, remove his hood," Arnold said.

His hood was whisked away. Campbell saw he was in a large, unadorned and dark hallway with a giant double door directly in front of him. He blinked and gazed around, but said nothing. Dr. Eto had accompanied him off to his left. The four heavily armed guards that flanked him on all sides shifted nervously on their clawed feet.

"Open the door," Arnold commanded from behind Campbell. One of the guards pushed a button on the wall next to the door and it opened.

TWO

Suddenly the noise level of screaming fans went up ten-fold. It was deafening. Campbell gazed out with wide-eyed amazement at the most bizarre circus of horror that he'd ever witnessed. He mindlessly stepped forward to peer into the circular arena inside a bubble dome beneath bright lights. There were three levels of deeply set stands surrounding the sandy arena floor. The stands were full of a massive army of raving fans excited to the point of near hysteria. The insane crowd was cheering, booing, and hissing foul oaths at the combatants competing in the walled arena below them.

"Remove his cuffs and guard the door," Arnold ordered.

Campbell felt his hands freed before someone pushed him out onto the sandy arena floor. A deafening roar went up from the crowd as Campbell stumbled forward. He could literally feel the sound and excitement of the crowd beating down upon him like a physical force. It was extremely exhilarating and terrifying at the same time. He guessed the fans were twenty-five thousand strong. He saw men, women, and an assortment of Arnold's creatures. But all the creatures were of human form, dressed in black military uniforms. He noted none of the unruly trolls, bats, or spider creatures from the hangar in the stands.

"Where're the children?" Campbell asked no one.

"We have few children here on the moon base, Campbell," Arnold said right next to him. "Those that we have are prohibited from the games. If you watch the arena action for a moment, I think you'll see why."

Campbell turned his attention toward the center of the arena as another mad roar went up from the crowd. He saw that there were six combatants fighting in three separate groups of two. Each of the combatant groups was fighting in different sections of the level arena floor. He immediately noted none of the combatants bore weapons, but decided they didn't need any.

This looks like the deadly gladiator contests that took place on Earth twenty-five hundred years ago, Campbell thought. *But those combatants are nothing like anything ever witnessed in Rome.*

Campbell turned to his left to spy two huge winged demons like George fighting in a vicious claw-to-claw struggle. They were wrestling, biting, kicking, and slashing with their talons with an insane madness to kill each other. As he watched, one bat-faced demon landed on the back of its rival and tried to sink its fangs into the exposed section of its opponent's neck. The rival managed to get its huge arm around its attacker's head and flip it to the sand. Another insane roar rose from the crowd.

The fans to the right of Campbell yelled and screamed even louder. He gazed in that direction to see a creature that appeared like a single muscular black wing the size of a personnel clipper. It had powerful human-like legs, and a tiny bird-like head. It was swooping down to attack an immense ogre creature.

A piercing cry screamed out from the wing creature's hooked beak as it dove upon the ogre. Campbell estimated the ogre was at least twice his own height and three times as wide and muscular. Its hands were so large it appeared as if they could pulverize stone.

If not for the seriousness of the situation, Campbell thought he would have found the ogre's head amusing. It was disproportionately large compared to its body. It featured a huge bulb of a nose centered by overextended cheekbones. Its mouth was a gigantic hole that bellowed with rage through rows of dagger-like teeth. Its single enormous black eye was furrowed at its opponent beneath a mop of brown hair. Campbell saw that the ogre was bleeding profusely from ragged wounds torn into its bare chest, arms, and horrid face.

The fans' screaming reached a deafening level when the diving wing slowed above the ogre and slashed at it with its talons. The ogre was slow moving. The wing creature ripped terrible wounds into the ogre's flesh to add to its already blood-soaked body.

Suddenly the ogre reached out with a quickness it hadn't shown before. It lunged and grabbed onto the wing creature's muscular leg. Immediately the wing creature began to flap frantically in an attempt to free itself while letting out another earsplitting cry.

Campbell felt an unexpected thrill that the wing creature might escape. Its tremendous wingtips pummeled the ogre as it began to lift it from the ground. But the bellowing and enraged ogre wouldn't relent. It managed to grab hold of its opponent's other leg. Then, with an inhuman yell of rage, the ogre leaned back and pulled down with its massive arms, crashing its attacker to the ground.

The ogre instantly pounced upon its opponent's back with a mighty leap before it could take to the air again and escape. The crowd went crazy as the ogre threw down its powerful hand and ripped off the wing creature's head. Holding the severed head aloft, the ogre screamed a victorious cry.

The crowd was on their feet in their blood fever. The ogre yelled something unintelligible before throwing the bloody head high into the stands.

"Lord in Hades," Campbell murmured. The crowd swarmed around the tossed head when it landed among them. They fought savagely for it as if it was the prized trophy of a lifetime.

The ogre was inspired by the crowd's frenzy. Campbell turned back to see the ogre struggling to lift its headless opponent. Again, he was astounded by the creature's brute strength. The ogre lifted the wing creature's body above its head with staggering legs and trembling arms. It charged the arena wall and heaved the dead creature into the first rows of the stands. Fans screamed in terror and scrambled to get out of the way. Three or four fans weren't fast enough. They were crushed to death beneath the tremendous weight of the dead creature.

Campbell was sickened when the crowd frenzy increased over the demise of their fellow onlookers. They descended upon the corpses and began to rip the bodies apart.

"Damn," Campbell muttered. He was just beginning to understand the horrible implications of the army Arnold had created, and the effects it would have on the civilized world.

THREE

"Incredible, isn't it?" Arnold said at Campbell's side, as if misunderstanding his expression of horror.

"It's a nightmare . . .," Campbell started to say.

"Exactly, Campbell! I knew you would appreciate the intelligence of our creations."

"What the hell are you talking about?" Campbell asked.

"We created these creatures out of the images from children's fables, dreams, and nightmares with the belief that they are the basis of all men's fears. What men feared as children, they still fear as adults."

Campbell started to say that was an insane idea, but Arnold grabbed his arm and pointed toward the center of the arena. "Look over there, Campbell."

He started to turn to where Arnold was pointing when he noticed something he'd missed in all the excitement. Standing at attention around the arena walls were human guards in black environmental suits. The bright arena lights reflected off the clear plasma bubbles around their heads. The guards were carrying rifle-like weapons he'd never seen before. The weapons were larger than bulky sonic blasters, and they were attached to a tank on the guards' backs by a thin hose.

What are those weapons and why the hell do they need environmental suits? Campbell wondered.

"Campbell, watch this!" Arnold repeated, when he noticed he hadn't gotten Campbell's attention.

Campbell turned toward center arena. One of the massive trolls he'd seen earlier in the hangar carrying clipper engines was standing over the mutilated corpse of its opponent. It was obviously the victor of its battle, but now the creature seemed confused and insane. It was bellowing madly as it whirled around in circles and peered intently at the sandy floor. There were no other living creatures close to it.

"What's it doing?" Campbell asked.

"Just watch," Arnold said impatiently.

Campbell didn't see anything happening but a mindless creature spinning in a circle. His attention was caught by another crowd roar, and he peered toward the action to his left. He was just in time to see one of the George-like demons pull its blade-like talons out of the bloody back of its prone opponent. It stood up with a howl of triumph.

Suddenly, the guards in the environmental suits descended upon the victorious demon and quickly corralled it off to one of the side doors in the arena wall. As the crowd howled in fury at their champion being unceremoniously escorted off, Campbell turned back to where the victorious ogre had been. He was intrigued and confused to see that it had already been taken from the arena as well.

"Campbell, pay attention!" Arnold yelled.

Arnold's command seemed to penetrate into the core of Campbell's mind. To his surprise, he snapped to attention. An evil smile crossed Arnold's face.

Campbell had turned to watch the bellowing troll when suddenly, out of the corner of his eye, something rose up out of the sand to his left. The disturbance was over by the time he'd turned toward that direction. He saw that the dead demon's body had disappeared.

"What the hell just happened?" Campbell yelled.

Arnold was laughing insanely. Campbell could hear the remaining troll screaming in panicked terror in the center of the arena. It had apparently seen the demon's body disappear as well. Campbell glanced back in time to see the massive troll was charging them with huge round eyes. He quickly realized the beast wasn't after them. It was trying to escape through the only open doorway behind them.

Before the troll made it ten meters, the guards with the strange guns rushed out to surround the terrified creature. The beast slid to a stop and howled in rage at the guards.

"What are those weapons the guards are carrying?" Campbell asked. Arnold just waved at Campbell dismissively and didn't respond.

Whatever those weapons are, they scare Arnold's creatures enough to make them obey, Campbell thought.

Campbell turned his attention back to see the guards had returned to their positions along the arena walls. The troll was whirling around the center of the arena again while peering at the sand.

Suddenly, Campbell almost lost his balance when the arena floor began to shake as if they were experiencing a minor earthquake. The crowd must have felt it as well. They fell silent with anticipation. A chill ran down Campbell's spine. He had an incredible sense of impending doom. The only sound seemed to be the continued howling of the beast in the center of the arena.

The sand beneath Campbell's feet shook more violently.

"It rises!" Arnold yelled. The crowd responded with wild excitement.

Campbell started to step backward toward the doorway when he noticed that even the guards had plastered themselves against the walls in fear. Abruptly, the sand exploded in a huge circle around the condemned troll.

Campbell felt a scream of terror rise in his throat. Huge gray tentacles with enormous round suckers shot up toward the arena ceiling, surrounding the terrified troll. One of the tentacles slapped down on the beast and wrapped around it with such terrifying speed and force the floor shook again. Campbell could tell the troll had been crushed to death even before the tentacle lifted its limp corpse into the air.

For a moment, the tentacles seemed to dance in the air while one of them carried the smashed body of its trophy. Then the tentacles slithered below the arena surface just as fast as they appeared, while taking their treasure with them.

Campbell stood rooted in complete shock. Even the crowd had fallen silent with stunned amazement.

"What? What have you done, Arnold?" Campbell finally asked when his heart had stopped beating so hard and he caught his breath.

"Oh, you like my pet, Campbell?" Arnold asked. Campbell didn't respond. "I call them sand squids. Actually, they can live in just about anything, and that one is the smallest one we created. We designed them to attack bulky military vehicles from beneath the surface. We have some large enough to take down battle cruisers on the high seas. We even have a few outside this military compound to guard against a ground attack," Arnold ranted, as if he were bragging about one of his favorite projects.

How do they keep those giant things fed? Campbell wondered. *It'd be nice to see Arnold dancing around center arena with one of those squids . . .* Suddenly, a bolt of pain shot through his body and he doubled over.

"I see you don't appreciate my creations, Burt," Arnold said, and clapped Campbell's lowered back. "Fine, it's time for your combat test against the arena champion anyway."

Campbell snapped to attention. Terror struck through his heart as he considered Arnold's words. "I can't fight that thing in the sand!"

Arnold laughed. "Don't be stupid. That sort of death is reserved for humans and creatures that don't follow orders and can't be controlled. The death sentences carried out in the arena help quell the blood lust of my army and control them by reminding them that their deaths can easily be arranged."

That would do it for me, Campbell thought.

FOUR

"Bring the inspector his shield and mace," Arnold said to a guard.

"A mace?" Campbell asked in total confusion.

"I'll explain in a minute," Arnold said, and turned away from him.

Campbell jumped suddenly when he felt a slight prick in his right tricep. He turned and glared down to see Eto at his side. She had an injector in her hand that she quickly slipped into her pocket.

"What the . . .?" Campbell started to say. Then he stopped when he saw the pleading expression on Eto's face.

As Campbell gazed into Eto's features, he noticed that the disfigurement from her beating had healed. *She's a pretty woman. Have I been on the moon base so long that she's had a chance to heal, or has she been healed by some different method?*

"Eto!" Arnold yelled. "What're you doing?"

"Nothing," she said with a telling expression of guilt. She quickly backed away.

The goblin-faced guard returned with Campbell's mace and a circular metallic shield that he estimated to be about a meter in diameter. The guard handed them to him with an evil-toothed sneer. Campbell took the half-meter-long mace shaft in his right hand and let the heavy spiked ball fall to the sandy ground. He flicked the handle a few times with his arm. The metal ball whipped back and forth easily on its chain with deadly force.

"I don't know how to use these," Campbell complained to Arnold.

"Then you'll have to learn fast," Arnold laughed.

"General, please don't do this," Eto pleaded again. "George will kill the inspector."

"Guards, escort Dr. Eto back to her lab," Arnold ordered.

Eto gave Arnold a hateful glare that Campbell thought would get her another beating. She turned around with an angry huff and left the arena. Arnold watched her go with a thoughtful gleam in his beady eyes before he turned to Campbell.

"Campbell, you're about to fight George, our arena champion for its class. Naturally, it has never fought the sand squid, but it's never fought a human before, either. It has never lost in over a hundred fights, but since you're human, we're giving you weapons while George will carry none.

"Since you're new to arena combat, I'll tell you there are no rules. Combat lasts until one or both of the combatants are dead." Arnold paused to let these words sink in.

Is he telling the truth? Campbell wondered. *Why would Arnold go through so much trouble to get me here, condition me to obey orders, and then kill me? Can Arnold even control George during a real battle?*

"I'll also tell you that George, like many of the creatures here, is a silicon-based being. In other words, its outer skin is similar to flexible rock. George has no morals, and won't hesitate to kill you the second it has a chance."

"Then how do you keep it from killing you?" Campbell asked, with an evil smile of his own.

"I have my ways," Arnold said. "Listen, Campbell, if you want to come out of this alive, you'll have to be faster and smarter than George. Stay away from it. Its claws will gut you with a single swipe into your unarmored body."

"What good are these things?" Campbell asked. He flipped his mace handle against his metal shield with a bang.

"I chose those weapons for a purpose. The shield should deflect most of George's blows and protect you. But to hurt George, you're going to have to get close and strike it with that mace. Its spikes will penetrate George's outer layer and injure it. If you hit it right, you may survive by killing it."

Is it really possible for George to kill me? Campbell wondered. *If I'm wounded or die, will the technology in my blood eventually heal me the way it did Hedon Bohdan? What if Arnold has my body destroyed before I have a chance to recover? What if George rips my body apart, or tears off my head and it's impossible for me to recover?*

Arnold moved into the center of the arena. The murmuring crowd went silent with Arnold's advance.

Are they quiet out of anticipation of things to come or out of fear of Arnold? Campbell asked himself. He felt queasy with nervous excitement.

Arnold pulled a communicator out his pocket and brought it to his mouth.

"Now the event you've been waiting for," Arnold announced over the arena audio system. The crowd remained tensely quiet.

Campbell suddenly began to feel a lightness and strength surging through his muscles. His mood became almost euphoric, as if he'd had too much to drink, but he didn't feel light headed or dizzy.

He wondered what could possibly have brought on this mood when he recalled Dr. Eto's injection. He realized she'd injected him with some sort of enhancement drug. For some reason, her rebellious act gave him courage and hope. It was a strange feeling for him. He decided it was the first time since he'd been brought to the moon base that he might have a chance to retaliate and win. At least he was being given a chance to fight. He decided he would fight to the death rather than become Arnold's slave.

"Burt Campbell," Arnold announced, "the new commander of our army, has decided to prove his loyalty and battle worthiness by challenging George, the arena champion, in a battle to the death. Here is the challenger, Burt Campbell!"

Campbell was stunned by the announcement. The crowd remained subdued in quiet anticipation. Arnold turned to Campbell and waved him out to the center of the arena. When Campbell didn't move, an uppity guard pushed him from behind to get him going. A roar of laughter went up from the crowd as he stumbled toward Arnold.

"And now, here's your champion!" Arnold yelled. "Undefeated in one hundred and twenty-one battles! George!"

A door opened in the arena wall opposite Arnold and Campbell, accompanied by the deafening blare of trumpets. George entered the arena with its claws held high and its bat-like wings spread wide, as if it were a fan favorite deserving great honor. The crowd booed, hissed, and chanted: "Death to George!"

George roared in anger at the fans.

FIVE

Campbell turned around to say something to Arnold about George's popularity, but discovered that Arnold had already retreated to the opposite wall. Campbell was alone in the center of the arena.

What happened to that squid thing? Campbell wondered, as he glanced anxiously down at the sand.

George roared. Campbell glanced up. George was soaring down to land before him. Its right claw, with dagger-sharp talons, was arched over its hideous head to deliver a death blow. Campbell ducked while throwing up the shield to protect himself. George's claw slammed into the shield with incredible force as its momentum carried it by Campbell's lowered body.

Campbell whirled with inhuman quickness. He blindly swung his mace as George passed. He felt the heavy blow of the mace dig deep into George's back. George let out a roar of pain and anger. A mad cry went up from the crowd.

Campbell wheeled around. The mace was embedded in George's right shoulder blade. Its right wing was sagging, crippled and useless. Campbell ripped the spiked ball out of George's hide. He felt the intense excitement of battle flowing through his veins like never before. The fury of twenty-five thousand screaming fans drove his excitement to a fevered pitch. Black blood poured from George's wound. Its thick black tail was lashing back and forth, snapping like a bullwhip. He rushed George, hoping to take advantage of George's injury.

Raising his shield, Campbell brought down his mace aimed at George's repulsive black skull. George dodged beneath the swinging steel ball of death. Its snarling face was a mask of unbridled hatred. It threw out a wild punch, striking Campbell's shield.

Campbell was knocked sideways and off balance by the powerful blow. George was on him in an instant. Campbell could see George's red eyes flaming with an intense rage of madness to kill him. He brought up his shield to fight off blow after blow from George's claws, which kept him falling back in a desperate retreat.

Suddenly, George lashed out with its tail wrapping up Campbell's legs. Campbell fell hard on his back. He desperately threw up his shield and rolled as George dove at him with its claws extended.

George hit the empty sand face first with a shriek of angry frustration. Campbell sat up, swinging the mace at the base of the tail near his feet. The mace buried itself deep into the extended limb. George howled in pain while retracting its tail and ripping the impaled mace out of Campbell's sweaty grasp.

Campbell was immediately on his feet. He charged George as it rolled and struggled to its knees to face him with a hideous snarl of fangs. Campbell plowed into George's chest with all his weight and force behind his shield. As George was thrown back, Campbell regained his balance and yanked the mace out of its tail. He whipped around, swinging the spiked metal ball high above his head to deliver a deadly strike. George was too fast. It was on its feet and leaping away as the mace buried itself in the sand.

George rampaged toward Campbell while bellowing in mindless rage. Campbell leaped aside. He managed a wild swing with his mace that struck a savage blow to George's right shoulder. Again the crowd went wild. But now Campbell felt winded by his emotion and excitement. His longtime torture had drained his body. His fear was returning. The mace injured George's shoulder enough to stop the beast's onslaught for a moment.

Campbell lowered his shield enough to see the black blood pouring down George's naked torso. George roared in an anguish-filled howl. As its head was lifted back and its flaming eyes disappeared, Campbell saw his chance. He charged recklessly forward while aiming another strike toward George's head.

The mournful howl was a trick. George ducked beneath the vicious mace swing. It drove its stone-like left shoulder into Campbell's unarmored stomach. With a mighty heave, George threw Campbell over its massive torn back. Campbell flipped through the air and came down hard with his mace beneath him. He screamed in sharp agony as the spikes of the mace impaled his back.

Campbell arched his back with debilitating pain as he tried to reach the impaling mace. He couldn't breathe, as if the mace spikes had punctured his lungs. The crowd noise and his excitement for battle had evaporated with the blood and pain of his injury.

The deep growl of a vicious animal nearby returned Campbell's attention to his danger. He opened his eyes. George leered over him—drooling and showing its yellowing rows of sharp fangs. Campbell had time to wonder how a silicon-based creature could drool while he raised his shield for protection. George roared as it ripped downward with its right claw to deliver a blow that would tear out his throat.

The shield partially protected Campbell. George's deadly talons skipped off the shield to tear a nasty gash in Campbell's left bicep. George's claw caught beneath the edge of the shield, and hurled it out of Campbell's weakened grasp. Campbell lay exposed, defenseless. George threw out another powerful swing with its left claw aimed at Campbell's neck. With instinctive desperation Campbell rolled, making George miss. Campbell screamed as he rolled over on his back, driving the mace deeper into his flesh. He heard George's cry of anger as he struggled to his feet.

Campbell stood on shaky legs a few meters from George, sagging with pain and exhaustion. As he caught his ragged breath, his burning desire to kill George rekindled. He yanked on the mace handle and pulled the spikes out of his flesh and muscle. His eyesight darkened as he nearly fainted, but he saw George put down its head and shoulder in a charge. Drawing his remaining strength, Campbell barely had time to raise his mace in a tremendous swing as George hit him squarely in the chest. The blow hit Campbell like a sonic blast. He flew through the air with his arms thrown limply over George's damaged wings. He hit the sandy floor with the immense weight of George crushing him.

Campbell hoped he was dead, but his suffering was so great he knew he was still alive. He felt his hot blood flowing from his painful wounds, but he was confused by an icy liquid pouring on his face. He was even more confounded that George wasn't getting up to finish him off.

He mustered his strength and heaved the creature off him. George fell limply to his side and didn't move. Campbell struggled to his feet on wobbling legs. He became aware of the deafening roar of the crowd. He gazed around him with dazed confusion. The crowd was on their feet, going wild with excitement.

"Kill George!" they chanted in a deafening chorus that seemed to vibrate in Campbell's soul.

Campbell slowly turned back to glare down at George with weariness and confusion. The right side of George's face was a smashed mess of black gore. The horrid face was barely recognizable anymore. Campbell realized that his last mace swing had struck George's head.

Spurred on by the cheers of the crowd, the power of victory surged through Campbell's veins. He gazed stupidly down at his right hand as if to ensure it was still there. His arm was covered with George's cold black blood. Strength returned to his grasp.

"Kill George!" the chant continued at a fevered pace.

The anger over his capture . . . the agony and humiliation of his torture . . . the hatred of everything around him . . . It all came together. It focused on George.

Campbell slowly straddled George's torso and began to raise the mace behind his head to deliver the killing blow. He gazed down at the horrifying remains of George's face. George's flaming eyes suddenly flew open. Campbell and George stared at each other with a hatred born in Hell.

Rage surged in Campbell's chest. He screamed as he brought down the mace with all the strength his muscles could deliver.

"Campbell! No!" Arnold yelled.

The mace came down with all the power to pulverize a boulder. At the last instant, Campbell's aim swerved to the side. The spiked ball buried itself in the sand, barely grazing George's head.

Campbell wearily learned over in stunned amazement—confused with exhaustion. *How did I miss?*

It was too much. His weakened legs wavered and he fell onto his knees, still straddling George's torso. He blacked out and fell onto George's face.

SIX

Campbell awakened to see Arnold leaning over him about to slap his face. Sharp pain and his sweat-drenched skin told him he'd only been out for a moment. He was on his back, lying on the arena floor. He realized that Arnold must have rolled him off George.

"Don't do that," Campbell muttered. Arnold stopped his slapping motion.

Campbell gazed up at Arnold. He didn't like, or understand, the evil grin of small teeth on Arnold's weasel-like face. He turned his head to his right. Four human guards were loading George's devastated body onto a hover stretcher. Campbell thought he must be going crazy. George was returning his gaze. There was a grin on its destroyed features similar to Arnold's. Unnerved by George's glare, Campbell gazed back at Arnold.

"You passed the test, Burt! You passed the test!" Arnold yelled and laughed.

"What are you talking about?" Campbell muttered.

"That was the test, to see if you could be controlled in the rage of battle. I commanded you not to kill George when your life was threatened and you had George at your mercy. You obeyed,

Burt! You intentionally missed George's head when you could have killed it!"

Campbell thought Arnold was acting as giddy as a school boy who'd just lost his virginity. He was sickened by the thought that he was totally under Arnold's control.

I have lost my will to the devil.

Suddenly, an explosion rocked the arena.

IX

A WARM WELCOME

ONE

"Okay, the clipper's all loaded," Koko shouted over to Penelope from next to their huge black military clipper.

She was kneeling in deep depression before the seated dogs on the sloping black lava rock atop the Mauna Kea volcano. They were shrouded in the early morning shadows cast out from the ancient astrological center. A strong breeze chilled Penelope and blew aside her long blond hair. The four dogs were staring mournfully back into her tearing blue-gray eyes.

Penelope had been trying to say goodbye to the beloved dogs for the last twenty minutes. She hadn't been too successful, and she knew Koko was impatient to get away. They'd been on Mauna Kea for seven anxious days while Koko had been setting up their desperate rescue attempt.

Penelope slowly stood and tried to shoo the dogs away with a wave of her hands. Sergeant howled, Amber woo-wooed, Hana grrr'd, but Cala remained silent and moody. None of the dogs moved otherwise. She bent over, hugging them each in turn with loving embraces—stroking their long fur. She felt warm tears flowing down her flushed cheeks.

Koko walked over to Penelope and lightly grasped her arm. "Let's go. We agreed there's no way they'd survive on the moon without environmental suits. They have to stay behind."

Sergeant growled dangerously at Koko, either because of his words that they must be left behind or because of his hold on Penelope. Koko quickly released Penelope, and backed away while holding up his hands.

"Sorry, ole boy. I promise I'll take care of her."

Sergeant stopped growling, but he continued to glare at Koko, his golden eyes ablaze. Koko gave up with a sigh. He backed away toward the clipper to wait inside and get out of the chilly wind.

"Okay, you guys, we have to leave," Penelope said through her tears. "You're safer here than where we're going. I promise we'll be back for you."

I hate lying to you, Penelope thought. *How am I ever going to keep that promise? Don't look at me with those sad eyes. You're breaking my heart. At least I know you'll be safe, and can survive on the island until I return.* She abruptly turned and stalked back to the clipper.

Once she was crammed into the copilot seat, she gazed with great sorrow out the window. The dogs remained sitting where she'd left them. They were staring expectantly at her as if waiting for her to return. She had to look away.

Koko was in the pilot seat. As if he couldn't watch this mournful scene any more, he quickly closed the ramp to the clipper and programmed the computer for the trip to the moon base.

"Are you going to be all right?" he asked quietly. "You know they can take care of themselves."

"I guess," she sniffled. "It's just that besides Burt, they're the only family I have. I keep thinking I'll never see them again."

"Sure you will. Besides, you always have me," Koko said with mock enthusiasm and a laugh.

He sounded so much like Burt, she laughed between her sobs.

"Okay, here we go," Koko said seriously. The clipper engines began to whine.

Penelope gazed out to get one last glimpse of the dogs. They hadn't moved. Their sorrow-filled expressions remained. Penelope knew they were aware of her betrayal, that she was leaving them behind. Their pain stabbed at her heart, and she prayed that they understood her reasoning. Hopefully, one day they would have the chance to forgive her.

Out of the corner of her tearing eye she could see Koko shaking his head. She didn't know if it was over her sense of commitment and love for four mutating beasts, or her continued emotionalism. *He doesn't understand the loyalty and love between a person and a dog.*

TWO

The clipper shot away from the sun-drenched volcano top. Penelope remained subdued and lost in her dark despair. She didn't utter a peep for the first twenty minutes of their flight. Eventually she convinced herself that Burt needed her help more than the dogs did.

"So tell me about this Captain Larsson you've been talking to on the moon base," she finally said. The clipper left Earth's blue lower atmosphere and entered the star-filled darkness of space.

"Well, he kind of misled me about the captain part," Koko said, and shook his head. "When I last talked to him a couple years ago, he *was* a captain. Now I guess he's only a corporal. And that's after a recent promotion."

"Oh, no," Penelope said with dread. She stared out the window at the surrounding darkness that seemed to mirror her mood. "What sort of man are you getting us involved with?"

"The best," Koko beamed. "At least, he's the best for this type of operation, given our restrictions. It isn't like we had a lot of time, or could call just anyone for an illegal and treacherous assault on the military moon base."

"But do you trust him?" Penelope asked. She turned her gaze on the distant illumination of the pock-marked face of the moon that seemed to hang ominously in the dark void of space.

Koko seemed reluctant to answer at first. He was leaning back in his captain's chair as if lost in thought. Penelope asked again, "Well?"

"I'll just say that he has no love for the military, and he'd like to see their authority on the moon destroyed. He told me that conditions in the mines, and for the security force, have become increasingly worse since Arnold took over."

"You still haven't told me whether we can trust him."

"Well, no," Koko said with a frown on his pale face. His brown eyes darkened as he swept back his long blond hair. "Ulf Larsson is the kind of man that you're glad to have on your side, but you can never trust him. He's an excellent tactician and soldier, but Ulf has never taken seriously his position as a leader. He's highly intelligent, but he doesn't exactly obey authority or rules."

Oh, no, Penelope thought, and buried her face in her hands.

Koko ignored Penelope's gesture, and continued. "Larsson was originally sentenced to the moon security force when he was suspected of smuggling. I don't know all the details. Apparently the military couldn't prove their case, and Larsson angered someone high enough up to get him exiled to the moon."

This just keeps getting better and better, Penelope sighed.

"When I asked him how he got demoted, he said he killed a soldier in a bar. He claims he didn't start the fight, and some other security officers backed him up at the trial. Apparently the court ruled it was self-defense," Koko finished with a shrug.

"So why did you contact this rogue criminal? He sounds like he could get us into more trouble than we're already in."

"Because, if anyone on the moon can get us into that military base undetected, it's Larsson. He as much as admitted to me that he's smuggling goods from the military, and he has contacts that can get us into the base."

"What's his motive?" Penelope asked.

"Money, of course. A lot of money." Koko grinned. "You might say all the money that Burt gave me is finally going toward a useful purpose."

"If Larsson is smuggling goods from the military, why does he want to see them destroyed?" Penelope persisted in her suspicions

"You know, you'd make a good investigator," Koko said with a smile. "I asked him the same question. He said Arnold is restricting all the traffic on the moon base and inspecting everything. He claims he would have a brisk business going with Earth if he could get his stuff by the military barricade. So I guess he doesn't want the military gone. He wants Arnold gone."

"How are we going to get onto the moon base if the military is inspecting all the crafts?"

"We'll be landing at the mining colony to meet Larsson. We'll go to the military complex from there. Ulf says he has contacts that'll get us through, but that's another reason why we had to leave the dogs behind. They would've been a little hard to explain."

"Is that why we didn't bring any weapons?" Penelope asked. Koko nodded. "What about our plan? How do we save Burt?"

"Larsson said I should leave all the planning to him. He said something about an arena competition going on in a couple of days that will involve almost all the military personnel and clear the way for our attack."

"I don't like this," Penelope said, shaking her head. "We're going into a place and against forces neither of us knows. We're leaving the planning to someone we don't trust, and we don't even know if Burt is still alive. We could be walking into a trap."

Koko sighed. "You knew this was a desperate attempt from the start, Penelope."

THREE

Koko approached the moon base flying in low from the west, away from the military complex, to avoid immediate attention. Penelope peered out at the desolate gray landscape of craters and dust illuminated by a brilliant sun. At first she saw no sign of life before scattered clusters of small low-level buildings began to appear. Eventually, a massive multi-level complex, complete with dozens of mining ventilation stacks, communication and sensor arrays, and a fusion reactor, appeared on the horizon. As they neared, they passed over a huge transparent horticultural center and a gravity-generation power plant.

"Welcome to the moon base mining facility, Penelope," Koko said as the clipper slowed.

They landed in a dark and dirty little hangar at the security force compound near the edge of the mining colony. Penelope sat anxiously in the copilot seat while Koko opened the starboard ramp to allow the small military detail aboard to inspect the clipper.

"Remember, Penelope, let me do the talking. If they ask you any questions, you're a researcher working on a classified project and it's none of their damned business. Hopefully, they won't check your ID, and don't give it to them unless they ask."

Penelope gazed out the clipper window as four human guards in black military uniforms approached the clipper. They weaved around various types of small mining craft that had seen better days. The hangar was a mess of spare parts, burned-out drilling equipment, and broken-down haulers. She saw that the guards were being led by a striking and ominous figure in the gray uniform of a security agent.

"Come on, it's better if we meet them outside," Koko said.

Here we go, Penelope thought, her heart red-lining with adrenaline. *I hope Koko isn't leading us into a trap.*

Penelope hid behind Koko as they went down the ramp. They were met by the giant man she'd seen leading the guards. He towered over Penelope and Koko as he motioned the guards up the ramp into the clipper.

Where did Koko find this evil creature? Penelope wondered, as she stared fearfully up at the man she assumed was Larsson. *And what happened to him?*

Koko waited until the guards were out of hearing range.

"Larsson, how are you?" Koko asked the huge man. Larsson smiled a crooked smile of shiny metal teeth.

"It's good to see you, my old friend. Who's this beautiful thing?" Larsson asked in an electronically automated voice. Penelope realized Larsson's voice-box had been permanently damaged or destroyed.

Larsson glared down at Penelope with one bright-blue eye. She couldn't help staring back at him while she took in his facial disfigurements. The entire right side of his face and head was a steel skull. His right eye was a black marble that reminded her of Burt's implants. Based on the human left side of his face and head, Penelope thought he must have been a very handsome man of Swedish descent at one point in his life. The left side of his head was covered with a thick blond mane that extended down to his left shoulder.

If personalities are similar to appearance, this man is the Devil himself, she thought.

"This is the woman I told you about, Ulf," Koko said uneasily.

"I apologize if my appearance frightens you, ma'am. I had an unfortunate accident many years ago," Ulf said. Penelope heard Koko snicker nervously. "Come with me, we have no time for pleasantries out here in the open. The fewer who know you're here, the fewer questions asked."

Larsson turned about, and they followed him from the hangar. As Larsson weaved between the junk, Penelope watched him with interest. *He's more cyborg than human.* His legs and feet moved with the heavy, even stride of a bot. She saw that his right hand, arm, and shoulder were artificial. His head swerved from side to side with the steady, even movement of a bot as he observed his surroundings.

Koko walked at Penelope's side behind Larsson. Koko seemed unusually tightlipped and quiet, as if anxious in Larsson's presence. This deepened her apprehension. They followed Larsson through a hangar door and entered a dark hallway without turning back to see if they were being followed.

The security complex hallway was so dark Penelope had trouble seeing where she was going. As she tried to inspect their new surroundings, she noted the poor condition of the facility and the lack of personnel. It stank of sweat and poor ventilation.

"I had the area cleared of people to ensure your secrecy," Larsson said without looking back. "I run this area of the compound."

After a short walk, Larsson stopped at a metallic door, and entered a security code into the panel on the wall. The door slid open to reveal a small, dark storage area.

"Inside," Larsson said curtly.

What in Hades is going on? Penelope wondered.

Penelope gazed at Koko. He ignored her and slowly stepped around Larsson. She hesitantly followed, but stopped when she couldn't see in the darkness.

A dim light came on. Penelope stared around the small confines of a room that reeked of mold and dust. It was crammed with storage crates that were covered with moon dust and filth. She was horrified to see two folding cots and a small metal table along the right wall. There was a portable toilet in one corner. She guessed their purpose.

"Welcome to the Alfa-Tango Moon Base, Koko Sinopa and Penelope Preston. These are your accommodations for a time," Larsson said, laughing. His booming, animated voice held no emotion.

Koko and Penelope whirled on Larsson. He held up his human left hand. Penelope noted with heart-pounding terror that he was heavily armed; his huge bot body blocked the doorway.

"I'm sorry," Larsson said. "I wish I could put you in grand suites, but at the moment, this is the best I can do. This is one of my personal storage areas. You'll have to stay here and out of sight for the time being."

Penelope saw that the thin lips of the left side of Larsson's face were turned up in an evil smile that she found grotesque and inhuman.

"I have to get back to the military guards who're inspecting your clipper," Larsson said. "I paid them handsomely, but I want to be there in case they get any other ideas."

"You're just going to leave us in here?" Penelope asked.

"Please, Ms. Preston, you have to understand my position. I have to leave you locked up in here for your security as well as my own."

Koko started to object, but Larsson took a quick step backward and shut the door before Koko could reach him. Koko rushed forward and pushed the button to reopen the door, but it remained closed. They were trapped. Penelope's heart sank.

FOUR

"I can't believe you, Koko!" she yelled with fury. "How could you have contacted this . . . this monster? What's worse is that you told him my name! He has to know I'm one of the most sought after humans in the galaxy. You've betrayed everything we've fought for!"

"Penelope, you're overreacting," Koko said with a sigh.

"Overreacting? Look at this place," Penelope said, sweeping her arm toward the dusty crates and rubbish. "And you expect me to use that?" She pointed at the small toilet.

"It beats peeing your pants," Koko said with a weak smile. "Look, Penelope, what Larsson says makes sense. We can't be seen. No doubt the military has spies all over this place. If they run an ID on either one of us, Burt's rescue will be off. We'll be captured and killed."

Penelope was still furious. "Why'd you tell Larsson who I was?"

"I didn't. Larsson only did what I would've done in his place. He must have checked on what I've been doing, and what he's getting himself into. I had to tell him about Burt. He wanted to know why he was getting so much money and who he'd be rescuing. He obviously has access to all the security files and he recognized you.

"What were you expecting—a grand celebration with a band? You knew this was a desperate operation before we started. Imagine the position we'd be in if the dogs were here," Koko said. He moved closer to a crate to inspect its contents label.

Penelope continued to sulk. She paced the tiny compartment like a caged animal while she considered their hopeless situation.

"Hey, at least we'll have food and won't starve in here," Koko said. "The label says this container is full of dehydrated fruit."

Men! Always thinking with their stomachs, Penelope thought angrily. "What're we going to use for water? The toilet bowl?"

"I've had worse," Koko muttered, as he strained to pry open the crate.

Penelope huffed with disgust as she went over to check the toilet. "There's not even any paper!"

"Lord in Hades, look what we have here!" Koko whistled with surprise as he peered into the opened crate.

Penelope forgot about her personal hygiene and came over to Koko's side to look into the crate. It contained a neat row of ten military directed energy beam rifles (DERs) that appeared to be new, neatly packed, and ready for shipment.

Koko closed the crate and quickly moved over to another one. He opened it and whistled again. Penelope stepped to his side and saw the crate was full of more DERs. Koko carefully removed two rifles and hammered the crate closed. He sat down on one of the cots to inspect a rifle.

"These are fully functional," he said. "If this is one of Larsson's storage areas, I can see why he keeps the door locked. He must have smuggled these from the military, but I have no idea where he's selling them or to whom."

Koko tried to hand one of the rifles to Penelope. She crossed her arms and shook her long blond hair with a pouting frown. He gazed at her for a moment with his intense brown eyes before dropping the extra DER on his cot with confused resignation.

"Doesn't this make you feel any better about Larsson?" he asked. "He trusted us enough to lock us in here knowing we'd discover these weapons and arm ourselves. In fact, I'll bet we could destroy that lock from the inside and get out, but I wouldn't suggest it. That would set off alarms all over the compound."

Penelope continued to frown and pace.

"What's the matter now?" Koko asked with exasperated irritation.

"I have to pee!"

DEATH'S BEDROOM

ONE

Several hours passed. Penelope became more and more apprehensive about what had happened to Larsson and when, if ever, he'd return to release them from their storage-locker prison. Koko had stretched comfortably out on a cot and was soundly asleep. His loud nasal snoring was driving Penelope insane. At least there was a rifle on the floor within his close grasp. She glared at him with anger, hoping her nasty look would give him a nightmare.

She wondered: *How can he relax considering our situation and the fact that Larsson hasn't returned?*

Damn, I wish we had some toilet paper that I could stuff in my ears to get some peace from his snoring.

Penelope had barely sat down on the other cot to sulk when the door slid open and Larsson appeared. Koko was up in an instant with his rifle pointed at Larsson's hideous head. Penelope leaped to her feet in a defensive position.

Larsson pulled his DEP from his waist belt with cat-like speed. For a moment, Koko and Larsson glared at each other with suspicious hatred.

Great! Penelope thought. *These two idiots are going to kill each other. What a fine predicament that'll leave me in then.*

Koko relented first and slowly lowered his weapon as he broke into a nervous smile. Larsson put away his DEP and quickly stepped through the door before closing it.

"Still as fast as ever, huh, Koko?" Larsson said with the evil curl of his lip that Penelope was coming to hate.

"It must be your handsome appearance," Koko muttered, while clutching his pounding chest.

"Where have you been?" Penelope demanded.

Larsson glared at her, his mismatched eyes bristling with intensity.

"We have trouble," Larsson said.

"Already!" Koko said with anger and surprise.

"Ms. Preston's description is posted everywhere," Larsson said. "After the military had checked out your ship, their captain dismissed the squad and pulled me over to the side. He recognized you, Ms. Preston."

"Oh, no," Penelope said. She brought her long beautiful hands up to cover her anguished features.

"It gets worse," Larsson said. "The captain said that bringing you in could mean a big promotion for him. He demanded a larger fee to keep quiet."

"Larger fee?" Koko cut in.

"The captain was originally a big part of my plan to rescue Campbell. I had already paid him a great deal. He was going to get us into the military prison compound where Campbell is being kept."

"So pay him what he wants," Koko said.

"It's too late for that. I killed him and threw his body in a garbage vaporizer."

"How are we going to get into the military compound now?" Penelope asked.

"I took his ID and his clothes. We're going to have to figure out something else. Right now we're going to have to get you out of here and find a different hiding place. If the captain doesn't check into his post when scheduled, the military will come searching for him here.

Desertion is rampant at the military base. That's one of the reasons they search every vessel leaving the moon."

"Where are you going to hide us?" Koko asked with a worried expression.

"I have just the spot," Larsson said with the return of his lip curl, "but first you're going to have to return those weapons to their crates. I have bots coming down here right now to load those crates in underground storage outside where the military won't look."

Koko and Penelope both gazed at Larsson with suspicion, but he waved off their expressions. "Move it! We don't have time for this now. I wasted too much time disposing of the captain's body. I'm sure they're looking for him by now."

Koko quickly put the weapons back in their crate. Penelope continued to glare at Larsson's horrid disfigurements while trying to decipher his true motivations and intentions. Larsson glared right back at her, his expression unreadable.

"I need each of you to bring along your cot, and make sure you haven't left anything behind," Larsson said when Koko was finished.

Penelope huffed, but she grabbed her folding cot and moved to the door. Koko did likewise, minus the insolent huff.

Larsson nodded his hideous head, and then turned and opened the door. He peered both ways down the dark hall, and motioned them to follow. Koko and Penelope exited quickly after him, since once again he didn't wait for them.

Penelope had only scampered a few hurried steps down the hall when she heard the heavy tread of bots behind her. She whirled around in terror of imminent capture, but saw nothing. The heavy sounds were apparently echoing around a corner in the hall.

"Hurry," Larsson whispered. He painfully grasped her thin arm in a vise grip.

Larsson yanked Penelope past Koko and raced for a metallic hallway door a few meters away. He threw the heavy door open and unceremoniously shoved Penelope toward a barely lit stairway that went both up and down. Penelope clumsily stumbled over her cot and started to topple headfirst down the stairs. She only regained her balance when she caught the stair railing.

"Don't ever touch me again," Penelope hissed angrily as she whirled around on Larsson.

Larsson appreciatively patted Penelope on the butt before rushing down the stairs. "I love it when you're mad," he said over his shoulder.

Penelope turned on Koko with burning rage. "Do something. You hired this animal," she whispered.

"Well, he's right. You *are* beautiful when you're mad." Koko smiled and quickly followed Larsson, as if afraid Penelope would smack him.

"Oh," Penelope scowled. She scurried after them, dragging her cot.

Larsson went down one flight of stairs and opened another hall doorway. He peered both ways and exited the stairwell, going to his right without looking back. Koko and Penelope raced after him. She saw that the hallway was even darker than the one they'd just left.

"Where are we going?" she hissed to the giant shadow of Larsson in front of her.

"It's the night shift now and this floor is unused." Larsson said, no longer whispering.

"But where are you taking us?" she repeated.

Larsson quickly opened and entered a doorway to his right. As Penelope followed, she realized it was so dark in the room that she couldn't see anything but the small amber lights of power switches that lined the left wall. The smell was so horrendous it almost overpowered her. She heard the door close behind her before bright lights snapped on and blinded her. As her eyes adjusted, she saw she was in a large laboratory that wasn't much cleaner than the storeroom they'd just left.

"Where are we?" Penelope asked fearfully. But much to her horror, she thought she already knew.

"The morgue," Larsson said flatly.

Penelope absently leaned her cot on the wall next to where Koko had left his. She gazed around wearing an expression of squeamish disgust. There was a series of dissection bots leaning ominously over the gleaming slab tables that ran down the center of the room. Much to her relief, all the tables were empty and the bots were powered down. No one else was in the room.

Penelope took in a sharp intake of breath and half-hid behind her elegant fingers as she turned to her right. There were high shelves of large glass specimen bottles. They contained torn and pale human body parts, including screaming heads with lifeless, staring eyes floating in cloudy liquid. She quickly glanced away to see several coffin-shaped quarantine containers. She was relieved to note there weren't any bodies visible through the container windows. Glancing around for any other hideous human atrocities, besides Larsson, she saw that the wall on the right contained a full body analyzer, research equipment, and several computer stations.

"There's no place to hide, Larsson. Where are we supposed to go if the military searches here?" Koko asked.

"Oh, ah," Larsson started, "well, I don't think you'll find it as glamorous as the storage room, but it's definitely a better location."

"Where?" Koko repeated.

"In those body storage lockers there in the wall on the right."

"What!" Penelope nearly screamed. "You're not getting me in one of those death traps."

"Hush, woman," Larsson said. "There isn't anywhere else that you can hide on such short notice. The military will search here, and if you're not in one of those containers, they're going to catch you."

Larsson grabbed Penelope's already bruised arm and whirled her around to face his frightening features. She was too terrified to stare up at Larsson's gleaming skull half, so she centered her hatred on the fairer human side of his face. She found its furrowed pale expression and glaring blue eye just as frightening.

"Look, lady," Larsson said with emotionless automation, "you people came to me and I'm trying to help you. Personally, I don't really give a damned what happens to you. I've been paid already. But if you get caught, that will lead the military to me. I can't afford that, so you're going to hide where I tell you."

Larsson released her arm and turned away. Penelope's anger quickly evaporated into embarrassment as she realized Larsson was right. She gazed at the grimy floor, lost in loathing introspection. She realized how naïve and childish she'd been acting—how little she understood the harshness of men outside the likes of Burt or Koko.

She was about to apologize to Larsson when she heard him say to Koko, "Here's a torch, Koko. Turn out the lights and make yourselves comfortable for the night, but get her into one of those containers. They *will* search here sometime tonight, but they never look at the dead bodies. Squeamish, I guess." He laughed his emotionless laugh before he walked to the door. "I'll return when the search is over. Don't leave this room! I *will* be back."

Larsson left.

TWO

Koko turned to Penelope, who was still staring at the closed door after Larsson. "Let's find some place to hide before the search makes it to this floor."

Koko silently ambled about, searching the reeking morgue for a few moments. He checked the larger cabinet spaces, the deeper recesses of the lab, anywhere they might be able to hide other than the dead body storage cabinets. Finally, he turned to Penelope and shrugged.

"It looks like Larsson was correct," he sighed. "We're going to have to use the body storage units. Help me find a couple of empty ones."

Penelope didn't want anything to do with the filthy storage units. She stood by and watched while Koko started opening the one-by-one meter doors that were stacked three high and four across in the right-hand wall. He was about halfway through his hideous search when he turned to Penelope. His normally pale features were haggard, almost green with repulsion.

"They must be having an epidemic of death here. I think all these things are full."

Penelope didn't move or respond, so Koko continued with his grisly search. She could tell by his hesitant motions that he wasn't enjoying his discovery process.

"This is like searching a morgue in a war zone," Koko groaned. He opened another refrigerated coffin. "All these people died violent deaths. I wonder if they recently had an accident in the mines."

Koko reached the bottom drawer of the last column and opened it. He leaped back with a loud hiss when he viewed the ghastly occupant. Shaking his ashen features with closed-eyed disgust, he reached forward with his foot and kicked the door closed.

"Lord in Hades, what happened to these people?" he whispered. "That one had a crushed skull!"

He hesitantly moved to the next drawer up, peeked in.

"Good, this one's empty."

Koko left the drawer open and moved to the next one.

"Well, this is the last one. If it isn't empty, it looks like we're going to have to share, and I think it'll be a tight fit. Wish me luck," Koko said with a poor attempt to smile.

"Luck," Penelope said weakly. Her stomach felt so queasy she began scanning the room for an empty bucket or container she could use in a hurry to vomit.

Koko slowly opened the last container. He peeked inside with one eye closed as if expecting the worst. "Hey, hey, you're as good as your word. It's empty."

"Oh, joy," Penelope said sarcastically.

Koko pulled out his newly acquired torch before switching it on. It only gave off a weak beam no brighter than a candle. Becoming angry and frustrated, Koko vigorously shook it with no improvement in the radiance of the light.

"Damn, leave it to Larsson to give us a faulty torch." He glanced up at Penelope and shrugged in resignation. "Penelope, would you please switch off the overhead lights, and come over here?"

She didn't move.

"Come on, Penelope," Koko begged. "I don't like this any better than you, but Larsson is right. They're going to catch us if we don't hide, and I don't think we'll find a better spot than this. There's nothing to be afraid of in here—really."

Penelope was filled with indecision as she gazed long into Koko's pleading brown eyes and mournful expression. His long blond hair was a tangled mess, his proud erect posture slumped with exhaustion and worry. Yet his features showed only compassion and concern for her welfare. He was doing his best in an impossible situation. How could she ignore his pleas? With a great show of reluctance, she turned around and turned out the lights. Near complete darkness fell on the room. Penelope rushed toward the weak light in Koko's hand.

"We're going to have to close these cabinet doors when they come in here," Penelope said. "Can you open them from the inside after they leave? I don't want to be stuck in there until Larsson comes looking for us . . . if he comes looking for us."

"Good thinking."

Koko peered inside a cadaver cabinet with his light. Penelope could see he was shaking his head. "I'll have to find some adhesive tape," he said. "I think I saw some in one of those cabinet drawers. Stay here."

"I'm going with you," Penelope said. She rushed after Koko to the storage cabinets on the opposite wall.

Koko rummaged through some drawers before standing up with a victorious smile. "We're in business. I found a roll of skin adhesive."

After moving back over to the two drawers they would use, Koko went about taping down the latches so they wouldn't lock when the doors were closed.

"Okay, I think the tape will hold, but I could only put it partially over the latches. If I put it on the outside part of the door, someone would notice. Come on. I'll help you into this middle drawer."

Again Penelope was reluctant and fearful, but Koko waved her on. Penelope realized she was being childish and selfish again. Finally, she relented and allowed Koko to assist her into the cold, foul-smelling container. As she stretched out and lay back, she realized she must appear like a corpse in a casket. She tried to dispel these terrifying images, but a new terror arose.

"What if they decide to open these things and examine the bodies?" she asked. "We don't look like corpses."

"I have an idea about that, but I don't think you're going to like it," Koko muttered.

"What is it?" Penelope asked, already hating the idea.

"Well, we have plenty of blood and gore from these other corpses that we could use to spread on our bodies to make us appear as if we're dead."

"That's a horrible thought!" Penelope snapped, as a violent shudder ran through her body.

"It won't be so bad, and it may save your life."

Penelope continued to scowl with disgust, but didn't object.

Not waiting for Penelope to protest further, Koko promptly turned and opened the container right next to her. It contained a gruesome victim of some terrible mining catastrophe. Horrified, but unable to tear her eyes away, Penelope squeamishly watched as Koko plunged his hands into the cadaver's torn torso. The rotting stench of dead flesh and bile assaulted Penelope's senses, making her gag. Through watering eyes, she saw Koko extract his blood-covered hands, grasping what she hazarded to guess was a torn liver. Feeling her stomach in full revolt, Penelope turned away when Koko began to smear the bloody organ over his head, chest, and arms.

"Okay," Koko muttered without enthusiasm. "It's your turn."

Penelope jumped and let out a gasp of horror when she turned back to look at Koko's gruesome features. His upper body was the vision of a terrible death. His matted long hair stuck out at every conceivable angle. His bloody mask was made even more frightfully eerie by the movement of his white eyes and smiling teeth. Before she could move or object, Koko slapped the cold piece of decaying liver on her flushed cheek and started to push it around her face. She violently gagged and spat when Koko accidentally pushed the bloody, wet organ into her protesting mouth. She nearly threw up when she tasted the cold blood on her teeth. Her skin felt sticky and defiled. She'd never felt so disgusting in all her long years.

God, she thought, *I hope I don't catch some vile disease.*

As Koko finished wiping down her upper body, she noticed he seemed to linger around her breast area.

"Are you getting a good feel, Captain Sinopa?" she protested.

"Well, ah, they are kind of nice," Koko said, with a smile that sliced through his blood-covered face.

After giving Penelope one final look-over, Koko at last appeared to be satisfied. "You even make a beautiful corpse," he said pleasantly.

"Don't get any ideas, Captain," Penelope muttered.

Scorned, Koko turned around, replaced the donor's organ, and closed the body's drawer. When he finished, he returned to Penelope's side before he heaved himself, grunting and groaning, into the drawer above hers. Without another word, he closed the drawer until only his spiked hair was visible.

Penelope followed his example and closed her drawer almost completely. She was surprised and frightened when the dim light coming from Koko's drawer suddenly went out, throwing them into darkness. An irrational panic began to pound in her chest as she thought about her cold confinement and grisly location.

There's nothing to fear, she tried to assure herself. *No bodies are going to come back to life and attack me. It's just drying blood. It won't hurt me . . . I don't think. Stop it, Monica! I can make it through this. I can. I just have to keep positive thoughts.*

"These drawers are awfully cold," she whispered.

Koko didn't answer.

Good god! That man can sleep through anything!

"Koko?"

"Yes, Penelope?" She thought he sounded weary or lost in thought.

"I was just wondering if you were still alive."

"Very funny. No, I was just lying here thinking. Do you think Burt is still alive?"

It was Penelope's turn to remain silent and thoughtful for a moment. "I don't know, and that scares me. You understand that, through me, Burt and the dogs were changed, don't you?"

"I know that something happened between all of you, but I don't understand it." Koko's soft voice drifted down through the darkness. Its presence gave Penelope comfort and confidence.

"There was a mental connection of some kind that formed between all of us. I developed a kind of sense about their well-being. Even though we're on the moon, I know the dogs are fine."

"I had a similar sense about Burt until just after he was brought here. But every day it has been growing weaker, as if he were dying. Now it's as if the connection is nearly gone. It's like he's just a memory of someone I once knew and loved dearly. The feeling scares me."

Koko didn't answer.

"Koko? I've been getting another feeling since we landed—a feeling of a powerful dark presence here. It's as if something horribly evil is trying to get into my mind. Do you feel it?"

"I think this morgue is getting to your imagination, Penelope," Koko said after a moment. She got the impression he meant to say something else.

"Koko, do *you* think Burt's still alive?"

"I have to believe so; otherwise I won't go through this. I keep telling myself that it's logical for Arnold to want Burt alive or he wouldn't have gone to so much trouble or risk exposing his plans. Still, I have to wonder if Burt has proved too troublesome and Arnold simply killed him."

They went silent again. Eventually, Penelope found herself dozing off, despite her cold stiffness and the creepiness of their surroundings. She thought of how long it had been since she'd really slept, and realized it had been the night before Goro Sen's kidnapping. She felt partly responsible for the death of the Sens, and sleep continued to elude her for a while.

THREE

"Penelope! Penelope!" Koko whispered harshly. She was startled awake in the frigid darkness of the morgue. "Someone's coming. Close your drawer." She heard him quietly slide his drawer closed.

Penelope was terrified about being trapped in the metal coffin, but she closed her drawer until there was just enough room for her to see out a crack. As she did so, someone threw open the morgue door. Men were talking in loud voices. She peeled over at two men silhouetted in the light from the hallway. There was a giant shadow towering behind them. There was no mistaking the horrid shape. It was Larsson.

One of the shorter men moved to the wall and snapped on the lights.

"Sergeant, I seriously doubt the captain would hide in here if he was trying to make it off the base," Larsson said in his automated voice.

"Arnold will have our heads if we don't catch this guy. We're to search everywhere until he's found," another voice said.

As the three men started to enter the room, Penelope quietly closed her drawer completely. She was terrified when she heard the drawer latch closed. Koko's tape job hadn't worked. She panicked in the cold darkness. She frantically tried to open the drawer again. It was locked.

In her panic, she felt as if a tremendous weight was pressing on her heaving chest. She stifled back a scream of claustrophobia as she realized she was trapped in a cold tomb, surrounded by death. She sucked in great gasps of air as she hyperventilated. Frantically kicking and clawing at the metal sides of her cold coffin, she didn't care if someone heard her—almost praying that someone would.

An image of Burt suddenly appeared in her mind. It was a sign of duty and peace. *I have a job to do. Burt needs me. I can't save him if I panic and get caught.* She stopped her struggling and tried to relax. Finally, she was able to control her breathing by imagining Burt and the dogs in the wide-open spaces of their Hawaiian sanctuary.

Penelope lost herself deep in concentration. Suddenly, she heard her door latch click open. Larsson had been wrong. They were even checking the corpses. She took a deep breath and held it. Abruptly, the drawer was pulled open and light burned into her brain.

Oh, no! My eyes are still open!

She fixated her stare on the stained morgue ceiling while fighting back the instinctive desire to blink. A dirty face with a week-old beard stubble and dark brown messy hair appeared over hers.

"Max!" grinned the face right above Penelope's. "Take a look at this one. She's gorgeous!"

Max came into view. His clean-shaven face was lean and wrinkled. His black hair was streaked with gray. His dark eyes seemed to peer into hers. Penelope was terrified they would notice she was alive. She could feel her panicked heart pounding against her ribs. Her chest was burning to take a breath.

"You're sick, Corporal," Max said. "She's dead and covered with blood. She isn't who we're looking for. Move on to the next one." Max disappeared from Penelope's view.

To Penelope's horror, a smile of brown teeth appeared on the corporal's young face. He reached in and groped her breasts with both hands. Abruptly, the corporal leaped back as if he'd stuck his hands into a roaring fire.

"This one's alive!" yelled the corporal.

Penelope shot her arms up and grabbed the top of her drawer. Throwing it open, she scrambled out to defend herself. As she hit the morgue floor, she was already whirling with a roundhouse kick as the corporal reached for his weapon.

Penelope's kick connecting with a satisfying crunch into the man's nose and threw him off his feet. Max and Larsson both drew their DEPs. She turned on Max knowing he was her closest danger.

"Hold it right there!" Max yelled, before Penelope had taken two steps in his direction.

Penelope halted. She had no defense against Max's pistol. She watched Larsson out of the corner of her eye with anguished disbelief as he put away his weapon.

Traitor! she mentally screamed.

"Who are you and why are you hiding in here?" Max asked breathlessly.

She glared with intense fury at Max, but said nothing. Larsson swiftly approached Max from the rear. He wrapped his artificial arm around Max's neck, and heaved the startled man off the floor with little effort. Max's eyes bulged with shock and fear. He dropped his DEP to grasp the arm snapping his neck.

"You know, Sergeant, I never liked you," Larsson whispered in Max's ear. He viciously twisted Max's head around until it was pointing backwards.

Larsson dropped the dead body without interest. He quickly stepped over to the corporal, who was frantically struggling to stand while grasping his blood-gushing nose. Larsson booted the guard in the face. The corporal's head snapped back with a sickening crack. His entire body was lifted from the grimy floor. He was dead before he landed.

Penelope stood there aghast at the speed of the guards' demise. Her heart was wildly pounding on an adrenaline high. She realized how close they'd been to discovery and capture. If not for Larsson, she would have been dead or worse.

"Where's Sinopa?" Larsson asked emotionlessly.

"You just killed those two men," Penelope whispered.

Larsson glared at Penelope, and then shrugged. "Would you like to switch places with them? They were about to kill you."

Penelope said nothing. She couldn't read the expression on Larsson's misshapen face.

"You need to get a grasp on reality, lady. Now, where's Koko? We have to get out of here."

Penelope turned and pointed at Koko's container with a trembling hand. Larsson stepped forward and opened Koko's drawer.

"Have a nice rest, Captain?" Larsson asked.

"A little chilly for my personal liking, but it's wonderfully peaceful in there," Koko said with a huge yawn as he started to climb out. He immediately noted the limp bodies and the shock on Penelope's face. "What happened?"

"They opened Penelope's container," Larsson answered. "The corporal there proved to be a necrophile. He copped a feel off Penelope and discovered she was alive." He didn't say anything else as if the rest was obvious.

"Oh," Koko said.

Larsson moved over to Max and lifted the sagging corpse with ease. "Koko, open your container the rest of the way so I can get the body in there."

Koko quickly did as he was told, still wearing an expression of stunned silence. Larsson haphazardly tossed the body into the space before shutting the container door. Koko reopened the door, and removed the tape that had been holding the door latch open. As Larsson retrieved the other blood-soaked body, Koko peeled off the tape from Penelope's drawer.

"I see the tape didn't keep your door from locking, Penelope," Koko said.

"No, it didn't," she said quietly.

"Ms. Preston," Larsson commanded, as he put the other body in her container. "Find something to clean up that blood. There mustn't be any evidence of a fight here."

This man is insane! Someone's going to find the bodies soon anyway. It's going to be obvious the two military guards don't belong here. Still, she kept her mouth shut, and did as she was told.

When she was finished, Larsson inspected the morgue. He seemed satisfied that it appeared as disgusting as it had been before they'd entered.

"Oh, you better clean yourselves up as well," Larsson said. "I can't be seen walking bloody corpses down the hall."

Penelope and Koko cleaned themselves as best they could.

"The search is still on for the captain," Larsson said. "When these guards don't report in, the search will intensify. We have to get you two out of the compound. Come on, I know just the place to hide you. I guarantee you'll be safe there."

Penelope groaned at the thought. "I suppose it's even worse than this," she muttered.

"Beautiful *and* intelligent. I like that in a woman," Larsson said. "Oh, and that was a hell of a kick you've got."

"Wait a minute," Koko said. After he'd retrieved the guards' weapons, he said, "Okay, now I feel better."

"You better give those weapons to me," Larsson said. "If we run into more search groups, I want to be able to explain your presence by telling them I'm moving prisoners down to the prison cells."

Koko reluctantly gave up the weapons to Larsson. Penelope shook her head.

This is getting worse by the minute, she thought. *There's something evil about Ulf Larsson.*

FOUR

Larsson left the morgue with Penelope and Koko close on his heels. Penelope wondered if maybe they shouldn't be in front of Larsson if they were supposed to be acting like prisoners, but she didn't say anything.

They returned up one floor and back to the original hangar they'd used when they'd arrived. When they came to the hangar door, Larsson pulled out his weapon and pointed it at Koko. Penelope's heart leaped. She was sure Larsson was about to kill Koko.

"Okay, there's a small jail clipper on the other side of the hangar. It's beyond your clipper," Larsson said. "I want you two to march in front of me as if you're my prisoners. Let's go."

Larsson opened the door and waved them ahead with his pistol.

Koko quickly stepped to the front. Penelope followed closely behind with Larsson bringing up the rear. Penelope nearly halted when she peered across the dark hangar and saw four military guards supervised by a military captain searching crates off to their right. She jumped when Larsson stabbed her in the back with the point of his weapon.

"Keep moving," Larsson whispered. "Keep your head down and don't say anything."

Penelope walked forward at a brisk pace with her head down in submission. They made it beyond the guards and were halfway across the junk-filled hangar.

"Larsson! Where are you taking those people?" a man yelled behind them.

"Prisoners, halt!" Larsson commanded.

Koko came to a halt so suddenly that Penelope almost walked into his back before she stopped.

"Stay here!" Larsson said, so the captain could hear him.

Penelope glanced up, and was terrified to see the captain was approaching them with a no-nonsense expression on his stern features. Larsson marched off to meet the captain before he could get close enough to recognize them.

Penelope turned her face away while Larsson met the captain in the middle of the hangar. She saw that Koko was examining the grimy floor with great interest and hiding his face.

"I know that man," Koko whispered.

Penelope strained to overhear the conversation between Larsson and the captain. She couldn't make out anything specific from their muted speech. After what seemed like an eternity, she heard loud, automated laughter. It was followed by movement behind her. She shyly glanced up. The captain was casually walking toward his work detail. Larsson was coming back.

"Move it, prisoners!" Larsson yelled. He shoved Penelope forward with such force that she stumbled and nearly lost her balance.

"Oh, I'm going to . . .," Penelope started.

"Shut up, whore!" Larsson snapped. He pushed her forward again.

Koko grabbed Penelope and pulled her toward him.

"You're going to get us killed," Koko whispered. He dragged Penelope toward the other side of the hangar.

When they reached the jail clipper, Larsson put away his DEP and opened the ramp. As Penelope started up the ramp, Larsson grabbed her arm and whipped her around to face his fury.

"Look, Ms. Preston. I'm getting the distinct feeling you don't realize the gravity of our situation. One more screw-up out of you and I'm going to kill you myself. Got it?"

Penelope glared up at Larsson's hideous face with furious heat radiating from her flushed cheeks and blue-gray eyes. She could hear her heart pounding in her burning ears.

"You . . . I . . .," she started. She looked down and took a deep breath. *Stop it! Think of Burt. Larsson's right. He did save my life, and I've been acting like an idiot. I can do this. I have to do it for Burt.*

She glanced shyly back up at Larsson. "I must apologize for my behavior. I thank you for saving my life. I won't cause any more problems."

"I doubt that," Larsson grumbled. He marched aboard the clipper without looking back.

Penelope slowly followed. *Will we ever see the end of this nightmare?*

XI

TUNNEL TO HELL

ONE

"What is this place?" Penelope asked Larsson.

They entered a gigantic round facility from a deserted attached hangar where they'd just landed their jail clipper. Koko followed closely behind the other two with his newly acquired DEP drawn. Larsson had remained relaxed as if he didn't expect any trouble.

"This is the Dust Compression Water Creation and Recycling Facility for both the mining and the military complexes," Larsson said, loudly enough to be heard over the whining noise echoing through the spacious factory and its towering ceiling. He swept his human arm around at the huge refining tanks, noisy pumps, and thick pipes that crisscrossed everywhere like tossed spaghetti. As seemed universal on the moon base, it was dark, deserted, and stank. But Penelope noted that it was the cleanest facility she'd seen so far.

"Where is everyone?" Koko asked anxiously.

"The plant is completely automated," Larsson said. "No one works here. But they do spot inspections a few times a day for preventive maintenance, so you can't hide up here."

Penelope glanced at Koko with a worried expression. Larsson led them round an enormous gray tank that was making loud gurgling noises to a door on the opposite wall. He turned on one of two powerful torches that he'd taken from the clipper. Satisfied that it worked; he opened the door and led them down a dark staircase. Penelope was immediately hit with an overpowering stench that pinched her nose.

"What's that awful smell?" she asked.

"These stairs lead to the tunnels where the raw sewage from the mining and military complexes enters the facility for recycling or disposal as fertilizer in the horticulture facilities."

Penelope and Koko exchanged disgusted looks behind Larsson's broad back. Larsson reached the stairway landing and opened another door. The devastating stench slapped Penelope's sensitive senses like a sharp smack from a wet towel. She refused to follow Larsson and Koko when they entered the total darkness beyond the door.

Larsson stepped back through the door, and waved Penelope to follow. "Come on. You can't hide in the stairwell."

"I think you brought us here intentionally to get back at me," she muttered.

"It's nothing personal, Ms. Preston. I just know all the best places to hide things . . . or dispose of them." Larsson laughed his automated laugh.

Seeing she had no alternative, Penelope reluctantly followed Larsson through the door. She wondered what Larsson meant by "dispose of them." Directly in front of her, Koko was shining his light around the huge underground tunnel. She was immediately reminded of the underground monorail systems of the inner cities on Earth. But where the rail would have been, she saw a black river of sludge and sewage flowing slowly from her right to her left. In the background, she could hear what she assumed were the whining pumps that struggled to move the thick, lumpy sewage along.

Larsson stepped up next to Penelope and handed her his torch.

"Okay, I want you two to stay here today and tonight. No one enters these tunnels unless there's an emergency. That only happens when the filters clog. Stay by the door and don't go exploring. There are things in these tunnels that will eat you alive."

"What kind of things?" Penelope asked anxiously. She was terrified about what might be large enough to clog the filters and eat them alive. She gulped as she frantically showed her light around the repulsive dark tunnel.

"I don't know," Larsson said quietly. "I've never seen them, but maintenance men have disappeared down here and never been found. The rumors are that things occasionally escape the labs at the military base and make their way down here."

"Oh," Penelope whispered. She continued to whip her light around as if trying to see everything at once.

"Okay, here's the plan," Larsson said. "I'll pick you up tomorrow morning with a military clipper and our rescue force of approximately thirty men and women. That's when most of the military personnel will be at their main arena to witness battle competitions and the carrying out of death sentences. The complex is least guarded then, and most vulnerable to an attack. I hope to get in and out of the prison facility where Campbell is being kept before an alarm is set off and they know we're there."

"How do you plan to get in undetected?" Koko asked. "There have to be guards."

"It's not going to be easy even with everyone in the arena, but I was thinking of two ways of entry," Larsson said. "I doubt Ms. Preston will like either one. First, we could follow these tunnels. One leads directly to the prison. We could enter and exit through the sewage access in the middle of the prison."

Penelope was vigorously shaking her head.

"The other way is through the garbage collection system that's also in the middle of the prison. It's more hazardous, since there will be people working there that'll have to be eliminated before they raise an alarm."

"What about the method you suggested earlier about entering the prison as if you were transferring prisoners?" Koko asked.

"I think that'll be too risky. The only ID I had to get us authorization into the prison without being questioned belonged to the captain that I killed. By now, they've rescinded his authority and put out a warning about anyone that tried to use his ID."

Koko nodded, but Penelope didn't like the plan. It seemed too vague and simple to her.

"How are we going to escape?" Penelope asked.

"We'll leave the same way we entered, and then leave the moon base on the clipper before heading back to Earth," Larsson said.

Koko just nodded again.

Koko! Penelope wanted to scream. *Take control of this situation. Poke some holes in Larsson's plan. It sounds too spur of the moment, with no contingencies figured out. We know nothing about what we're about to confront. Nor do we have any idea of what we'll do if we get into trouble, which I'm sure will happen.*

"Look, I have to get back," Larsson said. "I have to gather the force and the weapons to prepare for tomorrow. You two just sit tight until the morning." He turned to leave.

"Will you bring us some food in the morning? I haven't eaten in a while," Koko said.

Larsson nodded with his evil-looking smile before he left and closed the door behind him.

"Koko! Food? We're stuck in this godforsaken sewer for an entire day, and all you can think of is food?" Penelope yelled.

Koko shrugged. "Look at the bright side. At least now you have some place to pee."

"Oh, you're more frustrating than Burt Campbell," Penelope said, before she hauled back and punched Koko in the arm.

TWO

Time became Penelope's eternal tormentor while she sat leaning against the filthy wall of the underground sewage tunnel. She felt desperate, depressed, but most of all frightened. She sat as far away from the reeking river of refuse as she could get and still felt a galaxy too close.

Penelope wasn't worried about some meager maintenance crews. She and Koko could easily escape and hide in the darkness of the tunnel. She was more afraid of the tunnel itself. She kept her torch lit at all times while anxiously searching the evil-smelling sewage flow. She imagined all sorts of terrible monstrosities slithering out of the black river and tearing them apart as if they were a midnight snack. Above all, the powerful feeling of some malevolent presence trying to invade her mind was greatly increased by the total darkness surrounding them. Sometimes, it even seemed to appear before her as an immense dark cloud. She dismissed this vision with great difficulty as simply her heightened imagination.

They'd agreed that someone should remain awake at all times, alert to danger. To Penelope's increasing frustration, Koko had quickly nodded off while seated next to her. His incisive snoring was infuriating. He seemed completely relaxed, while she felt terrified and lonely for Burt and the dogs. She desperately longed for the clear sea breezes of Hawaii, as the nauseating stench of the tunnels seemed to clog her every pore.

Above the obnoxious sound of Koko's nasal snoring, the tunnels were filled with weird echoing noises that frequently had Penelope jumping to her feet in preparation to flee. She often thought she heard inhuman cries and whispering voices in the darkness, but when she searched the area with her light there was never anything in sight. Once she thought she saw something dive back into the sewage when she turned her light in that direction, but she was unsure.

After a while, Penelope gave up trying to wake Koko about her fears. The first few times he got up and helped her search the area with his DEP drawn. Eventually he waved her off and told her to relax. He told her the noises were probably her imagination, and Larsson had just been trying to scare her with boogeyman stories.

THREE

"Well, I see you're still alive," Larsson said, standing in the doorway.

Penelope and Koko leaped to their feet with breathless surprise. Penelope was astounded to discover that she'd actually fallen asleep in the midst of her fear—and they *were* alive!

Koko sleepily rubbed his eyes with the heels of his hands before roaring with a huge yawn. "Is it morning already? Time flies when you're having fun," he muttered.

Penelope jabbed him in between the shoulder blades.

"Come on, we have to get moving," Larsson said. "The clipper is in the hangar without authorization and I don't want a maintenance crew showing up and asking questions."

Penelope eagerly followed Larsson onto the stairway landing, anxious to get away from the evil, reeking tunnel. She was surprised to see a towering man and slender woman standing there waiting. They were dressed in armored environmental suits and carrying sonic blasters. Larsson stopped and made the introductions.

"This is former security sergeant Edward Chester. We call him Chester the Molester. He's been demoted to a prison guard for his criminal obsession with women."

Penelope was gazing up at the wide and smiling childlike face of the huge man who she figured weighed in excess of a hundred-and-fifty kilos. She'd been holding out her hand to shake Chester's immense paw, but she quickly withdrew it when Larsson announced Chester's offenses.

"How do, ma'am? I like you already," Chester said with a deep laugh.

"Ah, yeah," Penelope muttered. She retreated behind Koko when he stepped forward and greeted Chester the Molester.

Penelope noticed that Larsson hadn't given their names during Chester's introduction. She thought that was for the best.

"And this is Prison Supervisor Valerie Emerson," Larsson said.

Penelope reached around Koko and shook the wiry little woman's hand. She quickly withdrew it as Emerson crushed Penelope's soft palm with knuckle-grinding strength. Penelope was taken by the no-nonsense stare from the woman's large brown eyes.

"Koko!" Valerie smiled a beautiful smile of real teeth that she hadn't shown for Penelope. "Long time no see."

"Ah, Valerie," Koko muttered, with what Penelope thought was teenage-like bashfulness or embarrassment. His normally pale features were flushed, and he ducked his head to hide beneath his long, still matted hair. "How have you been?"

"Like you care, you bastard! Come here and give me a hug," Emerson said. She threw herself on Koko like a long lost and sex-starved lover.

"Break it up, you two," Larsson said. "You can renew old relationships after we rescue Campbell." He started up the stairs.

Penelope followed closely on Larsson's heels. She felt eyes boring into her head, and turned to see Chester staring at her with a wet grin on his greasy lips. He winked at her. Penelope ducked her head. She quickly retreated to the rear behind Koko and Valerie, who had their heads together and were whispering in each other's ear like a couple of kids.

As they marched through the dark, noisy facility, Penelope kept her head on a swivel, expecting trouble to pop out from every corner. They never encountered a soul and reached the hangar without incident. She saw a black, disk-shaped military clipper parked in the center of the dusty floor.

The group quickly scrambled up the clipper ramp before Penelope stopped with surprise. The clipper was crammed with men and women dressed in identical environmental suits and armed with various types of heavy weapons. She saw people of every race and description, but they all had the same look in their eyes. It was a look of uneasiness and suspicion. The clipper had been filled with the noise of their talking, laughing, and oaths, but the group went silent as soon as Larsson stepped aboard.

Penelope felt the heat of embarrassment on her cheeks as she glanced around and noticed that all eyes were on her with expressions of interest. Larsson must have noticed the looks as well, since he quickly grabbed Penelope's arm and pulled her toward the cockpit.

"Come on," Larsson said. "You too, Captain."

When the three of them were crammed in the instrument-filled cockpit, Larsson turned and closed the door to give them privacy. Then he motioned Koko toward the copilot seat while he eased his stiff bot-like frame into the pilot seat. He immediately set about making the preparations to get underway.

"Larsson!" Koko whispered harshly. "What's going on here? I recognized some of those people. They're convicts doing hard time on the moon for their crimes. And Valerie Emerson! She was tried for aggravated assault for killing her husband!"

"What did you expect?" Larsson asked, glaring at Koko. "You asked for a group of people who were willing to attack the military base, and this is what you get. Every one of those twenty-five people out there is willing to risk their lives to get back at the military.

"All of them are serving hard time on this rock for some crime they allegedly committed. They all agreed to fight for a chance to escape back to Earth and regain their freedom. Do you want to deny them that opportunity and give up on your attempt to save Campbell?"

Koko sighed and turned to glance up at Penelope. It was obvious he was having serious misgivings. He turned back to Larsson, who was ready to take off. "Do you trust them?"

"Koko, I don't even trust you. I just know they'll fight. They all know they'll die violent deaths on this forsaken place if they don't escape."

Penelope liked this whole deal less and less, but she was finally realizing that they'd been at Larsson's mercy since the moment they'd landed on the moon. She sighed with resignation about her fate.

"Well, I guess we don't have a choice, do we?" Koko said angrily.

"Not anymore," Larsson said, confirming Penelope's dismal thoughts.

Larsson reached over the side of his seat and pulled out a blue refrigerated container, which he handed to Koko before he took off. Koko opened the small container and peered inside.

"Hey, food," he said with childlike glee.

Penelope brought her hands up to her beautiful yet soiled face and shook her head in despair. Larsson flew out of the green plasma hangar doors and over the desolate landscape toward the military base.

"I didn't forget you, pretty lady," Larsson said. "There's another container there behind me. There are also two armored environmental suits in there, one for each of you. You both need to put one on."

"Why? Are we going outside?" Penelope asked with an anxious voice. She'd never walked outside on the moon, and was terrified of the dangerous implications.

Koko continued to wolf down his food, as if he expected as much.

"Since you didn't like the idea of using the underground sewage tunnels," Larsson said, "I figured we better go through the garbage collection and hauling area.

"I couldn't get a hold of a garbage vehicle. We can't land a military clipper in the area without attracting attention, so we're going to have to land the clipper outside the complex and walk the rest of the way."

"Won't someone notice a large group of armed people walking around outside?" Penelope asked.

"No, armed patrols are always walking around, and those are military environmental suits. We should fit right in."

Penelope didn't like Larsson's overconfidence, but she silently slipped into her suit. Koko finished eating and burped with satisfaction. Penelope noticed he hadn't offered her anything. She realized she couldn't have eaten anyway. She sat in the copilot seat as Koko got into his suit.

Larsson flew the clipper just above the dust- and rock-covered moon surface beneath the brilliant sunlight. He was swooping up and down through the sloping craters so close to the surface that Penelope feared they would crash and die before they even reached the military base. Within minutes, they cleared the rocky ledge of a huge dust-filled crater. Larsson expertly slowed their clipper near the far side.

"Okay, we're here. We have to climb that ridge in front of us. The garbage-disposal area is just beyond it," Larsson said, as he smoothly landed the craft. "You two are in my lead group, so stick to my side."

FOUR

Larsson exited the cockpit with Penelope and Koko behind him. Larsson made a quick right out of the cockpit and stopped at a weapons locker. He handed Koko a directed energy beam rifle. He tried to hand Penelope another one, but she refused any weapon with a pouting frown. Larsson gave her a nastier look than usual.

"Why exactly did you come here?" he asked with frustration. "You're more of a liability than an asset."

"You know nothing about me or my abilities, Larsson," Penelope said with a scowl. "Your life may come to depend on mine."

"I hope not," Larsson muttered, and turned to the force. They were standing silently at the ready. "Okay, people, this is it. Chester, your group will follow mine. Emerson, your group will cover the rear. After we recover Campbell, we all return immediately to the clipper. Don't delay or you'll be left behind. We wait for no one once our task is completed."

Larsson forced his way through the cramped group toward the ramp with Penelope and Koko right behind him. Penelope noticed that the rescue detail was tensely silent as if they were all considering their mortality.

The clipper suddenly shifted violently. Penelope let out a frightened scream as she was thrown onto Koko.

"What was that?" she said anxiously into Koko's ear above the other questioning voices.

"It wasn't a strike from a weapon. It must just be the landing skids settling in the rocks and moon dust," Larsson answered. "The dust can be pretty deep in some of these craters."

Larsson reached the ramp and pushed a button on his shoulder pad. A clear plasma bubble appeared over his head, stemming from the neck of his environmental suit.

Penelope desperately searched her shoulder pad in fear that Larsson would open the ramp door before her suit was sealed. Koko calmly reached over and pressed her shoulder button before he did the same with his suit.

Total silence fell on Penelope's ears after the bubble formed around her head, but then she heard Larsson ask, "Is everyone ready?"

No one answered. Larsson reached up and punched the ramp door button. Penelope felt herself sucked forward in a brief yet powerful wind as the clipper depressurized.

As she regained her balance, Larsson said, "Let's move out, people."

Abruptly, the clipper was shaken more violently than the first time. Penelope was thrown back into Koko and Larsson with another fright-filled scream. The three of them toppled forward and rolled down the ramp out onto the dusty moon surface. The inside of Penelope's helmet erupted with panicked screams and foul oaths as everyone yelled at once in their confusion.

Penelope came to a sudden halt sitting up with her back leaning against Koko. She gazed back up the ramp, trying to ignore her own fear and the confused clamor in her helmet. Everyone else had been hurled back into the clipper and away from the ramp door.

Penelope was paralyzed with terror and confusion as she gazed around her. Slithering snakes the size of building columns were erupting through the moon crust around the base of the clipper. The thick gray snakes danced about in the atmospheric void with slow uncoordinated motions as if blindly searching for something. They rippled with smooth scaly muscle that flowed like liquid stone. One of the snakes slapped on the surface with a dust-filled thud that shook Penelope's bones. It started to slither toward her. To her ultimate horror, she saw it wasn't a snake, but a squid-like tentacle with huge fanged suckers as large as her head.

"Lord in Hades, what are those things?" Koko yelled.

"Run for the ridge!" Larsson screamed.

Penelope was up and bounding through the low lunar gravity before Larsson had finished his warning. She covered the two-hundred meters to the ridge as if she had on a space jetpack. She didn't come to a breathless halt until she was halfway up the rocky ridge.

In the close confines of her helmet, Penelope heard the terrible screams of people dying as if they were right next to her. She whirled around to view the devastating scene of destruction and death. Larsson and Koko had barely reached the sloping base of the ridge. The clipper and its screaming occupants were completely engulfed by the massive tentacles of some tremendous nightmare out of the ocean depths of Earth. The clipper was being heaved to and fro as if it were a toy. To her horror, she realized that no one else had escaped.

Penelope's screams joined those of the dying rescue team as the tentacles bulged with terrifying strength and crushed the clipper walls as if they were paper. The monster in the ground held the crumpled ball of metal and human remains up in the airless atmosphere for a moment as if showing off a grand trophy. Suddenly, and with incredible quickness, the moon squid hauled its terrible prize back into an immense hole in the surface crust.

As Penelope watched with open-mouthed amazement, the hole began to fill itself. By the time Koko and Larsson had breathlessly reached her and turned to see what had happened, the hole was filled. Except for the lingering dust cloud, the moon surface appeared as if nothing had happened. The whole deadly disaster had taken only moments to occur. The screaming in Penelope's helmet had gone silent. Twenty-five vital men and women, their entire rescue force, were dead.

Penelope was so devastated by the loss of life, and the uselessness of their whole rescue operation, that she sat heavily on the ridge and cried. To further her despair, she couldn't touch her face through her helmet to wipe away her tears.

"Larsson, what . . . what was that?" Koko asked, sounding out of breath from his exertion and fear.

"I don't know," Larsson said; his automated voice without tone.

Penelope glared up at Larsson's back as he gazed down at the crater. Something in his emotionless voice told her that he knew exactly what that monstrous thing had been, and maybe even had been expecting it. Koko turned to face Larsson.

"What do you mean, you don't know?" Koko asked with heated anger. "How could you have lived on the moon for so many years and not know that a creature like that exists?"

It was Larsson's turn to glare down at Koko with anger. Penelope feared Koko might have gone too far.

"Don't be stupid, Koko!" Larsson yelled. "I just about lost my life as well. Do you really think I'd land somewhere if I knew something like that thing existed out here?

"I can only guess that it was one of Arnold's pets. I've heard rumors that Arnold is creating some kind of army out of creatures from some sort of experiment. I think we just saw one of his creatures."

Larsson turned and slowly started for the rocky top of the ridge. Penelope got to her weary feet. She gazed after him while desperately wishing she could wipe away her tears and the snot that was leaking from her nose.

"Where are you going?" she asked.

Larsson turned and stared down at them for a moment.

"To save Campbell," he said.

"Just the three of us?" Penelope asked.

"Koko and I will save Campbell," Larsson said sarcastically. "I also have an associate on the inside that'll guide us to him, but I don't see how you're going to do us much good without a weapon. I will say, however, that I've never seen anyone run as fast as you did across that crater."

"Koko, say something," Penelope turned on Koko.

Koko shrugged with slumped resignation and started up the ridge. "I think he's right, Penelope. Where else are we going to go? It's kilometers back to the mining colony, and we'd never make it walking through all the military patrols and the checkpoints. If we're going to get caught, it might as well be while trying to rescue Burt.

Besides, do you want to try and walk across that crater with that creature down there? I don't think that even you could outrun that thing."

"Oh, men!" Penelope scowled. She started her slow leaps up the ridge.

XII

THE RESCUE

ONE

Penelope stared down in amazement when she reached the top of the ridge. The military moon base was far larger than she'd imagined. Most of it appeared to be made from lightweight prefabricated modular buildings that had been attached together to form the main complex. While it might have once been a cream color, it now appeared the dingy gray of moon dust shining dully beneath the bright sun. Gazing past the vast array of antennas and rotating scanning disks, Penelope saw a huge, domed structure in the middle of the complex. It was obviously the death arena Larsson had talked about.

Penelope squinted against the blinding sunlight and spied what appeared to be a small city off to her left, away from the military complex. The city contained tall buildings and a monorail system. She even spotted large garden areas or parks. The whole scene was eerily similar to an urban area on Earth, and she wondered about its purpose.

"What are they doing up here?" Koko asked in an awestruck tone when he reached the ridge top and stared down at the military base.

"Arnold is getting a huge budget from somewhere," Larsson said. "They've been building like crazy for the last few years. That's where we're going right down there."

Larsson stabbed his index finger at a low single-level extension of the base down below. It was less than half a kilometer away. Penelope could see a few abandoned garbage-hauling vehicles in front of three huge red-plasma doors, but there was no one about.

"Where is everyone?" she asked.

"Hopefully, they're all at the competition in the arena," Larsson said. "The competitions are a sort of holiday here. Attendance is mandatory for all but a few guards. Let's go."

Larsson led them down past the haulers to an entrance into the compound. Penelope continued to feel anxious and surprised by the lack of personnel. Koko said nothing as he brought up the rear with his DER leveled and ready for anything.

When they reached the base personnel door, Larsson stabbed a button on the dust-covered wall next to a man-sized metal entrance. The door to a large vacuum chamber opened with a dust-blowing hiss of escaping air. They quickly stepped into the dust-filled chamber and the door hissed closed behind them. They were now trapped and blind behind the solid door leading into the complex.

"Okay, people, this is it," Larsson said. "Koko, get ready with that rifle. I don't know if anyone is working on the other side."

Larsson waited until a light above his head went from red to green. Koko pushed in front of Penelope with his rifle in the ready. Larsson leveled his rifle and pushed the button to open the door.

"Clear," Larsson said. He quickly moved into a brightly lit, hangar-like area with his head swiveling in all directions. Koko raced to fan out around the first of three garbage haulers that were parked to their right. Penelope followed closely behind Koko, skirting huge containers full of heaped trash. Larsson disappeared around the immense balloon-like rear wheels of the filthy hauler to their left.

"Blake! What in Hades have you done?" Penelope heard Larsson say in her helmet.

Penelope raced after Koko. They rounded the corner to the rear of the haulers before coming to a sliding halt when confronted by a horrifying scene. A grotesque massacre had obviously just taken place. To her revulsion, Penelope saw what she assumed had been the bodies of human beings sprawled on the puddled floor.

Penelope felt her empty stomach spasm in revolt at the sickening sight. It appeared as if the bodies had been liquefied by some kind of pink slime that had engulfed them. The only way she could even tell that the pink puddles had once been people was because there was an occasional clawed hand or booted foot still bubbling away in the acid-like pools.

"Oh!" Penelope moaned. She saw a partially dissolved head at the top of a puddle. Based on the head's hideous expression, she realized what horrible pain the person had suffered while being liquefied.

Penelope reached up and turned off her plasma helmet as she bent over and gagged. Her empty stomach convulsed with dry heaves until she couldn't breathe.

"Are you okay?" Koko asked with a comforting hand on her heaving back.

Penelope stood up wiping the spittle, tears, and snot from her face. She glared across the floor to see a short, overweight, Caucasian male in an environmental suit standing next to Larsson. He wore a tank on his back connected to a huge rifle that was still oozing pink goo. She knew immediately who'd murdered these people. Penelope was physically and emotionally sickened by the actions one human being would commit against another.

"You, you did this?" Penelope said with rage to the man standing next to Larsson.

"I had to," said the man. "You people set off an alarm outside. They sent a team down here to investigate. I raced down here knowing this was where you were coming in. If I hadn't stopped the guards, they would have killed you before you even got through the entrance."

"This is Dr. Blake," Larsson said. "He's the associate I was telling you about."

Penelope raced around the liquefied bodies and confronted Blake's fat smiling face with her enraged features on fire.

"I suppose you think you're a hero?" Penelope snapped.

Blake nodded dumbly. "I *did* save your lives," he said. His greasy grin widened, revealing his unclean teeth.

Penelope hauled back and slapped Blake's jowly unshaven cheek hard enough to rock him off balance. She leaped forward with a vicious snarl to punish Blake further, but Larsson quickly grabbed her and pulled her back.

"Slow down there, lady. He's on our side," Larsson laughed. "I see you have some fight in you after all."

As Penelope struggled briefly and glared at Blake with fiery eyes, Koko walked up to Blake to examine his weapon.

"What kind of gun is that?" Koko asked.

Blake rubbed the side of his flushed, wounded face. He stared at Penelope with a hurt, childlike expression to ensure she was safely in Larsson's clutches and couldn't attack him.

"It's a simple compressed air sprayer," Blake said. "It's loaded with a nano-type acid that liquefies biological silicon entities. But as you can see, it works rather well on carbon-based life forms as well."

"What silicon entities? I've never heard of anything like that," Koko said.

"You haven't told them yet, have you?" Blake asked Larsson.

After ensuring Penelope had calmed down, Larsson released her, and said, "I told them Arnold was creating an army, but I haven't told them of what. I don't even know myself."

"You'll all find out soon enough, but come on," Blake said. "We have to get out of here. I don't know if they're sending more guards. You all have to remove your environmental suits, and leave behind your rifles. There are guards patrolling the halls because of the alarm you set off. I'm going to have to escort you as if you were my prisoners if we're going to get through the prison block."

"What's to stop you from killing us the way you killed these poor people?" Penelope asked.

"If I was going to do that, I would've done it already," Blake said.

Penelope glanced at Koko, and saw he didn't like the idea either. Larsson started to strip out of his suit, so Penelope and Koko did likewise.

"I thought you said there was a force of twenty-five to thirty coming with you, Larsson," Blake said.

Larsson ignored Blake and picked up two DEPs lying on the floor next to the massacred guards. He handed one to Koko. "Hide this on your body someplace where you can reach it fast."

Blake started to object, but Larsson turned on him and said, "Let's move it."

"We have another problem," Blake said. When Larsson didn't say anything, Blake continued. "You got here too late."

Oh, no! Penelope thought. *Burt might already be dead.*

"What do you mean?" Larsson asked.

"Campbell isn't in his prison cell anymore. Arnold took him to the arena already. Assuming we get that far, we can't march into the middle of the arena and demand Campbell be released in front of an army of Arnold's creatures."

Thank God. At least Burt's alive. Penelope sighed with relief.

Penelope saw Larsson's frustrated expression. She realized Larsson didn't trust Blake any more than she did. She was anxious to get moving in her fear for Burt's life.

She wondered: *Why did Arnold take Burt to the place where they're executing prisoners?*

"Blake, you have to get us to that arena," she said anxiously. "What if they're going to kill Burt?"

"They won't," Blake said, "at least not unless his conditioning has failed. Campbell represents too much to Arnold's plans."

"Conditioning?" Penelope asked, now really confused.

"Can you get us into Campbell's cell?" Koko asked. "They'll probably take him there after the competition. We can wait for him there."

"Then we'll be confined to a cell," Larsson said. "What if he isn't brought back right away, or not at all?"

"We'll either have to fight our way out, or become Arnold's guests until he decides to kill us," Koko said. "Do you have a better plan?"

Penelope noticed that Blake was slowly shaking his fat features at this suggestion.

God, she thought, *either Blake has terrible body odor or he just let a raunchy fart.*

"Let's go," Larsson said forcibly.

"Get in front of me so you look like prisoners," Blake said. "Turn right outside the doorway over there." He pointed his rifle at a door off to their right.

TWO

Larsson led the way with Koko and Penelope following. Blake brought up the rear. They exited the door and turned right. Penelope saw they'd entered a long, well-lit, crème-colored corridor that veered off to their left toward the main compound. She stopped suddenly when she glanced up and spotted cameras and directed energy beam cannons on swivels in the hall ceiling.

"Keep moving," Koko whispered urgently in her ear. Penelope didn't move. The sound of marching boots came echoing down the hall. Blake shoved her forward.

"Move it, prisoners!" Blake yelled.

Penelope slowly started walking forward again with her heart pounding against her ribcage. A formation of five human guards led by a sergeant rounded the corner at the far end of the corridor and continued to march toward them.

"Sergeant Ozona," Blake said confidently as the guards neared, "Captain Peña caught these prisoners trespassing in the west garbage hangar. He asked me to escort them down to the prison block."

The guards stopped in front of Penelope's group while leveling their sonic blasters at them.

"What are you doing here, Doctor?" the dark-faced, black-haired Ozona asked, while he peered suspiciously down the hall behind Blake. "What happened to Captain Peña and his detail?"

"Ah, I was just passing by when there was an accident with one of the guard's weapons that killed most of his group and wounded Peña," Blake said. "Peña called for a med group and is waiting with the wounded. He asked me to escort these prisoners to the checkpoint and ensure they got to the prison block."

Ozona's brown eyes darkened and his brow creased as he eyed Blake suspiciously before he turned to his guards.

"Okay, you first three take up the rear. You two take the forward position with me. We'll go back to the checkpoint and see what Lieutenant Broderick wants to do with them."

The black-uniformed guards silently took up their positions, and the group continued forward. Penelope was terrified. She glanced behind her. Blake was evilly staring back at her as if enjoying her obvious discomfort. He smiled and winked. Penelope turned forward again and glanced sideways at Koko. Koko was staring ahead with a grim expression. His right hand was at his side where he'd hidden his DEP.

They rounded the corner into another corridor. Penelope thought it appeared exactly the same as the last except for the checkpoint and blockade at the end of the hall. She glanced up and noticed there was another battery of cannons and security cameras in the ceiling. The cannon barrels noiselessly swiveled and followed their every movement.

How did Larsson think we could penetrate such security and get in with such a large force? Penelope wondered. *It would have been impossible to escape after Burt's rescue when the base had been alerted to our attack.*

Their marching steps echoed as they neared the fortified blockade and the adjoining checkpoint. A tall, light-haired brute of a man stepped out of the guardhouse on the left-hand side of the hall. His thick chest, leg, and arm muscles bulged out of his tight black uniform.

"What do we have here?" the man said with a small grin, as the group halted before him.

"Lieutenant Broderick," Ozona said, "this is a group of prisoners that Captain Peña took down in the garbage hangar. We were taking them down to the prison block."

"Where's Peña?" Broderick asked suspiciously.

"He's been wounded," Ozona said.

"Ha!" Broderick roared with laughter. "The bastard deserves it."

Penelope thought the guards became uneasy over Broderick insulting a superior. *I wonder what Broderick will think when he discovers Peña is no more than a sludge puddle now.*

Broderick pushed aside everyone and came to a stop in front of Penelope. She glared defiantly up into his brown eyes and pale, freckled features.

"My, my," Broderick said with a crooked smile, "you're awful good looking for a traitor. Sergeant, have you searched these prisoners?"

"No, sir," said the sergeant with a tremble in his voice.

"It looks like I'll have to search you myself, pretty woman," Broderick said. "Turn around, put your hands on the wall, and spread your legs."

Penelope didn't move. She continued to give Broderick a venomous stare.

"Don't make me get rough with you, lady," Broderick said, menace in his voice.

Penelope glanced at Koko, but saw no hope in his down-turned face. Reluctantly, she turned around and placed her hands on the wall above her head. Broderick kicked her feet aside until they were spread to his satisfaction. He kneeled with his knees popping in protest and placed his hot paws on her left thigh. Blake came up beside Broderick.

"I wouldn't do that, Broderick," Blake whispered. "This woman is wanted by Arnold. You defile her, and you'll be the next contender to face George in the arena."

Broderick quickly stood and glared angrily down at Blake.

"That's a laugh," Broderick said. "Just before you showed up, I was watching the competition on my monitor. George just got his head beat in by the new army commander, Burt Campbell. I don't think I have anything to fear from that damned devil anymore."

"Maybe not," Blake continued to whisper menacingly, "but Arnold has worse things than George to punish a meaningless lieutenant for ruining his precious prize."

Penelope's heart soared with happiness and confusion. She was ecstatic that Burt had survived a fight against whoever this George was, but she was confused by Burt's title of army commander. *Burt would never fight for Arnold. What have they done to him?*

"Well," Broderick said, "Ozona, take these prisoners to the arena if Arnold wants them so badly."

"But Peña wanted them to be taken to the prison block," Blake protested.

"Peña isn't here, is he?" Broderick growled, "I give the orders here, not you, Blake. Get them out of here, Ozona."

"Yes, sir," Ozona said. "Move it!"

THREE

The group of three prisoners, six guards, and Blake marched down the hall toward the arena. Penelope stepped back into line beside Koko with Larsson directly in front of them. Ozona and his two guards led the way with the other three guards and Blake bringing up the rear.

They made multiple turns and walked down long, heavily guarded hallways. Penelope continued to be surprised by the number of checkpoints and security personnel along the way. She also noticed the lack of non-security personnel. Most of all, she worried about how they were going to get out of this one. She began to resign herself to the fact that they were trapped. But for all their dismal circumstances, Penelope remained uplifted. At least her worst fears had been averted. Burt was alive.

After what seemed like an eternity of anxious walking, Penelope's sensitive ears picked up the fevered roar of a crowd. She realized they were close to the arena. Her time was running out. Once they entered an arena filled with Arnold's army, she knew they were lost. Her only hope was that somehow Burt had the leverage and power with his new position as army commander to save them.

They rounded the final corner. The arena doors were open before them. Her heart sank in deep despair when she saw there was thousands of screaming military personnel in the stands. There was no escape.

Koko made a sudden move at Penelope's side. He leaped beside Larsson while pulling out his hidden pistol. He jabbed his weapon barrel into Ozona's eye and fired.

"Halt!" a guard yelled.

The guard stepped next to Penelope and leveled his sonic blaster at Koko's exposed back. Penelope viciously kicked sideways and knocked the guard's blaster out of his grasp as he pulled the trigger. The wild shot splattered the guard next to Larsson. Penelope followed through with a whirling roundhouse kick that slammed the surprised guard in the head. He hit the floor unconscious.

Penelope regained her balance in a defensive stance while desperately searching for more victims to assault. Larsson and Koko had been blown to her right by the errant sonic blast. They were both scrambling to their feet with their pistols drawn.

"Koko, watch out!" Penelope yelled. The remaining guard from the front group was leveling his blaster on Larsson and Koko. Koko instinctively ducked and rolled while firing his DEP. The guard's head exploded.

Larsson pointed his pistol at Penelope. She dropped on the ground to her right. The blazing heat of Larsson's death ray seared just past her ducking head. A guard behind Penelope screamed in agony. Larsson quickly stepped forward and fired again. The scream was silenced.

A terrible cry suddenly reached Penelope's ears from behind her. She leaped to her feet as the last guard withered on the floor covered in pink slime. She watched with horror as the guard's body dissolved before her eyes. She'd never witnessed a person die in such a horrible, agonizing manner. She glanced up. Blake's spray gun was dripping with pink goo. Penelope was sickened. A sadistic grin had appeared on Blake's jowly face while he stared with greedy eyes at the pink bubbling puddle on the floor.

"You're a sick . . .," Penelope started to yell at Blake.

She was cut off by Larsson's quiet, menacing voice. "Drop your weapon."

Penelope continued to glare at Blake, expecting him to lower his spray gun. Blake's grin only seemed to widen. He slowly turned and leveled his sprayer at Penelope.

"Drop the weapon, Koko!" Larsson snapped.

It finally hit Penelope like an emotional sledgehammer. She whirled and stared with shocked disbelief at Larsson. He was drilling his DEP into Koko's ear. Koko gazed back at Penelope with a painful expression of surprised sorrow. Slowly, Koko lowered his DEP to the floor and pushed it away.

"What're you doing, Larsson?" Penelope whispered.

Larsson's half mouth curled in a sneer. "Collecting my reward, bitch," he yelled angrily. "You can't be so stupid that you didn't realize what a huge reward there is on you and Koko."

"But why the elaborate set up?" Koko asked. "Why not turn us in when we arrived?"

"You know, Koko, sometimes I wonder how you ever made captain," Larsson continued, leering with hatred. "I wouldn't have received much credit or a reward if I didn't turn you over to Arnold myself. I had to kill all those people or they would have wanted in on the deal." Larsson gloated over his prize.

"Don't forget me," Blake said, still pointing his sprayer at Penelope. "I get twenty percent of the reward. Without me, you would never have gotten this far into the base."

"You almost got us all killed, Blake!" Larsson yelled, as he turned toward Blake with fury in his disfigured face. "You must have known about that squid thing in the crater that killed the rest of my force. It was your idea that we land there."

"It was a risk I was willing to take," Blake laughed.

Larsson turned on Blake and fired his pistol with amazing quickness. It happened so fast that by the time Penelope turned back toward Blake, he was already falling to the floor with most of his head gone. Penelope whirled back to face Larsson, but he was already pointing his DEP back at Koko.

"Hold it right there!" shouted a voice from the direction of the arena.

Penelope glanced behind Larsson. Four human military guards had appeared in the arena doorway. They had their rifles pointed in Penelope's direction.

"It's all right," Larsson said. He lowered his weapon away from Koko. "I'm Ulf Larsson. Go tell General Arnold that I'm here with the two prisoners I promised, Penelope Preston, and Koko Sinopa."

"Throw aside your pistol, Larsson," said a guard.

Larsson did as he was told. Two guards got behind Penelope while the other two guards continued to point their weapons at Larsson and Koko. The guards motioned them toward the arena door.

Penelope sagged in defeat. *I have failed you, Burt. Only you can save us now.*

XIII

GOODBYE OLD FRIEND

Campbell struggled to sit up on the sandy arena floor. He groaned as a wave of pain, nausea and dizziness passed through him from the wounds in his back and bicep. He felt exhausted and mentally drained with depression. He turned toward the sound of the sonic blast explosion that had come from the arena entrance. The once excited crowd had gone quiet with murmurings of curiosity. Arnold stood up next to Campbell, and glanced with interest in the same direction.

The guards at the entrance had disappeared down the hallway leading into the compound. Campbell fought to his weary feet when he saw flashes of weapon fire. There was obviously an unscheduled battle taking place. Arnold seemed as surprised as he was.

Campbell saw a chance to rid humanity of a terrible evil. Arnold had his back to him. He moved stealthily toward Arnold.

"Don't even think about it," Arnold said calmly. He turned to face Campbell.

Suddenly, Campbell's brain and body burned with fiery pain. He was driven to his knees again, groaning in agony.

"You see, Campbell, it's impossible for you to attack me," Arnold said with a grin. "Your mind and body are so conditioned that they refuse to obey your treacherous thoughts."

"I'll kill you yet, Arnold," Campbell managed through tremendous pain. He fell forward onto his hands gasping for breath.

"Ah, Campbell, you're just the way you should be, kneeling before your superior," Arnold said with a sinister laugh.

Arnold's laugh was drowned out by a new roar from the crowd.

"How can this be?" Arnold had to yell to be heard. Campbell caught the tone of amazement in his voice. "Look up, Campbell, your slavery to our cause is complete. You will do whatever I wish or see your loved one die a horrible death."

Campbell wearily lifted his sweat-covered head, his drenched long black hair hanging loosely around his face. He peered toward the arena entrance through a pain-filled haze.

Oh, no! How? Campbell wondered with horrified amazement. *This has to be some sort of trick. You promised me you wouldn't do this. Now all is lost!*

A new pain, greater than anything George or Arnold had been able to inflict upon his torn mind and body, pierced his heart and soul. Penelope was being driven into the arena by Arnold's guards.

"No!" Campbell howled. He slammed his fist and head into the sand. "No, no, no!"

"Larsson, I knew you wouldn't fail me!" Arnold yelled above the crowd.

"Stuff it, Arnold. I only did it for the reward," said an automated voice close to Campbell's lowered head.

"Halt!"

"Oh, let her go," Arnold said.

"Burt! Burt! Oh, my God, I found you at last," he heard Penelope's anguished voice just before he felt her warm comforting arms around him.

Campbell gazed up into Penelope's face. He saw his agony reflected in her pain-creased expression. It was still the most beautiful face he'd ever seen. Her high cheekbones and normally pale, smooth complexion were rosy and rugged in pinched excitement.

Her intelligent blue-gray eyes were blazing with fire, pain or anger. Yet he felt deep sorrow at seeing her there. He'd fought so long and hard to save her. Now their love was doomed. He knew he was powerless to save them.

Campbell's anger roared when he heard Arnold laughing in his victory. His mind was filled with retaliation as he struggled to stand. He was driven to the ground again by intense pain.

"Burt, you're injured," Penelope cried.

Campbell felt Penelope's hand searching his back before he felt heat from her touch. He realized she was trying to heal him.

"No, Penelope, not here," Campbell whispered. He grabbed her tender hand and held it tight.

He used Penelope's hand for support while he tried to stand. Koko was suddenly in front of him lifting him to his feet. Koko appeared anguished, mournful beyond words, as if he realized what their capture meant not only to him, but to Burt and Penelope.

"Koko, what're you doing here?" Campbell whispered, knowing how this must end.

"Koko Sinopa," Arnold said, "thank you for your help. I knew you would eventually lead us to Campbell and the elusive Penelope Preston. Or if you prefer, Monica Yamamoto."

"Burt, I tried to persuade her from coming," Koko said, his eyes pleading for Burt to forgive him for his failure to protect Penelope. "But she said she would come by herself with or without me."

"I know," Campbell said weakly. He patted Koko on the back in the only way he could comfort his friend.

"She's a pain in the ass," Larsson muttered.

Campbell gazed at the disfigured half human, half cyborg with confusion. The horrid half-steel face, crooked metal mouth, and mismatched eye repulsed him. The man oozed evil. Campbell hated him immediately.

"This is the man that betrayed your friend and your lover, Campbell," Arnold said. "Ulf Larsson has been working for me for years as my agent in the mining colony after I caught him stealing weapons from the military base."

Arnold stepped over to Larsson and wrapped his arm around Larsson's huge shoulder. "He contacted me after Sinopa reached him trying to find a method to rescue you. I offered him a very handsome reward for Penelope's capture, and I see he threw in Sinopa as well. Good work, Larsson, you earned your reward."

Campbell glared at Larsson with hatred burning his face. Larsson bowed his head as if ashamed, and wouldn't return his look. Campbell lurched toward Larsson with a ferocious snarl, but his legs buckled beneath him. Koko steadied him, and held him back. The crowd had gone deadly silent with interest.

"Sinopa, come here," Arnold commanded in a menacing tone.

Koko calmly turned toward Arnold as if resigned to his fate. He didn't move from supporting his longtime friend.

Arnold turned to the guards by the arena door and motioned for them to come to him. Two human guards in environmental suits approached with the bulky weapons and tanks that Campbell had noticed before. Terror struck his heart. As the guards neared, Arnold motioned them toward Koko. The guards came forward and pointed their weapons at Koko.

"Come here, Sinopa," Arnold repeated in a calm, yet sinister voice.

Koko glanced up a Campbell. Koko's brown eyes were filled with sorrow, yet were strangely calm. They showed no fear. A small smile curled his pale thin lips. Campbell reached up and grabbed Koko's arm, but Koko slipped away and moved to confront Arnold.

"Why did you come here, Sinopa?" Arnold asked with a sneer. "You must have known your mission would fail."

Koko laughed at Arnold. His eyes twinkled with hatred. "Arnold—Benedict, as Burt likes to call you—if you have to ask such a question, then you'll never understand the answer."

Koko stepped menacingly forward. Arnold leaped back with wide eyes and a mouth opened in fear. Koko laughed again before he spat in Arnold's face.

"You were always a coward and a traitor!" Koko yelled for everyone in the silent arena to hear. The crowd responded with wild jeers and laughter.

Arnold went crazy with rage, "Guards! Kill him! Kill him!"

The guards stepped forward with their guns leveled. Campbell shrugged off Penelope's arm and leaped to his left in a blur of motion. He had his arm around the first guard's neck as he snapped the guard's spine. He was too late to save Koko. The second guard sprayed Koko with a pink liquid before Campbell could untangle himself from the body in his arms.

"No!" Campbell screamed as he dropped the dead guard.

Campbell was horror stricken, rooted motionless as he watched. His close friend withered spastically on the sandy ground in horrifying agony. Koko's body disintegrated into unrecognizable sludge in seconds before Campbell's astonished eyes. Koko never uttered a word. Campbell rushed forward.

"No! Campbell, don't touch him!" Arnold yelled. "That liquid will eat you alive just like him."

Campbell sagged to his knees beside Koko. His shoulders slumped in deep despair, his hands hanging loosely, useless, at his sides. He gazed at Koko for a long time. Hot, unashamed tears rolled down his burning cheeks. Eventually, Penelope kneeled beside Burt and wrapped her comforting arms around him. She lowered her head in tearful sorrow upon his shoulder.

"I'm sorry, Burt, so sorry. He was a great man," she whispered through her sobs.

"He was a great friend. I will have my revenge," Campbell said loud enough for Arnold to hear.

"Guards, take Commander Campbell down to the medical unit," Arnold commanded.

"I'll kill you!" Campbell roared, and tried to stand. His body wouldn't obey, and he collapsed.

"Guards," Arnold said.

Campbell saw the feet of two guards appear before his head. They pulled him out of Penelope's arms. He screamed in fury and tossed aside the guards. He whirled on Arnold with death burning in his black eyes. Suddenly, he felt a terrific blow on the side of his head. His body sagged to the ground in defeat and despair before everything went black.

XIV

THE MASTER

ONE

Campbell awoke back in his dimly lit cell when he heard the door open. He glanced up from his bed as Arnold entered. *What? No guards?* he wondered. *I will* kill *you, Arnold! I will avenge Koko's and the Sens' death somehow. God forbid if something should happen to Penelope.* He struggled to sit up as intense pain shot through his brain and body. Arnold didn't seem to notice.

"You have been summoned, Campbell," Arnold said.

"By whom?" Campbell asked with his face buried in his hands.

He gazed up at Arnold. It'd been a day since his battle with George. His back and bicep were almost completely healed by the nanotechnology and genetic engineering flowing through his blood. His body still ached. His mind was lost in deep depression.

"How are you feeling?" Arnold asked.

"Like you care, you bastard, but I'll bet I'm faring better than George," Campbell said with a small smile over George's demise.

"You *do* seem to have amazing recuperative powers, Campbell. Too bad we don't have time to do some more tests on you. Don't worry about George. He's been repaired. Come with me."

"I'm not going anywhere until you tell me what you've done with Penelope," Campbell growled.

"Don't make me hurt you, Campbell. You know I can do it with a word."

Campbell didn't move.

"Let's just say that Ms. Preston has been interrogated and is under the loving care of Dr. Eto for the moment," Arnold said with a smile. "I know she has some amazing powers, and since she isn't important to our immediate goals, we're conducting a few tests on her."

Rage exploded through Campbell's heart. He lurched at Arnold, but only fell on the floor twisting in pain.

Arnold laughed. "Campbell, you are a glutton for punishment. Now, get off the floor. Your lover won't be injured permanently. I doubt that's even possible. Now, get up. You have an appointment, and we can't afford to be late."

Campbell slowly struggled to his feet. He approached Arnold with an expression of deadly hatred. Arnold stepped back. Campbell saw an expression of doubt and fear on Arnold's face before Arnold turned and left the cell.

Good! Campbell thought. *He still fears me. This battle isn't over yet.*

He painfully followed Arnold down the wide, well-lit hall. "Who are we going to see?"

Arnold slowed until Campbell was alongside. "Your new boss."

"You mean your boss . . . the Master?" Campbell asked.

Arnold stopped suddenly and glanced up at him with surprise. "How do you know about the Master?"

"Something I picked up from you and Blake."

"That doesn't surprise me. Blake always talked more than was good for him, but it's just as well. You were destined to meet It sometime," Arnold said, and started forward again.

"You mean the Master is one of your creations?"

"If you must know, the Master was our first creation in the teleporter. It was more of an accident than anything else," Arnold said with his head down, as if he were wondering where his plans had gone wrong. "We were greedy at first. We tried to create something that could read and control human minds. We thought that if we could control the minds of the world leaders, we could take over Earth without a fight."

Campbell was amazed he was getting so much information out of Arnold, so he pushed on. "What went wrong?"

"Wrong? I wouldn't say things went wrong. They just took another direction. The goals remain the same, but what came out of the teleporter wasn't what we intended."

"You were successful, weren't you? You created something that could read and control minds. It took control, didn't It?"

Arnold clammed up at this point.

It's obvious that whatever Arnold created took over the moon base. What in Hades am I about to meet? Campbell thought. His anxiety deepened; his physical pain and depression forgotten.

Arnold's revelations explained a great deal to Campbell, since he'd never gotten the impression that Arnold had either the intelligence or the ambition for world conquest. On the other hand, the idea of an unknown something that *did* have the ambition and intelligence to come up with a plan to conquer Earth struck renewed fear in his heart. He'd always felt that somehow he could defeat Arnold. What about the Master?

TWO

They followed the hallways, and went through the checkpoints until they came to the entrance to the arena. Before they reached the arena door, Arnold directed Campbell down a hallway to the right. After a short walk, they passed through another checkpoint that was more heavily guarded than the others. After he and Arnold were searched by human guards in long black robes, they were allowed into an elevator.

"Where are we going?" Campbell asked. The elevator seemed to take a long time to descend.

"The Bunker," Arnold said absently.

The elevator abruptly stopped and the doors opened. Arnold stepped out. Campbell stayed behind him while gawking about the empty black stone-walled chamber they'd entered. It appeared to be a checkpoint. Behind the checkpoint area was a long dark hallway lined with guards in ankle-length black robes over black armor. Campbell saw a battle turret built into the stone at each corner of the hallway entrance. Each turret had a heavy cannon that was pointed at the elevator. Campbell was quick to move out of the line of fire.

"General Arnold, the Master is ready to see you and Commander Campbell," said a voice from the ceiling. "Please step down to the viewing area."

Campbell glanced around for the origin of the voice, but only saw viewing cameras and remote cannons in the ceiling. The cannons were all pointed at him.

"This way, Campbell," Arnold said. He started across the chamber to the hall with his footsteps echoing off the stone walls.

Campbell hurried after Arnold down the hallway. As he walked by what he counted as fifty guards standing at attention along the walls, he saw they carried rifles similar to the one that had killed Koko. Great sorrow returned to his heart over Koko's death.

This place is more heavily guarded then a military fortress, Campbell thought. *What kind of attack is the Master expecting?*

They came to the end of the hallway, and entered another empty chamber similar to the one they'd left. Campbell noticed the ceiling was just as heavily armed, and all the cannons were pointed at him. He took a step forward and saw that the cannons followed his movement.

"Please step through the doorway in front of you, Commander," said the same voice from the ceiling.

Campbell examined the chamber again, but did not move.

"Aren't you coming with me?" he asked Arnold.

"No, this is a private viewing," Arnold said solemnly.

Damn, he sounds almost jealous. "Viewing?"

"You have nothing to fear, Campbell," Arnold said. "The Master has no form in the physical sense that you would recognize. You are going into a small soundproof room where the Master will communicate with you. Now, move along."

Campbell was confused, but intrigued and just a little anxious. He moved to the single door in the center of the front wall. He stepped forward. The black metal door slid open. He stepped inside a tiny room with the same black shining walls as the chambers and hallway. The room was completely empty. There were no weapons, no viewing cameras, and the walls were bare.

THREE

The door closed behind Campbell. He was enclosed in complete darkness. Fear swelled in his chest. He wasn't alone. He felt a presence, a tremendous evil, beating on his mind and his body from every direction with great power like nothing he'd ever felt.

In his tremendous fear, Campbell panicked. He found he couldn't move. His feet felt cemented to the floor. His arms hung useless at his sides. He wanted to scream, but discovered his voice wouldn't obey.

In the depths of his panicked mind, Campbell heard whispering and hissing that sounded like faint voices that weren't his own. While he couldn't make out the words, he knew he was being questioned, studied, and probed. He found the pain of the voices unbearable. He knew he was answering every question, revealing his entire life, his every secret, with the plea to stop the pain. His every fiber was laid bare before the Master.

He lost all sense of time and space in the void of his personal hell. Suddenly the agony was gone. He collapsed on the cold stone floor a whimpering child bathed in sweat. Abruptly, a new emotion arose in his mind. One that was soothing, forgiving, and euphoric.

Campbell heard the whispering in his mind again. At first he panicked, but the whispers continued and filled him with a feeling of happiness and wellbeing. As his body relaxed, he even felt his lips spread in a smile.

Just as suddenly, the euphoria was stripped away. His mind and body erupted in agony as if his body had been dropped into molten lava. The whispers turned into screams in his mind that seemed like daggers ripping apart his brain. Yet he understood the screams. He was being warned. He was being told that if he ever betrayed his new Master, his immortal body would suffer this agony for eternity.

The pain stopped. Campbell vaguely heard the door open. He was dimly aware of Arnold leading him back to his cell in silence. His mind was shattered. He was unable to articulate a single thought. He passed out on his cot.

XV

BATTLE STRATEGIES

ONE

Campbell awoke in complete darkness. At first his body clenched in pain and fear as the memory of his meeting with the Master returned. Then he realized he was back in his cell. His tensed muscles eventually relaxed, but his mind continued to race. He lay on his bed for a long time reliving his incredibly terrible experience and thinking of the awesome power that was about to be unleashed on the unsuspecting world.

God help us, he thought. *I have met the true Lord of Hades.*

He was surprised that, despite the warning of eternal agony for betraying the Master, he could contemplate the Master's destruction. But he quickly discovered this was a futile exercise. He didn't know or comprehend what the Master was, or if It could even be destroyed.

His thoughts were disturbed when the cell door opened and Arnold appeared.

"Don't you ever knock?" Campbell moaned as he sat up.

"I see you've recovered from your interview with the Master," Arnold said, and entered the cell. "An interesting experience, wasn't it?"

"That's putting it mildly."

Arnold nodded slowly as if he were contemplating Campbell's reaction.

"The Master has learned a great deal from Its interaction with you. Most interesting was your history and physical make-up after the Yamamoto experiment. Although we now understand what you are, and what you're capable of, the Master was unable to determine how it was accomplished. Apparently you don't understand it yourself, and the Master was unable to determine the details of your transformation.

"More important is that the Master has determined you're satisfactory for our operation. It has approved the plan to go ahead with you as the field commander of our forces."

Campbell nodded with resignation and renewed depression. "Why me? Why don't you, or some other commander, lead your forces?"

Arnold started to pace the cell. Campbell noticed he left the cell door open and there were no guards.

"Part of the Master's abilities is that It is psychic," Arnold said. "It can see the future, or at least part of it. Have you ever read the Bible?"

"I'm a historian, but I never really studied the Bible. I've never seen anything in the galaxy that supports an all-powerful god."

"Well," Arnold said slowly, "the Master foresees an apocalyptic end of the Earth soon, very soon. Yet It claims It doesn't know the method. The Bible says that evil will rise from this destruction and control the planet."

"And the Master sees Itself as the leader of this evil, huh?" Campbell said, with a small smile of disbelief.

"Exactly. Once the old order is destroyed, the Master has foreseen that It will rise from the chaos, organize the survivors, and control Earth under Its central rule."

"People have been foreseeing the end of the world as long as there have *been* people," Campbell said. "What makes you think now is the time? And what about the current leaders? Some of them will survive to fight you."

"Oh, but they won't," Arnold said. "We're going to kill the most powerful leaders now so there isn't anyone left to organize the survivors. That's the plan you're going to help put into motion."

"You still haven't answered my question: Why me?" Campbell asked, disregarding Arnold's statements as rubbish.

"Besides your excellent military leadership in the past, the Master has foreseen that you and a woman will be leaders in the new world order. Rather than allow you to rise to power against It, the Master has decided to control you both now."

"Why not just kill me rather than take a chance?" Campbell asked. *I don't believe any of this. The Master is using Arnold. He doesn't even know the Master's real plans.* Still, Campbell played along to see where it went, and to learn more of Arnold's plans with the hope of discovering a weakness.

"That would have been my choice," Arnold said, "but the Master thinks you'll be a great asset who'll lead our forces to victory and assist It in controlling the post-apocalyptic world."

"What makes the Master believe that I won't be able to defeat Its control over me and find a method of destroying It?"

Arnold didn't say anything for a moment. Campbell got the impression that this was at least one of Arnold's concerns, if not the Master's.

"The Master has not seen Its own end," Arnold finally said. "Personally, I believe It can't. It thinks that since It cannot see an end, that there isn't one. It believes that It is indestructible."

Campbell immediately saw major flaws in the Master. It was a trait that he'd seen throughout history in all dictators who had tried to take over the world: vanity and the belief that they couldn't be defeated.

"Forgive my ignorance," Campbell said, "but didn't the Bible also say something about the second coming of Christ to counter the antichrist?"

Arnold blew out his cheeks. "Look, Campbell, I don't believe in this biblical crap any more than you do. I just do as I'm told."

"Just another toady licking his master's boots, huh, Arnold?" he asked sarcastically.

Arnold's cheeks burned with rage.

Ow, hit a sore point with that one.

"No more than you, Campbell," Arnold said hotly. "Now follow me. We're going down to the military strategy room to discuss our plan of attack and your part in it."

TWO

Arnold was silent as Campbell followed him thoughtfully through the well-guarded halls to the strategy room. His most immediate concern was the apocalyptic end of the Earth that the Master had predicted. How was it going to happen, and when?

From what Campbell had gathered from Arnold, if the end of the world did happen, it wasn't going to be caused by something coming from the moon base. Neither did he think it would come from something the people of Earth did to themselves either on purpose or by accident. There were simply too many safeguards in place for that to happen. *Of course, anything is possible,* he thought.

The other thing that concerned him deeply was Penelope. She was an ever-present thought in his mind. He was worried about what Arnold had said—that the Master had predicted that a man and a woman would be leaders in the new world. It had predicted that he was that man. He could only assume that the woman was Penelope.

"Can I see Penelope Preston?" he asked.

Arnold laughed. Campbell got a sinking feeling in the pit of his stomach.

"She's with the Master now," Arnold said.

Fear surged through Campbell's body. *Her incredible body might survive the Master's torture undamaged, but her vulnerable mind will never withstand Its mental onslaught.*

"Don't worry, Campbell. She's safe for the moment. Like I told you, the Master believes that a man and a woman will be a key to Its successful rise to power. It believes Penelope is that woman. As long as It continues to believe that, and you do what you're told, Penelope Preston will be treated like a queen around here."

There's something false in Arnold's statement, Campbell thought. *Was that a tone of envy in his voice? Does Arnold see us as a threat—his replacement? Will Arnold try to eliminate us to save his position of power with the Master?*

They reached a huge double door that was heavily guarded. He noticed, like all the doors in the complex, it was unmarked. He figured this was for security reasons, but he wondered how anyone found their way around the complex.

They entered into the large, well-lit, three-tiered room. Campbell noticed it was similar to other military strategy rooms in which he'd been. There were twenty-to-thirty technicians and military personnel in black uniforms seated at or crowding around communication and computer centers. The technicians were engrossed in their intense activities while calling back and forth at each other with commands or giving instructions into their communication devices. Campbell saw what all the agitation was about when he glanced up at the three huge monitors covering the front wall before the consoles.

The monitors showed different areas of the small urban Earth-like city that he'd seen upon arriving at the moon base. The city was a chaos of simulated fighting between Arnold's creatures and human soldiers in environmental suits. Men and creatures packed the scenes while struggling in hand-to-hand combat, firing harmless light-ray weapons, or simply standing around watching.

"We're running simulated battles for an attack of an earthly urban environment right now," Arnold said. "We've run thousands of simulations on our computers for the best method of attacking areas of any type. My army has been training in our mock city for the last year and a half. You'll be leading some of the best-trained troops ever assembled into battle."

"Troops? You call those things troops?" Campbell asked sarcastically.

"Campbell, they're the best fighting force you'll ever find. They live only to fight, and die fighting."

"Yes, but can you control them?" asked Ulf Larsson as he stepped up behind Campbell and Arnold.

Campbell whirled at the sound of Larsson's mechanical voice.

"Ah, Campbell, I want you to meet your second-in-command. He's . . .," Arnold started to say.

"You bastard!" Campbell screamed. He lunged at Larsson growling like a wild beast.

Larsson leaped back in surprise. Campbell brought up a right hook into Larsson's stomach with inhuman force. Larsson doubled over with an explosive groan of pain. Campbell drove his knee into Larsson's metal and bone forehead with enough force to flip Larsson's heavy cyborg body over and send him crashing to the floor on his back. He was on Larsson in an instant with his powerful hands wrenching at Larsson's throat in a death grip.

"Campbell, no!" Arnold yelled.

Campbell felt Arnold's scrawny hands on his huge shoulders desperately trying to yank him off Larsson. A terrible pain electrified his mind and body as he struggled to disobey Arnold. Insane rage to kill the man who'd betrayed Penelope and Koko won over his agony. He continued to throttle Larsson's cybernetic neck.

"Campbell, stop!" Arnold screamed in Campbell's ear.

Campbell continued to pummel Larsson with a single mindedness that obscured all else but seeing Larsson dead. But as hard as he squeezed with his powerful grip, he couldn't crush Larsson's bot neck. As he glared into Larsson's mismatched eyes and gleaming metal teeth, Campbell thought he detected a smile in Larsson's expression.

"Ah!" Campbell screamed. He felt crushing pain as Larsson reached up with his artificial hand and grabbed his chest. It was as if Larsson was trying to rip away his huge chest muscles to tear out his wildly beating heart. He released Larsson's neck and began to pound Larsson's head with little effect.

Larsson heaved upward and threw Campbell off his chest. He landed heavily on his back. Larsson was on him immediately. Campbell was amazed at the weight of Larsson's bot body. It pinned him to the floor like a frail insect. He struggled for a brief moment, but knew he was defeated. He glared up to see the smug, disfigured smile remained on Larsson's face.

"Don't try that again, Campbell," Larsson whispered.

"Guards, guards!" Arnold yelled.

Campbell raised his hands in surrender.

Arnold appeared over Campbell, his beady eyes flaring in anger. "Have you calmed down enough for us to let you up, Campbell?"

Campbell glared at Arnold with enough hatred for Arnold to retreat a step.

"Let him stand, Larsson," Arnold said. "Guards, stay out of reach, but keep your rifles pointed at his head."

Larsson heaved himself off Campbell. Burt slowly got to his feet, still winded with exertion and pain. He continued to glare hatefully at Arnold.

"Remember, Campbell, it's not only your life that's at stake here," Arnold said. "Any more outbursts like that or any sign of disobedience, and Penelope Preston will suffer. I think you know what kind of pain the Master can inflict. Do you understand?"

Campbell glared at Arnold for a long moment. "Yes, sir," he muttered.

"That's better, Commander. Now shake hands with your second-in-command."

Campbell turned his glare on Larsson, but finally did what he was told.

"By the way, Larsson's your bodyguard as well," Arnold said.

Campbell huffed and turned away, but he thought Arnold had made a good choice of bodyguards if he wanted him alive. Larsson wasn't as powerful as George, but he figured he was quicker and a hell of a lot more intelligent.

At least he's part human. Too bad he doesn't have any human morals, Campbell thought.

"Gentlemen, if you'll follow me please, we'll discuss our general plan of attack," Arnold said, and waved off Campbell's guards.

THREE

Arnold moved off to the right, down the stairs of the strategy room. Campbell turned to Larsson to let him pass first. He didn't like the idea of having the murderous Larsson behind him.

"No, after you, Commander," Larsson said. "Superiors first."

"I see this is going to be a long, loving relationship," Campbell muttered, and followed Arnold.

"More than you know," Larsson whispered.

What in Hades does that mean? Campbell wondered.

He followed Arnold into a small, windowed room off to the right of the main strategy area. After he and Larsson entered, the door closed behind them. Arnold waved to the chairs surrounding a large black-metal conference table with inlaid monitors, communications and computer controls. Campbell also noted a large monitor on the back wall.

He took up a side chair at the table while Larsson went to the other side to sit opposite him. Arnold plopped himself in the seat at the head of the table opposite the wall monitor. He nimbly typed in some commands on a keyboard. The monitor lit up with a detailed three-dimensional map of a military base. Campbell recognized it immediately.

"Fort Knox! You plan to attack Fort Knox!" Campbell said with amazement. "You're even crazier than I thought!"

"That's right, Campbell. We plan to attack Fort Knox, and you're going to lead us to victory," Arnold said with a smile.

Campbell glanced at Larsson to see him glaring at Arnold with an equal expression of surprise on his disfigured face. Arnold glanced back and forth between them with a grin.

"Why the astonished expressions, gentlemen?" Arnold asked. "It's the perfect opportunity. In five days, the North American War Games will commence at Fort Knox. This year I got us invited to participate in an attack game on an urban environment."

"You're a lunatic, Arnold," Campbell said. "I was trained in armored warfare at Fort Knox for the Yarv War. It's the most modern military facility in the world. They design and test their latest weapons there. Only the most elite soldiers will be there for the war games."

"Exactly, Campbell, and all the top military staff will be there as well observing the proceedings. If we can defeat the forces at Fort Knox, and eliminate the leadership, we'll basically have paralyzed the effective abilities of the North American fighting force."

Campbell was stunned. *The plan is insane, but it also shows a sign of genius. If Arnold can take over Fort Knox, not only will he have access to the most modern weapons in the world, he'll control a strategic foothold in North America from which to launch attacks on the rest of the world.*

"How do you plan to defeat their advanced weaponry and elite soldiers?" Larsson asked.

"The plan's simple, gentlemen. All the forces but ours will be armed with nonlethal weapons for the war games. We plan to attack with lethal weapons and destroy their forces before they can be rearmed. One of our first priority targets are the weapons depots. Once we have control of those depots, they'll have no choice but to surrender or die."

"What's to stop the leaders for calling for help once they see what's happening?" Campbell asked.

"All the leaders will be in the command bunker observing the games. I will also be in the bunker with a few of my assistants. When the time is appropriate, we'll take control of the bunker to ensure no one escapes and no assistance arrives."

Campbell nodded, as he could see how this could work. He'd participated in the games before and knew they were for training purposes only. The soldiers participating would never expect a real assault, and most of them were inexperienced in actual combat conditions. Once they were leaderless, it was likely that the inexperienced soldiers would panic under the threat of live ammunition and death.

"What about these creatures of yours?" Larsson asked. "As soon as they appear, someone will set off the alarms."

"Our forces will be made up of approximately four thousand human or human-like soldiers that'll start the initial assaults in case anyone wants to make an initial inspection of the troops. Once the battle is underway, *if* I feel it's necessary, we'll unleash the creatures from a second carrier force."

"Four thousand troops?" Campbell asked with surprise. "There'll be at least fifty-to-sixty thousand troops there from other units performing in various games. Do you really have so much confidence in your forces? I haven't seen anything here on the moon base that could defeat an armored division."

"You've seen very little of our secret arsenal, Campbell, but even you've seen the power of a small sand squid in the arena. There are many surprises we can unleash on our unsuspecting enemy."

"He's right, Commander. I personally saw one of those giant squids destroy a full-size military clipper with ease," Larsson said, and described the attack of his clipper in the crater.

Rage flowed through Campbell's heart when he thought of how Larsson had endangered Penelope's life in their confrontation with the squid. He realized she was damned lucky to be alive, yet he remained tightlipped. Instead, he concentrated on poking holes in Arnold's plan.

"Remember," Arnold said, "even their hover tanks are training vehicles that will be armed with only light rays, smoke, and paint munitions. Their armor is defenseless against some of our creatures."

"What about the air forces?" Campbell asked.

"These exercises are to be carried out with little air support other than small medical clippers, but you know that already, Campbell. Like I said, there's much you and Larsson don't know about our forces."

"If you already have all this planned out, why do you need Larsson and me?" Campbell asked.

"As I told you, Campbell, your participation was not my idea. The Master insisted on your presence as a method of cementing the relationship between you and It. Once you have been introduced as a leader of the forces that will destroy Fort Knox, there will be no going back for you. You'll be considered a traitor."

"Like the rest of you," Campbell muttered. He chanced to glance over at Larsson. He was surprised by the bitter anger in Larsson's horrid features. He didn't think Larsson was faking his intense emotion.

"The other reason for your participation, Campbell, is because you've trained at Fort Knox. You know the complex and their training methods. We don't know the strategies we'll face. We need your wartime leadership experience during combat to lead our troops during the chaos of battle."

"You have a lot of confidence in me, my abilities, and your troops, Arnold. What makes you think I won't lead your troops into defeat?"

"Like you could, Campbell. I have confidence in you, because if you fail, you know what awaits you and Penelope Preston. Even if your own eternal hell wasn't enough to convince you that you must succeed, the Master has predicted our eventual victory, and It has never been wrong,"

Based on his tone, I don't think Arnold really believes that, Campbell thought. *Why did he say* eventual *victory?*

"Give me one example of what the all-powerful Master has predicted that's come true," Campbell said sarcastically. "It didn't even help you find where I was hiding for the last two years,"

"Oh, but the Master did lead me to you. It told me of your relationship with Goro Sen. There're many predictions It has made that wouldn't make sense to you. It did predict that you and Penelope Preston would be brought here, and It predicted that Ulf Larsson was a traitor. I'm convinced the Master can accurately see the future."

"I am not a traitor!" Larsson shouted with fury. He pounded on the metal table so hard Arnold jumped and let out a high-pitched squeal.

Campbell ignored Larsson's outbreak and Arnold's cowardly reaction while considering something Arnold had said.

"It might be that your master can see events in the future like many have been able to do in the past, but can it accurately read *what* It sees in Its visions? Future seers are notorious for misreading signs in favor of their own beliefs."

"I guess you'll have to stick around to find out," Arnold said. "But enough of this. We have four days to familiarize you with the forces you'll be leading, and develop plans of attack based on what we know."

"Four days is hardly enough time to prepare an attack against the most powerful force in the world," Campbell said, "but why all the preparation if you already know you'll win?"

Arnold gave him an evil glare of frustration. "There's always some chance for failure. We need to keep our losses to a minimum. This is only the first of many battles."

Campbell was thinking again about Arnold's lack of confidence when Larsson asked something he'd been wondering about.

"What about the other nations of the world? They aren't going to stand aside for you to take control of the planet."

"Those plans don't concern you and Campbell," Arnold said dismissively. "Now, let's review our plan for Fort Knox, and familiarize you with your forces."

Campbell didn't like being kept out of the entire plan of world conquest, but he decided there wasn't anything he could do about that for the moment.

Damn us all to hell for what we are about to do, Campbell thought with dismal resignation.

FOUR

For the next few hours, Campbell sat uncomfortably in his conference room chair while being continually amazed as Arnold went over the plan of attack and the forces he would be leading. He was terrified to discover that his force would mainly consist of humans and similar creatures, yet they would also include different types of ogres, trolls, squids, and demons like George.

What surprised and frightened Campbell the most was when Arnold introduced his deadly dinosaur creatures. Arnold wore a smile of pure evil and pride as he showed images on the main monitor of mutated beasts that hadn't walked the Earth in millions of years.

There were triceratopses, raptors, and pterodactyls, but they were all mutated in more deadly ways than Campbell had seen in illustrations or museum reconstructions. All of the dinosaurs had heavy scale-like armor for skin except for the pterodactyls. The pterodactyls continued to have huge bat-like wings and elongated heads with sharp wicked beaks. Yet they also had oversized legs with nasty-looking clawed feet that Arnold claimed could tear through armor.

Campbell thought the tank-like triceratopses appeared unstoppable. He figured their heavy armor plating, three massive horns surrounded by an armored head crown, and spiked tails could take on even the heaviest armored ground vehicles with no problems. He hated to think what kind of damage a gang of man-sized and lightning quick raptors could inflict on ground troops with their razor-sharp talons. He wondered if these creatures' intelligence and aggressive personalities had been enhanced to fit their horrifying appearance. He was sure they had been.

Finally, Arnold changed the image to the most terrifying creature Campbell had seen yet. He gawked with awe and fear.

"What is that?" he whispered.

"The ultimate destroyer," Arnold said with a broad smile on his weasel-like features. "I can see you're impressed. It's a spinosaurus. At over twenty meters in length and eleven metric tons in weight, it's the greatest carnivore to ever walk the face of the Earth. It's even bigger and badder than a tyrannosaurus rex."

As Campbell leaned forward to examine the image of the terrifying creature, he immediately noted the spinosaurus had a similar body style to the tyrannosaurus rex, with two exceptions. While the spinosaurus walked on two muscular legs similar to a T. rex, it had two long and powerful arms. At the end of the arms were wicked-looking three-fingered claws with long talons for tearing apart victims. The second exception was the huge spiked sail along the spine.

"Notice the long and low head of the spinosaurus," Arnold said. "It's similar to a crocodile's. Crocodiles have the most powerful bite force of any modern animal, and this creature has a mouthful of razor-sharp teeth that are thirty-six centimeters long."

"Lord in Hades!" Campbell muttered. "How do you plan on controlling those things?"

"Well," Arnold said, "you've hit on a sore point there. We can't control them. They destroy everything in their path including friend or foe, and we have no way of recapturing them once they're loose."

"In other words, they'll be loose in the world forever once you release them," Campbell said.

"Yes, and to make matters worse, they're asexual and amazingly reproductive. We could be unleashing the resurgence of the dinosaur age," Arnold said with a smile.

I don't see anything worth smiling about, Campbell thought. *Those things could kill millions of people. What am I getting involved with here?*

"Then why use them? Why even create them?" Larsson asked.

"They were originally created as an experiment," Arnold answered. "Having created a few of them, we found they were a great crowd pleaser in the arena, so we created more and more of them. Eventually, the Master integrated them into our plan in case all else failed. They'll only be used as a last resort."

Campbell thought, *I wonder how earnest Arnold is about only unleashing these horrors as a last resort. At what point will he feel it necessary? I'll bet he releases them whether the battle is won or lost. It only adds to Arnold's desire for world chaos.*

"What other terrible surprises do you have in your arsenal?" he asked.

Arnold smiled and pointed eagerly to the monitor like a child showing off his latest toy. "I saved the best for last."

Campbell reluctantly turned back to the monitor and saw a dim image of a nearly translucent cloud. "What is it? I don't really see anything?"

"That cloud is similar to how the Master often appears. Naturally, that isn't the Master, and doesn't possess all the Master's abilities and mental powers. But these things can inflict the same kind of mental torture on the human mind that you experienced during your interaction with the Master.

"The biggest difference between them and the Master is that while the Master can withdraw from human interaction without inflicting much damage to the human mind, these cannot. They take possession of the victim's mind and consume their mental energy until the person dies in agony. Then they move on to the next victim. They seem to have an unquenchable appetite."

Campbell was stunned and speechless.

"That's not the worst thing about these clouds," Arnold continued. "They're uncontrollable and indestructible as far as we know. They're captured when they're created in a controlled environment and not released until they're needed."

"Then how do you get them to attack anything?" Larsson asked quietly.

"They appear to be attracted to the electro-kinetic energy of living beings. Brain impulses from human beings send them into a feeding frenzy and they attack."

Campbell remained quiet while he contemplated his own survival on the Fort Knox battlefield, and the fate of the world if these things were allowed to roam free.

"Come, come, Campbell," Arnold said. "I'm sure you'll lead our soldiers successfully in battle and none of these creations will ever have to be released. I only showed you these things to reinforce your desire for victory. I can see from your expression that you understand what will happen to you if things don't go our way."

Yeah, I'm going to die, Campbell thought grimly.

Larsson finally turned away from the monitor and said to Arnold, "Why not simply ask the world leaders to surrender? I think if you show them the horrors that you're about to unleash that they might listen."

Even Campbell knew this plea was lame, but he hated Larsson less for suggesting it. Arnold just laughed.

"Larsson, even you can't be so stupid to believe the world leaders would capitulate under a terrorist threat. They must be shown the real dangers of our forces by example. That's one of the purposes of this Fort Knox attack."

"Even then I doubt they'll surrender, Arnold, and you know it," Campbell said. "You're hoping for an all-out war and the destruction of the world governments."

Arnold tuned to Campbell and nodded. "Now you're beginning to see the whole picture," he smiled. "Let's move on to the strategies of our attack that we've run in simulations and are testing on our mock city at this very moment."

FIVE

Arnold led them through various scenarios while Campbell and Larsson occasionally commented on the feasibility of and problems with the strategies of attack. Campbell kept most of his opinions to himself, but he was surprised at Larsson's intelligent input and his ability as a tactician. He realized Larsson would've made an excellent field officer, and that Arnold hadn't made his choice of Larsson as his second-in-command on a whim.

Campbell was also surprised with the knowledge Arnold showed of Fort Knox from what he could remember of the facility. He knew the fort was one of the most secure and fortified facilities on Earth, and yet Arnold had specific data about the whole complex.

"Arnold, how do you come by such detailed information about what's going on at the fort?" he asked.

Arnold took a moment to answer. "You were very outspoken when you retired from the military about the corruption and idiocy of its leaders," he said. "Nothing has changed since you left. In fact, it might even be worse now than it was during the Yarv War. Not all the military commanders are happy with the current leadership and their status. There're many that would welcome a change."

Campbell went silent while deep in thought. Arnold continued with his plan of attack. Campbell glanced up with the feeling that eyes were upon him. Larsson was staring intently at him with a thoughtful expression. He couldn't imagine what Larsson was thinking, so he returned his attention to Arnold's presentation.

"Any questions?" Arnold asked when he finished.

Campbell thought there were many faults in the plan. Mostly, he worried about how he and Penelope were going to survive this ordeal. He kept quiet as he examined the tabletop.

As he thought about Arnold's strategies, he knew there were too many variables out of his control. There was too much they didn't know about the opposing forces, their weapons, and the type of countermeasures that would be used against them. He felt Larsson examining him once again, but he didn't look up.

"Excellent," Arnold said, apparently taking Campbell's silence as agreement with the strategy parameters. "Now, if we can all move back out to the situation room, you can watch the rest of the battle taking place in the mock city. You can witness a truly elite fighting force at work."

Arnold eagerly got up, and led them back out into the main room. They took up command seats in an area at the top and back of the strategy room, where they could see everything that was happening in the battle on the three large monitors on the wall.

Arnold rambled on nonstop like a child at show-and-tell while they watched the action unfold on the monitors. Campbell acknowledged Arnold when spoken to, but he offered no advice. The battle taking place before him was like nothing he'd ever witnessed. The combatants' movements were slow and clumsy in their environmental suits and the low-lunar gravity. The thrusting attacks seemed uncoordinated and without leadership.

Often soldiers on the same side could be seen dropping their weapons and starting to fight hand-to-hand amongst themselves. Campbell was horrified to see that frequently these small vicious conflicts resulted in the death of one or both of the combatants.

Campbell thought: *What sort of chaos is going to result when these soldiers are given real weapons and put in real battle situations? Will my own troops, who don't even know me, kill me and then desert the battle?*

I wonder how many of these soldiers are fighting for the Master and Arnold under their own free will. What's the soldiers' reward for fighting? It certainly doesn't appear to be honor or patriotism. What's stopping these unwilling soldiers from deserting to roam free on Earth as soon as they land at Fort Knox?

Campbell was jolted by a loud bell. He glanced up at the monitors to see most of the fighting stop. A few small scuffles continued that appeared to be more personal than a coordinated effort, but most of the soldiers began to return to the complex.

"Well, Campbell, what did you think? Have you ever witnessed a better fighting force?" Arnold asked with childlike excitement that demanded approval.

"Oh, they're good fighters," Campbell said. *In a bar brawl.*

"I knew you'd see things my way," Arnold said with enthusiasm. "Tomorrow you and Larsson will be out there as well. You'll practice the plans we've discussed and fine tune our effort. I'm sure that with you at the helm our forces will be unbeatable."

Arnold got up and gestured Campbell and Larsson toward the exit. As he did so, Campbell glanced up at the monitors. A new force was exiting the complex and heading for the mock city.

"Who are they?" he asked while pointing at the monitor.

"Oh, don't worry about them. We're practicing twenty-four hours a day, since time is of the essence."

Arnold pushed them from the room in a hurry. Arnold's rush made Campbell wonder: *Is the Fort Knox attack the only assault that's going to take place? Reason says that it's not. I saw much more than four thousand troops when I was in the arena. Where are the other troops going, and who are they going to attack?*

Campbell was lost in thought as Larsson and Arnold escorted him back to his cell. He said nothing. He noticed that Larsson appeared equally thoughtful.

"Goodnight, gentlemen, I will see you in the morning." Larsson said when they reached Campbell's cell. He slowly ambled away without waiting for a response.

Campbell watched Larsson leave while wondering where Larsson spent his spare time. Arnold ignored Larsson as he clapped Campbell on the back like a close friend.

"Goodnight, Campbell. I'm glad to see you cooperating with our efforts. I feel much better about our chances now that we have you on our side."

There's that lack of confidence again in the Master's prediction for victory, Campbell thought, before he turned to stare down at Arnold. "Did I ever have a choice?"

"Don't think of it that way, Burt. Think of it as the future. You have a great future ahead of you on our side. Your experience is invaluable to us."

"Yeah," Campbell said without enthusiasm. He turned to enter his cell. "That's why I'm still locked in this cell."

"Ah, Campbell?" Arnold asked with a wide grin on his rodent features. "How would you like some companionship tonight? We have pleasure creatures beyond your wildest dreams."

Campbell whirled to glare down at Arnold with malice in his black eyes. "Arnold, don't ever put me in the same slimy category as you."

Arnold's face reddened with anger or embarrassment. He huffed, and punched the button to close the door to Campbell's cell.

Campbell lay on his uncomfortable cot for hours after Arnold was gone. He thought long and hard about his situation and the possible outcomes. Most of all, he anguished over Penelope and wondered how she was faring.

I wonder what the hell Penelope did with the dogs. I'm sure they're someplace safe stuffing their furry faces. Lord, I miss them.

Eventually, he fell into a dreamless, uneasy sleep.

XVI

MEET THE TOADIES

ONE

Campbell was awakened by the noise of clanking metal accompanied by the stinging smell of rotting meat and low-grade acid. A clumsy human orderly barged into his cell carrying a metal tray before setting it on the cold floor and leaving without a word. Campbell peered down at the tray with sleep-crusted eyes. He was repulsed to see another stenchy breakfast of some kind of dried meat and mud-thick coffee. *Damn, this stuff isn't fit to feed George,* he thought, but his stomach growled with hunger. He dressed and gnawed on his putrid cold coffee while contemplating the Fort Knox attack. He shook his weary head. The whole idea was insane.

"Good morning, Campbell," Arnold said with too much enthusiasm when he opened Burt's cell.

Campbell wondered: *Is he on stimulants or something?*

"Morning," he mumbled, not finding anything good in the new day.

"The first thing we'll do this morning is meet the sub-commanders that will be leading your forces," Arnold said while leading him back to the strategy room. Campbell tugged at a piece of dried meat, praying he didn't break a tooth.

As Campbell entered the already bustling strategy room, he glanced up at the activity on the monitors. The war exercises were already in full progress. The mock city was a beehive of simulated and not-so-simulated combat. The technicians in the strategy room were still running all over, shouting back and forth, as if they'd never left.

All this activity only confirmed Campbell's belief that Fort Knox wasn't the only point of attack. He decided there were going to be strategic attacks all over the world. It was the only way the Master could eliminate all the world leaders and their governments.

He followed Arnold down into the small side room they'd used the day before. Two men and a woman were already seated silently at the table. Larsson was brooding in his usual seat while wearing an expression of even greater disdain than normal. They all glanced up as he and Arnold entered.

"Commander Campbell, I'd like to introduce you to your immediate support staff," Arnold said.

This can't be true! "Don't bother. I know everyone," Campbell said in a scornful, repulsed tone.

He walked up to the man who was seated closest to him. The man rose with a crooked smile on his full, unshaven face.

"Marcus Kingsley, when did they let you out of prison?" Campbell asked the balding man, who was of average height, had a muscular build, and wore eyeglasses over his dark, round eyes. Kingsley was the only man Campbell knew who still wore eyeglasses to correct his vision. The rumor was he was terrified of undergoing the painless and routine transplant surgery necessary to get eye implants. Kingsley was a coward. He tentatively extended his hand to Campbell in wary greeting. Campbell ignored it.

"General Arnold had me released when I was transferred here last year from New Detroit's death row," Kingsley said. He broadened his smile of large, crooked teeth.

Campbell gave Arnold a nasty glance. "This man was one of Bohdan's cronies. How could you turn him loose again?"

"Well, number one, he did lead forces in the Yarv War, so he has leadership experience . . .," Arnold said.

"Yeah! He led his troops to their deaths, and then ran away! He was running so fast it took Koko Sinopa a year to catch him!"

Arnold ignored Campbell's interruption.

"Number two, Kingsley has great motivation for joining our cause. He hates the military and he was on death row, where he'll return if he fails you."

Campbell huffed in disgust. He turned back around to glare down at Kingsley.

"I was so sorry to learn of Sinopa's demise," Kingsley said sarcastically with his ugly grin.

Campbell swung at Kingsley so fast that Kingsley had no time to react. Campbell's fist hit Kingsley hard enough to knock him spread-eagled across the tabletop, unconscious. Kingsley was no longer smiling.

Campbell turned his burning eyes on his other two sub-commanders, who were staring at him with wide-eyed terror. "What about these two, Lydia Lewinski and Brent Garrett? They're both mercenaries!"

"I served you well in the Yarv War," Lydia said in the husky voice of a longtime hemp smoker. She leaped to her feet with a look of brave defiance to confront Campbell. Her squinting bloodshot eyes told him she was probably high.

"That depends on your definition of serving well, Lewinski." Campbell said to the tall robust woman with chopped black hair, dark brown eyes, and a bloody dagger tattooed on each of her temples. "You were disobedient, and I'd say just a little overzealous with your killing methods. I think you killed more of our troops than theirs with your crazy shooting sprees."

Lydia's cheeks flushed scarlet as she glared back at Campbell, but she said nothing. She plopped down in her seat again with a disgruntled huff while staring at Kingsley's prone form on the table.

Larsson reached across the table and slapped Kingsley's bruised cheek a few times in an attempt to either revive him or just beat him some more. Campbell noticed that Larsson's lips were curled in a disfigured smile. Kingsley didn't notice anything.

"And Garrett!" Campbell pointed at a wiry and short bird-faced man with a scruffy black beard and long black hair. "He's totally unfit to lead troops into battle. He's a backstabber who runs away at the first sign of trouble."

Garrett seemed to shrink under the table at this accusation.

"Oh, don't worry, Garrett. I'm not going to hit you," Campbell said. "I'd have to catch you first!"

Larsson roared with mechanical laughter.

"Despite what you think, Campbell, these people have led our troops successfully in our battle trials," Arnold said. "They're well paid and motivated to succeed much the same way as you. They will not fail our efforts."

Campbell merely shook his head with disgust and resignation again. Kingsley started coming around with a pain-filled groan. Campbell leaned forward and hauled him off the table by his lapels. Kingsley cringed and whimpered at Campbell's brutal handling. He quickly retreated across the table to sit at Larsson's side.

Larsson leaned close to Kingsley. He gave him an evil grin with his horrid face before he said, "Boo!"

Kingsley squealed and quickly scurried to a seat away from Larsson.

Campbell sighed and faced the dysfunctional group at the table. "I'm warning you all now! If you don't follow my orders exactly and immediately from this moment forward, I will kill you without hesitation." He glanced around the table to ensure everyone face was turned toward him with the appropriate concern and seriousness.

I doubt I would do it, Campbell thought, *but it's good they believed me.*

"We will be facing some of the greatest forces ever assembled," Campbell said. "Any disobedience by any of you could mean failure and our deaths. I don't know what Arnold has threatened you with, but I guarantee you that I'm an even worse threat if you fail me. Is that understood?"

"Yes, sir!" Kingsley, Lewinski, and Garrett responded sharply in unison.

"That includes you, Larsson," Campbell said with authority.

"Yes, sir," Larsson said. He glared back at Campbell.

"Good," Arnold said. "I'm glad to see we all have an understanding and a working relationship."

Campbell huffed. He was angered to see the crooked smile return to Larsson's face.

TWO

"I received good news this morning," Arnold said. "The commander of Fort Knox has sent us our preliminary orders for the war games. Our forces will attack a fortified urban environment to capture a command post in the center of a mock city. The defending force will consist of ten thousand troops supporting light armor.

"These orders have played directly into our plans, since this is exactly what we've been training for. This means we can use our current simulations and tactics to determine the best method to reach our goals."

As Arnold said this, he pushed some buttons in the table and a colorful holographic model of the moon base mock city appeared on the table. Campbell could see tiny figures scrambling around the buildings in a training battle. He realized this was a virtual representation of what was occurring outside at that very moment. He was stunned that Arnold intended to attack a fortified army over twice the size of his own.

"As you can see," Arnold said, "under this current battle plan we split our forces to attack the city from all directions. This way, we can surround the enemy and annihilate them as we fight our way towards the center of the city."

Campbell was slowly shaking his head while he watched the holograph. The whole battle was a scene of chaos and mayhem that showed no coordination, direction, or leadership.

"You disagree with the plan, Campbell?" Arnold asked.

Campbell thought: *How much should I say to Arnold? If I say nothing, and allow him to continue by himself, it will lead to our defeat. But if Arnold is defeated, won't that lead to Penelope's death as well as my own?*

"Campbell?" Arnold asked again.

"Well," Campbell said slowly, "it goes against all military rationale to attack a fortified force under siege with less than ten times the number of soldiers as the defending force. If you wish to surround a force of ten thousand troops, I wouldn't attack with less than a hundred thousand. With only four thousand troops, I would avoid the enemy at all costs."

"That is not an option," Arnold said with an irritated expression.

"Then I would say that to attempt to surround a fortified enemy supported by light armor is insane." The comment caused Campbell some mental pain for calling Arnold insane, but he continued. "Yet if you insist on attacking, I would launch my main force against one location, and attack one of the enemy's flanks with a small diversionary force. Your odds of success would be much greater.

"The enemy will be forced to keep its forces spread out in defensive positions around the city in fear that you might be attacking from other directions. That way, you'll have nearly your entire force attacking only the small fraction of the enemy that's stationed on that side of the city. The odds for success are greater for reaching the center of the city without having to fight much of the enemy forces still defending other portions."

"Excellent, really excellent," Arnold said, beaming from ear to ear, "but I disagree. How will we keep enemy forces from escaping us and heading for the weapons depot if we don't surround and eliminate them?"

"I thought you only wanted to capture the command post with the fewest losses," Campbell said while shaking his head.

"Okay," Arnold said after a moment, "I suggest a compromise. We send small forces to the other three sides of the city to harass the enemy into maintaining their positions and prevent them from moving against the main force. That way we can keep their main force in the city and keep them from counter attacking toward the weapons depots."

Campbell still shook his head in useless disagreement. He knew that in real battle circumstances Arnold's small split forces, his forces, would be wiped out. Four thousand troops just weren't enough, and there were still too many unanswered variables.

"What is it now, Campbell?" Arnold asked.

"I never enter a battle without asking myself a few questions," Campbell said. "First, are our forces in complete accord with you, our leader, regarding the goals of the battle? Are they willing to die for you? Why should they follow me, a commander they don't even know, much less respect?"

"Because they'll die if they don't follow orders," Arnold said simply.

"What's to stop them from deserting and just disappearing when they reach Earth?"

"They wouldn't dare," Arnold smiled. "But we're prepared for the possibility of deserters. Don't worry. Your elite forces will be there, and they will fight for you."

He's a fool believing his forces will fight, Campbell thought. *They have nothing to fight for, and they're as undisciplined as spoiled children. But my concerns and strategies are useless. Nothing I say will dissuade Arnold.* Still, he continued on for his own edification. The more he knew, the better his chances of survival. "Do you know anything about the forces we will be fighting or their commanders?"

"No," Arnold said, starting to show some irritation, "but you said yourself all the military commanders are incompetent. That's why we picked you to lead our forces. I have great confidence in your abilities, Campbell."

"You only picked me because you had something you could use against me," Campbell said angrily. "There are still some excellent generals in the military. Even their sub-commanders are far better trained than these buffoons you've given me." He glared at those around the table. "What I'm saying is that without knowing anything about the commander or the forces we're facing, we could be heading into disaster. You must always know and respect your enemy. *You* show no respect for your opponent at all!"

"You worry too much," Arnold laughed. He dismissed Campbell's outburst with a wave of his hand. "Are you forgetting that the enemy will be armed with harmless laser-lights, while our forces will be carrying the most devastatingly lethal weapons?"

"No," Campbell said quietly, "but war is the art of deception. Be prepared to face some deception from your opponent."

"You know, Campbell," Arnold said in an equally quiet voice. "I'd say you were scared."

"You're damn right I'm scared. Not only am I scared of facing an unknown opposition unprepared, but I'm terrified of what's going to happen when this all goes wrong and you lose your temper. I'm terrified of how anyone will survive the battle when you unleash those uncontrollable creatures on the world."

"You'll just have to make sure that doesn't happen, won't you?" Arnold smiled insanely.

Campbell slumped and hung his head in frustration and defeat.

"Okay, let's move ahead," Arnold said. "Campbell, we'll try your strategy first and run a computer simulation of your attack plan to see how it works."

Arnold quickly went about inputting his battle strategy command parameters into the computer simulator and ran the mock battle at high speed on the tabletop holographic city. Campbell watched the simulated battle with a mixture of amusement and terror. Arnold had used insanely overoptimistic parameters that allowed Arnold's forces to sweep away the enemy with ease. There was little resistance and no unexpected variables.

The man really is a lunatic, Campbell thought miserably. *He has no concept of reality.*

"Your plan is a complete success, Campbell, thank you," Arnold said.

Campbell sagged with disgust, but Arnold didn't seem to notice.

"It's time to get out and test this plan on the field, people" Arnold said, and got up to leave. "We have three days to perfect it and plan for anything unforeseen."

As they filed out of the strategy room on their way to prepare for the simulated battle on the lunar landscape, Larsson pulled Campbell aside and away from the others' earshot.

"You showed some insightful thoughts and strategies back there," Larsson said. "I can see why you came back from the Yarv War such an honored commander."

Campbell was shocked by Larsson's compliment, but said, "Regardless of my knowledge and experience, you know we're all going to end up dead."

"Just stick close to me. I'll keep you alive," Larsson said with his disfigured smile before continuing down the hall.

Campbell remained behind, lost in thought. He was intrigued and confused by Larsson's words and motivations. The man was a fascinating combination of repulsive disfigurement and a lonely personal honor that didn't appear to have any love for the military or Arnold. Yet here he was fighting to destroy humanity.

Why does he want to keep me alive? Campbell wondered.

Arnold popped out of the strategy room with a gleam in his beady black eyes and a sinister smile on his weasel features. Campbell quickly scrambled after Larsson before Arnold could catch up to him.

XVII

STRENGTH AND HONOR?

ONE

It took Campbell and Larsson four long sunbaked hours outside trying to get all the wandering disorganized troops unified on the dusty
lunar plain before the mock city. To Campbell, their movements
seemed slow and tedious in their armored black environmental suits
and the low gravity.

First, they met the lieutenants under Captains Kingsley, Lewinski,
and Garrett. To Campbell, the lieutenants were a band of useless rab-
ble even more poorly trained and incompetent then their captains.
He glared at them in disgust while offering little encouragement. He
sought their fear and respect, not their friendship. Many were obviously dark-faced human-like creatures of limited intelligence. But he
was surprised when the troops showed some military discipline and
obeyed their commands—at least they didn't get into too many fights
while getting into formation.

Campbell formed his four thousand troops into four groups.
He and Larsson took command of the larger center group of fifteen
hundred troops directly in front of the city. Captain Lewinski covered his left flank and Garrett his right flank with a thousand troops
apiece. Kingsley was in command of the small diversionary force of
five hundred troops on the far left side of the city. Campbell figured
the less he saw of the bastard Kingsley, the better.

Campbell gazed across the desolate moon plain at the rank upon
rank of troops standing loosely in formation. The heads-up display on

the left side of his plasma helmet showed him a miniaturized overhead image of the battlefield and the overall casualty statistics generated by the central battle computer. Directly before his eyes were his weapons status, aiming device, and magnification vision that also showed the distance to the target. To the right of his view was his communications status. It contained images of the faces of Lewinski, Garrett and Kingsley, as well as their heart monitors so he could tell if they were dead or alive. He noted Garrett's heart was beating as fast as a hummingbird's.

As Campbell examined the line-by-line formations of semi-attentive troops, he was reminded of historical images of Roman legions preparing for conflict with a city under siege. His stomach churned with tension as he realized he'd never led such a large force of untrained and unruly troops. He also realized this could be his last command performance. He could easily get killed even in this simulated attack. Swallowing his nervous tension, he turned toward the mock city before him.

Now that he was so close to the city, he could see that it was merely a crude mock-up. The tall buildings were flimsily fabricated shams, their windows painted around shabbily cut holes. There were no cars on the elevated monorail system. The gardens were trampled stalks of some green plastic. The trees were two-dimensional fabrications. The whole scene appeared eerie, silent, and uninhabited on the gray, rocky landscape. A million stars twinkled overhead.

"Good luck," Larsson said at his side.

Campbell turned and peered over at Larsson. Larsson wore a strange expression that he couldn't read. He realized again what a damned enigma Larsson was to him—a traitor who had vowed to protect him. He decided it wasn't the time to worry about it, and returned his attention to the battle that was about to begin.

"Captains, check in when you're in position and are ready to commence the attack," Campbell commanded over his helmet intercom.

After the three captains had checked in, Campbell called Arnold, who'd remained in the strategy room to view the mock attack on the monitors.

"Commence attack on your order, Campbell," Arnold said in Campbell's ear.

Arnold had told them they would be facing an army of ten thousand human troops dug in around the perimeter of the city and hidden in the city buildings. Their goal was to capture a building in the center of the city that'd been designated as the command post.

The enemy was armed similarly to the assailants, with harmless light-ray guns. The weapons would trigger sensor targets on the soldiers' chests or backs when they were hit. When a soldier was hit, he or she was to lie down and would be considered out of the battle. A central computer kept tally of the casualties.

At Arnold's insistence, armored vehicles and heavy weapons like artillery were not to be used in this initial assault. Campbell agreed with this. He simply wished to see how his troops obeyed orders and maintained their groups during the chaotic confusion of battle.

"Captains, commence your attack when you see the light ray from my rifle in the sky," Campbell ordered over the command frequency.

The captains acknowledged.

Campbell took a deep breath, and gazed at the city. It appeared silent and peaceful, a dead corpse surrounded by a valley of death. Again, he examined his flanks to see all the troops at the ready. He could almost feel the troops' pumping adrenaline. Their ranks had become tighter. Some already had their rifles lowered for action. Others were bouncing up and down in the low gravity with unrestrained excitement. Their hooded expressions appeared eager and anxious. Campbell wondered what their emotions would be if they thought they were really about to die.

Still, Campbell felt a heart-pounding surge of adrenaline as he thought of all the power at his command. All these men and woman were awaiting his order to fight for him. He felt the resurgence of the intoxicating feelings of awe and responsibility that he hadn't known since the Yarv Wars. *Damn, I missed these feelings.*

TWO

"Attack!" he yelled. He raised his rifle and fired. A bright red beam sliced through the dark, star-laden heavens.

Initially, Campbell felt the start of the attack was anticlimactic. He skip-hopped forward in slow motion with his troops flowing behind him like the rolling waves of the sea. He found the silence unnerving. He'd never fought a battle within an enclosed environmental suit. The only sound he would hear was the now silent command frequency.

The entire landscape before the city suddenly erupted in a spectacular light show of what seemed like millions of red, yellow, blue, and white light beams aimed at him and his battle formations. He found the blinding experience strange and unreal. The simulated destructive barrage wasn't followed by earsplitting explosions, screams of the dying, fire, or dense smoke. The attack was unobtrusive and completely silent.

A brilliant red flash zipped just over Campbell's head. He instinctively ducked. He immediately felt foolish knowing no human reaction was quick enough to avoid the speed of light. Glancing up again, the simulated effects of the defensive measures were evident all around him. Soldiers everywhere were falling to the moon dust with their targeted sensor shields lit to show they were dead.

Larsson was suddenly at his side, painfully grabbing his arm and hauling him forward. Campbell yanked his arm free. He started bounding through the dizzying light rays as the troops behind him started returning fire.

Almost immediately, the battle unraveled into chaos and disorganized mayhem. The once tight formations of his attacking force had vanished. Most of the troops were madly surging forward without rank or orders. Some clumsily tripped over the fallen. Personal fights broke out everywhere. Some of the troops were rapidly advancing with wild bounds of insane fury. Others simply stood there as if lost in watchful contemplation. The lieutenants, sergeants, and corporals had completely lost control over their individual groups.

"Keep those ranks close and organized," Campbell called out. Only Lewinski offered a breathless acknowledgment.

A trooper went bounding by them, firing his weapon with mad abandon and wildness in his eyes. As the soldier's feet landed on the moon surface with a dusty poof, he was hit squarely in the chest by a light ray. To Campbell's amazement, the stricken soldier continued his frantic attack as if nothing had happened.

Campbell raced ahead as fast as he could. He switched his weapon to rapid fire and aimlessly blasted away at the defensive perimeter. Even as he closed on the defensive positions, he had yet to spy a single enemy soldier. The defenders were too well entrenched. His own troops were dropping all around him from very accurate enemy fire.

"We're getting slaughtered," Larsson yelled.

Campbell slid to a halt and dropped to a knee in frustrated anger as he considered what to do next. Larsson kneeled at his side. Abruptly a light ray reflected off Larsson's armored shoulder. The shot didn't set off Larsson's chest monitor.

"It must have been a flesh wound," Larsson laughed.

Soldiers swarmed by Campbell and Larsson. More fell to the surface in mock death as the fire from the city intensified. Campbell immediately realized that the enemy had brought up their reserves knowing this was the main attack. He could see that none of his forces had even reached the city perimeter. Their casualties were mounting at an alarming rate. The plan was obviously a complete failure without the powerful armor and artillery support to wipe out the perimeter defenses.

"Do we retreat and regroup?" Larsson asked.

"There will be no retreat!" Arnold yelled in Campbell's helmet. "We must learn all we can from this simulated attack."

Campbell gazed out at the simulated destruction. The overhead image of the battlefield showed him that the chaos was complete. He shook his head at the complete disarray of his forces. His "dead" soldiers littered the landscape.

"The casualty percentage of our attacking force is fifty-one percent," Campbell muttered to Larsson after reviewing the casualty statistics in his helmet. "Computer, what's the casualty percentage of the defending force?"

"Four percent."

"General Arnold, I suggest we retreat," Campbell said. "This battle is lost."

"Quit being a coward, Campbell," Arnold yelled. "There will be no retreat!"

Now Campbell was sure that Arnold was insane. There was no strategic purpose to continue. His troops were an unruly mob of children playing cowboys and Indians. Campbell saw no way of reorganizing them to make an effective assault. If this had been a real battle, they'd all be dead. He glanced over at Larsson, who was shaking his head with disgust.

"You heard the man, Larsson," Campbell yelled with mock enthusiasm. "We fight to the last man."

THREE

"They're mounting a counteroffensive from the center of their line of defense!" Captain Lewinski announced.

Campbell glanced at his battlefield display with dismay. A sea of frantically firing enemy soldiers was pouring into his disorderly ranks from the middle of the city. The intense coordinated fire from the enemy slaughtered his attackers and began to spread out. Even as Campbell watched, his attackers turned and fled from the rout. They were massacred before the rapidly advancing defenders.

"Captains, reform your groups and concentrate all your fire on this counteroffensive," Campbell ordered. He knew he was too late. Already, the heated combat was at hand. Defenders beat back a small group of attackers that were grouped together only meters away from him.

One of the attackers from behind Campbell raced by him. Campbell saw the look of insane rage on the man's face. The attacker ducked beneath the close-quarter fire of two defenders, plowed them aside, and made for a lieutenant of the defending forces. Campbell caught the reflective flash of a knife blade materialize in the mad attacker's hand. He knew instantly the lieutenant was about to die for real.

"No!" Campbell shouted. Then he realized the attacker wasn't even on his frequency and wouldn't hear his order.

He quickly leaped up and bounded after the wild attacker. He was on the madman's back and throwing him down even as the attacker was viciously swinging at the lieutenant's neck with his sharp blade. The lieutenant ducked away, unharmed.

Campbell was tangled up in the attacker's limbs as they hit the ground and rolled in a dusty scuffle. The man's insane rage surprised him with its ferocity. Effortlessly in the low gravity, the madman whirled over and tossed Campbell's weight off him. As Campbell landed on his back, the attacker was on him slashing at him with his knife. Campbell flung his arms to and fro, frantically trying to defend himself from the savage knife thrusts. The man's enraged features were so close that Campbell could see the craziness in his wild eyes while the man screamed silently behind his helmet.

Suddenly, Campbell felt the rapid decompression of his environmental suit deflating. One of his attacker's knife thrusts had punctured a hole in the right arm of his suit. The attacker rabidly continued his ferocious assault, not allowing Campbell a chance to recover. Campbell knew that if he didn't rid himself of this insane assailant and get immediate attention, he would be dead.

Campbell caught motion out of the corner of his eye. Larsson was standing only two meters away with a mad gleam in his mismatched eyes. He was swaying with the savage motions of the struggle while attempting to aim a DEP at Campbell. A new terror arose in Campbell's frantic heart that Larsson was going to kill him.

Suddenly, a burst of light flashed from Larsson's DEP. The attacker's head exploded before his body fell on Campbell. The body continued to feebly attack him with uncoordinated muscle spasms.

Campbell let his exhausted limbs fall limp. His chest hitched and began to burn as all the air was depleted from his suit. He saw Larsson hover over him still holding the DEP. He knew Larsson would kill him now. Larsson holstered the weapon, bent over, and threw aside the attacker's body.

"Don't worry, Campbell, I'll get you out of here," Larsson said.

Larsson quickly reached into his accessory pack, and pulled out an adhesive suit patch and a small emergency canister of compressed air. Campbell was growing lightheaded, almost euphoric, as his consciousness drifted away. Still, he tried to retain his concentration as he watched Larsson expertly patch the puncture hole in his suit. He felt the instant relief of fresh air washing over his sweaty face after Larsson plugged in the emergency air supply.

After a few moments of relishing huge gasps of air, Campbell was able to sit up. His head felt as if it might split open like a rotting melon.

"Come on," Larsson said. "It's time to get out of here, unless you want to be captured."

Larsson hauled him to his feet as Campbell anxiously gazed around him. Larsson had been correct. His attacking forces were scattered, bounding away in full retreat. New forces were pouring from the city to finish off any stray attackers that still had the will to fight. He wondered how many of them would still be fighting if the attack had been real.

He motioned Larsson to follow him as he quickly bounded across the dead lunar landscape back toward the huge military complex. When he deemed they were far enough away from the retreating battle to be safe, he motioned Larsson to a halt. He changed his communicator to a low-range personal frequency, and then reached over to Larsson's suit to do the same.

Campbell gazed into Larsson's black implant and blue eye. "I want to thank you for saving my life back there, Larsson. Where did you get that DEP?"

Larsson laughed. "I've been watching the monitors during these mock battles, just like you, Commander. I noticed that these soldiers don't fight by the rules. I thought it was necessary to be prepared."

"Good thing you were," Campbell said, "but for a moment there I thought you were going to kill me instead."

Larsson stared at him. "For a moment there, I *was* going to kill you. What better way to stop this insanity than eliminate their field commander?"

"Huh," Campbell grunted. He turned and headed back toward the compound.

As Campbell hop-skipped forward in the low gravity, he considered Larsson's words. He decided to let it pass. The man *had* saved his life, no matter what his intentions had been. Still, Larsson's true motivations perplexed him deeply.

After returning to the complex and removing their equipment, they went straight to the strategy room where Campbell knew Arnold would be anxiously awaiting their return. Campbell dreaded the heated confrontation with Arnold, but he knew there was no escaping it.

He wasn't disappointed. Arnold was fuming with rage when he saw them.

"Your tactics were a total failure!" Arnold screamed at him. His face was nearly purple with anger; pulsating veins ready to rupture were popping out of his creased forehead.

"I warned you that there was no defeating a fortified position with that many men," Campbell said calmly. "Your troops are undisciplined and uncontrollable. And as you requested, we didn't have any armor or artillery support to destroy the fortifications."

Arnold's features went ashen while he stalked back and forth waving his arms around and saying, "Your fault, your fault . . ."

Campbell thought: *He looks like a child having a temper tantrum.*

Finally, Arnold stopped and jabbed a shaking finger at Campbell. "This is all your fault, Campbell. This is your failure. I will take none of the blame. You disobeyed my orders and allowed those troops to retreat. I knew I could never trust you!"

Campbell remained silent and calmly watched Arnold continue to pace. He'd expected no less from the irrational lunatic. Suddenly, Arnold stopped and took a deep breath. A semi-lucid smile had appeared on his quivering lips when he turned toward Campbell. He laughed as if his rage had never been there.

"Come, gentlemen," Arnold said. "Let's go into our room and make plans for tomorrow. I think the problem with our assault today was that we didn't have armor or artillery support."

I just said that, you idiot. Campbell felt his mouth drop open at Arnold's transformation.

"Shouldn't we review the recording of today's attack and the casualty statistics?" Larsson asked.

Arnold just waved off Larsson's request and entered the side room. Campbell and Larsson followed after exchanging confused glances.

XVIII

A BRIEF VISIT

ONE

The following two days were pure hell for Campbell. He and Larsson spent frustrating, exhausting, wasted hours sweating in their cumbersome environmental suits, repeating their assaults on the mock city. While they'd incorporated armored vehicles and artillery m the attacks, they still met with varying degrees of failure. The additional equipment only added to the disorganization and chaos. The added light rays fired by the artillery above the desolate landscape caused a confusing multicolored strobe effect that reminded Campbell of a lightshow run amok, the struggling mass of bodies around him an orgy of death. The lack of discipline and infighting among his disorganized forces became epic. Campbell felt lucky to have survived the two days.

Campbell's forces were often decimated by the defenders' artillery in the open field before they even reached the city perimeters. It was only after the attackers were allowed into the defenses, and the defenders were unable to use their artillery, that Campbell's forces showed marginal success. Yet Campbell knew these were unrealistic circumstances.

On the final morning before their departure to Fort Knox, Arnold requested Campbell's and Larsson's presence in the strategy room to go over the results from the previous days of trial battle. To Campbell's surprise, Arnold remained upbeat and even happy about the results. Campbell considered them total failures. If the enemy troops at Fort Knox had access to real weapons, he knew his forces would be wiped out.

Arnold continued to wave off Campbell's concerns by saying, "We have the element of surprise on our side, gentlemen. We'll be using real weapons, while the defenders will only be using harmless flashlights. They cannot hurt us. Our casualty statistics during these training attacks are irrelevant."

"You're ignoring that your troops are undisciplined, Arnold," Campbell pointed out. "They retreat and fight among themselves at the slightest provocation. What's going to happen when we issue them real weapons and they start killing each other . . . or worse, me?"

Arnold immediately went into another fit of rage. "Campbell, you persist in blaming me for your mistakes! It isn't my fault that your troops are improperly trained and don't obey your orders. You had three days to train them!"

Campbell took in Arnold's response in complete silence and resignation. He'd given up on getting any sort of rational reaction out of Arnold.

When Arnold had settled down, they went over the final plans of assault again. Campbell noticed that no mention of the use of Arnold's deadly and uncontrollable creatures was made or discussed. This worried him greatly. He knew Arnold planned to use the creatures at some point, and Arnold was keeping him in the dark about it. He decided it was useless to bring up his concerns. He doubted Arnold would tell him the truth anyway.

As they got up to leave, Arnold said, "Campbell, will you stay for a moment?"

Larsson gave them a curious glance before he shrugged and left the room.

"Campbell, the Master thinks you need a little incentive to motivate you to success. It has graciously allowed you a brief visit with Penelope Preston."

Campbell was amazed and immediately excited. Even with all the tension and commotion over their upcoming attack, he'd thought of little else other than Penelope's welfare and what the Master was doing to his love.

"Are you saying she's okay?" he asked anxiously.

"Of course, Penelope has become the Master's prize possession. She's being treated like a queen. She will continue to be treated as such as long as you succeed in your mission. Come on and see for yourself."

Prize possession? What in Hades does that mean? Campbell's apprehension deepened.

He didn't care for the terrifying implications of Arnold's statement, but he was too excited about seeing Penelope to ask what Arnold meant. He quickly followed Arnold down the hall, lost in eager anticipation and anxiety over what he would find.

TWO

Campbell recognized that they were following the halls toward the Master's bunker. When they reached the bunker area, they took the elevator up instead of down. The elevator door opened. Campbell gazed out into a small foyer with black stone walls that reminded him of the entrance to the Master's bunker. There was a single door in the center of the rear wall that was guarded by two black-robed guards.

Both the human guards raised the barrels of their spray guns to their shoulders and snapped to attention when they recognized Arnold.

I wish my own troops showed such discipline, Campbell thought.

"The commander is here to see the woman," Arnold said to the tall, brutish guards. He turned to Campbell, and said, "You have ten minutes to visit Penelope. I believe that you'll find the experience enlightening, but don't make me send the guards in after you. I'll wait here. Guards, open the door."

Campbell quickly stepped forward through the darkened doorway with tightlipped excitement. His heart was beating hard more out of fear of the unknown than from the joy of seeing his love.

Campbell waited a moment for his eye implants to adjust to the poor light. From what he could see the room was large, airy, and had vaulted ceilings that disappeared into the darkness. There were shadow-filled corners that contained lavish chairs and couches. Large framed paintings covered the walls, but he couldn't make them out in the dim light. The ventilation was poor, and it stank of human occupation and illness. There were no windows. It was a luxurious jail cell. Still, he thought it was a vast improvement over his lodgings. He couldn't find any way to activate the lights. His heat-sensing eyes picked up a muted heat signature coming from the rear of the room where he thought he could see a huge bed with a posted canapé.

"Penelope?" Burt asked softly, his heart pounding wildly.

No one answered.

"Penelope?"

"Go away," Penelope said in a sleepy voice without recognition.

"Penelope? It's me, Burt," he said with deep anxiety.

Burt started to move slowly toward the luxurious bed. His fear deepened when the lax figure on the bed didn't appear to move.

"Burt who?" she asked in a faraway voice.

Burt was terrified. *How could she not know who I am? What have Arnold and the Master done to her?* He rushed forward.

He reached the bed, and saw Penelope was lying with her head on a pillow and a rumpled sheet covering her body up to her chin. Her once beautiful blond hair was a tangled mess tossed about above her head. Her pale face was gaunt, lined with pain. Her cheeks were hollowed out.

Dark, ugly circles rimmed her sunken eye sockets. But what terrified him most was that her blue-gray eyes were huge unblinking orbs that stared at the ceiling without recognizing his presence.

"Penelope?" he whispered. His heart was breaking. His worst fears were coming true. The Master had tortured her into a mindless zombie.

"Yes," Penelope answered in a slow and vague voice.

He sat tenderly on the bed at Penelope's side. She still didn't acknowledge him with any movement. He reached down with a trembling hand and stroked the top of her head. Her hair felt dirty, greasy. He softly caressed her forehead and down the left side of her pale face. Her skin felt cold and clammy. She didn't respond to his touch. Her eyes remained vacant and fixed on the ceiling.

"Penelope, please, it's Burt Campbell. Don't you remember me?" he asked softly. His voice was breaking with emotion.

"Burt Campbell," Penelope repeated from some distant place.

I can't stand this!

He reached forward with both arms and began to lift Penelope's limp body to his chest. Penelope first went rigid before she started flailing madly at him with her fists.

"No! No! Don't touch me!" she screamed.

He hugged her tightly to his chest, both in self-defense and to try to show her he meant her no harm.

Penelope struggled with amazing strength for a moment. Burt held her tightly, speaking softly in her ear. Penelope's panic slowed. Her struggle seemed to exhaust her. Suddenly, she stopped her assault. She allowed Burt to lovingly hold her while she leaned her weary head on his shoulder and sobbed uncontrollably.

Finally, Penelope reached up and wrapped her thin arms around Burt with a fierce hug. He held her close with loving tenderness. He moved his hand up to the back of her head to press it into his shoulder. For a few moments they rocked back and forth, lost in their intense love and desperation.

He was aware of his time limitation. He knew Arnold was closely watching this whole scene in search of ways to torment them even more. He moved away from Penelope and placed his hands on her wet cheeks to lift her pain-racked face up to his.

"Penelope?" he asked softly. "Do you recognize me?"

"Burt?"

He still thought she acted as if she were in another world. He gently wiped the hot tears away from her cool, wasted cheeks and swept back her lank hair.

"Penelope, what have they done to you?"

Penelope only leaned forward again and limply rested her head on his shoulder in a sign of resigned agony. Her bony body felt fragile and exhausted as if she were at a point of total physical and mental breakdown.

Burt was lost in a desperate world of depression thinking Penelope was near death. He saw only loneliness and darkness without her in his purposeless life. He was stroking Penelope's head in deep sorrow when Arnold entered the room.

"Oh, what a touching scene. Time is up, Campbell. Personally, I would have spent my ten minutes ravaging her body, but let's go."

Campbell's heart awoke with savage rage. His body tensed like a coiled snake's ready to strike, but he didn't move. Penelope clung desperately to him.

"Move it, Campbell!" Arnold yelled from the doorway.

Penelope hugged him even more tightly.

"Guards! Remove the commander!"

"Don't leave me. Don't leave me," Penelope pleaded in his ear.

Campbell heard footsteps approach him from behind before a hand fell heavily on his shoulder. Penelope clung to him as if she were drowning.

"Don't worry, sweetheart," Arnold said snidely. "He won't be gone long. Until then the Master will see to all your needs."

"I will never leave you, my love," Burt said loud enough for everyone to hear, his voice filled with trembling emotion.

Arnold's roaring laughter echoed through the room. Campbell was struck with a blinding rage. As his body tensed, Penelope loosened her grasp. Campbell whirled and struck the guard behind him in the right ear with a crushing blow. The guard was thrown across the room where he hit the floor in a loose pile.

Campbell turned in a raging search of the other guard, but found him far out of reach with the barrel of his spray gun already leveled. Careless of his own life, Campbell started an insane rush on the remaining guard until he realized the spray gun was leveled at Penelope.

"Such anger, Campbell," Arnold said, and laughed softly. "Good, that's very good, but save it for the battle ahead. I have a feeling you're going to need it."

Burt turned to Penelope. She had remained on the bed in a slumped, uncaring position. Her head hung limply on her sunken chest, as if she'd fallen asleep again. Campbell felt his heart tearing to pieces. Seeing Penelope this way was the most pitiful sight he'd ever witnessed. Burt sagged in defeat.

"Move it, Campbell!" Arnold barked.

Anger soared through Campbell's veins again. He snapped to attention and raised his head high. He quickly stepped back over to Penelope and raised her head between his palms. He softly kissed her quivering lips.

"I will be back," he whispered.

Burt moved his head back and stared into Penelope's teary eyes. Life and hope soared into his heart. She was staring back at him with intensity and intelligence. It was like gazing into the vivid blue-gray eyes of the Penelope that he'd always known and loved. Then she shut her eyes and lowered her head again.

Burt leaned over and whispered in Penelope's ear so Arnold couldn't hear, "I love you. Don't give up hope. I will be back to save you after I kill Arnold."

Penelope reached up and squeezed Burt's hand once to acknowledge that she understood. Burt stepped back, turned around, and marched by Arnold.

THREE

Campbell and Arnold returned to his cell in a tense silence.

"I'll be back within two hours to take you to your clipper. We'll be leaving for Earth shortly afterwards," Arnold said curtly. He closed the cell door after Campbell had entered.

Campbell slumped on his bed with his head in his hands as he thought about Penelope. *It's obvious that the Master has been torturing her since her capture. I can't imagine her mental state. Just one interaction with that terrible creature nearly killed me. She's apparently experienced the Master's will on numerous occasions. Still, she's alive, and she hasn't lost all her will.*

"Hang on a little longer, Penelope."

Campbell got up and began to undress to get into a fresh battle uniform. As he began to fold his soiled shirt, he felt something crumple in the shirt pocket. He reached into the pocket, and pulled out a wadded piece of paper. Not remembering what it was, or how it had gotten there, he opened it up. To his amazement, it was a hastily scribbled note in Penelope's handwriting. He realized she must have stuffed it in his pocket when she was hugging him.

He read the note over and over again. It read: "Help me, Burt! Time is short. The end is near. The dogs are stargazing."

He slumped on his bed again wondering about the meaning of the note. He found it unclear and vague. He realized Penelope must have had some foreknowledge or hope of their meeting, and that she'd written the note in a hurry, since she knew she was being watched.

The obvious meaning is that Penelope doesn't think she's going to last much longer under the Master's torture. I don't see how she's lasted this long. But she must have known she didn't have a lot of time to write this note. Why did she waste time repeating herself? The phrases about her need for help and the dogs are obvious. Penelope needs help and the dogs are on the big island of Hawaii, where we often spent the long nights talking and gazing at the stars.

She was apparently worried that someone else might read the note, and she didn't want them to understand where the dogs were hidden. Only I would understand the meaning of stargazing dogs.

He smiled as he thought only Penelope would be concerned about the dogs in her time of dire need, but then he wondered: *Penelope had to have known that when I went looking for the dogs again, Hawaii would be the first place I would have searched. Why did she waste time and words on the dogs?*

Campbell concentrated on the phrases that time was short and the end was near. *What if she wasn't referring to herself, but of the dogs? If she was referring to the dogs, why would she think their time was short or their end was near? The dogs have no problems taking care of themselves. They have enough food on the island to last indefinitely. Penelope has to know this as well, or she would have never left them on the island.*

He was more and more confused in his search for inner meanings to the note until he recalled the Master's prophecy. *What if Penelope knows and believes the Master's prophecy that the world is about to end? She must believe it, and she thinks the dogs are in danger.*

After running this and other possibilities through his head, he wondered if maybe he wasn't attributing too much thought to the words. Penelope hadn't appeared to be in a condition to be able to generate much of a coded message. At the very least, he thought the message confirmed his beliefs that he must survive the attack on Fort Knox. He had to return to the moon base in a hurry to find some way to save Penelope. At the moment, things were still out of his control.

After Campbell had changed clothes, he put the note in his breast pocket close to his heart.

XIX

A STRANGE RECEPTION

ONE

The elegant Fort Knox Reception Hall reeked of the honor and glory of military history. Loyalty, unity, and bravery against insurmountable odds hammered one from every direction. While Campbell still held these virtues close to his heart, he wondered how many of those that surrounded him still believed in them. *Larsson, maybe, on some deep personal level, but certainly not Arnold.*

"Burt Campbell, I must say that you're the last person I expected to see leading the forces of the Alfa-Tango Moon Base, or any military force for that matter," said General Brian Scott. Scott was standing erectly before Campbell, Larsson, and Arnold. They were attending the formal reception during the evening of their arrival at Fort Knox.

"Why is that, General?" Campbell asked.

He refused to meet Scott's intense stare. Instead, he gazed around at all the military personnel dressed in their formal uniforms, their chests covered with heroic battle ribbons. The men and women of various races and ages were scattered around the luxurious reception hall chatting quietly while holding glasses of champagne or plates of food. The hall's wall-high windows were covered with heavy red drapes of fine fabric. From the vaulted ceiling hung twinkling crystal chandeliers. The walls were covered with huge oil paintings of historical battle scenes and grim-faced generals. Between the impressive paintings hung distinguished divisional battle flags.

Campbell recognized many of the people there, and thought it was a very impressive group. *If Arnold wanted to kill some of the most powerful military leaders in the world, he couldn't have picked a better gathering place to do it.*

"Burt," Scott said, "I've never had a more capable leader and strategist under my command, but when you retired you were very outspoken about your disdain for the military and its leaders. The rumor here is that you've returned to take your revenge, and make fools of us all," Scott said, with a quiet, disarming laugh.

Campbell gazed up at the tall, fit, silver-haired general before him. He struggled to find an appropriate response.

"Well, I see you have your own thoughts as usual," Scott said, and turned to Arnold. "I saw your troops were noticeably absent from the inspection this afternoon, General. I hope they will arrive in time for the morning maneuvers."

"I just received word that they're arriving as we speak." Arnold said with a broad smile of small teeth, obviously feeling out of place. "We had some logistical problems earlier, but they appeared to be solved now."

Campbell gave Arnold a nasty glance, knowing he was lying. Arnold had not trusted his forces enough to allow them to be reviewed. He'd delayed their departure until it was too late for the inspection.

"Well, if your forces were trained by Burt Campbell, I'm sure they'll be some of the finest troops on the field tomorrow," Scott said cordially. "A toast to your success, gentlemen."

Scott raised his champagne glass, but Campbell was too ashamed and disgusted to continue the lie. He turned and briskly walked away from the group. He heard Larsson's heavy steps following closely behind him.

"He's so temperamental, General," Campbell heard Arnold saying to Scott as he departed. "I don't see how you ever put up with him during the Yarv War."

"You know, Arnold, I've never understood how you got command of the moon base," Scott said icily behind Burt. "When I heard they were establishing a prison there for the world's most despicable criminals, I thought that was a good thing, and that you should be placed in that prison."

Campbell choked on his laughter. He glanced behind him to see Scott glaring down at Arnold with obvious mistrust. Scott abruptly turned to Campbell, came to attention with clicking heels, and held up his glass again in a respectful salute. As Campbell acknowledged with a nod, Scott winked at him with a thin smile. The general's gesture filled Campbell with confusion and foreboding. He watched the general turn and stroll away, leaving Arnold standing alone as if dismissed.

"I see the hate and distrust of Arnold is universal here," Larsson said at Campbell's side. "I just wonder if they hate and distrust Arnold enough."

"Total betrayal is a difficult thing for even the most distrusting mind to fathom, Larsson," Campbell said. "Loyalty, honor, and unity are the cornerstones of military training. They are deeply imbedded in most of these people here. They might mistrust Arnold, but I don't think they understand the evil that's about to befall them."

"Shouldn't we try to warn . . .," Larsson started to say.

"Here comes Arnold," Campbell silenced Larsson.

Arnold stepped up to Campbell and Larsson. "Well, gentlemen, it doesn't appear that we're welcome here. Should we make it an early night and retire from this snobbery? We have a big day before us tomorrow."

Campbell smiled evilly down at Arnold's weasel face and beady eyes. "No, you go ahead, General. I get the feeling that it's *you* that's unwelcome here. It's a feeling that you should be accustomed to receiving, since I'm sure you get it wherever you go."

THE SOUL CAGE II

Larsson snickered. Scarlet rage and embarrassment filled Arnold's pinched features. Campbell turned away from Arnold with a smile of satisfaction while he made his way back to the well-stocked bar for another drink. It'd been some time since he'd had anything alcoholic. He was feeling rather tipsy and happy with himself.

TWO

Campbell spent the rest of the evening moving about the reception and mingling with those he'd never met as well as others that he'd known for years. He was surprised by the warmth, interest, and respect he received from all those with whom he talked. Yet he found he had to steer the conversations away from the allegations that he'd been involved in an attack on a naval vessel and then disappeared. There were also some probing questions regarding a secret military experiment that he'd been involved with that he found rather disturbing. He deflected the questions as best as he could, but he found it odd and frightening that no one questioned him about his current duties. Neither would anyone discuss the upcoming war games.

To his dismay, Larsson and Arnold followed him everywhere he went like unwanted shadows. While he was grudgingly content to introduce Larsson to everyone, he refused to acknowledge Arnold's presence, hoping he'd get the hint that he wasn't wanted. Unfortunately, Arnold stuck to his side as if he were afraid that Campbell might reveal his plans and treachery.

Toward the end of the evening, Arnold finally had to use the facilities and disappeared for a few minutes. Campbell suddenly found himself next to Scott again as if Scott had been waiting for Arnold to vanish.

"I don't know what Arnold is holding against you, Burt," Scott whispered, "but it must be something of tremendous value for you to side with such trash."

Campbell quickly glanced around. Even Larsson had taken the hint and left them alone. His mind whirled for what to tell Scott. *How can I prepare Scott for what's about to be unleashed on the world in the morning? If he doesn't already think I'm insane for joining with Arnold, he'll know I'm crazy when I start talking about devil creatures, mutated dinosaurs, and invisible clouds that torture peoples' minds.*

"Burt, we've been friends through many difficult times," Scott said, "and I can see you're in a very bad situation. I pray that you can resolve your issues. Good luck tomorrow."

Campbell opened his mouth to respond, but Scott quickly turned and walked away. He was about to follow Scott when he heard Arnold behind him.

"What did that old windbag want?" Arnold asked in an acid-filled tone.

Campbell was infuriated that he hadn't been able to warn Scott. He turned his rage on Arnold. "Windbag! Arnold, you're not even fit to lick that man's boots!" he shouted.

Campbell furiously stalked out of the crowded hall, conscious of the shocked silence that had fallen and the stunned stares that he was drawing. He marched into the warm night, infuriated at his inability to warn someone. He wondered if his interaction with the Master and Arnold's conditioning of his mind hadn't subconsciously made it impossible for him to betray them. He heard heavy footsteps behind him.

"Larsson, must you follow me everywhere?"

Larsson stepped abreast of Campbell. "I've been ordered to be your bodyguard. I wouldn't want anything to happen to you."

Campbell huffed. They walked together through the wide, well-lit street surrounded by low drab-colored military buildings, toward their assigned barracks. The street was strangely devoid of people.

"It looks like our troops are arriving," Larsson said, gazing up at the multitude of clippers and transport vehicles that were passing through the clear, star-filled night overhead.

A small force of soldiers marched by them doing double time. They were wearing military police uniforms and carrying directed energy beam rifles. Campbell noticed the moon base insignia on their sleeves. He realized the police force was heading toward the spaceport to meet the moon base arrivals.

"It looks like Arnold doesn't even trust his own troops not to desert as soon as they arrive," Campbell said dryly.

"Would you?" Larsson asked with an automated laugh.

Campbell didn't answer. He was wondering about Larsson and his motives for being there. *Will Larsson make a break for it during the night? I doubt it. He has some sense of personal honor that will make him stick to it through to the end. But then, Larsson hasn't really been tested. He did betray Penelope and Koko. That led to Penelope's capture and Koko's death. Then again, he saved my life. Oh, hell, I don't know what to think. Until he proves otherwise, I don't trust him.*

They walked to their barracks in silence. Campbell saw a group of disheveled and disinterested moon-base troops being led by a throng of their own military police to their barracks. None of the soldiers was armed, and they appeared like a shabby, undisciplined mob compared to the elite Earth forces Campbell had seen. He hadn't realized it while on the moon, but it occurred to him that these troops were as much Arnold's prisoners as he was.

They entered the single-story barracks that housed the room they were sharing. They walked down the long deserted hallway, passing many doors on their way to their room. Campbell saw Kingsley, Lewinski, and Garrett talking quietly in the hall outside their rooms, but the threesome did a vanishing act as soon as they noticed Campbell and Larsson. He noticed the silence that fell on the barracks and decided that, besides them, it was vacant.

"You know, those three are going to be a problem," Larsson said, as they entered their small sparsely furnished room with bare walls and no windows.

"They're the least of my worries," Campbell grunted.

Larsson disappeared into their connecting bathroom while Campbell gazed around their room. It contained a cot against each side wall with a small beaten-up metal desk and chair in the middle.

Campbell eyed the communication equipment and computer monitor on the battered desk. He wondered if it was possible to get a warning to someone on either the communication equipment or the computer. He decided against it. He didn't know who was monitoring his communications or computer usage. He was going to have to get away from Larsson and find someone he could trust to deliver the warning. That meant finding one of the generals who would be defending Fort Knox.

Larsson came out of the bathroom. "I'm going out to do a little reconnoitering. Do you want to come along?"

Campbell thought about this for a moment. He did want to have a look around, but he wanted to do it without Larsson.

"No, thanks," he said. "I might go out later, but I want to rest first."

Larsson gazed at him as if considering something he wanted to say, but then he turned around and headed out the door without a word.

Campbell decided to wait a few minutes to make sure Larsson was out of the area. He got up to leave when there was a soft knock on the door.

"Come," he said.

A young human lieutenant in a moon-base military police uniform hesitantly opened the creaking door. Campbell saw two other sinister-looking goblin-faced guards in police uniforms standing behind him carrying DERs.

"What do you want, Lieutenant?" he asked. The lieutenant nervously shuffled his feet before glancing up at him.

"Sir, orders from General Arnold. You are required to remain in your room under guard until the briefing in the morning."

"What?" Campbell yelled, but he wasn't as surprised as he acted.

The lieutenant's Adam's apple bobbed with fear. "I'm sorry, sir, but the general ordered that you remained confined to your quarters and have no visitors," said the lieutenant, gazing at the wooden-planked floor. "We are to maintain guard at your door until morning, sir."

Campbell felt pity for the terrified lieutenant, but approached the door. "I want to see the general right now."

"General Arnold said you might want to see him, sir. He said that he was indisposed for the rest of the night, and not to be disturbed. We will be waiting right outside your door if you want anything, sir."

Campbell opened his mouth to object, but the lieutenant quickly retreated and closed the door behind him.

"Damn," Campbell muttered in frustration.

He plopped on his flimsy cot while he considered trying to defeat the guards and escaping. He decided against it. Even if he was able to get by the well-armed guards unharmed, a warning would go out to find him. It was unlikely he would escape long enough to give anyone his warning. He lay back and closed his eyes while he considered his dwindling options. They didn't appear good.

THREE

Campbell was abruptly awakened long after midnight. There was a heated argument taking place just outside his door.

"I'm Sub-Commander Ulf Larsson, you idiot! Who are you?" he heard Larsson yelling.

266

Campbell heard a high-pitched yet muffled response that he couldn't make out.

"Fine, Lieutenant. Now get your skinny ass out of my way!" Larsson ordered. He threw open the wooden door with a crashing bang.

Campbell sat up. He watched with a stifled grin as Larsson stomped into the room with a furious expression that would have frightened George with its deadly rage. He slammed the door hard enough to nearly splinter it.

"How do you like that?" Larsson muttered. "They had the nerve to question me about my whereabouts, and then confine me to this room until morning."

"Well, where were you?" Campbell asked anxiously.

Larsson's disfigured face turned from a hideous scowl to an expression of softened concern.

"I've been all over," Larsson said. He went over to sit on his cot opposite Campbell. The cot screeched in protest beneath Larsson's tremendous weight. "First, I wandered down to our landing zone. There were far more transports there than would be needed to carry our troops. Arnold must have emptied all the military police out of the moon complex. The zone was crawling with them."

"Were they the standard troop transports?" Campbell asked.

"Some of them were, but most of them were the big, heavy equipment kind, and they were surrounded by police. I couldn't get anywhere near them."

"Sounds like Arnold's creatures have arrived," Campbell muttered with mounting concern.

"That was my guess, but I wonder how he plans to use them? They would have to transport them forward to the target area to be used in the battle. If he releases them in the rear area, they're just as likely to run away from the battle as they are to run into it."

"That would also mean they would have to run through us to get to the front. I don't relish the thought of being run over by an armored spinosaurus or eaten by one of those raptors."

"That's not the worst of it," Larsson said.

"What else did you find out?" Campbell asked, glancing over at Larsson's unreadable features.

Larsson's lips curled in his usual evil smile. "After finding out what little I could about our forces, I commandeered an observer's ground vehicle and drove as close as I could get to the battle area.

"I couldn't get too close, because they have the perimeters guarded even more heavily than Arnold has us boxed in here. But I did get a view of the mock city we'll be attacking."

"Do you have a point to all this?" Campbell asked impatiently.

Larsson gave him an uglier frown than usual. "They're planning something big over on the other side. I got close enough to see they're rushing to complete some heavy fortifications around the city perimeter.

"The city was flooded with lights, and I could see bulldozers and cranes digging deep holes that looked like tank and artillery trenches. The field before the city appeared to be covered with all sorts of anti-personnel and vehicle traps."

Campbell thought about Larsson's news, but decided it wasn't anything he hadn't expected.

"There's one more thing that I noticed," Larsson said. "It might be nothing, but I thought it was odd."

"What is it?" Campbell asked wearily. He didn't know how much more bad news he could stand.

"I saw a lot of military police from both sides, but I didn't see any enemy troops. I mean, I didn't manage to get close enough to the city to see much, but I didn't see any troops at all. Don't you think that's kind of strange?"

"Well, maybe they're enforcing a lockdown like us," Campbell said, but he didn't believe it. He'd never heard of soldiers being confined to their quarters before a training battle.

"Burt, all the preparations I've seen go far beyond anything our troops have faced before, and that's just the things I could see before I was caught."

"Caught, by whom?" Campbell asked with smirking surprise.

Larsson appeared embarrassed if possible. "Well, someone called in that their observation vehicle had been stolen, and the military police caught me as I tried to bully my way past one of the checkpoints to get a closer look at the fortifications. They escorted me back here before I could see anything else."

Campbell laughed, but then got thoughtful again.

"What're you thinking?" Larsson asked.

"I'm thinking that this battle might go worse for us than I'd thought. When Arnold sees the kind of forces and fortifications he's up against, he might panic and simply release his creatures. If that happens, we've all lost. No one can defeat those things once they're loose."

"Why do you continue to be so naïve, Campbell?" Larsson sneered. "You were lost the moment Arnold snared you. The only thing you and I can hope to do is somehow survive this ordeal. But you're right about one thing. When Arnold releases those creatures, survival is going to be very difficult in the destruction that follows."

Campbell went silent after that, and reclined on his cot. He closed his eyes and thought about what Larsson had told him.

FOUR

Campbell woke up with a start when he felt someone shaking his shoulder with an iron grip. He cracked open his eyes to see a horrid face leaning over him, and he let out a small yelp of fear.

"Very funny," said Larsson. "You're no beauty queen the first thing in the morning, either. Come on, we're wanted at the briefing shortly. We better go eat breakfast."

Larsson waited silently for Campbell to dress in his battle gear. When they opened the door to leave, Campbell was surprised to see the guards were gone and they weren't getting a personal escort to the briefing. They went to eat.

Campbell and Larsson were the last to arrive at the crowded briefing room. Campbell gazed around the long, narrow room that was filled with bright sunlight coming from the large open windows. For the first time, he noticed the chirping of birds above the low murmuring of the seated men and women crammed in the room. The air was hot and stuffy, trembling with excitement. Campbell was surprised to see only the moon-base leadership in attendance. He'd expected the briefing to include all the leaders involved in the battle.

He and Larsson moved to the front row of metal folding chairs and sat down next to Kingsley, Garrett and Lewinski. The rows behind him were filled with the approximately one hundred lieutenants and sergeants who were below the captains in command. The entire room went silent with tense expectancy, making the birds' morning ritual sound loud and out of place.

Arnold, who was seated at the podium at the head of the room, stood up and walked to a huge detailed map of the battle area. Using a laser pointer, Arnold went over the main points of the attack. It was basically the same strategy Campbell had suggested the first day that had failed so miserably. The exception was the inclusion of the artillery and armored vehicles. There was still no mention of the creatures.

The main objective was to capture a building in the center of the city that was designated as the enemy command post. The real command post and strategy room, from which the generals would watch the battle on monitors and give their orders, was well away from the field and the fighting. Although the leadership from both opposing forces would be in different areas, they would all be in the same building. That was how Arnold planned to capture and kill them all. Arnold had left Campbell ignorant as to how he planned to achieve that goal.

As Campbell listened to the briefing, he examined the topography map closely.

"Excuse me, General Arnold," he said, standing up, "but I see heavily wooded areas on three sides of the city. Rather than start our troops out in the open field before the city, why not keep them under the cover of the wooded areas until our directed energy beam cannons and hover tanks can clear the perimeter defenses? Once the perimeter is breached, we can move our armor ahead to spearhead our troops through the city."

Campbell could see that Arnold was furious at being interrupted.

"What's this, Campbell?" Arnold snapped. "Are you questioning your own plan at this late hour? A change in plans will only confuse our troops at this point. We will stick with how they have been trained. Now, sit down and don't interrupt me again."

"But, General," Campbell persisted, "when we made the initial plan, we didn't know there would be cover available to protect our forces against their armored forces. If we leave them out in the open field during an armored attack, there might not be any troops left to lead into the city."

Arnold's face turned bright red. "You forget, Campbell, we'll be fighting against a toothless enemy. Any troops hit by the enemy's harmless fire will just continue the fight. Sit down!"

Campbell glared back at Arnold for a moment with furious frustration. He opened his mouth to say something, but then turned back to his seat and sat down. He figured it was useless talking to a madman. Arnold settled down, and continued the briefing as if nothing had happened. Behind Campbell, he heard a murmuring of agreement with his suggested change of plans.

At the end of the briefing, Arnold made what Campbell thought sarcastically was an overconfident pep talk that finished on a highly motivational note.

"If you see any soldier fighting within the ranks, disobeying orders, or attempting to desert, they're to be killed immediately. Please pass that message along to your troops. Good luck."

After everyone was dismissed, they noisily filed out of the briefing room to get their troops into position. Campbell stayed behind and walked up to Arnold. He wasn't surprised that Larsson followed him. Arnold appeared extremely nervous.

"Have some pre-battle jitters, Arnold?" Campbell asked, and then got serious. "I noticed you never said anything about releasing those creatures of yours. How can you expect your troops to fight effectively if they think their own leader will unleash hell on them and kill them all?"

"What makes you think those creatures are even present, Campbell? No one here even knows those creatures exist except you and Larsson. So as long as you do your job, there will be no problems."

"Every one of your troops has seen those creatures, or ones like them, fight in the arena," Larsson said. "Even your dumbest soldiers can figure out those things are here."

Arnold ignored Larsson. He turned away and started to leave the building. As Arnold reached the door, he turned again. "By the way, gentlemen, that order about disobedience and desertion applies to you two as well. Fail me, and I *will* have you killed."

Arnold left the room.

"He just inspires so much hope and love," Larsson muttered. "A regular ray of sunshine on a stormy day."

"Him I at least understand," Campbell said, as he made for the exit. "But what the hell are you doing here?"

"Don't you know?" Larsson laughed in his emotionless manner. "I'm just along for the fun-loving ride."

XX

"THE ART OF WAR"

ONE

"Ten minutes before the battle starts, Commander," Larsson said at
Campbell's side. They stood before rank upon rank of moon-base
forces on the open grassy field in front of the mock city. Trickles of
sweat ran down Campbell's back beneath the savage morning sun.
His nervous excitement and the greasy eggs and bacon he'd wolfed
down at breakfast were making him queasy. He definitely shouldn't
have had that second cup of coffee.

"I know," Campbell said nervously.

He flipped down the visor to his battle helmet. It showed him
the same heads-up displays that his moon helmet had. He glanced at
the overhead satellite display of the battlefield to ensure all his forces
were in position. Lewinski's troops were to his left again. Garrett's were
to his right. He couldn't see Kingsley's smaller diversionary force. They'd
disappeared into the dense woods to the right of the city.

Damn, I don't like this, Campbell thought. *There could be all kinds
of enemy forces hiding in those woods, and we're sitting out here in the open
with no protection.*

He didn't like this dead calm before the battle, either. The sweat
was rolling down his squinting features now, and everything was too
quiet. The air felt oppressive and alive after the stale artificial atmosphere of the moon base. He glanced anxiously to both sides. His
black uniformed troops were crammed into tight formation by the
dark and dense forests covering their left and right flanks. Nothing

could be seen beneath the shadows of the trees and underbrush. Again he thought they were too exposed with no way to maneuver.

Arnold is an idiot. Our troops should be using the cover of the woods while our armor should be up front leading the battle.

He turned to the soldiers close to him. They appeared stern faced and silent beneath the shadows of their black helmets. None of them showed the wild enthusiasm they'd exhibited before the mock battles on the moon. Each man and woman wore heavy body armor like his. They were armed with directed energy beam rifles or sonic blasters as their main weapons. Each carried directed energy beam pistols and some sort of a knife or machete as a side weapon for close combat. He also saw that many carried grenades—both sonic and shrapnel.

Campbell glanced down at his own DER and DEP before turning to Larsson. "You think you can use these weapons against defenseless men?"

Larsson smiled. "Campbell, you keep forgetting that I always look out for me, myself, and I."

Campbell nodded and turned toward the city. The small city, more like a town, he thought, had obviously seen many war games. Under the bright morning sky, the small low-level brick buildings appeared burned and ruined. Other than the rusting hulks of some burned out troop carriers, the dirty side streets were deserted, no trees, no gardens. It was a shelled-out war zone. Most ominous to him were the heavy earth-mound and trench fortifications forming the defensive perimeter. These could contain all sorts of hidden horrors for his exposed troops. Even with the magnified vision of his helmet, he couldn't spot a single person moving about in the city ruins or the fortified perimeter. This worried him greatly.

"Captains, are your troops in formation?" Campbell asked through his earplug headset.

Garrett, Kingsley and Lewinski acknowledged they were ready. He noticed their heart monitors were blinking wildly. The commanders of the directed energy beam cannons and the hover tanks in the rear area also acknowledged they were in position and ready.

According to the plan, the cannons and tanks at the rear of the troops would begin the attack by destroying the defensive fortifications. Arnold had kept the tanks back so that no one from the city could get close enough to examine them and see that they were armed with real 500-kilowatt cannons. Once Arnold's cannons had destroyed the fortified perimeter, the tanks would move through Campbell's forces and lead the assault on the city. The troops would follow behind under the protection of their armor and firepower.

"General Arnold, you can inform the opposition that our forces are in position and ready for battle. We'll await your order to open fire," Campbell said.

"God help us and forgive us," he said to Larsson

Larsson roared with laughter. "You don't need a god to protect you, Campbell. You've got me!"

Campbell started to shake his head in disgust of Larsson's blasphemous jest when he heard a soldier close by say, "Commander, look at the city. What's that?"

Campbell quickly glanced up. He heard Larsson softly swearing in amazement. He couldn't believe his own eyes. A huge, nearly transparent dome now covered the entire city. Dimly reflecting the early sunlight, the dome extended so close to the ground just past the perimeter defenses that even a squirrel couldn't scurry beneath it to retrieve a lost nut.

"Lord in Hades," Campbell muttered in awe. "I've heard that huge plasma shields were theoretically possible, but I didn't know anyone had built one."

"We don't have anything that could possibly penetrate . . .," Larsson was saying. He was suddenly silenced by the explosive sound of muted thunder coming from somewhere behind the city.

TWO

"Down!" Campbell screamed. All his fear was forgotten as his long-time war experience and training took over. The deadly battle had begun.

He fell to his stomach just before a series of massive explosions walked down their crowded and cramped ranks. Campbell felt the very ground beneath him heave up and toss him atop Larsson's prone body. Deafening explosions ripped apart his screaming and dying troops. Dirt, blood and body parts were flying everywhere through the dense smoke.

"Campbell, this is Kingsley! We're under attack by some sort of bots that were hidden in the woods. The bots have shields our weapons can't penetrate. We're getting slaughtered . . ."

Another round of huge explosions erupted around Campbell, deafening him to Kingsley's report. He felt dizzy and disoriented from the close blast concussions.

"Are you all right, Campbell?" Larsson yelled in his ringing ear.

"Yes, I think so!" he yelled.

"What the hell was that?" Larsson shouted to be heard over the screams of the wounded and dying soldiers surrounding them.

Campbell cautiously sat up, and glanced at his satellite display of the battlefield. The forest of trees behind the city had suddenly disappeared. In their place was row after row of enemy artillery cannons.

That enemy artillery battery is too close to the plasma dome protecting the city, Campbell thought. *The directed beams of our cannons can't hit them.*

"There's an enemy artillery battery behind the city that's using live ammunition," Campbell yelled. "They're lobbing explosive projectiles over the protective dome, and we can't return fire."

"What?" Larsson asked

Another series of muffled explosions could be heard in the background. Campbell grabbed Larsson and hauled him to the ground as the earth all around them erupted in fiery destruction and death. The horrific concussion of the sound waves seemed enough to rip Campbell's body apart. The intense smoke choked him, but spared him the horrible blood-filled vision of his slaughtered troops.

"Campbell! Campbell! What's happening out there?" Arnold screamed in his ear.

Campbell was surprised to hear laughter exploding from his throat as he shouted, "Arnold, you idiot! We've been had! They know about your treacherous plan and they're trying to kill us all!"

"But, but . . .," Arnold stammered.

"Kingsley!" Campbell yelled. "Try to get your troops out in the open area . . . Kingsley!"

He glanced up at his heads-up display. Kingsley's image and heart monitor were dark.

Damn, he's dead. Good riddance, you bastard.

Campbell gazed back toward the rear area when he heard a whine of engines in the smoke-filled sky. To his terror, a dark line appeared over the horizon that approached their position with incredible speed.

"Come on, Larsson!" Campbell screamed. He jumped up and grabbed Larsson's arm.

Campbell paused in mind-ripping horror as he witnessed all the dead and dying soldiers. Through the flames and choking smoke, he saw that the previously green field was now a tortured burial ground of blood and gore. He began to run for his life.

He leaped over the torn dead and screaming wounded as he sprinted toward an explosion crater nearby. He dove into the smoldering pit with Larsson landing heavily on top of him. Campbell crawled out from beneath Larsson and up to the crater lip. He was just in time to see the line of torpedo-shaped, short-winged drones pass through the still blue sky over their rear area.

The sky erupted with an intense lightshow when red directed energy beams blazed upward from the rear area and vaporized many of the drones. Campbell realized that their cannons hadn't been destroyed yet. Their artillery had opened fire on the deadly drones as they sped over.

He heard another series of muffled explosions and quickly ducked into the crater, fearing another murderous assault in his vicinity. To his surprise, the projectiles landed far to the rear of his area. He peeked out of the crater to see billowing black smoke and flames rising from where their artillery and hover tanks had been.

"Lewinski! Garrett! Regroup your forces and try to make it to the cover of the woods!" Campbell yelled.

The enemy's artillery began to fire more rapidly and out of sequence. Campbell knew they'd been given the order to fire at will. Massive explosions began at the rear area and worked their way toward the open field, destroying everything and killing everyone in their path.

"Get down!" Larsson yelled.

Campbell peered upward when he heard the rapid fire of small-caliber cannons. The entire sky was ablaze with fiery destruction and death as the remaining drones opened fire on the exposed troops with their nose cannons.

Campbell watched with horror while his troops were torn apart by the pouring flood of exploding shells fired by the drones. He sat exposed and mesmerized as a line of small eruptions sprinted along the ground directly toward him. He felt himself yanked into the cover of the crater just as the cannon fire from a drone passed over his head.

Campbell felt an inhuman punch in his back that momentarily numbed his legs. It knocked the wind from his lungs and slammed him to the ground. Panic raged through Campbell's mind as he fought for breath and struggled to control his paralyzing agony. He got himself under control as the feeling returned to his legs. His back was on fire while he crawled back to the crater lip and heard more drones scream over his head.

"Campbell! You're hurt!" Larsson yelled.

"You always were the observant one," he said breathlessly with a pain-filled grimace. He reached around to the wounded area of his back. He grimaced again when he brought his hand around to see that it was covered with fresh, dark blood.

"Let me take a look," Larsson said.

Larsson's powerful hands pulled back his torn armor. Campbell sucked in his breath with agony. Immediately, he felt the painful pressure of Larsson's hand on the wound. Larsson quickly reached into his belt for a healing laser.

"How bad is it?" Campbell asked.

"It's probably not as bad as it looks. It appears that it wasn't a direct hit. That would have cut you in half. It's probably only a piece of shrapnel. There's a good size hole in your back, but I think I can stop the bleeding with the laser."

"Do it quick. We have to get out of here," Campbell whispered, and prepared for the searing heat of the tiny laser.

Larsson expertly went to work while Campbell bit back his screams of pain.

"Okay, Campbell, I think that's the best I can do here. I've stopped the external bleeding, but I'm sure you're still bleeding on the inside. This wasn't supposed to happen."

What in Hades does that mean? Campbell wondered.

THREE

Before he could question Larsson, the devastating shelling started again now that the drones had cleared. Campbell painfully crawled up to look around. The scene was the most horrible massacre he'd ever witnessed in all his wartime experience. Burning, smoking craters littered the tortured landscape. There were dead and dying as far as his smoke-filled, watering eyes could see. It was only getting worse as the artillery continued to pound their positions.

"Are you okay to move?" Larsson shouted to be heard above the deafening explosions and the screaming of the dying men and women.

Campbell ignored him.

"Captains Lewinski and Garrett, what are your situations?" he called. He couldn't make out any response. A heavy artillery shell exploded nearby, throwing him and Larsson to the bottom of their crater. A shower of rocky dirt rained down around them.

"Lewinski, acknowledge!" Campbell yelled when he caught his breath and his ears stopped ringing.

Three breathless soldiers piled into the crater next to them. Campbell hardly noticed the newcomers.

"Garrett, acknowledge!"

Campbell listened intently above the terrifying sounds of the battle. He received no response from the captains. He checked his heads-up display. The images and heart monitors of Lewinski and Garrett were dark.

"They must all be dead," Campbell said to Larsson.

"That's right! Everyone's dead!" shouted an enraged soldier. He was lying across from Campbell on the opposite side of the crater about three meters away.

Campbell glanced over at the earth- and blood-covered soldier. He wasn't entirely human. His horrid face and misshaped head had a goblin appearance. Black blood streamed from the huge nostrils of his bat nose. His misaligned eyes burned with red flames from hell.

"It's Commander Campbell and his lackey Larsson!" said the huge human soldier next to goblin face.

"They're the ones who led us into this trap to get us all killed. It was their plan all along. They're traitors!" yelled the third soldier. Campbell saw he was breathing heavily and bleeding badly from a ghastly shoulder wound.

Campbell's heart leaped into his throat when the three soldiers started to raise their weapons.

"Let's kill . . .," goblin face was saying. Suddenly, his head exploded like a wet ripe watermelon from a blast of a directed-energy beam.

Campbell instinctively rolled to his right with lightning speed to avoid the fire from the other two soldiers. Their heads exploded in rapid succession.

"Maggots!" Larsson roared, as he jumped to his feet with his DEP still aimed at the headless corpses. He leaped across the crater and began to viciously kick the limp bodies with mindless rage.

"Stop it, Larsson!" Campbell yelled.

As the echoes of his voice died away, he realized he could only hear the screams and oaths of the dying.

"Larsson, listen. The shelling has stopped." He painfully scrambled out of the crater to see what was going on. "Damn," he muttered in awe.

There didn't seem to be a meter of earth that wasn't burning or pitted with giant smoldering craters. The sunlight was blocked by dense smoke. The disheveled ground was splotched crimson with the blood of the dead and dying. To his amazement, there were still a large number of his soldiers alive and unhurt. They were cautiously crawling out of whatever cover they'd been able to find.

"Look! Over there coming out of the woods to your left!" Larsson yelled. He smacked Campbell in the shoulder to get his attention. "What're those things?"

Campbell turned to his left. Then he painfully whirled toward the city to see the same image appearing out of the perimeter trenches.

He made another quarter turn to peer anxiously toward the woods on their right flank, but his vision was obscured by the thick smoke that filled the battlefield.

"Those are armored bots of some kind I've never seen," Larsson said.

"Those must be the type of bots that were attacking Kingsley," Campbell muttered with dread, while wondering what other terrifying modern weaponry their enemies could release upon them.

He turned back to the forest on their left flank in confusion and curiosity. There was line after line of bots weaving out of the dense tree line. The bots were like nothing he'd ever seen.

"I can only assume those things are one of the many wonder weapons that Fort Knox is famous for creating," Campbell said. "The enemy commanders have released their latest surprises to field test on Arnold's forces."

Campbell watched with more curiosity than fear as the bots formed close-line ranks and began to move across the field with surprising speed. The bots seemed to hover a half meter above the ground and moved smoothly over the rough terrain. They were shaped similarly to a small hover tank with a wide, disk-shaped base and a rotating cannon turret on top. But what captivated his attention was that a plasma-bubble shield surrounded each bot.

The surviving soldiers immediately noticed their new enemy. Sporadic groups laid down a murderous barrage of fire on the bots as they screamed with rage at finally having a visible enemy to attack. Campbell wasn't surprised when their directed energy beam shots reflected harmlessly off the protective bot plasma bubbles. The only weapons that appeared to have any effect were the sonic blasters, but even these proved useless. The dense sound waves blew the bots out of position for a moment, but they remained undamaged and quickly returned to their ranks.

Campbell's attention was caught by explosive fire and screams from both behind him and to his left. He turned to see that a murderous fire had erupted from the bubble bots. The bots were ripping apart the remaining troops with their rapid-fire cannons. The carnage was horrifying and total.

Campbell turned again toward the city. Thousands of bubble bots were firing on the tattered remains of his forward ranks. It occurred to him that the enemy was using only explosive armor-piercing ammunition as opposed to directed energy beam weapons, which were far more customary and accurate. It was as if the enemy wanted to inflict the worst kind of carnage and ensure their opposition's death in the most horrifying and bloody fashion.

"Campbell, we're surrounded. We have to get out of here!" Larsson shouted.

Campbell couldn't agree more. *With our remaining force scattered, and most of the leadership dead, this battle is lost.*

FOUR

"General Arnold," Campbell hailed over his microphone. "Our forces are surrounded and taking heavy casualties. What are your orders?"

He received no response.

"General Arnold! What are your orders?" he repeated more urgently. He could see the bubble bots were cutting through his slim defenses and would be on them at any moment.

"Campbell, we have to move now!" Larsson shouted. "Look to the rear. Those are hover tanks closing in and I doubt they're ours."

As if in response to Larsson, the tanks started firing volleys of explosive shells with pinpoint accuracy and devastating effect on those that remained fighting.

"Okay, it's time to retreat and save ourselves," Campbell said. "Let's move toward the rear and the tanks. Maybe we can surrender before they kill us."

"The treachery is complete, Campbell!" Arnold screamed in his ear. "There can be no surrender. We fight to the death!"

Debilitating pain shot through Campbell's brain and body when he thought of an appropriate negative response to Arnold's command. He was driven to his hands and knees by nauseating agony. His jaws clenched together, he couldn't respond.

"Speak for yourself, Arnold!" Larsson screamed. "To all moon-base troops, this is Sub-Commander Larsson. Retreat toward the rear! Save yourselves!"

"Thanks; Larsson," Campbell managed between breaths. "I can't . . . can't . . ."

"Come on," Larsson shouted.

Larsson hauled Campbell to his feet. They stumbled and ran toward the tanks, dodging right and left to avoid bodies, craters, and being made easy targets for the bubble-bot cannons. The agony in Campbell's mind and body subsided as he ran. He could feel the nanotechnology in his blood hard at work. Already the pain in his back was reduced.

"Code Red. I repeat, Code Red," Arnold said calmly in Campbell's ear.

Campbell was confused and came to a sliding halt. "Code Red? What does that mean?"

"You'll see, Campbell. I'll see you in Hell!" Arnold yelled with an insane laugh.

"Oh, no," Campbell muttered. He turned toward the rear area as explosive cannon fire hit all around him.

"Get down!" Larsson shouted. He knocked Campbell to the ground. Larsson covered Campbell with his body when cannon fire from the bots ripped apart the ground to their left.

"Let's move it! We have to get to those tanks now!" Campbell yelled. He heaved Larsson off him and leaped to his feet.

Larsson cautiously stood up in a bent defensive position. "That's what I've been trying to tell you."

"No, you don't understand. Arnold just gave the order to release the creatures," Campbell yelled. "We're doomed if we don't get out of here now."

Without a word, Larsson continued running in a zigzag pattern toward the enemy tanks with Campbell close behind him. They hadn't gotten ten meters when Campbell picked up the screaming sound of an approaching tank shell and dove headfirst into a ditch he was passing.

Earth rained on Campbell when the shell exploded where he'd been running. He dug himself out and anxiously peered about to see that Larsson was lost in the smoking debris.

"Larsson? Larsson!" he shouted. His voice was drowned out by a series of heavy explosions nearby.

When the earth stopped shaking beneath him, Campbell lifted his head and crawled out of the ditch. He immediately spotted Larsson's prone body a few meters away.

"Oh, no," he muttered. He scrambled to Larsson's side and kneeled next to the lifeless body.

He reached for Larsson's neck to see if he could find a pulse. He only found armor plating. He swore at himself, and began to quickly search Larsson's body in an attempt to discover if he was alive. Larsson didn't even appear to be breathing.

"What do you think you're doing, Campbell?"

"Ah!" Campbell yelled with shock and surprise.

"Does playing with bodies in the middle of a battlefield turn you on or something?" Larsson asked. He laughed as he sat up.

"No, you bionic idiot. I was worried that you were dead."

Larsson smiled with crooked lips baring his metal teeth and was about to respond. Campbell quickly glanced up at the smoke-filled sky when the roar of huge engines caught his attention. Larsson wheeled around and got to his feet to follow Campbell's gaze.

"Those are the transports I saw in the rear area last night. The ones I thought contained the creatures," Larsson said. He pointed at the dozens of huge transport carriers that filled the sky and were approaching their area. "What're we going to do?"

"Let's keep running for the tanks. Maybe we can make it to the rear area before any of the transports land," Campbell said anxiously, not believing his own words.

He started his sprint without waiting for Larsson to respond. They didn't make it far. The air exploded with deafening shock waves as the approaching hover tanks fired another volley.

"Down!" Campbell yelled. He hit the devastated ground without seeing any immediate cover.

To his relief, he heard the shells scream over his head and explode somewhere behind him. Campbell peered to his rear. Larsson was already on his feet and leaping forward over dead bodies. He got up and followed after Larsson, but the tanks erupted with fire again. Larsson skirted to a nearby crater and landed with Campbell right behind him. Again, the deadly volley went over their heads.

"We're never going to make it at this rate," Larsson muttered.

Campbell quickly scrambled to the top of the crater and peered over. The huge black creature transports were already starting to land. The tanks were pounding the landing ships with heavy fire, but their shells had little effect on the heavy armor plating of the transports. Again he wondered why the opposition had chosen explosive ammunition over the heavy energy beam cannons that would have destroyed the transports.

Campbell watched with fascination while a transport briefly landed. One of the twenty huge doors that were built along a line in the side of the rectangular craft flew open. He heard the monstrous roar of a wild beast over the whine of the transport engines, but he couldn't see the creature that had emitted the terrifying cry of rage.

Suddenly, Campbell experienced a sight no human had seen on Earth. A spinosaurus leaped through the open door and landed with an earth-shaking thud. Campbell gazed with open-mouth horror at the mutated creature that he estimated stood between ten-to-twelve meters in height.

FIVE

The spinosaurus roared again while it gazed at the carnage that surrounded it. It bent with amazing speed and scooped up a screaming soldier with its deadly sharp talons. The mutated monster popped the already limp body into its tremendous mouth. Without stopping to chew, the creature swallowed the soldier whole. It quickly moved forward on its two huge muscular legs, its crocodilian mouth gaping, to attack a group of terrified soldiers that were aggravating it with DER shots and sonic blasts.

Campbell watched the DER shots reflect harmlessly off the dinosaur's armor. The sonic blasts only seemed to increase its instinctive fury. The spinosaurus quickly dispatched the helpless soldiers by either squashing them beneath its huge three-toed feet or grabbing them in its deadly claws to squeeze the life out of them before consuming their bodies.

Campbell turned back toward the transport that'd just dropped off the spinosaurus. Its engines roared as it took off to a new location to offload another creature. Everywhere he looked around the smoldering battlefield transports were stopping briefly, unloading a single dinosaur, and then quickly moving on to a new location. In the few moments he watched, at least one hundred creatures of all kinds were unleashed and roaming free in all directions.

He wasn't surprised that while many of the dinosaurs where roaming about the battlefield reaping a tremendous amount of havoc and destruction, many of them were fleeing the noisy chaos through the woods off to both sides. Some went rampaging toward the rear area. To his relief, he noted that most of the pterodactyls wanted nothing to do with the deadly battlefield. They simply took flight upon being released and flew off. While Campbell was worried about the carnage these escaped monsters would inflict upon an unsuspecting world, some hope grew in his heart that the random terror and disorganization caused by the dinosaurs might allow them to escape.

"What do you see?" Larsson asked from the bottom of the crater.

"We're too late. The transports have already started to land between us and the rear area. The dinosaurs are everywhere. We might be cut off."

The roaring sound of transport engines abruptly grew closer. Both Campbell and Larsson peered toward the darkened sky in time to see a group of huge transports pass over their sheltered position as they came in to land nearby. Campbell quickly considered their options.

"Now we're surrounded by Arnold's creatures," Campbell said. "It's no use heading back toward the cover of city or the wooded areas. Even if we made it that far, those bubble bots would cut us down before we could surrender. We have to make it to the rear area through the chaos the dinosaurs are causing."

Larsson nodded. "Sounds like a plan to me. Let's go."

They scrambled out of the crater only to come to an immediate halt.

"Lord in Hades," Campbell muttered, frozen in terror. He stood rigid, bug-eyed, and open mouthed while staring at a spinosaurus leg the size of a tremendous tree trunk. The muted leg was so close he could count the muddy gray scales of its armor. The bloody, pointed nails at the end of its huge toes were as large as his torso.

Campbell started to gaze upward when a tremendous roar, accompanied by a terrible wind of foul breath, nearly blew him off his feet. As he regained his balance, he suddenly found himself nose to snarling snout with row upon row of huge dagger-like teeth. Beside the blood-red curled tongue, he spied the remains of a soldier's crushed head jammed between the dinosaur's fangs. The blank dead eyes were staring back at him as if to accuse him of their final fate. The tremendous elongated head of the spinosaurus swooped down to swallow him whole.

Suddenly, the monster's hideous head disappeared toward the darkened sky while roaring with surprised pain.

"Get away!" Larsson screamed, as he continued to fire his DEP at the injured dinosaur's huge yet unarmored eye.

Campbell didn't waste time considering his fate. He spotted open space between the dinosaur's wide stance and raced between its legs. He didn't stop or turn around to check on Larsson until he was well beyond the thick trashing tail of the terrifying creature. The spinosaurus was whipping its head to and fro in rage and agony as it stumbled off, crushing everything in its path.

Campbell bent to his weary knees, breathing heavily. His heart was pounding wildly as his body reacted to his near escape. He saw Larsson's giant feet appear next to him.

"You owe me another one, Campbell. Let's keep moving."

Campbell stood up and glared at Larsson. "I owe you nothing, Larsson! If not for you, Penelope Preston might still be safe!"

"If you believe that, you're even dumber than I thought. Now, let's move it. You can thank me later."

SIX

Larsson raced off toward the rear area before Campbell could reply. He angrily glared after him for a moment before following.

Larsson ran a few hundred meters, and then turned sharply to the right. Caught off guard, Campbell was wondering what Larsson was doing when he spotted two three-meter tall raptors briefly hidden in the smoky haze. His already struggling heart leaped into his throat again as he skidded to a halt. The horrid bird-like raptors, with muscular clawed arms instead of wings, were bent over while ripping apart the torn body of a soldier. They appeared so intent on their bloody feast, they hadn't noticed them yet. Campbell raced after Larsson, turning every few steps to see if the raptors were pursuing him. When he turned back around, Larsson had vanished.

Campbell whirled around in terror, searching for Larsson. His fear only increased when he spied a squat tank-like triceratops staring at him with blood-red eyes from a hundred meters away. The triceratops dropped its armor-crowned head and three massive horns toward Campbell. The very ground trembled as the beast hoofed the earth and snorted like an enraged bull in preparation for a stampeding charge. Campbell frantically searched for cover. The triceratops let loose a tremendous trumpeting sound as it rampaged forward with surprising quickness. Campbell spotted a small ravine and dove into it. Larsson was already hiding there with several other tattered and muddy soldiers.

"Stop following me, Campbell!" Larsson muttered jokingly with his metal-toothed smile.

I think that madman is actually enjoying this, Campbell thought.

The three-quaking soldiers next to Larsson were speaking with excited but low voices. They appeared human and miraculously unhurt. Campbell ignored them and crawled to higher ground to see if the triceratops had taken further interest in the hidden men. He reached level ground and peeked over. The triceratops was only about twenty meters away. Its armored sides were heaving in and out in angered frustration as it searched for its elusive victim.

"Damn," he grumbled, and ducked his head.

"What is it?" Larsson asked.

"There's an enemy hover tank coming up fast in this direction," he replied. He peeked cautiously over the rocky ridge again just in time to see the long tank cannon erupt with destructive fire as it targeted the triceratops.

A terrifying explosion of flames engulfed the triceratops. The shot was a direct hit into the armored-plated side of the massive drab-colored beast. The tremendous weight of the dinosaur was thrown into the air by the blast. It landed not ten meters away from their position with a ground-shaking crash. Campbell ducked as a mound of loose dirt rained down on him.

Campbell heard a great angered bellowing from the beast, followed by a loud commotion. The torn earth continued to shake beneath him. He hurriedly unburied himself, and peered over the ravine lip with terrified curiosity. To his amazement, the triceratops was alive and on its feet again. The dinosaur slowly shifted its tremendous weight to turn toward the whirling sound of the approaching tank. It lowered its gigantic armored head with its three horns pointing towards its enemy. The mutated animal had a ghastly gaping wound in the side. Black blood flowed down its armor.

The triceratops charged the tank like a monstrous raging rhinoceros. The earth trembled beneath its weight.

"Shoot!" Campbell yelled at the tank. He knew he was too late even if those huddled inside the protective tank could hear him.

The deadly horns of the triceratops smashed into the tank straight on, accompanied by the screams of tearing metal and armor. The tank was tossed backward with seeming effortlessness before it was flipped over onto its turret. The triceratops was stunned. It staggered back and forth like a drunk on shaky legs. The crumpled tank spun slowly around on its topside.

The injured dinosaur seemed to recover as it regained its insane rage at the sight of its wounded enemy. Campbell could see dazed men frantically trying to scramble out of the tank escape hatches. The enraged triceratops charged again.

The triceratops smashed into the side of the tank with terrifying and reckless speed. The battered and smashed tank rolled side over side as the dinosaur continued its violent and thundering rampage. It trampled the fleeing tank crew beneath its huge, flat-toed feet. The dinosaur continued to ram the crushed tank over and over again. It finally collapsed either from exhaustion or from its wounds.

Campbell watched for a moment longer as his pulse returned to a near-normal pace. The triceratops did not move again. Campbell's attention was caught by the words being spoken beneath him in the ravine.

"You are Larsson, and that is Commander Campbell, correct?" Campbell heard a soldier ask. He slowly slid down to rest next to Larsson alert for more trouble.

Campbell jumped when Larsson grabbed his DEP and pointed it at the three soldiers. The threesome quickly raised their hands in surrender. Their dirty human faces appeared shocked and wide-eyed, their hands were trembling. They were weaponless.

"Yes, I am Commander Campbell and this is Sub-Commander Larsson," he answered. "All of you are deserting, aren't you?"

The soldiers vigorously shook their heads with rapid words of denial.

"It's okay," Campbell tried to reassure them. "This battle is lost. Larsson and I are trying to escape as well. You're free to come with us. I think if we stay together as a group, our chances of survival are better."

Suddenly, a deep sound of rolling thunder seemed to come from beneath the earth. The already disheveled ground shook so violently that Campbell was tossed into the air. As he landed, he tried to scramble to his feet, but he was hurled down again.

"What new devilry is this?" Larsson shouted over the protesting earth.

"I don't know?" Campbell yelled. He tried to regain his feet, but only made it to his hands and knees before losing his balance again.

The convulsing earth was more violent than Campbell had experienced during the explosive shelling. He couldn't imagine a weapon that could cause such massive destruction short of something nuclear. The soldiers next to him were screaming in terror. It was as if they were being tossed about by some invisible force.

Abruptly, a shaking fissure started to crack open in the earth between him and Larsson. Streaming gases and noxious fumes began to hiss out of the opening.

"Campbell!" Larsson yelled from the other side of the rapidly widening gap. If possible, there was fear in his mechanical voice.

Campbell couldn't see him through his burning, watering eyes and all the smoke-like vapors. He hacked and gagged as he was surrounded by the sulfur-smelling fumes. He tried to scramble away from the widening fissure, but he was knocked off his feet again. Suddenly, he found himself on the very edge of the opening while staring into the intense heat of rising lava.

"Campbell," Larsson repeated weakly from very close.

SEVEN

Campbell realized that Larsson had been incapacitated by the noxious fumes, and probably didn't know about the potential danger of the rapidly rising lava. Fighting down his own fear, Campbell managed to get himself into a crouch. Gathering all his strength, he leaped into the fumes over the fissure unable to see the other side. For an instant, he didn't think he would clear the opening. He'd fall into the fissure and instantly combust in the superheated magma below. Then suddenly he was landing hard on the other side right next to Larsson.

He quickly discovered the thick sulfur fumes were much more toxic in this area. In near blindness and with burning lungs, he rapidly examined Larsson to find him nearly unconscious. Grabbing Larsson beneath the armpits, he held his breath and began to haul Larsson's tremendous weight away from the spewing crevasse. He'd pulled Larsson about ten meters, and was becoming exhausted when two of the terrified soldiers from the ravine joined him to haul Larsson free of the fiery danger.

Just as suddenly as the rumbling noise and trembling ground had started, it stopped. Campbell gave Larsson's heavy body one more yank before he fell back heaving for breath, mentally and physically drained. He didn't know how many more of these deadly surprises he could stand.

The two soldiers dropped down in breathless exhaustion next to Campbell. One of them said, "Listen."

Campbell listened for a moment, but he couldn't hear anything except the continuing wails of the dying.

"Everything has gone silent," said the soldier.

"Where's Markus?" asked the other soldier.

"He lost his balance and fell into that crack," answered the first soldier, seemingly unconcerned with the other man's fate.

"Damn! The man owned me money. Are you sure he's dead?"

Campbell tried to ignore the two squabbling hens while he studied the landscape with great interest. It was a vision from the fiery pits of Hell. All around him wide cracks split the already tortured earth. Dark billowing smoke was intermixing with hissing white fumes. Dirty sand was spewing from mini volcano-like eruptions. To his relief, he didn't see any of the molten hot lava rising to ground level, but intense fires were blazing everywhere. The foul atmospheres reeked of aged, rotten eggs.

He turned to the surrounding forests. Many of the mighty trees were uprooted and toppled. Many others roared in crackling fire near where gaping fissures had cracked open. Soon the entire forest would be a raging inferno. Already, great towers of black and gray smoke were billowing from the flames, blackening out the struggling sunlight.

Campbell turned to the city and was filled with confusion and awe. It lay in complete ruins. A great cloud of smoke and ash or dust was hanging above the toppled edifices. The buildings were leaning crazily or had collapsed altogether. Even while he watched, another building relented and crumbled with a loud crash and a cloud of dust. But what surprised him the most was that the protective plasma dome that had surrounded the city was gone. It occurred to Campbell that the destruction he saw couldn't have been caused by some weapon from the opposing forces.

Campbell had lived on the Hawaiian Islands long enough to think he knew what had happened. He just wondered if nature could deliver such an incredible coincidence during a major battle or if this universal destruction was manmade. Did Arnold possess a weapon that he hadn't told anyone about?

The loud angry roar of a nearby spinosaurus immediately reminded him that they were far from out of danger. The battle may have come to a stunned silence for a moment, but now Campbell saw the dinosaurs were running amok as if they were terrified by some instinctive danger he couldn't see. As he kneeled beside Larsson to revive him, the earthly thunder returned. The ground began to vomit and shake violently all around him.

"Commander! What's happening?" one of the soldiers cried.

"I think we're having an earthquake," Campbell said while he struggled back over Larsson. "Larsson." He slapped Larsson's half-metal face. "Ouch! That was stupid. Larsson, come on, get up!"

Great vents in the earth continued to rip open all around them. A small, sand-spewing volcano erupted just meters away. Choking fumes fouled the superheated air, sending Campbell and his companions into violent coughing fits.

"Larsson, get up!" he yelled between coughs as he desperately shook Larsson's shoulders.

Larsson's eyes suddenly popped open. He quickly sat up and stared around him with a mixture of fear and confusion. The groaning earth trembled again followed by the sharp sound of cracking rock.

"What in Hades is happening?" Larsson asked.

"I think we're having an earthquake or a volcanic eruption," Campbell yelled. "Come on, we have to get out of here while we have a chance."

The trembling earth opened another yawning fissure not ten meters away. Roaring flames licked at the rocky edges of the new crevasse while great clouds of vapor hissed out of the opening. Larsson was immediately on his feet. Campbell shakily rose with him as they used each other to keep their unsteady balance.

Campbell whipped to his right when he heard a terrifying bird-like screech nearby. Through the dense fumes he spied two ravenous raptors standing on the other side of the newly formed crevasse. The sharp nosed, muscularly built raptors glared fiercely back at them with wide dark eyes filled with terrible hunger for anything living. They scrambled back and forth along the fissure edge, frantically searching for a bridge across the steaming void to get at their prey. All the while, they chattered in excited voices, chirping and squawking. Their terrible hooked talons slashed at the dense, dirty air.

"Do something, Commander!" yelled one of the soldiers. "They'll kill us if they get across."

Campbell turned around. He found both the soldiers behind him and Larsson as if they were trying to hide. He turned back to Larsson when he saw him drawing his pistol.

"That won't kill them!" Campbell yelled.

"Maybe not, but it might persuade them to leave us alone," Larsson said.

Larsson carefully aimed and fired at the nearest raptor. The 150-kilowatt energy beam struck the horrifying creature behind the right eye before reflecting off its armored head and slicing harmlessly through the dense smoke. Campbell wasn't surprised to see that the raptor remained unhurt, but at least the power of the shot knocked the relatively diminutive dinosaur off its pins. The raptor screeched with wicked anger, but was instantly back on its feet. It was furious as it clicked and squawked at its partner. Abruptly, the two raptors turned and disappeared back into the cloud of vapors.

"See, it worked," Larsson said with a broad grin of metal teeth.

"Look out!" a soldier cried in terror.

The raptors raced back through the cloud and made a tremendous leap in an attempt to jump over the wide fissure. Campbell stood in mesmerized panic as the arm-flapping raptors landed on the lip of their side of the fissure. One of the raptors lost its balance when the ground beneath it crumbled. It wheeled frantically back and forth, screeching with fear, before it toppled back into the crevasse and disappeared.

Larsson began to pummel the remaining raptor with shot after shot of his DEP. The raptor hissed at them with venomous fury. It frantically tried to retreat, only to find itself caught between Larsson's onslaught and the fiery opening in the earth. The creature tried to escape by leaping back over the fissure. As it jumped, Campbell knew it wouldn't make it. With a terrified screech, the raptor plummeted to a burning death.

"Let's go before more of those things find us," Campbell commanded. He dashed off to his right. As he did so, he noticed the earth had stopped rumbling and shaking. The fierce roars of wild beasts and the whirling engines of enemy hover tanks could clearly be heard though the dense and blinding smoke.

EIGHT

Campbell ran doubled over and almost completely blind. The cloudy vapors choked him and made visibility impossible. He could only hope he was still running toward the rear area. On a positive note, he figured no one else could see them, either.

"We have to slow down," Campbell said, after he nearly dropped them into a magma-filled crevasse.

As they marched forward with caution, Campbell witnessed the carnage of the battle and the earthquakes. There were mutilated bloody bodies everywhere. Many of them were consumed by flames, their body fat sizzling and popping. The smell was horrid and revolting. The ground was littered with torn and screaming wounded. Although Campbell felt fleeting sympathy for the retched wounded, they were Arnold's treacherous army, and he didn't stop to help them.

Campbell did take pleasure in one gruesome sight. He stopped next to a smoking crevasse filled with molten lava when he saw a huge tentacle lying shrived and burnt over the crevasse edge. The rising lava had claimed one of Arnold's squids.

Maybe there's a god after all, he thought.

As he hurried forward, Campbell also saw numerous hover tanks destroyed by the quakes, ripped apart by some huge creature or simply abandoned as if their crews had panicked and fled.

"Do you think we could get one of those abandoned tanks going?" he asked Larsson.

"We probably could with some time to defeat their security systems, but I think it would take too long. Besides, there's a good chance we'd end up in one of these fissures," Larsson answered, so they moved on.

They came across other soldiers moving silently in and out of the vapors like ghosts. Many had ghastly wounds, but most wore vacant stares with dirty lax expressions of horrified shock. Their will to fight was gone. Their will to survive wasn't far behind. Campbell knew their feelings all too well.

They were moving into an area that was free of vapors and smoke. Suddenly, Campbell was startled by horrible screaming. On his left, he spied a black-uniformed corporal who was writhing on the ground in terrible pain. He was tearing madly at his bruised and bleeding face and head. But the wounds appeared inflicted by the corporal's insane self-torment. Campbell could see nothing else physically wrong with the soldier. He couldn't understand what was happening. He started to move toward the soldier when Larsson grabbed his arm.

"Leave him alone," Larsson warned. "We have to get out of here before he dies and it escapes."

"What're you talking about?" Campbell asked quietly while still staring at the horrifying sight.

After a cresting shrill scream, the corporal abruptly went still. With his final exhalation, a cloud of vapor seemed to seep from his bloody nose and gaping mouth.

"Run!" Larsson yelled. He was already sprinting away.

Campbell stood transfixed with confusion and fear until he realized what he was seeing. Arnold had unleashed the mindless mental vampires created in the Master's image. Vivid memories of the torturous pain the Master had inflicted upon him got Campbell moving again.

Campbell ran as fast as he could, pumping his arms and lifting his knees. He quickly caught up to lumbering Larsson, and twisted around to see the two soldiers sprinting behind him with wide-eyed expressions of terror.

"Hurry up," Campbell yelled. The tormenting cloud was catching up to the soldiers at a rapid pace. It seemed to glow red, either because of its excited state or from its recent feast.

Adrenaline pushed Campbell on to greater feats of speed, but he knew they could never outrun the unquenchable hunger of the cloud. He legged by Larsson as he heard the high-pitched screeching of the soldiers when they realized the creature was almost upon them.

The relative silence was suddenly shattered by the terrified shrill of a man in horrible pain. Campbell slowed down, knowing the vapor-like creature had found another victim to torture to death.

He ran, huffing and puffing, in and out of another sulfur-reeking cloud of vapor before sliding to a halt. The agonizing screams of the dying soldier were still clearly audible, and he prayed the feeding creature would be occupied by its human feast long enough for them to escape.

The remaining soldier ripped out of the vapor cloud with Larsson chugging along right behind him. They both stopped next to Campbell, and wearily dropped their hands to their knees while heaving for breath. He didn't let them rest long.

"We have to get out of here while that thing's busy," Campbell said breathlessly. "Let's hope we don't run into any more of them."

NINE

They moved cautiously forward. Campbell swiveled his head to and fro with a sharp eye for new dangers. He waved the other two on to hasten their pace when the high-pitched screams of the dying soldier came to a sudden halt.

Campbell felt a cooling easterly breeze upon his sweating face. He stopped for a moment to gaze around and reconnoiter their position. The refreshing breeze had ripped open a vent in the dense smoke and vapors. He could see they were nearly at the rear area where their hover tanks and artillery had been stationed.

The enemy's explosive shelling had been particularly fierce and effective here. The moon-base cannons and hover tanks had been completely decimated by the enemy's artillery barrage. Smoldering explosion craters pitted the tortured landscape. Burning and smashed armored vehicles were tossed everywhere like unwanted toys. Campbell was sickened by the number of torn and charred bodies. The useless slaughter of the personnel was complete.

"What a waste," he muttered.

"Not quite, Campbell. This may mean your freedom," Larsson said at his side.

Campbell wearily nodded before he raced forward with a subdued glimmer of hope rising in his heart. His companions were close behind him when he heard the remaining soldier cry out with renewed fear. Campbell slid to a stop. A huge shadow materialized out of a smoke cloud to his right.

"Damn," Campbell muttered. His shoulders sagged in pending resignation. He was totally drained and exhausted. His will to fight flickered like the weakest flame. He couldn't face another insurmountable obstacle.

A hulking enemy hover tank had appeared. Its 125-millimeter cannon was pointed directly at him. It couldn't miss from this close range. He wearily raised his blood and mud-covered hands above his sweat-soaked head knowing there was no escape. His only hope was that they would accept his surrender, but so far the enemy had shown no mercy.

"What're we going to do?" Larsson asked at his side.

"Wait and see," Campbell muttered.

The huge battle-gray tank continued to approach until Campbell was staring right down the deadly black hole of the cannon barrel. He felt a small degree of hope, since the tank commander hadn't killed them outright and moved on. Suddenly, the remaining soldier made a desperate run for it.

"Halt!" a voice commanded from the tank loudspeaker.

The soldier kept sprinting toward the protective cover of a nearby crater as the ominous tank quickly swiveled its deadly guns in that direction. Campbell immediately saw his chance to bolt and escape his imminent death, yet he stood rooted in horror at what he knew was about to happen. The tank opened fire with the two rotating small caliber cannons affixed to its nose area. The escaping soldier was ripped to bloody pieces by the explosive shells.

"Waste, another wasted life," Campbell muttered, and slumped.

Feeling the tremendous burden of useless despair, Campbell turned from the carnage toward the awaiting annihilation. He wasn't surprised to see the hovering tank had quickly returned all its forward weapons upon him and Larsson. He stared back at the ominous tank fearlessly awaiting his death.

"Why don't they kill us?" Larsson whispered.

"They're probably terrified by your horrifying face. Don't push your luck."

"Inspector Burt Campbell?" someone in the tank asked through a loudspeaker.

Campbell was shocked that someone had not only recognized him, but they had used his real title. He was so dumbfounded he didn't respond.

"Answer them before they kill us, you fool," Larsson muttered.

"Oh, yeah," he stammered. "Yes, I'm Burt Campbell," he said in a loud voice.

"You treacherous bastard!" the voice in the tank shouted.

Campbell shuffled nervously from foot to foot while he tried to think of an appropriate response to the accusation. He had none.

His anxiety turned to curiosity while he watched the top hatch of the tank turret unlock and open. The heavy hatch top was heaved back, and a small man in a dark green uniform began to climb out. Campbell's curiosity turned to stunned amazement and then to happiness beyond his wildest dreams.

"Goro," he whispered, still not believing his eyes. "Goro Sen!"

Campbell forgot about his exhaustion and pain. He raced toward the tank as Sen clumsily clamored down to the ground. They came together exchanging beaming grins. Burt couldn't contain his bursting happiness any longer. He leaped forward and crushed Sen in a huge hug that lifted the little man off the ground. He roared with laughter before setting Sen down.

"You're really alive, Goro!" Burt yelled, and laughed again.

Goro gazed into his black eyes. "Burt, Burt Campbell. I can't tell you how happy I am to see you alive as well. I was terrified that you'd be dead before we found you and Major Larsson."

Burt's smile dropped from his face in confusion. "What'd you mean? What're you even doing here? How did you escape from Arnold? Is . . ."

"Burt, shut up! There's plenty of time for questions later. We have to get out of here now."

Campbell thought about the horrible cloud creature they'd just escaped, and said, "You're right."

Larsson stepped up beside him. "Sen, I'm glad to see you. Your timing couldn't have been better. I've been having a hell of a time keeping this friend of yours alive."

"What?" Campbell yelled. "You keep *me* alive? Who're you . . .?"

"Burt, shut up for once," Sen said. "Larsson, get Campbell onto the back of the tank. We're getting out of here before all hell breaks loose."

Campbell knew when to shut up. He and Larsson scrambled onto the rear of the tank and grabbed hold of troop-carrier handles. Sen climbed back into the turret hatch while speaking into his microphone.

"General, this is Sen. I have Campbell and Larsson. They're alive and I'm moving to the rear area now. You can commence fire in a moment."

A multitude of questions whirled through Campbell's excited mind. The hovering tank turned and moved quickly out of the battlefield.

"Who are you?" Campbell asked Larsson as the tank sped away.

"Ulf Larsson," Larsson said with his crooked smile.

"General, this is Sen. We're clear," he said into his microphone.

Campbell ducked behind the armored protection of the tank turret when the world around him erupted in the most incredible artillery barrage he'd ever heard. The clapping thunder of the initial firing vibrated through his body and numbed his mind. He covered his ears, fearing they would burst. He peeked up from his protection to peer back at the battlefield.

"Lord in Hades," he whispered. He squinted as the entire battlefield was lifted in explosive fire and destruction as if from a massively erupting volcano. Nothing could have survived the devastation. Arnold's forces were wiped out, but what about his creatures?

XXI

QUESTIONS ANSWERED

ONE

Their immense tank slowly hovered through the disorganized rear area, which was crammed with scrambling soldiers and equipment. Campbell felt his body and senses reverberating from the concussion blasts of the seemingly eternal artillery barrage. From the rear of the tank, he tried to peer through the fiery black smoke and earth-filled eruptions on the destroyed battlefield, but nothing appeared alive. Even the mock city had disappeared into the blazing devastation. As mentally and physically exhausted as he was, he still felt pain over this waste of life. All of this was originally caused by Arnold's insane mission to conquer the world.

The tank came to a rocking halt. Campbell turned forward to find they were parked next to a huge black disk-shaped clipper with military markings. He slowly crawled off the tank before making room for a fast-marching column of heavily armed and grim-faced soldiers heading toward the battlefield.

As he rounded the rear of the tank, he found Goro already waiting for him and Larsson. The air was thick with drifting smoke. The tortured ground beneath them shook with each destructive blast.

"So we're not under arrest or anything?" Campbell asked Goro as they trotted to the waiting military clipper. Larsson was lumbering silently along beside him.

"No, Burt," Goro laughed. "Actually, I think you're a hero of sorts."

"Sit down, Campbell," Larsson said, when they entered the long, thin fuselage along the center of the disk-shaped clipper. "I want to check that wound."

"I'm fine," he said, while giving Larsson a nasty look for pestering him like a mother hen.

"Just do it, Campbell," Larsson persisted. "I was ordered to deliver you in good condition, and I'm not going to have you bleeding to death on me."

"It's a little late for that now," Campbell muttered, but sat down in a seat against the fuselage wall.

Larsson sat next to him and explored his back wound with a sudden intake of breath. "I've never seen anything like this. The wound has completely healed, Campbell. The piece of shrapnel has been rejected from your body."

Campbell felt Larsson flick his finger across his itchy wound. He heard a piece of metal clink on the clipper floor. He looked down to see a bloody piece of shrapnel lying at his muddy feet.

"Campbell," Larsson said with awe in his voice, "they briefed me about you, but I never . . ."

Suddenly, the metal floor beneath Campbell's feet shook violently almost knocking him out of his seat. He anxiously grabbed the seatback to steady himself as the clipper shook back and forth. Goro rushed to grab a seat opposite Campbell and Larsson.

"We have to hurry and get out of here," Goro yelled above loud groaning from the ground. "Things are only going to get worse."

"Is this an earthquake, or have they released a new weapon that can torture the Earth this way?" Campbell shouted.

Goro gestured for them to strap themselves into seats before he leaned forward and yelled. "No, Burt. It's an actual earthquake, and we had nothing to do with starting it. There's a fault line in the Midwest that is centered in Missouri. It's called the New Madrid

Line. This quake is just a small part of what is happening right now, but its effects are being felt from Texas to the East Coast and as far north as New Detroit. It has started, Burt!"

Just as suddenly, the earthquake stopped and the clipper settled. Silence fell all around them as even the artillery barrage had stopped momentarily. Campbell found the sudden silence eerie.

"What has started?" he asked, almost afraid to know.

"I don't understand the whole thing, but the President will brief you," Goro said. "We're going to Lincoln, Nebraska, right now to meet her."

"The President?" Campbell said with amazement. "You mean *the* President, Elizabeth Cathcart?"

"That's right, Burt," Goro laughed. "You've made it to the big show, and I understand she has grand plans for you. That's why she sent me to find you."

Goro disappeared up front to tell the pilots to get underway while Campbell sat there in stunned silence. He turned to Larsson only to find him staring back at him while nodding with his horrid grin. Campbell turned away, not liking the look from those mismatched eyes. Goro returned to his seat and strapped himself in as the clipper engines began to whine. They took off almost immediately.

TWO

"Okay, Burt," Goro said as they ascended into lower orbit, "we've got about twenty minutes to catch up on things before we land at the capital. I imagine you have a million questions."

"You bet," he said quickly while trying to organize his confused thoughts. "I'll try to keep them in order. First, tell me how you escaped. I was sure you and your family were killed."

Goro smiled. "I was sure we were dead as well. Let's just say that the security force you alerted when you returned to headquarters decided to make a counteroffensive. They were waiting down the hall when Oki, Akio, and I rounded the corner on the way to our deaths. You probably heard the sound of the sonic blast that killed that sergeant, and that's why you thought we were dead."

Campbell nodded. "What'd you do next? You knew about Arnold's treachery."

"I knew Arnold planned something serious, so I contacted some friends in the federal government. They contacted some *more* powerful friends, and I soon found myself in front of the President, explaining our whole ordeal. I mean everything, Burt, from Yamamoto's teleporter experiments to my beliefs about Monica Yamamoto's recreation. I also told her I thought Arnold was creating creatures like that George thing using the moon base teleporter, which Koko obviously failed to destroy.

"I was in luck that day, since Major Larsson here—" Goro pointed at Larsson. "—just happened to be there briefing the President on the moon base situation. She called me into the briefing. What I told her only confirmed what Larsson was reporting."

Campbell turned to Larsson with openmouthed astonishment. *How could I have been so wrong about this man? Well, half a man?*

Larsson laughed. "You see, Burt, I'm not the kind of traitor you thought I was. Yes, I betrayed Arnold, but I've been working for Cathcart all along. There have been weird rumors coming from the moon base ever since Arnold took over and those teleportation experiments began. I was sent there undercover to investigate."

Campbell nodded in understanding while he thought about the Master's prediction that Larsson was a traitor. The Master had been right. It just hadn't understood the extent of Larsson's betrayal.

Suddenly, Campbell's astonishment turned to burning rage. "Why did you betray Koko and Penelope?" he yelled.

Larsson peered at the floor. His expression had always been hard for Campbell to read, but he thought he saw anguished pain in Larsson's disfigured face.

"That was, and is, a very complex situation, Burt," Larsson said slowly. "I'm truly sorry about Koko's death. Believe it or not, he was my friend. But the whole thing was unavoidable once Koko and Penelope decided to come to the moon base, and Koko refused to listen to my warnings. He insisted on coming.

"When Koko contacted me about saving you, I knew I had to oblige him and try to keep him out of trouble. If I didn't help Koko; he would have contacted someone else, which would have gotten them killed immediately.

"I knew that Arnold had plans for you and Penelope, and that he wouldn't kill you. I decided the best thing to do was to simply turn Penelope over to Arnold safely with the hope that we could save you both later. Then Koko muddled things by starting to kill the guards at the arena."

Campbell could see how the whole situation was complex, but he thought a man of Larsson's intelligence could've thought of a better scheme then turning Penelope over to Arnold. He realized speculation on what could've been didn't help. What happened had happened. It was out of his control. He moved on to other questions, realizing that Larsson had been an invaluable help in other ways less personal to him but for the greater good of all.

"So it was you that betrayed Arnold," Campbell said to Larsson. "You told the Fort Knox military forces what Arnold planned."

Larsson nodded. "Every day I reported about Arnold's plans. I kept them updated about our progress in training and the forces that were being used. Most important, I told them about the creatures Arnold was creating to use against them."

"I wondered why you disappeared every day after our briefings," Campbell said, nodding in understanding.

"You may also have wondered why we used explosive projectiles against Arnold's forces," Goro said. "Larsson informed us about the creature's indestructibility using energy beams. A plan was developed to surround the battlefield and to use explosives powerful enough to obliterate them. Unfortunately, we don't know if the plan worked. I fear many of the things escaped, since we held back our major fire-power until you were rescued."

"Rescued? I was almost killed!" Campbell said with emotion.

Larsson reached over to Campbell's belt and pulled out a small transmitter.

"See this?" Larsson asked, while holding up the transmitter. "I planted this on you before the briefing. It transmitted where you were the whole time. That's how Goro found us so fast. The artillery and the bots had specific orders not to fire in your area, even though I must admit there were some close calls. Besides that, I had orders to keep you alive."

"So you were just following orders, huh?" Campbell asked with a snide smile. "Here I thought you were trying to save me out of your adoring affection for me."

"Let's just say I'm a people person," Larsson said, with a mechanical laugh that sounded almost human.

Campbell gave him a thoughtful glance, and turned to Goro. "Why didn't you destroy all Arnold's forces before they even landed on Earth?"

Goro's Japanese features pinched together in an ugly frown. "There was the question about Arnold's real intentions, but that was a matter of heated debate. The military won the argument and convinced President Cathcart to let the battle take place. They claimed they had to see the kind of forces they might be up against in the future, since it's believed Fort Knox wasn't the only place being attacked today. We believe Arnold sent forces all over the world."

"I got that impression as well," Campbell nodded. "We only came with four thousand troops, and I know there were at least twenty-five thousand in an arena. Besides that, I saw other groups of troops training, and Arnold wouldn't tell me what they were training for."

"Well," Goro said, "my vote was to destroy the forces as they landed. I have to wonder about the true motivations behind some of the generals' desire to allow Arnold into Fort Knox."

Campbell nodded again. *Arnold said something about not all the military leaders being content with their situation and wanting to bring about a new order.*

"What happened to Arnold?" he anxiously asked Goro.

"He was captured even as he gave that Code Red order," Sen said. "Unfortunately, he was too heavily guarded before that and we were unable to capture him alive until then. I believe he's being questioned at this moment about the Master, the Master's plans, and Its whereabouts."

"That's one of the reasons it was so important to keep you alive, Burt," Larsson said. "I was under orders to learn as much as I could about the Master, but I could never get close to It. It is my belief that, other than Arnold, you may be the only one who's been in contact with the thing. You may be the key to understanding Its plans and how to destroy It."

"Penelope has been in much closer contact with It than I have," Campbell said, shaking his head in sorrow as he thought about the last time he'd seen Penelope. "I doubt I'll be much assistance in killing It. The reason It interacted with me was to keep me from betraying It. Even if I had a weapon that could destroy It, and was in the same room, I don't know if I could kill It."

Campbell noticed Larsson and Sen went quiet and thoughtful after this. *I wonder what they have up their sleeves. They aren't telling me everything.*

"So why does Cathcart want to see me?" he asked. "I didn't even vote for her, and I don't want to make a contribution to her reelection fund."

"Burt," Goro said seriously, "there isn't going to be another election. Maybe not ever, and as you well know, you have another job to do."

The clipper landed before Goro explained his words. Campbell felt more confused and anxious than ever.

⬤XXII⬤

THE BEGINNING OF
THE END

ONE

Campbell found himself alone in the expansive Lincoln Oval Office
with the tall and handsome Elizabeth Cathcart. They examined each
other for a moment with equal curiosity, and a little bit of awe on
Campbell's part. Campbell thought the sandy-haired president must
have been a stunning beauty when she was younger. Now the ninety-
year old woman's creased and worried face showed the wear and tear
of her seven years in the Presidential Office. She still carried herself
erect and proud, but now she appeared weary and frail beneath some
immense burden.

The office itself was a duplicate of the original Oval Office in
the now-submerged Washington D.C. area. Cathcart stood behind
her historic desk. The late afternoon sun peeked through a huge bay
window overlooking the west garden behind her. Campbell faced
Cathcart with his back to a large antique conference table surrounded
by high-back chairs. He stood with his muddy feet on a thick tan
carpet bearing the national seal. The bookshelf-lined walls were filled
with priceless historical documents that he was sure hid the high-
tech communications the President needed to stay in instant contact
with the world. A huge portrait of George Washington to his left
glared down at him. He was unnerved by the way Washington's eyes
followed his every move.

Campbell tried to shift out of George's gaze again, but failed. He was ashamed to be standing there with his disorderly and bloody appearance, yet he was still awed to be in the presence of the President.

"First let me say, Inspector," Cathcart started in her deep cultured voice with a Midwestern accent, "that I am aware of your past, and I consider you a hero."

"A hero?" Campbell blurted out while his cheeks flushed.

"Yes, you may have saved the world from a great catastrophe when you destroyed Yamamoto's teleporter experiment and his computer. If you had not taken such resolute initiative on your own, mankind might be facing an even worse situation than it is today. Furthermore, you stopped the mad ambition of the overzealous General Stenwood, and saved me from a major embarrassment."

"I don't suppose you condoned my actions against the *USS Smith*, and the usage of Stenwood's misappropriated funds," he muttered.

"Under the circumstances, those things are of little importance at the moment," said Cathcart, while she walked around her desk. Campbell noticed she still bore a fine, trim figure beneath her brown-tailored suit.

A minor earth tremor shook the office. Cathcart leaned against her desk. Campbell gazed around, afraid the walls might collapse. He gazed back into Cathcart's intelligent brown eyes. There was no fear, only a sad calmness.

"As you can see, Inspector, the world faces some grave problems, possibly the worst that have confronted mankind in modern history," Cathcart said when the tremor stopped.

"Captain Sen hinted at something like this. What's going on?" Campbell asked, his stomach still churning with anxiety.

"We're short on time, but it's important you understand what's happening. What you do with that information may be of vital importance to the future of mankind. Please sit down."

Cathcart directed him to a luxurious and cushioned seat in front of her desk that was obviously meant for heads of state. He sat gingerly, ever conscious of the permanent stains he might be leaving in a seat that was probably irreplaceable. Cathcart started to pace the large office.

"For centuries," Cathcart began, "prophets and astronomers have predicted the end of the world. That time may be upon us."

Oh, not this end-of-the-world crap again, Campbell thought. *First I get it from Arnold and the Master, and now from the President. People have been predicting catastrophes since the beginning of time, but mankind is still here.* He kept his mouth shut, and tried to appear attentive out of respect for where he was.

"As you know," Cathcart continued, "the Earth rotates on an axis stemming from the magnetic poles. The problem with this rotation is that the Earth wobbles. This wobble is further affected by the molten core of the Earth, the gravitational pull of the Sun. solar flares, and other astrological forces. Like a spinning top, the wobble has become increasing unstable and dramatic. Eventually, the top loses balance and falls down.

"In the Earth's case, the wobble has become so dramatic that the magnetic poles have begun to shift and reverse themselves. The reversing poles are causing the continental plates to move along the Earth's molten core. The movement of the continental plates is occurring much faster than many believed possible."

"Causing the earthquakes we're feeling," Campbell nodded. He still found it hard to believe what he was hearing.

"Exactly," Cathcart said, "but these quakes are only the beginning. To give you an idea of the kind of continental shifts that the scientists are expecting, the last time the poles reversed they believe Alaska used to be aligned along the equator.

"If you can imagine the kind of shift in the world's land masses that I'm talking about, you can imagine what will happen to all life forms as this is occurring. There will be devastating earthquakes all over the world. The earthquakes will cause giant tidal waves that will devastate our coasts. Huge volcanoes will erupt as the surface crust splits and opens up. These volcanoes will spew trillions of tons of toxic vapor and ash into our atmosphere, causing tremendous climatic changes. New mountains will form while others will be destroyed. Billions of people will die from the initial onslaught, while the survivors will have to scratch out a meager existence in the ruins of our world. We are talking about the end of modern civilization, and although it may not be the end of mankind, it will be the end of everything we know today."

An impressive speech, but I'm not buying it, he thought before saying, "Scientists have been arguing about this for years, and we've never had any major problems. Sure, earthquakes and volcanic eruptions have increased in number and magnitude over time, but I've always heard the shift would take thousands of years. Today's earthquakes could be coincidental."

Cathcart lowered her head and shook it with great sorrow in her eyes. Campbell could see that she honestly believed what she was saying. A great fear started to grow within him.

"I wish this were a local incident, Inspector Campbell. The scientific data and news pouring in from around the world prove that the catastrophe is starting. This is the real thing."

"Okay, assuming all this is true," Campbell persisted, trying desperately to find some hope, "you must have known this for years. Certainly you've formed a plan of action, a method of saving mankind."

Cathcart turned and stared at him as if she were gazing down at an ignorant pupil. Anger hardened her once-soft eyes.

"Inspector, what makes you think we could, or should, save mankind? You of all people know human nature. Human beings are bent

318

on their own destruction. They refuse to believe in their own mortality. Look at the past, the continual use of fossil fuels, global warming that nearly flooded the world and annihilated much of mankind due to its own stupidity. That doesn't even include the destruction caused by warfare and man's creation of weapons of mass destruction.

"What I'm trying to say, Inspector, is that even though we've known something like this has been coming for years, what makes you think the public would believe the end is coming or would do anything about it?"

Campbell didn't say anything. He saw this was something the President had thought about a great deal. It was a matter of great passion for her. Her pacing had become a brisk walk. There was an expression of pinched pain on her face.

Finally, his own passion stirred and he couldn't keep quiet any longer. "Why wasn't there an attempt to inform the public? Some of them would've believed you and tried to prepare."

"We thought of that, of course. Yet as scientists calculated the level of destruction that's about to occur, we saw there was no way to prepare the world population for nearly total annihilation. Inspector, they're predicting only about a one- to five-percent survival rate from this. Do you have any idea of the panic and chaos that would cause?"

Campbell shook his head sadly, knowing the entire world would come to a cataclysmic standstill while the population panicked, rioted, fought over resources, or just waited to die. Simply announcing the truth would mean the destruction of the world's economic systems and the death of millions in selfish wars for resources.

"I guess the thing that stopped us from launching a massive information campaign," Cathcart continued, "was hope—the hope that the destruction wouldn't be so great. No one wants to believe the world they're living in is about to come to an end."

"That's the kind of unrealistic thinking and hope that's led to all our world problems," Campbell huffed.

Cathcart whirled on him with fury in her eyes. "This is not the time to examine the morality of our actions, Campbell! That time is past."

The President paced for a moment while she regained her composure.

"Look, Inspector, some of us still believe there is hope for mankind and we have made preparations. Some scientists convinced my predecessor that this threat was real. He began preparations twelve years ago to secretly build a sanctuary deep in the Pacific Ocean for a small portion of mankind.

"He also convinced other world leaders to do likewise. Ten facilities have been built all over the world with the capacity to hold an approximate total of two-and-a-half million people. We don't have time to go into details, but we haven't forsaken all hope."

Cathcart came over to Campbell and softly laid her hand on his shoulder. He noticed her hand was trembling.

"Inspector, this is where you come into the plan."

Now Campbell was really confused. He gazed up at her concerned face with a questioning expression.

TWO

"When I read the reports about you and Monica Yamamoto, a new hope rose in my heart," Cathcart said with a warm smile. "I saw the chance for man's survival, the future in the form of the next step in man's evolution that could survive the horrible environment man will face in this new world."

"Penelope and I?" he asked with astonishment.

"Yes, Burt. When I read about you and Penelope, as you call her, and your extraordinary abilities, I saw a sort of Adam and Eve. You two could be the beginning of a new race of humans that could survive the turmoil of the new world. That's why I want you to go to the moon base and save Penelope. When you've done that, I want you two to escape to New Atlantis, the secret ocean city we've created."

Campbell was stunned into silence. The implications of what Cathcart was telling him were beyond his comprehension. He thought again of the Master's belief that he and Penelope would have something to do with the leadership of the world after man's demise. But this was the *President* suggesting that they were the beginning of a new human race, not the raving of an insane cloud Arnold had created in a teleporter.

"Burt, I know this is a lot to take in at the moment," Cathcart said.

"That's the understatement of all time," he blurted out. "Sorry," he continued after seeing Cathcart's angry expression.

"You have an even greater mission than saving Penelope when you arrive at the moon base. We need you to destroy this so-called Master and Its teleporter capabilities. If the Master brings Its creatures to Earth, mankind may not survive beyond this catastrophe."

"How am I supposed to do that?" he asked, thinking about the impregnable fortress on the moon.

"Ulf Larsson was not the only spy we had on the moon base. In fact, when we started to hear the rumors about what Stenwood was doing there, we sent an entire team to the base. Naturally, each team member acted individually without knowing about the other members."

"Naturally," he said. He received another angry glance from Cathcart, and decided it was time to keep his mouth shut.

"Unfortunately, the Master seems to have incredible powers, and It was able to identify and eliminate most of our agents. Before he was tortured and killed, one of our agents, a Major Nelson, was able to learn of the Master's intentions for the future."

"How was he able to do that?" Campbell asked. "It was my understanding that no one but Arnold was able to get close to the Master."

"Nelson was your predecessor. He was to be the commander of the forces that attacked Fort Knox. In fact, if he hadn't been caught, you'd still be living on Hawaii. We believe that after Nelson was killed, Arnold determined that he must find someone new from the outside.

"After the incident with the *USS Smith*, you were one of the most sought after men on Earth. Arnold knew you couldn't be working for us, and your abilities as a military leader made you an obvious choice. Your dislike of the military was well known, and there were a multitude of things he could use against you to make you do as he wished, including Monica Yamamoto."

"So I was recruited," Campbell grumbled.

"Yes," Cathcart said, "but before Nelson was killed, he told us that the Master's plans to come to Earth after the world's destruction and lead the survivors in a sort of biblical Hell.

"In fact, it's our belief that the attack on Fort Knox, as well as other parts of the world, was a method of eliminating many of the world leaders that may have lived through the destruction to oppose It in the future, including General Arnold."

"Arnold? Why kill Arnold?" he asked.

"Because Arnold has served the Master's purpose and is only a future threat to It. Arnold knows how It was created and maybe how to destroy It. Once Arnold created as much chaos as he could in the world, he became expendable."

"Won't enough world leaders survive this catastrophe to oppose the Master in the future?" he asked.

"That's hard to say, because it's impossible to predict what will happen in the next few months. But it will be better not to have to face that possibility, since we don't really know anything about this creature and its abilities."

"There's one big problem with your plan," he said. "The Master interacted with me in an attempt to make it impossible for me to betray It. It may be impossible for me to destroy It, but I guess I won't know for sure until I try."

The President became thoughtful for a moment, and then said, "This may still work. You can destroy It indirectly. What we really need is for someone to show a team where the Master can be located on the moon base.

"We did have one last agent on the base, but we lost contact with her. Did you meet a doctor by the name of Ai Eto while you were there?"

Campbell smiled weakly. "Yes, I did. She may have saved my life. Don't tell me she was your last agent. I think Arnold was on to her."

Cathcart frowned. "We feared as much. She knew she was in danger, but in her last transmission she said that the moon base was evacuated shortly after your main force left. She was supposed to contact us about the Master's location as well as Monica Yamamoto's, but all attempts to reach her today have failed. She was the last one on the base who could show us how to get to the Master."

"What about Ulf Larsson?"

"He'll be a member of your team, but Arnold kept a close eye on him. He never learned much about the Master. It was Eto and Nelson that gave us most of that information."

Cathcart went silent and gazed expectantly at him.

"If you're waiting for me to say I'll do it, I will," Campbell said with a grim smile. "I vowed to return for Penelope even before you requested my help. I just didn't realize so much depended on me rescuing her and returning safely. When do we leave?"

Cathcart gave him a warm smile in return. "I knew we could count on you, Burt Campbell. You leave immediately. There are two clippers waiting with your force. You'll be briefed on the way."

Campbell was surprised at the mention of only two clippers. That hardly sounded like a force capable of attacking the moon base, but he got up slowly to leave. His pain and apprehension returned with the weight of his new burden.

President Cathcart returned to her desk and picked up a slip of paper before handing it to him. He looked at the printout, and realized the numbers on it were coordinates to a location on Earth.

"That's the location of New Atlantis. Memorize it and destroy the paper. The base is one of our best-kept secrets."

Campbell stared at the coordinates. *Couldn't someone have come up with a more original name for a deep-sea city?* Then he realized Cathcart was holding out her hand to him. He gazed down into her deep brown eyes and saw her sadness.

"I'm not going to see you again, am I?" he asked.

"Who knows, Inspector? If there's anything I've learned in my long life, it's that anything is possible. For the moment, I plan on staying here for as long as I can and continue doing the job I was entrusted to do. I could hardly run away at a time when the people need me the most."

He reached down and shook the President's hand warmly while thinking she was a brave woman. *Maybe I should have voted for her.*

Naw.

"Good luck, Burt Campbell. Take care of that woman. You two may represent the future hope of mankind."

That's a scary thought.

He opened his mouth to say something, but then closed it again and quietly left the office. As he stepped into the outer office, he spotted Larsson and Sen waiting for him.

"Are we returning to the moon base now?" Larsson asked.

"It looks like it," he responded with a tired sigh.

"Well," Goro said, wearing a solemn expression, "it looks like it's goodbye again for a while, Burt."

"What're you talking about? I thought you were going with us," Campbell said anxiously.

"I wish I was, but my mission was only to retrieve you from Fort Knox. I don't know what's in store for you and Larsson. I only know you have to save Penelope, and I have a family to take care of."

Burt was deeply hurt and sorry, but he knew Goro was right.

"Goro, I don't know what to say."

"Just say till we meet again, Burt," Goro smiled, and grabbed his hand.

"Till we meet again, Burt," Burt repeated.

Goro laughed, turned, and walked from the room.

XXIII

RETURN TO DANGER

ONE

"Inspector Campbell and Major Larsson, I am Captain Mark Fellows of the Special Forces. I'll be leading the two teams for our assault on the moon base," said a tall, thin man with dark hair and a boyish face. But his hard, dark-brown eyes told Campbell that Fellows was an experienced warrior, probably a hardened veteran of the Yarv War. Campbell also noted that Fellows was wearing a dirty, nondescript black uniform and body armor. They were standing near two huge rectangular transport clippers at the Lincoln Spaceport. A moonless night was descending and the transports' engines were already whining in preparation for a quick getaway.

Campbell shook the captain's thick calloused hand as he gazed at the black troop transports and noticed they had moon-base markings.

Fellows caught his glance, and said in his deep, quiet voice, "We just captured the transports from Fort Knox. We believe the moon base has been evacuated, but there might be security systems still in operation. These transports should get us in. Now, gentlemen, if you'll step aboard, we'll get going. I'll brief you on the way."

Campbell and Larsson followed Fellows up the steep metal ramp into a voluminous transport. Campbell immediately saw the vast dark interior was devoid of people, but contained eight harnessed hover bots like those he'd seen on the battlefield at Fort Knox.

"Are these the only forces we're taking?" he asked with skepticism.

"Yes," Fellows said. "There wasn't time to gather much more. But we decided that if the base has been evacuated, we wouldn't need much of a force. Our mission is basically to get in, set the demolition charges, and get out again."

Fellows directed them to uncomfortable troop seats against the port wall behind the cockpit where they strapped themselves in. Then Fellows went forward to tell the pilots they were ready to take off.

When Fellows returned and had strapped himself in, Campbell asked, "What about Penelope Preston and the Master?"

"We have two teams, Inspector," Fellows said, as he leaned against the G-forces of their take off. "The mission of our team is to enter the base itself and rescue Penelope Preston. We also need you to show us the location of the Master, where I will set a fifteen-megaton nuclear device to go off shortly after we've had time to escape."

"Fifteen megatons!" Larsson said with astonishment. "That'll vaporize the entire base."

"That's the idea, Major," Fellows said with a grim smile that appeared out of place on his boyish features. Campbell thought he appeared like a twelve-year-old who'd just discovered a pile of fireworks and a box of matches. "That's the only way we can be sure the Master, the teleporters, and any of the creatures left at the base have been destroyed."

"What's the mission of the second team?" Campbell asked.

"Sergeant Miller, with another demolition team and hover bots, will enter the military fusion plant and set a second nuclear device."

"What about the mining colony?" Larsson asked. "Nuclear devices of that size will wipe out everything, leaving only a huge crater. I have friends there, close friends."

Fellows gazed at Larsson with a flicker of sympathy in his dark eyes. Campbell wondered if it was genuine. "There's nothing we can do for them, Major. Originally there were thoughts of trying to warn those in the mining colony so they could evacuate. But we were afraid that would alert those left at the military base that we were coming. We also feared that military personnel might be hiding at the mining colony, including the Master. That's why it was determined that the fusion reactor must also be destroyed to ensure the total annihilation of all human development on the moon."

"Incredible," Campbell muttered. "So we're committing a tremendous evil against humanity to save humanity from a tremendous evil. Is that about right, Captain?"

"A few must suffer so the many may live," Fellows said weakly.

"Stuff it, Fellows," Larsson grumbled. "From what I understand, no one will survive on the moon *or* Earth."

Fellows turned away from Campbell's glare, and said little more during the flight except when directly addressed.

After a while, Campbell asked something that had been bothering him. "Have you had any word on what happened to General Arnold after his capture?"

"Oh," Fellows said with his boyish smile, as if happy to redeem himself. "He died while he was being taken away, but I don't understand what happened."

"Tell us what you know," Campbell said, worried that Arnold had somehow managed to fake his death and escaped.

"From what I heard," Fellows answered with a creased brow, "Arnold was being led to a clipper from the command bunker where he'd been captured. Suddenly, he went crazy. He fell to the ground screaming, and began beating his head against the concrete road with enough force to fracture his own skull. He was dead before anyone could stop him."

Campbell and Larsson exchanged worried glances.

I wonder if anyone saw a small cloud of vapor around Arnold just before he went crazy. Campbell decided against telling Fellows that there might still be terrible things loose on the moon base that his small force couldn't fight.

TWO

Campbell was deep in thought about his brief and intense meeting with Cathcart when he was interrupted by the pilot over the loud-speaker. "Captain, we're coming up on the moon. The base computer has given us clearance to land."

Fellows quickly unstrapped himself and went to the cockpit. Campbell and Larsson eagerly followed close behind to witness the approach that could lead to their doom.

"Did the computer ask for a password or any kind of identification?" Fellows asked the pilot.

"No, sir, it recognized our computer identification, but that was it," said the pilot.

"That seems strange," Larsson said. "Normally, security is much tougher. Captain, we better be on our toes. This could be a trap."

Fellows adjusted his ear microphone toward his mouth. "Sergeant Miller, this is Fellows," he said to the second team in the other transport. "Be alert that Major Larsson believes this may be a trap. Go directly to the fusion reactor."

"Oh, Captain," Larsson said, "you better alert your sergeant to land as close to the reactor as possible and to go directly into the facility. Don't wander about on the surface. There are things that live beneath the surface that can swallow his transport whole."

Fellows gave Campbell and Larsson an odd glance of disbelief, but Campbell nodded at him. Fellows relayed Larsson's instructions, and the sergeant acknowledged.

"Fellows," Campbell asked, "we're detonating these nuclear devices by remote control once we escape, aren't we?"

"That's a negative, Inspector," Fellows said sternly. "It was determined that remotes were too unreliable, and we might not get a second chance to get back in to detonate the devices if a remote failed. The bombs will be set on thirty-minute timers to be initiated on my command. That gives us fifteen minutes to get back to the transports, and fifteen minutes to get out of the area."

"What if you're dead?" Larsson asked. "Who gives the order to detonate then?"

"Either Sergeant Miller, or one of you two," Fellows said, as if not considering his own mortality a problem.

"Can these devices be turned off once the timer has been initiated?" Campbell asked. He was worried that they were entering a situation where there were too many unknown variables. Once those bombs were set, they could be signing their own death warrants.

"No, sir," Fellows said. "For security reasons, once that timer is turned on, there's no turning back."

"We're preparing to land in a hangar, Captain," said the pilot. "You'd better return to your seats in case we're attacked."

Campbell took a quick peek out the cockpit window. The base appeared the same as when he'd initially arrived with Arnold and George. He found it hard to believe the entire base had been evacuated. Something was waiting for them, something terrible. He shivered.

"Come on, gentlemen, I want to give you your weapons in case we have to make a fast escape," Fellows said.

Campbell and Larsson followed Fellows back to a well-stocked weapons locker where he distributed each of them a directed energy beam pistol and a gun belt loaded with a .45-caliber pistol and ammunition. He also gave each of them an ear microphone so they could communicate. Both Campbell and Larsson still wore their somewhat muddy and torn body armor from the battle at Fort Knox.

Campbell grinned as he pulled the .45 out its holster. "Hey, I've got one of these at home. Great weapon."

"Good, Inspector. You know how to use one," Fellows said. "We found that the antiquated projectile-firing weapons were very effective against the armor of the creatures that we fought at Fort Knox. Let me add that Major Larsson was the one who provided the information that allowed us to destroy most of those creatures."

"You're well informed, Fellows," Larsson grumbled, "but there's a problem. I've never used one of those things." Larsson pointed at Campbell's handgun.

Campbell laughed. "Come on, you big dummy. I'll show you how they work."

Campbell and Larsson took their seats as he showed Larsson the basic mechanics of loading and firing his .45-caliber pistol.

"Sure is a clumsy weapon," Larsson remarked, while waving the loaded gun around and making Campbell duck for cover.

"Get ready everyone," the pilot announced. "We're entering the hangar."

Campbell anxiously held his breath. He expected the transport to be rocked by energy beam cannons at any moment. Time seemed eternal as he gazed around the dark interior of the transport waiting for something terrible to happen. If he'd learned anything on the Fort Knox battlefield, it was that death seemed to pop out and surprise him even when he was expecting it. He felt the sluggish motion of the huge transport stop, and then settle. He exhaled with relief.

THREE

"Okay, Captain, we've landed inside the hangar," said the pilot. "I see no sign of any real reception committee, but there're some small bat-like things flying around that look nasty."

"You better activate the ship's auto-defense system and kill them, Captain," Larsson said. "They aren't deadly, but their bites can be deep and painful."

"Do as he says," Fellows told the pilot.

Campbell heard the crackle of directed energy beam fire outside the transport as the automatic weapons found their targets. Fellows waved Campbell and Larsson toward the eight hover bots, and began to unharness them. Campbell marveled at the deadly advanced technology and weaponry on the tank-like bots, which stood about chest high to him.

"As you can see, each bot carries a directed energy beam rifle and a small-caliber cannon," Fellows said. "Four will travel in front of us, guarding our advance, while four will cover our rear."

Fellows reached down behind one of the bots and switched it on. Campbell watched with fascination as the bot began to hover slightly above the floor and go through its system diagnostics and weapons check. Finally, a nearly transparent bubble appeared around the bot.

"That, gentlemen, is a highly classified plasma shield that was recently developed to be small enough for bots," Fellows said. "Unfortunately, it's still under development for human usage, so we can't use them."

Fellows finished activating the rest of the bots. As they waited for the bots to get ready, Fellows retrieved a small black case from the weapons locker.

"Is that your nuclear device?" Campbell asked. He was amazed that such a small case could contain enough awesome power to wipe out a small city and kill thousands.

"Yes," Fellows answered. He set it down before them. "If something should happen to me, you use this simple timer here. It's preset for thirty minutes." Fellows pointed out a digital timer on the top of the suitcase near the handle. "Once the timer is set, you activate it by pushing the red button here." He pointed to a button on the other side of the handle.

"Captain," called the pilot, "the defenses have destroyed all the bats, but there seems to be something scurrying around the floor like large spiders."

"They're maintenance creatures," Larsson answered. "Normally, they're harmless, but we'll have to be careful outside the clipper."

"Damn," Campbell muttered. "I wonder what else is left around here." The terrifying feeling that something was waiting for them hadn't left him.

"Captain Fellows!" yelled an excited voice over the loudspeaker. Campbell could hear the sound of DER blasts and cannon fire in the background. "This is Miller, sir. We've managed to get into the reactor facility, but we're under heavy attack by guard bots. I'm not sure how long we can hold out."

Fellows exchanged worried looks with Campbell, and pulled his microphone to his mouth.

"Miller, you must set your charge, but under no circumstances are you allowed to activate your device before I give the order. You must give us time to find Penelope Preston and the Master. Do you understand?"

"I understand, sir," Miller yelled in a fearful tone, "but what if we're overrun?"

Fellows gazed at Campbell, his dark eyes turned to stone. "If all else fails, you must activate your device. The destruction of this facility is our first priority."

"Understood, sir. If we activate the bomb before your command, we will warn you. Miller out."

Campbell heard the screams of a wounded man before Miller signed off. He wanted desperately to dispute their priorities. As far as he was concerned, saving Penelope was the first order of business, but he knew it was useless to argue.

"We have to move fast, gentlemen," Fellows said anxiously. "Miller has eight bots that can defend themselves, but he only has two other men with him who can set off the device. If all three of them are killed, the mission may fail."

FOUR

Fellows pushed the button to lower the transport ramp. Campbell glanced out the yawning ramp and saw the dimly lit hangar floor outside. He was relieved to see a troop of goblin-faced guards hadn't somehow slipped by the ship defenses and was lying in wait.

"Bots one through four, exit the transport and form a protective perimeter around the ramp base," Fellows ordered.

Campbell watched with continued curiosity and anxiousness as four bots hovered down the ramp to the hangar floor. Immediately, brilliant light flashed as two of the bots opened fire with their DERs at something Campbell couldn't see. After a moment of tense silence, the four bots widened their perimeter and moved out of his sight.

"Let's move out, gentlemen. Bots five through eight, follow us out and protect our rear," Fellows ordered. He started down the clanking metal ramp with Campbell and Larsson close behind in crouched defensive positions.

Campbell glanced around the dark hangar with apprehension when he reached the hangar floor. His pain and fatigue disappeared as his heart raced. He spotted the first four bots stationed on each side of the transport pointing their weapons into the silent darkness.

Campbell jumped when a bot to his left fired its DER at something small and low scrambling across the littered and junk-filled floor. Whatever the ungodly thing had been, it was vaporized in an instant as the shot hit it with pinpoint accuracy.

Campbell nervously glanced around for possible assailants, but only saw a partially dismantled disk-shaped clipper and useless non-functioning maintenance equipment hiding in the dark shadows. The hangar appeared strangely empty and devoid of anything useful. The moon-base forces seemed to have evacuated any working clippers. He prayed there were none of those bestial one-eyed ogres or any of the other terrifying creatures he'd seen in the arena hiding in the deep recesses of the corners waiting to surprise them.

"Larsson, do you recognize where we are?" Fellows asked.

"Yes," Larsson said, "but I don't know where we're going." He turned to Campbell.

"Oh, ah, we need to get to the arena," Campbell said. "The Master's bunker is somewhere beneath the arena. Penelope was being held a few floors above it. The elevator is near the arena doors."

"Okay, we need to go that way to get to the door we want." Larsson pointed off to his right.

Fellows gave the orders to the bots to form a defensive perimeter around them and they moved quickly toward the huge double door. Campbell tried to peer everywhere as he expected some sort of attack. Suddenly, a small tool whizzed by his unprotected head before clanking harmlessly on the floor nearby. He whirled around to see who, or what, had thrown it. One of the rear bots had already targeted the assailant and fired. A huge spider, missing its human-like head, dropped from the ceiling.

The group rapidly moved forward and reached the door without further incident. Campbell was surprised when the double door slid open for them. He'd been expecting a security lockdown. The first two bots led the way through the door. Campbell abruptly felt himself being thrown to the floor by Larsson when directed energy blasts reflected off the plasma shields of the two bots in the hallway.

"Stay down!" Larsson yelled.

Campbell dared to lift his head as the battle sounds continued. Two more bots were nonchalantly hovering into the deadly energy beam filled hallway as if they were out on a stroll. The first two bots were taking heavy laser-like fire from opposite directions in the hall. Campbell realized the thick energy beams had to be coming from cannons fired from elevated locations. They were being attacked by the security cannons in the ceiling. The unharmed bots rapidly returned fire with their DERs and quickly dispatched the unarmored ceiling cannons.

"Let's move," Fellows ordered. He leaped to his feet and cautiously peeked out into the smoke-filled hallway.

Larsson and Campbell got off the floor and closed on Fellows.

"We need to go to the right," Larsson muttered to Fellows.

Fellows rapidly reorganized the bots into their formation and they moved forward as quickly as frightened caution allowed, with Larsson directing the way. He quietly warned Fellows whenever they were coming to a checkpoint where the automated security system would be active. At these points, Fellows directed the bots forward to eliminate any threat. The bots performed flawlessly, making Campbell wonder about the new state of warfare.

"I wish we'd had these kinds of bots on Yarv," he muttered. "There wouldn't have been a need for troops."

"What would be the fun of that?" Larsson asked with a horrid grin. Campbell favored him with a nasty glance.

They came to a halt at the end of another hallway.

"We have to turn left here, but I think there's another checkpoint around that corner," Larsson whispered.

Fellows gave his orders to the first four bots. They fearlessly hovered around the corner and immediately came under heavy fire again. There was a short, intense firefight while the ceiling cannons were eliminated before silence returned. Campbell was cautiously moving forward with the others when suddenly he heard the angry roar of some huge beast. One of the first four bots suddenly went soaring down the intersecting hall as if it had been shot from a cannon.

"What in Hades is happening?" Campbell shouted when another bot went silently sailing by him before crashing down the hallway with a loud din.

He precariously peeked around the corner. His eyes flew open wide when he spied one of the hulking one-eyed ogres that he'd seen in the arena. Based on its scar-rendered flesh, shabby clothes, and unruly mop of hair, Campbell thought it might even be the same ogre. Its massive body was blocking the hallway while glaring angrily down at the remaining two bots. The bots were hovering passively in front of it, doing nothing. Campbell couldn't comprehend why the bots weren't attacking such an obvious target. He quickly ducked back behind cover when the growling brute grasped another bot between its huge hands and heaved it down the hallway.

Campbell's fear turned to blind fury at having his quest to save Penelope stalled by some stupid beast. Screaming with rage, he raced around the corner while pulling out his .45-caliber pistol. The equally enraged ogre was in the process of picking up the remaining bot. It spotted Campbell, and hurled the witless bot at him as it thundered forward. Campbell ducked as the bot flew harmlessly over his head. As he straightened, the bellowing monster was nearly upon him. Its huge paws were stretched out ready to tear him apart. Campbell barely had time to raise and fire his pistol before the ogre's terrifying strength and weight smashed into him crushing him to the floor.

"Campbell, are you okay?" Larsson yelled. He and Fellows strained with loud grunts as they heaved the dead ogre's body off him.

Campbell painfully struggled to his feet, and gazed down at the ugly ogre's bloody features. He thanked his lucky stars that he'd had the .45 revolver. His wild shot had miraculously hit the ogre in the eye and blown out the back of its massive skull.

"Why didn't the bots kill it?" he asked breathlessly.

Fellows stared down with a horrified expression at the dead beast, as if trying to understand its existence. "I don't know. Their programming is new. Maybe they didn't recognize this thing as a target."

"It was attacking *them*," Larsson said. "How much more incentive do they need before they decide something is a target?"

"Captain Fellows, this is Miller." Miller sounded terrified, breathless, over Campbell's earphone. He could hear continued heavy fighting in the background.

"This is Fellows. What's your situation?"

"Captain, we're at the target point, and the charge is set. Hawkins is dead, and Martin is badly wounded. The bots are almost out of cannon ammunition. DERs have no effect on these guard bots. We can't hold out much longer."

"We're almost there, Miller. You must hold on as long as possible," Fellows said.

Campbell knew this was an optimistic lie. He felt panic stricken when he recognized this hall. They weren't more than halfway to the arena area.

"Miller out."

"We have to hurry," Fellows said anxiously. "If Miller feels his death is imminent, he'll set off that bomb and we're all dead."

FIVE

Without waiting for Campbell or Larsson to respond, Fellows collected his bots and ordered them forward as fast as he dared. Campbell trotted after Fellows and Larsson with the first four bots in the lead and the other four bots bringing up the rear. After the annoying delay of two more checkpoints, Campbell at last saw the doors to the arena.

"Okay, Campbell, we got you to the arena. Where to now?" Larsson asked.

"That hallway to the right," he quickly answered. They rushed down the hallway.

As they arrived at the elevator, Campbell realized with panicked frustration that it was too small to fit all of them aboard. "Where do we go now, Fellows?" he asked. "We have to go up to reach Penelope's quarters or down to the Master's bunker."

Fellows thought for a moment in indecision. "You and Larsson take two bots and go up to save Penelope. I'll wait here until the elevator returns and then take two bots down to the bunker to set the bomb."

Neither Campbell nor Larsson argued. They boarded the elevator and Fellows ordered two bots to follow them. As the elevator rose, Campbell anxiously wondered if the bots would follow his orders, or even fire on any guards waiting outside Penelope's quarters. He avoided thinking about the possibility of the guards carrying spray guns that dispensed liquid acid.

Larsson drew his .45-caliber pistol, and Campbell did likewise. Just to be safe, Campbell got behind one of the bots to use its plasma shield as cover. Larsson crammed himself in the cover of the front corner of the elevator.

The elevator doors opened. Campbell immediately spotted two giant guard bots across the foyer defending Penelope's door in the center of the black-walled foyer.

"Take cover!" Campbell yelled. The guard bots lowered their DERs and fired into the cramped elevator.

Campbell hid in terror, crouched on the floor behind the defensive shield of a hover bot. He was deafened by explosive cannon return fire from the hover bots. Just as abruptly as the shooting had started, it stopped. With his abused ears still ringing, he peeked up through the smoke-filled air. Larsson stepped out of the elevator with his gun pointing the way.

"It's okay, Campbell. These guard bots have been destroyed."

"I heard cannon fire," Fellows said over Campbell's earphone. "What's the delay with the elevator?"

"We ran into a couple guard bots," Campbell answered breathlessly, "but we're okay. I'll send the elevator down in a moment."

He tried to step around the hover bot in his way. It didn't move.

"Bot, move out of the elevator," he ordered, but the bot didn't budge.

"Bot, move!" Larsson yelled. Neither bot moved.

"Damn," Campbell muttered.

He bent over and tentatively poked the bot plasma shield with his index finger. Although the plasma shield resisted his touch with a tingly sensation, it didn't hurt his finger. Placing both his palms on the back of the shield, Campbell gave the hovering bot a mighty heave that sent it out into the foyer. He stepped over to the other bot and pushed it out of the elevator as well before stepping out himself. As the elevator doors closed, Campbell realized they were now trapped on this floor until the elevator returned. He prayed this wasn't some evil trap.

"Where's Penelope?" Larsson asked.

"Behind that door."

Campbell gazed down at the guard bots. They'd been cut to pieces. He kicked a severed bot head out of the way as he stepped up to the door. Before opening it, he stopped and hesitated. His heart was pounding wildly with anticipation and anxiety.

Larsson gazed at him as if he sensed his apprehension before turning toward their hover bots. He shook his head after a moment, apparently deciding it was useless to expect them to lead the way.

"I'll go first," Larsson said.

"No, this is my job," Campbell whispered. "I'm just afraid I'll find her in there dead." He stepped in front of Larsson.

After crouching down into a defensive position, Campbell drew his .45-caliber pistol and pushed the button to open the door. Diving in low with his head tucked, he hit the stone floor and rolled into the darkened room. He immediately came to his feet and whipped his body around searching for possible assailants. He found none. He desperately searched the shadow-filled room again. There was no one there. Larsson stepped into the room.

"She's not here," he muttered from behind Campbell.

Campbell rushed to the ruffled bed, his heart pounding with a new fear—one that he hadn't anticipated. He threw back the covers only to find it empty.

"No!" he screamed in an anguished howl of despair. He whirled around frantically seeking for something he'd missed. He saw a huge closed closet in the corner and raced to it in desperation. He threw back its doors to find it dark and bare.

"Campbell, I'm sorry, but she's not here," Larsson said.

"No," he whispered with anguished frustration. "She has to be here somewhere! She wouldn't leave. She knew I'd be back," He turned around in slow circles searching for anything she might have left behind telling him where she'd gone. He saw nothing.

"Campbell, Larsson," Fellows screamed in Campbell's earphone, "we're in the bunker, but something is down here with us. I'm under attack!"

Campbell was snapped back to reality when heard the loud explosions of small arms fire. He immediately recognized the sounds of the captain's .45-caliber pistol. He wondered what had happened to the bots that had accompanied Fellows to the bunker.

"Attacked by what?" Campbell asked. If the bots had failed to react again, he feared that Fellows might be facing the Master or one of the cloud creatures.

"It's huge! It looks like the devil itself with huge bat-like wings and red eyes!" Fellows cried out in fear as he fired more shots.

"George," Campbell and Larsson said in unison.

"Fellows, get back up here!" Campbell shouted urgently. "You can't fight that thing by yourself!"

Campbell suddenly heard a terrible human scream of a dying man over his earphone. It was quickly followed by a strangling gurgle noise as if Fellows was being choked to death. Then there was only silence in his ear.

"Fellows! Fellows!" Campbell called out. He received no response.

"Burt," Larsson said with urgency, "we have to get down there. It sounds like Fellows is dead and he didn't set the charge."

"But we haven't found Penelope. She has to be here somewhere. If the Master knew the Earth was going to be destroyed, why would It evacuate her?" he asked with fading hope.

"If the Master knew Earth was going to be destroyed, what makes you think It didn't know the moon base was going to be destroyed as well? That's why everyone was evacuated."

Campbell held his ground filled with maddening indecision. "But we don't know for sure," he said with a desperate tone. "Penelope and the Master could be hidden somewhere on this base."

"Captain Fellows," Sergeant Miller said over Campbell's earphone. He thought Miller's quiet voice sounded strangely calm.

"The battle is lost," Miller whispered in obvious pain. "I am mortally wounded and the bots are out of cannon ammunition. We can't hold off the guard bots any longer. I am activating my bomb. You have fifteen minutes to clear the base from . . . now. Good luck."

"Thirty minutes until detonation," said a computer automated voice in Campbell's ear.

"What in Hades is that voice?" he asked.

"Our communications system must be linked directly to Miller's bomb. It is giving us the countdown," Larsson said.

"Miller! No, Miller, wait!" Campbell yelled. "We haven't accomplished our mission!" He anxiously waited for Miller to respond, but his earphone remained silent.

"Come on, Burt," Larsson said urgently. "We have to get down to that bunker and set that other charge. It's still possible that the Master is holed up there."

Larsson turned to leave, but Campbell held his ground. He looked around Penelope's quarters again hoping beyond hope that somehow she would appear. She didn't.

SIX

It suddenly occurred to Campbell that Penelope might still be alive and hidden somewhere else on the base. Some hope, as desperate as it might seem, sprang into his wildly pounding heart. He raced after Larsson as he was calling the elevator. Campbell noticed that the bots made no attempt to enter the elevator with him when the doors opened. He waved at them in disgust and left them behind.

"If that's George down there, what's the plan?" Campbell asked while the elevator rapidly dropped to the bunker. "These DEPs aren't any good against its armor. Fellows must have missed George with his .45, or these guns are useless as well."

Larsson drew his .45-caliber pistol anyway. "Fellows must have either missed George, or didn't hit it in any vital areas. Remember, you crushed George's hideous skull using only a spiked mace, so the thing can at least be injured if not killed."

"You've got a lot of nerve calling someone hideous," Campbell smirked nervously. He avoided Larsson's scornful glare.

Campbell and Larsson crammed themselves into the protective front corners of the elevator as it came to an abrupt halt and the doors quietly slid open. To Campbell's surprise, their arrival wasn't met by a vicious directed energy beam attack from the turret cannon defenses. He held up his hand to Larsson and cautiously peeked around the corner into the dark bunker foyer.

Campbell could tell a serious battle had taken place. The cannons in the foyer walls, ceiling, and corner turrets had been blasted away by cannon fire. Explosion blast marks pitted the once smooth black walls all over the foyer. Neither George nor any other creature was anywhere in sight.

Campbell was pained to see Captain Fellows lying dead in a large crimson pool of his own blood. His body had been cruelly hacked and clawed through the body armor as if by some powerful beast with sharp talons. The captain's bloody features, screaming mouth, and bulging blank eyes showed he'd died a horrible death. His head was nearly squeezed from his stretched and purple neck. Two bubble bots hovered next to the body as if they were a useless memorial guard. Campbell wondered how the bots could have let this happen to Fellows.

He quickly slipped out of the elevator, waving to Larsson to follow. As Campbell neared Fellows's ghastly body, he heard Larsson hiss behind him. The small black case was still clutched in the captain's dead hand. Campbell bent over to retrieve it only to discover with horrified frustration that Fellows wouldn't release it.

Campbell stood up again while contemplating some delicate method of retrieving the case. Larsson came forward, and placed his heavy robotic foot on Fellows's wrist with a crushing snap. He bent over and ripped the case out of the dead fingers.

"Here," Larsson said. He shoved the bomb into Campbell's chest. "Where to next?"

Campbell grabbed the case handle in his left hand while holding onto his pistol with his right.

"Down that way," Campbell said, while pointing his pistol down the long dark hallway stretching away from the rear of the ruined foyer. He anxiously peered down the black-walled tunnel, but could see nothing. It filled him with apprehension that even the Master's black-robed sentries had been evacuated. He wondered if the Master was gone as well.

"Twenty-five minutes until detonation," the animated voice announced in Campbell's ear.

"Bots, move down the hallway in front of us," Larsson ordered.

To Campbell's surprise, the bots moved forward down the hallway as ordered. He followed closely behind them with Larsson at his side. Although he could see no obvious defenders, his head swiveled in search of George.

"Down!" Larsson shouted when the front bots were suddenly assaulted by heavy directed energy beams that reflected off their plasma shields.

Campbell hit the floor as he heard the explosive cannon blasts from the bots returning fire. He watched through squinted eyes while two ceiling cannons were destroyed by the bots' intense firepower.

"Any more of those little surprises waiting for us that you didn't tell me about?" Larsson grumbled while he slowly got to his feet.

"I don't remember."

"Bots, continue forward," Larsson ordered.

Campbell followed along, thinking they were moving at a snail's pace, but he decided it didn't do them any good to hurry recklessly and get themselves killed. They entered the dark-walled rear room with the bots in front of them. Hazy smoke from the brief battle further obscured their already darkened vision. Larsson rushed forward and pushed through the awaiting bots while he approached the only door in the rear wall.

"Campbell, this door has a security lock on it. We'll never get through," Larsson said while he turned around.

"Look out!" Larsson yelled too late.

SEVEN

Before Campbell could react, he felt the tremendous strength of a scaly armored arm wrap viciously around his neck. To his shocked horror, he realized that George must have been hiding around the corner out of their sight.

Campbell dropped his weapon and the bomb case. He grabbed George's rock-like arm with both his powerful hands in a desperate grasp. He heaved with all his fearful might, but the arm around his strangled neck tightened even more and cut off his wind. He frantically struggled and kicked at George's legs, hoping to throw the creature off balance. George heaved back on his neck, lifting his kicking feet off the ground. With the razor-sharp talons of its free claw, George ripped at the armor around Campbell's torso trying to tear open his stomach.

Campbell landed a savage kick with his assault boot heel into George's mighty knee. The devil's creature howled with inhuman pain. The breath-stopping noose around Campbell's neck loosened for a moment. His feet landed on the floor. Instantly, he hurled all his weight backward into George's torso, slamming it off balance against the rear wall. Campbell quickly ducked forward again while still grasping George's thick arm and used his momentum to flip George over his back. George's tremendous weight went sailing over him, but it took Campbell with it. They crashed hard on the floor lying side by side.

THE SOUL CAGE II

Campbell was suddenly deafened when two explosive blasts erupted behind him, so close and loud that the noise stunned his senses. Abruptly, the deadly grip around his neck went limp. He quickly rolled out of it and to his feet. George was lying on its side with black blood pouring out of neat puncture wounds in its enormous winged back. Its snake-like forked tongue hung loosely out of its gaping, fanged mouth. The fiery red light in George's eyes went dark.

Campbell glanced up breathlessly. Larsson was standing over and behind George, still pointing his smoking .45-caliber pistol at the downed beast as if waiting for it to get up.

"I think it's dead," Campbell whispered through his wheezing breaths.

"Looks like you owe me another one," Larsson muttered. He stepped forward and pummeled George in the back with a vicious kick. George didn't move.

"We can settle the score later," Campbell said, rubbing his wrenched neck. "Let's set this bomb and get out of here."

Larsson kicked George again for good measure and then followed Campbell. Campbell scooped up his gun and the bomb case before rushing toward the door.

"We'll never get through this door," he said. "It's about as close as I got to the Master anyway. We'll have to set it here. I just pray Penelope isn't trapped inside as well." Somehow he knew she wasn't.

"Do it. This place still gives me the creeps," Larsson said behind Campbell.

Campbell carefully set the bomb case down next to the black door, and finger punched the timer. It blinked thirty minutes at him in red digital numerals.

"Oof!" Larsson shouted with an explosion of breath.

"What?" Campbell asked while he began to turn. "No!" he screamed in horrified anguish.

Larsson's squirming body was elevated a meter off the floor. His arms and legs were jerking about in wild spasms. A huge blood-dripping claw had erupted through Larsson's chest. Larsson's torn heart was still struggling to beat within the grasp of the squeezing claw.

Larsson's head dropped to his blood-covered chest when he died. George was standing behind Larsson with its huge arm impaling Larsson through the back. George's eyes were ablaze with the fire from Hell. There was an evil, fang-filled grin on its horrid, bat-like face.

George savagely yanked its arm back through Larsson's sagging body, pulling out Larsson's heart. Blind rage flowed through Campbell as he reached for his .45-caliber pistol. George hurled Larsson's limp body to the bloody floor. It raised Larsson's still beating heart to the ceiling while howling in triumph. Burt shot George in the head three times.

George's headless body was thrown backwards before it fell limply to the floor. Campbell gazed down at the bloody claw and watched mournfully as Larsson's heart stopped beating. Campbell screamed with rage. He emptied his pistol into George's limp convulsing body.

Campbell quickly kneeled next to Larsson. He stared at Larsson's shocked and disfigured face with deep sorrow filling his already despairing heart. Campbell was stunned with disbelief. It had happened so fast he couldn't understand how his brief bodyguard and savior could be dead. He wondered if he could use the healing powers that Penelope had passed on to him to bring Larsson back to life. He quickly remembered that Penelope had only healed living beings. Burt sagged and dropped to the floor in defeat.

He reached forward and clutched Larsson's still hot human hand in between his own.

"I'm sorry, Ulf Larsson. I have failed you," Campbell whispered. He was surprised when his deep emotions overwhelmed him and his vision blurred with tears.

XXIV

THE SEARCH

ONE

Campbell could have sat there on the bloody bunker floor for days lost in his mournful sorrow and despair. First, Koko was dead. Penelope was either lost or dead. Now Larsson had been killed.

"Twenty minutes until detonation," the automated voice said in his ear. Campbell struggled out of his grief while clinging to his vow and the slim hope that Penelope was still alive.

He slowly turned toward his bomb. He was about to push the activation button when he considered the time difference between the two bombs. The bomb from the reactor would go off ten minutes before his bomb. *What if the explosion from the reactor damages this bomb so it won't go off and the bunker isn't completely destroyed? If the Master is in there, it might survive and escape before this bomb goes off.*

He reset the timer on the bomb case to nineteen minutes and pushed the activation button.

This bomb should go off before the reactor is blown. At least the bunker will be destroyed. Damn, that only gives me four minutes to get back to the transport, and I still haven't found Penelope.

"Nineteen minutes until detonation," said the automated voice of his bomb.

He fought back his grief and peril while he reloaded his pistol and wondered where Penelope could be. He quickly reached down and scooped up Larsson's fallen pistol.

"Goodbye, and thank you, Ulf," he said, and raced down the hall.

Campbell decided on his plan of action while he rode the elevator back up to the arena level. He knew that the moon base was so vast in size it would take him a week with an army to search the place for Penelope. He decided to go to the places he knew about on the way back to the transport and hope for the best.

When the elevator door opened, he was confronted by the remaining four bots. He stood there undecided about what to do with them, since the bots hadn't defended Larsson or Fellows against George. Nor had they fired upon the ogre.

"Oh, come on. Bots form a defensive perimeter in front of me, and proceed down the hall to the right," he ordered.

He was surprised when the bots did as ordered. He hustled after them back down to the central hall before the arena doors. Directing the bots to the left and then to the right, he followed them back toward his old cell. Whenever they came to a doorway, he quickly stopped and opened it to check for Penelope. To his increasing frustration and anxiety, Penelope was nowhere to be found.

After a brief firefight at a checkpoint with more ceiling cannons, Campbell was glad he'd brought along the bots. He kept a close eye on their rear, expecting an ogre or some other deadly creature to sneak up on them.

He checked more doors, and the bots took out two checkpoints before they reached the door to his old prison cell.

"Penelope?" he called out. He had little hope as he opened the door and peered around the dark cell.

The cell was empty. All hope of finding Penelope deserted him. Then he remembered the labs where he'd been tortured. He thought it was possible that they'd been experimenting on Penelope and had left her behind.

He rushed out the cell door to move down the hall. Throwing open the lab door; he whipped his head around desperately searching the room. Disappointment crushed his heart when he saw the lab was empty.

"Penelope, what have they done to you?" he cried out. He sadly turned back toward the hallway. There was a muffled response to his cry. He turned around searching in vain for the noise.

"Penelope?" he shouted. "Where are you?"

Again, he heard a moan. The sound seemed to be coming from the closed torture coffin they'd used on him. He rushed toward the contraption with hope rising in his heart.

Campbell searched frantically for a way to open the coffin until he found the controls and activated them. As the coffin lid slowly opened toward the floor, he saw there was someone inside.

TWO

"Dr. Eto, I thought you were dead." He rushed forward to release her restraints.

Eto only moaned in response. Campbell could see she was in terrible pain. Her thin body appeared bruised and broken as if she'd been brutally beaten, and then sealed in the coffin to die.

After he'd released her, Dr. Eto slumped into his awaiting arms. He gently lifted her out onto the floor. Her once beautiful Asian features were horribly disfigured and swollen with bruises. Blood was oozing out the corners of her mouth.

"Campbell? What, what're you doing here?" she whispered.

"I came to rescue Penelope and destroy the Master."

"They're gone," Eto hissed out with a ragged breath. She was broken up inside.

"Fifteen minutes until detonation," the voice of the bunker bomb announced.

"I have to get you out of here now. The whole base is about to be destroyed." He gently started to lift Eto off the floor.

Eto groaned in anguish and coughed up more blood. Campbell carefully lowered her back to the floor.

"Don't move me," Eto said in agony. "I'm dead. Save yourself."

"No, you saved my life. I'm going to get you out of here," Campbell said, but then saw that Eto had passed out and never heard him.

A strange sensation overcame Campbell. It occurred to him that he might possess the power to heal Dr. Eto's broken body like Penelope had healed his. He leaned forward and placed his left hand on her head and his right hand on her broken torso.

He closed his eyes and concentrated on healing Eto. He recalled the light and power that he'd seen emanating from Penelope's hands when she'd healed Sergeant Preston back at his home in Denver. He opened his eyes and saw that nothing was happening. For a moment, he slumped in failure, deciding the power to heal was beyond him.

"No! I can do this!" he shouted defiantly. Raging emotions surged through his body over all the useless waste of life he'd witnessed recently. He would not let another friend die.

Again, he closed his eyes and concentrated. He felt pulsating warmth spread through his palms and fingertips, and he concentrated harder. An electric tingling sensation flowed through his entire body. He felt a tremendous power of life surging through his hands into Eto's body. *This feels amazing! So powerful!*

The weariness of his mind and body seemed to slip away. His depression disappeared into an almost erotic euphoria. The powerful feeling of some life-giving force only lasted a few moments before he felt it returning back into his body. He suddenly felt great weariness from the exhausting effort and almost fainted.

"Fifteen minutes until detonation," said the reactor bomb.

Their deadly peril quickly got his attention again. He opened his eyes to peer down at Eto. She remained unconscious and appeared no different. He recalled that he'd slept an entire eighteen hours after Penelope had healed him. It took time for the nanotechnology she'd passed into his blood to repair his body's damage.

He gently lifted Eto into his arms. She uttered a soft moan, but didn't awaken. He raced out of the lab and found the bots waiting for him outside the doorway. He ordered them to the left and down the hall back toward the stairs he hoped would get them to the hangar where the transport was waiting.

They came to another annoying delay at a checkpoint. Campbell was ready to pee his pants with anxiety as he waited for the brief firefight to end. They hastened to the stairway door the second the checkpoint defenses were destroyed.

After rushing up the stairs to the floor where he prayed the transport was waiting, he stepped back to let the bots go out the door first. The bots stopped outside the door with no orders on which direction to turn. Campbell stepped out of the doorway and looked in both directions with confusion. Sweat was dripping down his face with the exertion of carrying his burden and the excitement of flight.

"Which way now?" he asked the bots, since he was lost.

The bots didn't respond. He readjusted his hold on Eto and ordered them to the right. He quickly followed them down the hall before they were suddenly assaulted by the base defenses at another checkpoint.

This can't be the way, Campbell thought. *We've destroyed all the checkpoints we came to on this floor.* He ordered the bots in the opposite direction and trotted clumsily after them until they came to the hangar door.

"Ten minutes until detonation," said the bomb at the bunker.

"Damn," he muttered. It was past time for their scheduled departure.

He punched the button to open the hangar door. His ears were immediately assaulted by the whirling sound of the transport engines. Fear leaped through his mind. Racing through the door, Campbell was just in time to spot the giant transport retreating out to the green plasma shield of the hangar.

He hastily laid Eto on the filthy hangar floor and sprinted after the fleeing transport while frantically waving his arms to catch the pilot's attention. He could clearly see the pilot staring back at him through the lit cockpit window.

"Captain, wait!" he yelled repeatedly in desperation.

"Ten minutes until detonation," said the reactor bomb.

"Wait, we're right here!" Campbell yelled as he gained on the transport.

The retreating ship, their only means of escape, kept moving out of the hangar. In desperation to catch the pilot's attention, Campbell yanked out his DEP and fired repeatedly at the cockpit window, scoring direct hits. The directed energy beams merely reflected harmlessly off the hull shields.

Campbell watched with frustrated rage while the transport left the hangar, turned around, and blasted away from the moon base. That was it! He and Eto were marooned with two fifteen-megaton nuclear bombs and a fusion reactor about to vaporize them.

THREE

A small tool flew by Campbell's unprotected head and clanked on the floor nearby. He whipped toward his left and saw a group of maintenance spiders scurrying toward him. There were far too many to shoot and he didn't have time. He raced back and scooped up Eto before rushing back into the hallway seeking the protection of the bots. After receiving their rushed orders to destroy the attacking spiders, the bots obediently hovered into the hangar while Campbell stayed behind.

"Nine minutes until detonation," said the bunker bomb.

Campbell's mind whirled desperately for another quick way off the deadly rock. There was the transport the second team had taken to the reactor, but he quickly realized they would never make it there in time. As his ears were blasted by the cannon fire from the bots, he recalled the old clipper he'd seen in the hangar undergoing maintenance.

He peeked into the dark junk-filled hangar when the cannon fire stopped. The spiders had either been destroyed or dispersed. Carrying Eto into the hangar, he peered through the darkness. In his desperation it seemed a miracle, but the black clipper was still there on the other side of the hangar.

"Nine minutes until detonation," warned the reactor bomb.

After rearranging the bots, Campbell chased them across the hangar toward the clipper while keeping a sharp eye for spiders or larger, more sinister creatures. As they neared the dilapidated clipper, his heart sank. His hope faded. The clipper was in terrible condition. He could see immediately that one of the two ion engines was completely dismantled. The armor plating was missing in areas where repairs had been underway on the outer hull. Even if he could get the piece of junk out of the hangar, he wasn't sure it was space-worthy. It also appeared that the weapons were missing, but that didn't concern him. He figured they wouldn't be fighting their way out anyway.

Still, he wasn't ready to sit down and die just yet, and that partially dismantled heap was their only chance at survival. He ordered the bots up the open clipper ramp and followed. As he entered the dark tunnel-like fuselage, he stumbled over a patiently waiting bot and nearly fumbled Eto. Unsure where to proceed, he glanced to his right and spotted faint light through the cockpit window. He headed in that direction, tripping and stumbling over maintenance tools and random junk on the floor.

"Eight minutes until detonation," said the bunker bomb.

Campbell had a violent urge to rip the ever-reminding earphone out his ear to silence the annoying warnings, but he knew he would need to know how much time he had to say his prayers.

When he reached the scattered cockpit, he gently sat Eto in the copilot seat and strapped her into the restraints. He gazed in mad despair and confusion at the partially dismantled control panel. He knew nothing about clipper maintenance, much less about the advanced electronics needed to reconnect the dizzying array of loose wires. The first thing he noticed was that the sophisticated weapons and shield controls had literally been torn out. Yet, to his elation, the computer appeared to be untouched and intact. He decided this made sense, since the maintenance crew would need the computer to make their repairs. His brief elation was quickly squashed with the ferocity of a swatted bug when he realized he didn't have the security code to run the computer or start the clipper.

"Eight minutes until detonation," said the reactor bomb.

"Damn! Damn! Damn!" he shouted with his voice echoing in the confined area.

In frustrated rage, Campbell slammed his fist down on the computer control panel. To his gleeful astonishment, the computer power came on. It occurred to him that the maintenance crew couldn't be bothered with knowing security codes so they'd been removed.

His brief victory turned sour when red lights began to appear all over the control panel as the computer powered up and did diagnostics on itself and the clipper.

"Computer, start the engines," Campbell ordered anxiously.

"Starboard engine nonfunctional," said the computer unemotionally.

This didn't surprise him. He'd already seen the dismantled starboard engine.

"Computer, start the port engine."

"Computer relays to port engine are disconnected," said the computer.

He fought down his rising panic that was threatening to drive him into useless lunacy.

"Computer, turn on interior lights and describe method to repair relays to port engine."

The cockpit light suddenly blinked on. Campbell was ecstatic to see that the clipper at least had power. The computer began to recite repair instructions for reconnecting it to the port engine. He scrambled beneath the control panel to find a tangle of loose, unconnected wiring. The wiring was coded. He worked at a frantic pace as he followed the rapid monotone instructions from the computer.

"Seven minutes until detonation," advised the bunker bomb.

Campbell worked with sweating desperation as he reconnected wires. He even reconnected wires the computer didn't bother to mention, since he figured they affected some other operations necessary to the clipper.

"Seven minutes until detonation," said the reactor bomb.

He was out of breath and sweating profusely when he crawled out from under the control panel.

"Computer, start port engine."

A slight vibration began to throb through the metal floor, followed by the muffled whirl of the port engine starting.

"Yeah!" Campbell yelled, and jumped to his feet.

"Port engine activated," announced the computer.

"Computer, shut ramp door and prepare for takeoff," Campbell ordered as he sagged into the pilot seat.

"Ramp closed. Warning," the computer said. "Hull integrity compromised."

Campbell's elation evaporated. He realized there must be holes in the ship's hull, making it impossible to pressurize the clipper cabin. This meant they wouldn't be able to leave the hangar and enter the atmospheric void in space.

He leaped up and raced to the storage lockers in the rear of the clipper. He prayed the lockers still contained environmental suits that he and Eto could wear to survive space without cabin pressure.

"Six minutes until detonation," said the bunker bomb.

"Yeah, yeah," he grumbled.

He ripped opened the locker door and found four suits inside. Tearing a suit out of the locker, Campbell quickly put it on. He tested the plasma helmet and ensured it worked.

"Six minutes until detonation," said the reactor bomb.

Campbell ran forward with an extra suit for Eto. After seeing that Eto remained unconscious, he unstrapped her and unceremoniously dumped her on the floor. He fumbled desperately with her suit. He became frustrated while he struggled to stuff her limp and beaten body into the tight suit.

"Dr. Eto, wake up. You have to help me." He gently slapped her already bruised cheek.

Eto only moaned in response. Campbell went back to trying to get her uncoordinated hands and arms into the suit sleeves. To make matters worse, Eto suddenly awoke and started to struggle with him before passing out again.

Finally, he managed to seal Eto's suit and activate her helmet. He lifted her back into the copilot seat and strapped her in.

"Five minutes until detonation," said the bunker bomb.

"Computer, activate launch sequence and exit hangar," he ordered, giving the computer the coordinates to the big island of Hawaii. The computer issued a long series of warnings.

"Just take off!" he shouted with frustrated rage.

"Five minutes until detonation," said the reactor bomb.

"We're never going to make it," he mumbled.

He felt the port engine increasing in power. The clipper started to vibrate from the unbalanced lift of only one engine. Everything suddenly went silent when the engine failed. Campbell wanted to scream with confused frustration.

"Relay to port engine failure," the computer announced without emotion.

"Damn this infernal thing." He slammed his fist down on the control panel in anger. Abruptly, the engine restarted.

"Some of the connections must still be loose," he muttered. His anger dissipated when the clipper began to rise from the floor and move toward the hangar door.

The clipper vibrated frightfully with the increase in engine power. He felt the computer compensating for the uneven lift by using the retro propulsion units. He was glad the retro propulsion was working, but he was worried about space flight when the port engine was at full power. His only hope was that the lack of gravity in space would level out the flight and reduce the stress on the hull and the struggling port engine.

"Four minutes until detonation," said the bunker bomb.

"Come on, come on, move it," he urged the clipper. It seemed to be taking an eternity just to reach the hangar door.

Finally, the clipper reached the green plasma door and was out. A storm of air rushed from the cabin as the clipper entered the void of space.

"Computer, full power to the port engine."

The engine abruptly failed again. Campbell screamed in terror as the clipper dropped the three meters to the ground just outside the hangar with a bone-jarring crash.

"Relay to port engine failure," the computer said.

FOUR

Campbell hammered the control panel with his fist again, but the engine remained quiet.

"Four minutes until detonation," said the reactor bomb.

He pounded the control panel again more out of frustration than utility, but nothing happened. After racing to release himself from the chair, he quickly scrambled beneath the control panel and began checking all the connections. He found several connections that had vibrated loose and reconnected them. Suddenly the engine restarted. The clipper lifted off the desolate moon surface.

"Computer, full power to port engine," he cried as he climbed back into his seat.

He felt the slight pull of the low lunar gravity as the clipper suddenly accelerated. The violent vibration through the clipper hull was terrifying.

"Hold together, come on, hold together," he prayed. "Computer, give distance from moon base every five kilometers."

It took so long for the computer to report the first five kilometers that Campbell was about to repeat the order. He figured they needed to be at least one hundred kilometers from the detonations for them to have any margin of safety.

"Port engine operating at maximum capacity of fifty percent," reported the computer.

"Three minutes until detonation," said the bunker bomb.

"Fifty percent?" Campbell asked incredulously. "We'll never make it with only one engine that's operating at fifty percent. Computer, increase power in port engine to one hundred percent!"

"Warning, port engine is at maximum safety margins," said the computer.

"Computer, increase power to one hundred percent on the port engine now!"

"Increasing power of port engine to one hundred percent," said the computer.

Campbell heard the whine of the engine slowly increasing. The moon began falling away at a greater rate.

"Ten kilometers from moon base," announced the computer.

"Three minutes until detonation."

The vibration in the clipper increased dramatically as the engine power increased. Warning lights on the control panel suddenly began to light up.

"Port engine reaching maximum temperature," reported the computer.

"Computer, fire retro propulsion units toward the stern to increase total forward speed," Campbell ordered.

He didn't feel any increase in speed, but decided they were far enough from the gravitational pull of the moon that they wouldn't feel any G-forces in such a stealthy craft. He held on to the seat arm rests with a white-knuckled grip while the engine whine grew louder and the clipper vibration grew worse.

"Port engine temperature is at critical level. Self-destruction in thirty seconds," said the computer.

"Two minutes until detonation," said the bunker bomb.

Campbell felt the port engine starting to shake itself apart. Still he anxiously waited and held his breath while the computer reported the passing kilometers with increasing speed.

"Fifty kilometers from moon base," said the computer.

He waited. His heart was pounding like a caged beast.

"Two minutes until detonation," said the reactor bomb.

A loud screech of tortured metal from the rear startled Campbell. The clipper was ripping itself apart. Annoying sweat poured down Campbell's face, but he was unable to wipe it away through his helmet.

"Sixty kilometers from moon base."

Campbell nearly jumped out of his seat with fear when he heard a loud cracking noise vibrated through the hull. He realized the port engine was breaking free from its mounts.

"Computer, shut down the port engine," he yelled, terrified he'd waited too long.

Almost immediately the clipper stopped its violent shaking as the engine noise wound down. Campbell hoped they'd reached their maximum speed and were completely free from the lunar gravity. He knew that as long as they were in the frictionless void of space, the clipper would maintain its speed.

"Seventy kilometers from moon base," reported the computer.

"One minute until detonation," said the bunker bomb. "Fifty-nine seconds, fifty-eight seconds, fifty-seven seconds . . ."

"Damn, we're not going to make it," Campbell muttered. "Computer, full power to rear plasma shields."

"Shields inoperable," the computer announced. "Eighty kilometers from moon base."

"What?" Campbell screamed. He glanced over at the tangle of wires where the weapons and shield controls had been and recalled they'd been torn out.

"Bend over and kiss your ass goodbye, Burt," he muttered.

". . . Three seconds, two seconds, one second, bomb detonation."

A flash of light, as brilliant as the raging sun, engulfed the clipper.

Campbell tensed his body in preparation for the tremendous explosion and shockwave that followed an atomic blast. He thought he felt a slight push on the ship hull, but then he wondered if he hadn't imagined it.

Suddenly, he heard a sound similar to hail hitting a window. He realized the clipper was being pelted by debris from the destroyed moon base. His heart was pounding with terror while he waited for something large enough to destroy them to slam into the clipper. His only hope was that the remaining clipper armor would deflect the debris.

He was beginning to think they would make it, when he heard the reactor bomb report one minute until detonation and begin its countdown in seconds.

"One hundred kilometers from moon base," reported the computer.

Campbell's muscles clenched with tension again while he listened to the countdown from the reactor bomb. He knew the explosion from the fusion reactor would be far more massive than the bunker bomb.

"One-hundred-ten kilometers from moon base," reported the computer.

". . . Three seconds, two seconds, one second, bomb detonation."

Another brilliant flash surrounded the clipper briefly blinding Campbell.

Campbell tensed in anticipation, but again nothing happened. He felt a slight push on the clipper, but nothing of massive proportions.

"Computer, what's our distance from the moon base?" he asked on a hunch.

"No longer able to scan the moon base," said the computer.

The moon base had been completely obliterated.

A tremendous bang suddenly reverberated through the clipper when something large struck the ship from the rear. Again, there was the sound of small pieces of the moon base striking all over the clipper hull. He waited with sweating fear for a large piece of debris to punch through their hull where the armor had been removed for repairs. It didn't happen. The sound of pelting debris quickly died away.

He wondered why the clipper hadn't been destroyed by the force of the massive explosions. It suddenly occurred to him that the moon didn't have an atmosphere. Atomic explosions wouldn't have the same effect as he'd seen on Earth, where there's a dense atmosphere. He knew a nuclear explosion on the moon would be just as powerful as it was on Earth, and thus destroying the moon base and sending out the debris. But he realized the destructive power of the atmospheric shockwave that occurred on Earth wouldn't happen on the moon.

"We made it!" he yelled with wild elation. "Dr. Eto, wake up! We made it!"

He turned to Eto. Her battered head was still slumped on her slowly rising chest. Her restraints were the only thing holding her in her chair.

"Party pooper," he muttered.

Campbell was ecstatic over their survival, but his ecstasy turned to deep sadness when he thought of the deadly cost and the loss of Penelope. The Master had escaped and had apparently taken Penelope with It. He had no clue where they'd gone, but he reasoned that the Master must have traveled to Earth. He didn't think the moon base had any intergalactic vessels at Its disposal. As he thought about the Master's plan to take over Earth, he was sure that was where the Master had escaped with Penelope. Some hope returned that she was still alive, but it was tempered with fear for what she was facing.

"I don't know how long it will take, Penelope, but I swear I will find you," he muttered with grim determination.

He turned his attention back to the crippled clipper. He knew he had to survive to rescue Penelope, and he had one more rescue mission before he could begin his search for her.

The End

SAMPLE CHAPTER OF *THE SOUL CAGE III: THE SURVIVOR.*

ONE

"Well, we might have miraculously escaped the destruction of the moon base with our lives, but I'm afraid we've only postponed our death sentence," Inspector Burt Campbell muttered to no one that could hear him.

He gazed solemnly out the cockpit window into the star-filled darkness of space through pure black eye implants as their crippled military clipper limped toward home. Partially silhouetted by the brilliant sunlight, the emerald-blue globe called Earth filled his vision. The 4.54 billion-year-old planet was consumed by wide white-gray brushstrokes of streaked, sometimes swelling clouds. Vast deep blue oceans eternally slammed against intermittent brown-green land masses. Earth appeared so awesome and immense in his vision, yet so small and lonely in the vastness of space. It was a humbling and beautiful sight that filled Campbell's heart with foreboding about their future. He also feared it might be his last.

Returning to the problems at hand, Campbell gazed down at the dizzying array of controls, instruments, scanners, and blinking red warning lights before him. His dark olive features and long black hair were surrounded by the protective plasma helmet of his military environmental suit. His hulking, genetically-enhanced frame was crammed into the pilot's seat. Thoughts of how they were going to get their crippled clipper back to Earth, and what they would find when they got there, sickened Campbell with worry.

He glanced over at Dr. Ai Eto strapped tightly in the copilot's seat. Her tall, lanky body was still slouched in unconsciousness. Her head rested on her slow-rising chest inside her plasma helmet. She was oblivious to their deadly situation. Campbell thought her once-fine Asian features remained badly bruised and appeared Mongolian-like with their black-blue swelling. Still, she appeared better than when he'd discovered her trapped the moon-base torture device in which he himself had suffered so much unbearable pain.

"Eto." Campbell reached over and gently pushed her shoulder. "Eto, wake up." She remained as motionless and limp as a recent corpse. "Okay, be that way," he muttered, and returned his attention to the ever-demanding control panel before him and their pressing problems.

"Computer, ETA to destination?" Campbell asked.

"Ten hours, thirty-four minutes, and twelve-point-five seconds," said the automated computer voice.

"Damn, I only asked for an estimate."

He took a moment to calculate the remaining air supply in their environmental suits. "Aw, crap! We won't even make it halfway to Earth."

He pounded his huge fist on the control panel, his face flushed with anger and frustration. Half the instruments on the panel blinked out.

"Oops."

Campbell quickly released his seat restraints and scrambled beneath the control panel. Struggling with the tangled disarray left behind by the moon base maintenance spiders, he found two of the connections had been loosened by his frustrated fury. He went about reattaching them. After crawling cursing and swearing back into his seat, he grunted with satisfaction to see all the instruments were operational again.

"Computer, restart port engine to fifty percent," he ordered.

Campbell heard the powerful deep-throated whine of the engine restarting. The disk-shaped clipper, with its long sausage-like fuselage stemming from bow to stern, began to vibrate slightly with the imbalance of only one working engine.

"Port engine restarted, and increasing power to fifty percent," reported the computer.

"Yeah!" Campbell pumped his fist toward the ceiling with elation. "Computer, what's our ETA to reach destination with engine at fifty percent?"

"Eight hours, forty-two minutes, and twenty-six seconds."

"Damn, that's still too slow."

His mind desperately searched for methods of increasing either their speed or their limited air supply.

"Computer, increase engine speed to eighty percent."

"Warning, maximum safety levels exceeded with port engine operating at eighty percent."

"Increase power level to eighty percent," Campbell persisted.

He quickly got up and headed back though the dark tunnel-like fuselage toward the equipment locker. After stumbling over the maintenance and parts debris and avoiding the four remaining hover bots, Campbell pulled the two spare environmental suits out of the locker. They were both functioning properly, and had enough air for them to make it safely to Earth—if they could use them.

But how are we going to change suits? he wondered. *The cabin won't pressurize. Our organs will rupture in the vacuum without their sealed protection. I don't even want to think about changing Eto's suit with her being unconscious.*

Digging back through the disheveled mess in the locker, Campbell was further frustrated to find only two full canisters of emergency compressed air. These wouldn't last more than thirty minutes—not nearly long enough. Sudden enlightenment struck him like a physical blow and he raced tripping and stumbling back into his seat.

"If they're not orbiting on this side, we're dead," Campbell muttered. "Computer, attempt to establish communications with the Hawking Space Station."

"Communication link established with the Hawking Space Station," the computer said after a moment.

"Hawking Space Station, this is Inspector Burt Campbell of the Global Police, come in please."

A handsome young man with dark features and unruly black hair appeared on the communications monitor. "Inspector Campbell, this is Corporal Enis of the Hawking Space Station."

"Corporal Enis, Dr. Ai Eto and I are in a crippled clipper attempting to reach Earth. Our starboard engine is gone, and our port engine will only operate safely at fifty percent. Our cabin will not pressurize, and we don't have enough air to reach Earth. We request an emergency docking with the space station."

The corporal's features pinched with indecision and he didn't respond.

"Corporal, did you hear me?" Campbell asked anxiously.

"Inspector, the space station is under emergency lockdown due to the situation on Earth," the corporal said with a worried expression. "We're under strict orders to destroy any vessel approaching or trying to dock with the space station, out."

"Corporal, wait!" Campbell shouted. "Please connect me with the space station commander. We're under orders from President Cathcart. We have to reach Earth. We mean you no harm. We don't even need to board the space station. We only need a pressurized area to change environmental suits."

Again the corporal only stared back at Campbell with concern. Campbell could see that Enis was lost with indecision.

"Corporal, please, let me talk to the commander."

A heavyset older black man with jowly features and intelligent dark-brown eyes appeared next to the corporal on Campbell's monitor.

"Inspector Campbell, I'm Commander Horton. I was listening to your communication. What was your point of origin?"

"Moon Base Alfa-Tango," Campbell said, and then mentally kicked himself.

"The moon base, huh? Sorry, Inspector," Horton said with a furrowed brow of suspicion. "We haven't allowed craft from the moon base to dock here for months, not even for emergency reasons."

"Commander, please," Campbell said with urgency, "if you contact President Cathcart, she'll verify that I was part of a military detachment that was sent to destroy the moon base. She will also verify that it's imperative that I return to Earth."

"Inspector, are you aware of the situation on Earth at the moment?"

"Yes, Commander," Campbell said with increasing frustration. "That was one of the reasons I was sent to destroy the moon base. You obviously have some knowledge of what was going on there, since you don't allow their vehicles to dock with the space station."

Horton's look of apprehension deepened. "Inspector Campbell, I recognize and believe you, otherwise we wouldn't even be having this conversation, but you must also realize my situation.

"Earth is destroying itself. Vehicles of all types, carrying all kinds of people, are trying to escape the planet. We have been ordered to destroy all ships that approach in order to save ourselves, and I happen to agree with that order . . ."

Campbell interrupted. "Commander, will you at least try to contact the President? I'm sure she'll rescind your orders and allow us to dock."

Horton's eyes softened, his brow relaxed. "Campbell, sensors show you're about half-an-hour out. I'll try to contact Cathcart to get my orders rescinded, but don't expect much. We have been having a great deal of difficulty getting through to anyone in all this chaos. I don't even know if we can reach her.

"If I don't contact you by the time you reach the station, don't approach within five kilometers or you *will* be destroyed. Is that understood?"

"Perfectly, Commander Horton. Thank you for your assistance, out," Campbell said with a measured degree of relief.

Made in the USA
Charleston, SC
13 February 2013